WHIPSER MY NAME

Francesca opened the door.

Sebastien wore the same low-slung jeans and black New Orleans Saints T-shirt she'd seen him in earlier, but now his square jaw was darkened with a five o'clock shadow that made him look ruggedly male, and more than a little dangerous. Especially with that Glock holstered to his waist.

Heavy-lidded gray eyes roamed across her face. "You didn't call," he said softly.

"I know." Her voice came out in a breathless rush. Mortified, she snatched a quick breath and tried again. "You were busy. I didn't want to disturb you. Besides, it's not your job to—"

He leaned down, cupping her chin in his hand and slanting his mouth over hers. She gasped a little as he kissed her slowly, deeply, drugging her senses. She let her lips part beneath the pressure of his, allowing him access, shivering as he took possession with hot, sensual sweeps of his tongue against hers.

When he drew away, she whimpered softly in protest and leaned into him, chasing the heat of his body. He chuckled low in his throat, brushing the pad of his thumb against her lower lip.

Also by Maureen Smith

WEAPON OF SEDUCTION

Whisper
My Name

Maureen Smith

Kensington Publishing Corp.
http://www.kensingtonbooks.com

DAFINA BOOKS are published by

Kensington Publishing Corp.
850 Third Avenue
New York, NY 10022

All Kensington Titles, Imprints, and Distributed Lines are available at special quantity discounts for bulk purchases for sales promotions, premiums, fund-raising, and educational or institutional use. Special book excerpts or customized printings can also be created to fit specific needs. For details, write or phone the office of the Kensington special sales manager: Kensington Publishing Corp., 850 Third Avenue, New York, NY 10022, attn: Special Sales Department, Phone: 1-800-221-2647.

Dafina and the Dafina logo Reg. U.S. Pat. & TM Off.

ISBN-13: 978-0-7582-1432-4
ISBN-10: 0-7582-1432-4

First mass market printing: June 2007

10 9 8 7 6 5 4 3 2 1

Printed in the United States of America

This book is dedicated to the men, women, and children whose lives were forever changed by Hurricane Katrina.

"It is a scientific fact that spiders are the natural predators of all insects."

Prologue

His masterpiece was nearly complete.

The needle bar moved across the woman's upstretched arm, piercing smooth alabaster skin as the tiny needles followed the path of an ink outline. With a methodical precision to rival any surgeon's, the artist worked swiftly and quietly in the dimly lit motel room, coloring and filling in the intricate lines of the tattoo.

As he watched his creation come to life, exhilaration sang through his veins, joining the heady flow of adrenaline that had seized him the moment he saw her.

Standing alone at the bus stop, wearing a gauzy blue sundress that clung to the ripe curves of her body, she'd practically beckoned to him from where he stood at a newsstand just inside the bus terminal. Transfixed, he'd tucked his newspaper beneath one arm and edged closer to her, needing to get a better look, to find out if she could be The One.

Frowning, she'd reached up and shoved a heavy curtain of hair off her face. Long and wavy, the strands gleamed pure and golden in the blistering afternoon sunlight. Nose buried in a city travel guide, she hadn't noticed him watching her, dissecting her.

Choosing her.

When the bus arrived, trailing a noxious cloud of exhaust fumes, the stranger boarded and sat three rows away from her. As the bus rolled through the clean downtown streets of the Alamo City, he'd watched her, never taking his eyes off her, silently staking his claim.

As if sensing the heat of his gaze, she'd glanced back, and her baby blue eyes collided with his. His breath had stalled in his lungs as he waited . . . for what he didn't know. And then she'd smiled—the polite, vacant smile reserved for strangers—before turning away again. He'd swallowed and felt the first stirrings between his legs.

And he'd known then that he had to have her.

When she disembarked from the bus, he made note of the motel where she was staying. When nightfall came, he returned for her.

Now, as he beheld his handiwork, he felt another surge of euphoria. She was perfect, her arm the right fit, her skin the right texture—

Suddenly he froze.

It can't be, he thought, even as he felt the first whisper of despair in the hollow of his stomach. Frowning, he leaned closer to get a better look, cursing the motel room's poor lighting, hoping his eyes were deceiving him.

But nothing was wrong with his eyesight. He hadn't missed, for example, a small brown stain on the multi-colored carpet that reeked of mildew. Nor had he missed the tiny initials someone had carved into the cheap wood-grain surface of the nightstand.

But somehow, *somehow,* he'd missed the one detail that would ruin everything.

There, nestled in the soft folds of the woman's underarm, was a strawberry birthmark the size of a sesame seed. A birthmark. Barely discernible, but there just the same.

An imperfection.

Fury swept through him, as swift and lethal as the white-hot flames of a brush fire blazing through a wooded forest. He lunged to his feet, away from the bed and the carefully arranged tools on the nightstand, and began pacing the floor.

How could he have been so careless? How could he have missed the imposter's traitorous blemish during his inspection of her naked body? *How?*

He'd been so sure of his choice, so sure of her perfection. But she *wasn't* perfect! Far from it! Just like the other ones. Once again, he'd failed.

Because he'd been too eager.

Because he hadn't been able to wait, to take his time and choose more wisely.

A soft, muffled moan from the bed interrupted his self-flagellating. He looked over his shoulder to where the woman, bound and gagged, was just awakening from a drug-induced slumber.

A fresh surge of rage overtook him.

He reached inside the breast pocket of his blazer, and the silver gleam of a hunting knife flashed in the dimness of the room. Slowly he advanced on the bed and stood over his victim. Terrified blue eyes met his cold, unforgiving gaze.

"I'm sorry," he said calmly, as if he were merely apologizing for dialing a wrong number. "I made a mistake. You're not the one I was looking for."

Before the imposter could utter another sound, he raised the knife high and slashed downward.

Chapter 1

"*What* in the world is that monstrosity?"

Without lifting her head from the textbook she'd been studying, Francesca Purnell chuckled softly. "What monstrosity are you referring to, Alfonso?"

A blunt-tipped finger stabbed at the glossy page in question. "*That* monstrosity. What is that thing?"

"It's a tarantula. A Colombian Giant Red Leg, to be exact."

"I don't care *where* it's from. It's ugly as sin."

"Think so?" Tilting her head thoughtfully to one side, Francesca studied the photograph of the long-haired, bright orange spider. "I happen to think it's quite beautiful."

Alfonso Garcia snorted rudely. "As they say, beauty's in the eye of the beholder. Of course, when the beholder is as nearsighted as *you* are, Frankie, one has to question everything." He regarded the photo another moment, then gave a mock shudder that shook his narrow frame. "Hope I never have the misfortune of running into *that* ugly creature."

Francesca pushed black horn-rimmed eyeglasses up

on her slender nose, deciding to ignore the crack about her nearsightedness. "The species is indigenous to the rain forests of Colombia, so unless you're planning a trip to South America, you should be safe."

"Thank God," Alfonso muttered, refilling Francesca's coffee cup. Automatically she reached for cream and sugar, dumping liberal amounts of both into her coffee.

"Honestly, Frankie," Alfonso continued, wearing a green apron with ESPUMA COFFEE AND TEA EMPORIUM stenciled in white letters across the front, "I don't know how you sleep at night with visions of those creepy-crawlers dancing in your head. It ain't natural. In fact, if you ask me, it's downright *un*-natural."

Francesca stirred her coffee slowly. "Insulting my profession isn't exactly the best way to earn a tip, Alfonso," she said dryly.

He took the hint. "Holler if you need anything else," he said, moving on to the next table. Nothing threatened Alfonso Garcia more than a hit to the wallet. A struggling writer, he took tips very seriously.

Shaking her head with a grin, Francesca lowered her head to take a sip of coffee. Midswallow, her gaze collided with a pair of piercing gray eyes set in the most arrestingly masculine face she'd ever seen.

Her breath caught in her throat, forcing the coffee down the wrong way. She choked and sputtered, setting her cup down on the tabletop with a loud clatter. Curious heads swung in her direction, and Alfonso hustled over to her table and hovered worriedly like a mother hen.

"What happened? Are you okay?"

"I'm fine," Francesca croaked out, feeling incredibly foolish for the minor commotion she'd caused. She accepted a handful of paper napkins from Alfonso and dabbed at her mouth and chin.

At Alfonso's summons, a young, pretty brunette

appeared with a glass of cold water and handed it to Francesca with a friendly smile.

"Thank you, Jennifer," Francesca murmured gratefully to the waitress. She took a careful sip of water, assiduously avoiding the other side of the room.

After Jennifer left, Alfonso continued to hover. "Are you sure you're okay?"

"Yes. I just swallowed too fast, that's all." As was her custom, Francesca masked her embarrassment with droll humor. "Don't worry, Alfonso. I'm not going to choke to death without paying my bill first."

He scowled and rolled his dark brown eyes heavenward. "Why do I even bother?" he muttered before shuffling away to tend to a more deserving customer.

Francesca picked up her cup of coffee, then reconsidered and set it back down, reaching for her textbook instead. But she couldn't concentrate on a single word of what she'd been reading, and after just two minutes, she succumbed to temptation and stole another glance across the room.

To her shocked dismay, the stranger was still watching her. Hard angles and planes carved in rich almond sketched a tough, compelling face that was softened by heavy-lidded gray eyes and a wide, sensual mouth framed by a neatly trimmed goatee. Even from this distance, Francesca could tell he was tall. The black cotton of his T-shirt strained against broad shoulders and sinewy biceps. His clean-shaven head only accentuated his rugged, undeniably dangerous appeal.

His focused, silent observation of Francesca sent heat crawling up her neck, and she couldn't help wondering what it was about her appearance that had so captured his attention. She was, and always had been, a realist when it came to her own strengths and shortcomings. With a Ph.D. in entomology, Francesca could discuss molecular biology and argue the ecological importance of arthropods with the best of them. She'd been called gifted, exceptional, even brilliant as she tenaciously climbed her way through the ranks in a male-dominated field of study.

But she was *not* the kind of woman who turned heads—especially not the heads of sexy strangers like the one across the room.

As he sat at a table in the corner drinking coffee and watching her, Francesca wondered who he was, and where he'd come from. She was a regular at the Espuma Coffee and Tea Emporium, and she'd never seen him before. She definitely would have remembered him, especially since he didn't strike her as the type to frequent a place like the Espuma. The quaint little café had been converted from an old house and featured cozy, well-lit rooms decorated with the works of local artists. The menu catered mostly to vegetarians, offering an eclectic blend of grilled vegetables and cheeses, and pita breads and pesto sauces served with iced Vietnamese coffees. Francesca, who lived within easy walking distance, scarcely let a day pass without making a trip to the Espuma, armed with her reading materials and papers to grade.

As the sexy stranger's silent appraisal continued, Francesca found herself wishing she'd had the foresight to wear something other than the shapeless tropical-print muumuu she'd thrown on before leaving the house that morning. And it probably wouldn't have hurt to actually *comb* her hair, instead of just shoving the kinky chestnut-brown curls into an unruly knot atop her head. As if to taunt her, an errant lock of hair suddenly sprang free and tumbled over one bespectacled eye.

One corner of the stranger's mouth curved upward, and Francesca's heart thudded in response.

What was going on here? Could this gorgeous man be flirting with *her*?

She threw a quick glance over her shoulder, half expecting to see some sultry-eyed, leggy vixen seated nearby. But the few tables behind her were empty.

She turned back around slowly. The man's gray eyes glinted with faint amusement. As Francesca watched, unable to tear her gaze away, he downed the rest of his coffee, dropped a large bill onto the table, and stood.

Francesca realized two things at once: The first was that she'd been right about him being tall. From where she sat, she judged him to be at least six-three, with a body that could have been hewn from solid rock.

The second thing she realized was that he was coming straight toward her!

Panic fluttered in her belly. She froze, cemented to the chair even as every gut instinct warned her to get up and run in the opposite direction. But she was powerless to do anything but sit and watch with mounting alarm as the handsome stranger sauntered toward her. Something about his relaxed, confident strides hinted at raw, unleashed power that quickened Francesca's pulse and turned her palms sweaty. He wore loose khaki trousers that hung low on his trim waist and rode his long legs in a way that would make Giorgio Armani proud.

A few feet away from her, he stopped suddenly and pulled out a cell phone clipped to his waist.

Francesca thought she heard him say "Durand," or something to that effect, but he wasn't near enough for her to be certain. And she was too distracted by the sound of his voice—a dark, smoky drawl that made her stomach clench in reaction.

He listened into the phone for a moment, his expression turning grim, and then he said, "I'm on my way."

Francesca held her breath as he sent her one long, final look before turning on his heel and striding purposefully from the café.

And somehow, inexplicable though it was, she knew she hadn't seen the last of him.

It was with some regret that Detective Sebastien Durand left the Espuma Coffee and Tea Emporium and climbed into the stifling heat of an unmarked Crown Victoria parked in the rear lot. He cranked the ignition and hoped to God the dysfunctional air-conditioning would kick in before he melted into the worn leather seat like a Nestlé chocolate bar.

He'd driven to the historic King William District that morning to interview a witness for a homicide case he was working. Afterward, on impulse, he'd stopped inside the little coffeehouse for a quick cup of joe while he read the morning paper.

He never got past the front page.

He'd been distracted by the arrival of a woman wearing the most god-awful dress he'd ever seen, an ill-fitting number garishly decorated with big colorful flowers. At her appearance, a few customers had looked up from their iced lattés and given the woman a cursory glance before turning away, dismissing her at once.

But not Sebastien.

His gaze had followed her as she walked unerringly to an empty table in the rear corner of the café. The way she claimed the table, and the promptness with which she was waited upon, told Sebastien she was probably a regular. After placing her order, she'd rummaged through a satchel, hefted out a whopper of a textbook, and promptly buried her nose in it. That should have put an end to Sebastien's interest in the dowdy librarian, but instead he found himself unable to look away, studying her as if she were a fascinating puzzle to be solved. She wasn't the type of woman who usually caught his eye—far from it. But there was something about *this* woman, something he couldn't begin to fathom, that held him riveted. Black horn-rimmed glasses perched on the bridge of a slim, upturned nose made him speculate about the color of her eyes. Her skin was a rich velvety brown and flawless to the point of perfection. Thick curly hair, a shade lighter than her complexion, had been carelessly swept into a poor excuse for a ponytail. Sebastien wondered what the woman would look like first thing in the morning, with that unruly mass tumbling about her face and shoulders in a glorious free fall.

More to the point, he mused, *what is she hiding beneath that hideous tent of a dress?*

When she looked up suddenly and met his gaze, Sebastien felt a punch to his gut that caught him completely by surprise. The woman appeared even more startled. After she recovered from her choking spell, he'd found himself willing her to look his way again. When she finally did, he'd felt, once again, that unexpected stab of desire.

The memory of it made him chuckle as he watched the coffeehouse shrink in his rearview mirror. "You definitely need to get out more, Durand," he muttered to himself. "Next you'll be camping out at public libraries to pick up women."

He left the King William District, passing block after block of elegant Victorians cradled by curved porches and manicured lawns that meandered along the south bank of the San Antonio River. He rolled down South Alamo Street and negotiated two left turns before hooking a right onto West Houston. Even before he reached the dingy Motel 6, the flashing swirl of red and blue lights announced the arrival of SAPD patrol officers who'd beaten him to the scene. Their radio cars idled side by side, hood to trunk, clogging the pothole-riddled parking lot as they conversed in low tones about whatever obscenity they'd encountered inside the motel room.

Sebastien swung into the lot and parked as close to the building as possible. He grabbed a notepad off the passenger seat and climbed out of the car, cursing the sweltering summer heat that rendered the idea of wearing a sport coat unthinkable.

Alerted by the heavy police presence in the middle of the morning, spectators gathered on steamy sidewalks across the street and around the perimeter of the motel, watching the unfolding drama with varying degrees of mild to morbid curiosity. Guests of the motel—those who'd judiciously decided to attempt sightseeing at night when it was cooler—hovered in doorways and leaned over rusty railings to peer at the action below. Sebastien felt their eyes on him as he made his way across the parking lot toward the building.

Two uniformed officers flanked the ground-floor door of the motel room, which was partially open and barred by a yellow ribbon of tape that warned: CRIME SCENE—DO NOT CROSS.

"Hey, Big Easy," the younger of the pair greeted Sebastien in a jovial tone that would strike some—namely those not belonging to the brotherhood of blue—as irreverent on such a grim occasion. "'Bout time you got here."

"What can I say?" Sebastien retorted in a lazy drawl. "It was a good cup of coffee."

The uniforms chortled and lifted the crime-scene tape to let him duck under. Sebastien stepped inside the tiny motel room and did not flinch at the stench of violent death that assailed his nostrils, preparing him for the gruesome display that awaited him.

A young blond woman lay upon the queen-size bed, the floral-patterned spread undisturbed beneath her nude body, the fabric stained crimson with blood that had spilled from deep, savage knife wounds across her neck and torso. She had been gagged and bound, her arms stretched taut above her head, her wrists tied to the center bedpost with the same kind of cord that had been used to bind her ankles.

A set of plastic key cards sat on the nightstand, joined by a pair of pink-tinted sunglasses and a wrinkled city travel guide. A gauzy cornflower-blue sundress had been flung across the back of a chair parked at a scarred round table near the window. The heavy floral-patterned curtains were drawn closed, keeping out the bright glare of the sunlight but doing little to diminish the heat and humidity that emanated from outdoors.

Sebastien took in the entire scene from his position at the door. Then, instead of moving directly toward the body, he walked around the perimeter of the motel room, looking along the floor, walls, and furniture, carefully making his way toward the victim in a slowly shrinking circle.

It hadn't taken ten years in homicide for him to learn that the body wasn't going anywhere; it would be there for as long as it took to process the crime scene. But the scene itself began to deteriorate as soon as the first person discovered the body; therefore it had become second nature to Sebastien to begin at the periphery and work his way methodically to the vortex of the violent storm—where the corpse lay. As he walked the room, he scribbled in his notepad, recording raw data that could prove useful in the ensuing investigation.

At length he stopped directly in front of the victim and, with clinical detachment borne from years of practice, sketched what he saw. He noted the absence of blood spatter on the wall above the headboard and followed the trajectory of the gaping knife wounds, concluding that the perpetrator had stood above the victim, to the right of the bed, and stabbed her in a downward motion, left to right. The angle of the wounds suggested that the killer was right-handed, which narrowed the scope of possible suspects to the majority of the city's population.

Watching where he walked, Sebastien rounded the bed and knelt beside the body. The woman's blue eyes were frozen wide in an expression of mute terror. In life she'd been beautiful, with long, wavy blond hair that blanketed the pillow and was now partially soaked in blood. She was young, in her early twenties, and moderately tall, no less than five-seven.

Sebastien glanced over his shoulder toward the doorway, where the two uniforms were still posted guard. "Who found her?"

"Cleaning lady," Lute O'Hara answered in a less jovial tone than before. His green eyes darted furtively to the ravaged corpse on the bed, then shot back to Sebastien's, as if he were afraid he'd turn into a pillar of salt if he looked upon the victim too long. "She says she was making her rounds this morning and entered the room when no one responded to her knock."

"Where is she now?"

"Giving her statement to Rodriguez in the lobby. He took the call at the station. He's also talking to the day-shift manager. Both women are pretty hysterical—he thought it best to keep them as far away from here as possible."

"Did anyone else enter the room after the housekeeper?" Meaning: *Who else may have contaminated the crime scene?*

O'Hara shook his blond head quickly. "Just Rodriguez. The crime lab is on the way."

"What about the ME?"

"Should be here shortly."

Nodding, Sebastien resumed his visual examination of the body. Although the brutality of the murder suggested that the perpetrator had been enraged, the incisions were surprisingly clean, inflicted with a controlled precision that sent a chill of foreboding down Sebastien's spine.

His gaze was soon drawn to a tattoo on the inside of the woman's right arm, an intricate engraving of a deadly-looking spider that measured about two inches in diameter. Elongated fangs protruded from the creature's head, and the body appeared to be heavily covered with thick black hairs and an abdomen that bore unusual red markings—three straight lines stacked over a small circle in some sort of hieroglyphic symbolism.

Frowning, Sebastien leaned closer to get a better look. The tattoo was still fresh. Had the woman visited a tattoo shop before returning to the motel yesterday?

Or had the killer left a calling card?

"Hope you're not messing up my crime scene, Durand," a voice warned dryly from the doorway.

Sebastien didn't turn around as Detective Juan Rodriguez entered the room and made his way carefully to where Sebastien knelt beside the bed.

"I heard you were on babysitting detail," Sebastien drawled, "comforting the cleaning lady and motel manager."

Rodriguez shrugged one broad shoulder, strong white teeth flashing in a quick grin. Thick black hair salted with silver made him look slightly older than thirty-seven, a fact he didn't mind since he'd been told on more than one occasion that he resembled Benicio Del Toro—a half-truth perpetuated by hookers attempting to sweet-talk their way out of the slammer.

After sixteen years in the San Antonio Police Department, twelve in homicide, Juan Rodriguez had earned the nickname "Don Juan" for the way he finessed witnesses and delivered bad news to unsuspecting family members. His soothing bedside manner had rendered him a favorite of grieving widows and made him the natural choice for the role of "good cop" during interrogations.

"So, what'd you learn about our victim?" Sebastien

prompted, still examining the mystifying tattoo. Of all the details that would be withheld from newspaper and television reporters, the tattoo was definitely one of them.

"Her name's Christie Snodgrass, twenty-four years old. She was visiting from Monterrey, California. Arrived two days ago."

"Helluva way to end a vacation," Sebastien said grimly.

"Tell me about it. I spoke to her parents—they're flying down today to identify the body—and Mrs. Snodgrass said Christie had just finished her master's program at Berkeley and wanted to treat herself to a trip to San Antonio before starting her new job at the university."

"Teaching?"

Rodriguez nodded. "Mathematics." He studied the mutilated corpse on the bed and grimaced. "She looked more like a Miss America contestant than a math professor. What a waste."

Sebastien didn't know whether the "waste" Rodriguez referred to was the victim's chosen profession, or her senseless death. Either way, he tended to agree. "Did she have a boyfriend?"

"Yeah, a med student by the name of Tad Cotter, who I'm still trying to track down. Her parents wanted to break the news to him personally, said they'll call me when they get in touch with him. But he didn't travel to San Antonio with Christie—desk clerk on duty says she checked in alone and was never seen with anyone else. And, according to her parents, she didn't know a soul in town. What do you find so fascinating about that damned tattoo?"

"It's new, for starters. Less than a day old."

"How do you know that?"

"See those tiny black specks around it?" Sebastien angled away from the body so that Rodriguez could peer over his shoulder. "During the application of a tattoo, the skin secretes fluid, forming droplets on the surface.

If the blood particles in the fluid dry on the surface, they stick to the skin in the form of those little black specks you see. If allowed to remain—that is, if they're not cleaned off immediately—they adhere strongly to the skin, dry, and begin to form a scab. These specks haven't started scabbing yet, which leads me to believe the tattoo is fairly new. Less than twelve hours old, I'd say."

Rodriguez eyed him speculatively. "How do you know so much about tattoos?"

One corner of Sebastien's mouth curved wryly. "My uncle owned a tattoo shop back home. He taught me everything he knew, whether I cared to learn or not."

"Well, now, aren't you glad you paid attention?" Rodriguez's gaze returned to Christie Snodgrass's savaged remains, and after a moment his lips thinned to a grim line. "All right, here's what I'm thinking. She was out partying last night, had one too many margaritas, and wound up in a seedy tattoo parlor. Afterward she came back here with some horny bastard she met at the club. He ties her up, they have rough, kinky sex, things get out of hand, and he kills her."

Sebastien frowned. "It's possible—except that I'm having a hard time picturing some schmuck showing up at the club wearing Cole Haan loafers and armed with a hunting knife, or whatever was used to carve up Miss Snodgrass."

"What if he's a psycho who hangs around clubs to choose his victims? What if he specifically targeted Christie and followed her back to the motel? I checked the window and door, and there's no sign of forced entry. The creep probably knocked on the door and announced himself as room service."

Before Sebastien could respond, the sound of new voices outside the room signaled the arrival of the crime scene unit. Rodriguez turned and started for the door, saying over his shoulder, "I've got uniforms knocking on doors and talking to motel guests to find out if anyone heard or witnessed anything out of place last night. And I'm guessing one, or both of us, will be making our rounds to local tattoo shops."

"You guessed right." Sebastien got slowly to his feet, his gaze still narrowed on Christie Snodgrass's arm. He couldn't shake the feeling that the key to the young woman's brutal murder lay in the intricately designed spider tattoo.

As he and Rodriguez stepped from the motel room to let the crime lab techs process the scene, Sebastien pulled out his cell phone and called Esther Rivera, their secretary at the police station, to ask her to compile a list of all local tattoo parlors.

As he hung up the phone, Rodriguez said under his breath, "Don't look now, but MacDougal's here."

The two men watched in silence as their supervisor, Sergeant Clive MacDougal, detached himself from a group of uniformed cops and made his way across the parking lot with the brisk, determined strides of a man on a mission. At forty-eight, MacDougal was a tall, barrel-chested Irishman with stern, craggy features, a steel-gray cap of hair, and piercing green eyes that had been known to reduce grown men to tears. Twice divorced, the twenty-three-year veteran of the SAPD had four children whom he only saw on holidays and the occasional weekends when he wasn't working. During the nearly two years he'd been with the department, Sebastien couldn't remember the last time MacDougal had ever taken a weekend off.

In the Homicide Unit, murders and attempted murders were assigned to the detectives on a rotational basis by the sergeant, who assigned a lead investigator. Other than to periodically review each case, MacDougal was generally hands-off, spending the bulk of his time completing administrative paperwork, keeping the brass at bay, and letting his detectives do their job. So when he showed up at a crime scene demanding answers, everyone sat up and took notice.

"I just got the call," MacDougal said without preamble as he reached his waiting detectives. "A tourist? Christ, the media's gonna be all over this like flies to a hot pile of shit."

Mouth twitching, Rodriguez hitched his chin toward a white KENS-5 news van that had just barreled around the corner. "Let the feeding frenzy begin."

MacDougal scowled, shaking his head in patent disgust. "Just what we need. A dead tourist at the height of tourism season. The mayor's not gonna be too happy about this." He nodded toward the open doorway of the motel room, now bustling with the activity of crime scene technicians. "How bad is it?"

"Pretty bad," Sebastien said grimly. "Victim has multiple stab wounds across her neck and torso. Looks like someone tried to carve her up like a Thanksgiving turkey."

"She also has an unusual tattoo of a spider on her right arm," Rodriguez helpfully supplied. "Durand thinks it was left there by the killer."

MacDougal's shrewd gaze settled on Sebastien's face. "How much do you know about tattoos?"

"Enough to know it would have taken the perp at least two hours to apply the type of tattoo found on the victim's body."

"Two hours?" Rodriguez echoed in disbelief.

Sebastien nodded. "The amount of detail involved, the size of the tattoo, the use of several colors, not to mention the time needed for preparation and setup. Two hours, easy."

MacDougal exchanged vaguely amused glances with Rodriguez. "How does he know so much about tattoos?"

"He used to work in his uncle's tattoo shop back in

New Orleans," Rodriguez drawled wryly. "Uncle taught him everything he knew."

"I see." The sergeant's gaze returned to Sebastien. "I'm making you the primary on the case, Durand. Apply your 'wealth of knowledge' to helping us find the son of a bitch who did this."

Chapter 2

The tall, lanky kid behind the counter of the tattoo parlor Sebastien and Rodriguez visited that afternoon couldn't have been a day over sixteen. His hair was long and dark, hanging past thin shoulders that were covered in a black T-shirt featuring heavy metal group Korn. His arms were heavily tattooed, and every inch of his narrow face seemed to be pierced—eyebrows, eyelids, nostrils, lips. When he opened his mouth to greet them, a flash of silver confirmed Sebastien's suspicion that the boy's tongue was also pierced.

The minute he and Rodriguez showed their badges, the kid began to fidget, straightening a stack of business cards on the glass countertop, glancing uneasily around the dingy shop as if willing one of the other four tattoo artists to come to his rescue. All were with customers.

"Relax, kid," Sebastien said drolly. "We're not here to give you a hard time. We're trying to find out if anyone has ever come into the shop and asked for a tattoo like this."

The boy hesitated, then leaned across the counter to examine the photo Sebastien held up. "Nope," he mumbled after a moment. "Never seen that one."

"Are you sure?" Sebastien pressed, although it was the

same answer they'd received at the other three shops they'd already visited.

"I'm positive. I would've remembered someone walking in here and asking for a tat like that."

"How long have you worked here?" Rodriguez asked.

"Well, uh, I don't exactly work here," the kid hedged. "I'm an apprentice to the other artists. I've been here about eight months."

"An apprentice, huh?" Rodriguez said. "So you're learning how to apply tattoos?"

"Yeah, but not just that. I'm also learning about sterilization, needle making, prepping, making stencils. Stuff like that."

"Nice gig," Sebastien said, speaking from personal experience. Though he hadn't always relished working with his pushy, loudmouthed uncle, he'd enjoyed learning about the art of tattooing. He'd even been allowed to practice his skills on a few customers—mostly his uncle's half-drunk buddies who were already covered with so many tattoos, one more wouldn't have made a difference.

"That's a really cool tattoo," the boy said, nodding toward the photo in Sebastien's hand. "Who did it?"

"That's what we're hoping to find out," Sebastien murmured.

"I've never seen it before, but you can ask the others. They've been here a lot longer than I have."

As expected, none of the other tattoo artists recognized the elaborate spider design etched onto Christie Snodgrass's arm.

Sebastien thanked them for their time and left the shop with Rodriguez.

"How the hell does that kid sleep at night or wash his face in the mornings?" Rodriguez demanded as they climbed into the sweltering interior of the Crown Vic parked outside the nondescript one-story building.

Sebastien chuckled, starting the engine and fiddling with the air conditioner settings. "You're showin' your age, *mon ami.*"

Rodriguez laughed. "So you think there's nothing wrong with that kid having more holes in his face than an overcrowded pincushion?"

"I've seen worse."

"Of course. At your uncle's shop." Settling back in his seat, Rodriguez eyed him curiously for a moment. "Did you ever get any tattoos?"

Sebastien shook his head as he backed out of the parking space. "Not because I didn't want to, though. My grandmother despised tattoos and threatened bodily harm to my uncle and anyone else who even *thought* about giving me one. My uncle was smart enough to know she meant business."

Rodriguez grinned lazily. "Why didn't you just give yourself a tattoo?"

"I didn't trust my skills. Besides, what part of my grandmother threatening bodily harm to anyone who gave me a tattoo didn't you understand?"

Rodriguez chuckled. "She must be quite a pistol."

"Yep. Owns a few, too. Where to next?"

Rodriguez glanced at the computer printout they had retrieved from the police station before starting their rounds that afternoon. "Our next stop is a place called Tats Galore." His lips curved in a lascivious grin. "Substitute one of those letters, and I'd be a much happier camper right now."

Sebastien shook his head, mouth twitching. "You're sick, Rodriguez."

"Not as sick as the bastard who's got us on this wild-goose chase. If I never step foot in another seedy tattoo shop again, it'll be too soon."

* * *

"Love between spiders is a matter of life or death for the male species. Why? Because female spiders are generally larger than males, and they have the peculiar habit of turning their sexual appetite into normal hunger. After copulating, female spiders eat their mates with no sense of guilt whatsoever."

Francesca's matter-of-fact explanation induced loud male groans mingled with triumphant cheers from her female students, some of whom exchanged high fives across the aisle.

Suppressing a chuckle, Francesca continued. "For that reason, it's understandable that some male spiders exercise the healthy precaution of tying up females with threads of webs. This way they can mate properly and survive the, uh, romantic interlude without being eaten."

This time her male students celebrated, whooping and high-fiving one another as the girls glared at them in disgust. Someone in the back of the classroom made a lewd reference to S&M, and one grinning sophomore audaciously declared, "Just goes to show that even in the world of arachnids, males are still smarter than females!"

"You wish, Craig!"

"All right, all right," Francesca intervened before a riot erupted. "We'll see how smart *all* of you are when you take the unit exam next week."

The blithe reminder was met with muffled groans as the students gathered their belongings and slowly filed from the room. As they passed Francesca's desk, she overheard one student joke to another, "I think Professor Purnell was a spider in a past life."

"Oh yeah?" came the amused response. "Well, I hope she had better fashion sense!"

As the students' laughter trailed them from the room, Francesca glanced down at herself and grimaced, more than a little stung by the rude wisecrack. It wasn't the first time she'd found herself the butt of jokes, and it certainly wouldn't be the last. She knew that her students, and even some of her colleagues, called her the Spider Lady behind her back. In a department dominated by award-winning scientific researchers and academicians committed to advancing entomological studies in areas of ecological importance—such as integrated pest management and biological control—Francesca's singular obsession with spiders made her something of an oddity. The fact that she was the youngest faculty member, and the only African-American female, all but solidified her status as an outsider.

On most days Francesca didn't mind being invisible to her peers, and she most assuredly never gave a second thought to whispered jokes about her nonexistent fashion sense.

But that was before today.

Today she'd found herself the object of frank male interest by the most gorgeous man she'd ever seen. And for the first time in years, Francesca Purnell had longed to be someone she wasn't. Someone who took more pride in her appearance. Someone who *didn't* leave the house wearing unflattering muumuus and . . . Oh God, was that a raspberry preserves stain disguising itself as a tropical flower?

Heaving a sigh of disgust, Francesca stuffed her lecture notes inside her satchel and left the room.

The entomology department at Texas Agriculture and Business University, or TABU, was housed in the Eugene H. Kirby Center, named after a wealthy philanthropist and descendent of William Kirby, who'd been dubbed the father of entomology in the late nineteenth century. The Kirby Center comprised two large buildings that were connected by an atrium, and provided an abundance of laboratory, office, and classroom space. Specialized facilities within the center included a photographic darkroom, a temperature-controlled chamber containing a vast collection of insect specimens, three greenhouses, federally approved maximum quarantine areas, and an NIH-approved containment facility equipped for a full range of biochemical, physiological, and toxicological research and experiments. Everything Francesca had ever needed for her work could be accessed within the elaborate confines of the Kirby Center. The entomology department was well funded, as was the private university, attracting researchers and scholars from around the world.

With summer underway, many faculty members were off completing fellowships abroad or enjoying extended vacations with family. Francesca passed few familiar faces as she made her way through a labyrinth of brightly lit corridors and cubicles to reach her office, a long, narrow room she shared with three of her colleagues.

Only Peter Ueno occupied the room when Francesca entered. His straight black hair was mussed, as if he'd been jamming his hands through it. His fingers flew nimbly over the keyboard as he typed at his computer, transcribing raw data into scientific annotations he would later ask Francesca to proofread. Peter, whose concentration was in forest entomology, had a brilliant mind, but was a woefully bad speller.

Noiselessly Francesca dropped her satchel to the floor and sank into the chair behind her gray metal desk, the entire surface of which was covered with research papers, scientific journals, dog-eared logbooks, and department memos—much like the other three desks in the office. In fact, were it not for the oversize plastic tarantula perched upon her computer monitor—a gift from Peter when she won an outstanding alumnus award last year—Francesca could easily have mistook one of her colleagues' desks for her own.

Especially on a day like today, when her mind was light-years away.

Grimacing at the thought, Francesca logged on to the

computer and opened her e-mail. Bypassing junk mail from her younger sister, Tomasina, Francesca scrolled through a series of messages until she reached one from the editor of *The Black Entomologist.* In addition to teaching full-time and pursuing her postdoctoral studies, Francesca was an active member of the Entomological Society of America and served on the editorial boards of *The Southwestern Entomologist* and *The Black Entomologist,* the latter of which was preparing for the September issue.

She rummaged through her desk for a red pen, settled for a black ballpoint, and reached for the pile of manuscripts that had already been accepted for publication.

At length the furious typing behind her ceased, and Peter spoke. "How'd class go?"

Without turning around, Francesca answered, "Fine. I successfully averted a battle of the sexes."

Peter chuckled dryly. "Let me guess. You've started the *courtship, mating, and reproduction* unit."

"Bingo. At no time do my students pay more attention in class than when I'm discussing the mating habits of spiders. Every last one of them will probably ace next week's exam."

"That's a good thing, right?"

Francesca considered for a moment. "I suppose. But sometimes I just wish my students exhibited *half* the enthusiasm for entomology that I did as an undergrad."

"*You* were an entomology major," Peter reminded her. "Less than two percent of the students you teach are entomology majors. Most of them take the class to fulfill an elective and make what they think will be an easy A."

"I know," Francesca said with a weary sigh. It was the bane of her professional existence as a junior faculty member, being consigned to teach one- and two-hundred-level courses to freshmen who had no more interest in entomology than she did in learning how to build a nuclear weapon. In the four years she'd been teaching, not a day passed that she didn't wonder if she really had what it took to educate, enlighten, and engage today's college student.

"I think you're being too hard on yourself," Peter said, intercepting her thoughts, as he frequently did. "Don't forget that I had to observe your class last fall for peer reviews, and from what I could tell, your students were very excited about what they were learning. They asked a lot of questions, took notes, and seemed genuinely interested. And that was Introduction to Entomology—no mating habits were discussed." He paused meaningfully. "Not of spiders, anyway."

Francesca laughed, swiveling around in her chair to face her colleague.

She'd always thought Peter Ueno was attractive, in a scholarly sort of way. Dark, keenly intelligent eyes glinted with mirth behind rimless glasses. His olive-toned skin was mildly sunburned from hours spent outdoors conducting research into insect-plant interactions, as part of a grant funded by the USDA. He was medium height and kept himself in great shape, and at forty-two—ten years older than Francesca—he still boasted a head full of gray-repellant black hair.

"Seriously, Frankie," Peter continued, arms folded across his chest as he leaned back in his chair. He wore a faded western shirt, jeans that strained white at the knees, and scuffed brown boots. "I think your students realize what a great instructor you are. Your vast knowledge of arthropods comes across loud and clear."

"Of course it does," Francesca said, a rueful smile playing about her lips. "I'm the Spider Lady, remember?"

Peter's expression softened with mild sympathy. No one knew who had started the nickname, but once it was out there, like flies to flypaper, the moniker had stuck.

"It could be worse," Peter pointed out thoughtfully.

"You could be called Bug Lady, Bug Doctor, Little Miss Muffet, or—"

Scowling, Francesca held up a hand. "I get the point."

Peter grinned. "In comparison to those other nicknames, I'd say Spider Lady is pretty damned cool. Now all we have to do is make you a red-and-blue spandex costume, and you can relocate to New York City to crusade around town as Spider-Man's sidekick."

"Very funny," Francesca grumbled. As she swiveled back to her computer, she shuddered at the mental image of herself garbed in spandex.

Over my dead body.

In the deep cover of night, he searched for his next victim.

He had been hasty before, too hasty, and his mistake had cost him precious time.

For a moment the memory of that other one—the imposter—taunted him, causing his long, lean fingers to clench around the steering wheel in anger.

But just as quickly the anger dissipated, leaving him with renewed conviction. A renewed commitment to his purpose.

He had not chosen wisely before.

He would not make the same mistake twice.

Perfection, like a diamond buried deep in the earth's mantle, would take time and effort to uncover.

As he sat in the shadowy darkness of his car parked across the street, windows rolled halfway down to permit an occasional sultry breeze, he watched them.

Scantily clad in midriff-baring tank tops and micro-miniskirts, their laughter wafting toward him like sinuous curls of smoke, they sashayed across the parking lot in stiletto heels, following the seduction of neon lights emblazoned upon a nondescript one-story building.

SIRENS AND SPURS GENTLEMEN'S CLUB, the sign proclaimed, beckoning customers from the highway. Promising pleasures of the flesh for the right price.

Just looking at them, he felt his senses heightening, and his blood pounded through his veins. Surely he would find perfection in their midst, these beauties who offered their glorious bodies as temples to be worshipped. Two brassy blondes, a fiery redhead, and an exotically beautiful black princess.

At the entrance to the club, the princess paused and glanced over her shoulder.

He froze, his heart thudding in his chest. Not with fear of discovery.

With anticipation.

Her wide, dark eyes swept the darkness. As if she knew he was there. Watching. Waiting.

He held his breath as she hovered uncertainly in the doorway, biting her lush bottom lip. Then, with a toss of her head, she turned and disappeared inside the building.

A slow, satisfied smile crawled across his face.

Soon he would go mining for diamonds.

And soon he would make his selection.

Chapter 3

"Hey, Durand, what's with all the library books? You know they ain't gonna pay you more for getting another bachelor's degree."

Sebastien barely glanced up from the textbook he'd been scouring as Rodriguez, carrying a paper cup of coffee, sauntered through the open door of his office and sat, uninvited, in one of the visitors' chairs opposite Sebastien's desk.

"Who says they're paying me for the *first* one?" Sebastien muttered, turning a page in his book. He barely flinched at a graphic image of a man whose face had been ravaged after being bitten by a brown recluse spider. After the night Sebastien had spent poring through tomes filled with vivid photographs of every spider species known to man, nothing shocked—or disgusted—him anymore.

Rodriguez sipped his coffee, shaking his head at Sebastien behind the books piled haphazardly upon his desk. "So you still think you can solve the Snodgrass murder by tracking down a tattoo artist?"

After accompanying Sebastien to every tattoo and

body piercing shop within a forty-mile radius of the Motel 6 where Christie Snodgrass had been murdered, Rodriguez was a little sour on the whole tattoo angle. Sebastien supposed he couldn't blame him, since no one they'd questioned had ever seen anything resembling the artwork etched into Christie's arm.

"Maybe she treated herself to the tattoo before she left California," Rodriguez suggested, not for the first time. "Chicks do that kind of thing all the time—you know, to declare their independence, celebrate some sort of milestone in their lives."

Sebastien shook his head. "I already told you. The tattoo was fresh, less than a day old. The ME confirmed it as well."

Rodriguez shrugged. "Maybe Christie hooked up with some freelancer who gave her the tattoo. Doesn't mean it's the same psycho who butchered her." His mouth curved ruefully. "Don't you just love it when I play devil's advocate?"

"Of course," Sebastien muttered. Pushing out a deep breath, he closed the book and rubbed his unshaven face, feeling the bristly whiskers rasping against his hand. It had been a long day, though it was only two o'clock in the afternoon. In the forty-eight hours since Christie Snodgrass had been found brutally murdered, they'd learned very little, certainly not enough to provide any potential leads or suspects.

Of the thirty-odd motel guests they'd interviewed, no one had seen or heard anything amiss on the night of the murder. According to the credit card receipts they'd obtained, Christie Snodgrass had enjoyed a final solitary meal at Boudro's, one of many restaurants that lined the Riverwalk. The Alaskan salmon she'd ordered was barely digested at the time of death, a detail the ME—a self-proclaimed seafood connoisseur—had provided with a mournful shake of his head. There were fibers inside her mouth, mostly on her tongue, from the strip of cloth that had been used to gag her. Lab tests showed traces of a common sedative in her bloodstream, but not enough to confirm that she'd been drugged. There was no vaginal penetration, no seminal fluid, no fibers or skin cells embedded beneath her fingernails to reveal signs of a struggle—nothing to hint at the terror she'd endured before the violent massacre.

It would be another week before the crime lab reported the results of trace evidence collected at the scene, but on that score, Sebastien wasn't too optimistic. Any recovered hair strands or DNA samples could just as easily belong to a previous motel guest as to the perp. The crime scene technicians had gone through the motions, dusting the walls and furniture for latent prints, paying special attention to objects that could have been moved and those that were closest to the body. In reality, Sebastien could count on one hand the number of cases in his career that had been solved by lab work, contrary to what Hollywood wanted people to believe.

"I just spoke to Mr. and Mrs. Snodgrass," said Rodriguez, breaking into Sebastien's dark musings. "They agreed to stay put at the hotel today."

"How'd you manage that?" Sebastien asked, thinking of the grief-stricken couple who had haunted the police station since arriving in town two days ago.

"I convinced them that they needed the rest, and that the time we spent answering all their questions was time *not* spent finding their daughter's killer. They seemed to accept the truth of that logic."

"Thank God," Sebastien muttered grimly. He couldn't have handled another gut-wrenching day of fielding the couple's tearful demands for justice—especially not on two hours of sleep.

Outside his office, the noise of phones ringing, conversations buzzing, and keyboards clicking could be heard from the maze of cubicles and desks.

"They invited me to join them for dinner tonight," Rodriguez said. "I think I'll go. Might give me a chance to question them more about Christie's boyfriend, who's been too busy with surgical rotations to return any of my phone calls. Her parents seem to think he's in major denial about Christie's death."

Sebastien quirked a brow. "And you disagree?"

"Not necessarily. But I intend to find out one way or another."

Sebastien rolled his cramped shoulders and thought fleetingly of the killer massages an old girlfriend used to give him. He could use one right about now—the woman *and* the massage. "I think the boyfriend is a long shot."

Rodriguez gave a dismissive shrug. "Probably." He drained the rest of his coffee, then stood. "I'm going to finish calling Christie's friends and colleagues back home. If we get lucky, someone might be able to shed some light on what the last few days, or hours, of her life were like. If we're *really* lucky, Christie may have called one of her girlfriends to fess up about a cute guy she met at the Riverwalk, or to complain about a weirdo she caught staring at her."

Sebastien nodded, picking up another book from his desk. "Sounds like a plan."

Rodriguez lingered in the doorway, grinning. "Don't study that stuff too hard, *mi amigo,* or before you know it, you'll be mumbling to yourself about your tingling Spidey Sense and trying to shoot silk from your wrist."

"Very funny. Don't quit your day job, George Lopez."

After the detective left, Sebastien set aside his book, logged on to the Internet, and performed a search on Google using the key words "spider morphology." A few minutes later, after viewing a series of spider identification charts and Web sites dedicated to the study of arachnids, he came to an article entitled "The Role of Spiders in Modern Society."

The article, which had been published in a leading trade journal two years ago, was authored by a local entomologist who taught, of all things, spider biology at Texas Agriculture and Business University.

Suddenly alert, Sebastien quickly read the article, making note of the author's name at the bottom. F. Lee Purnell, Ph.D.

He printed out the article, made a couple of phone calls, then grabbed his jacket and headed out of the office.

For the second time that week, Sebastien found himself cruising the idyllic, tree-lined streets of the historic King William District. The town that had been established by wealthy German immigrants in the late nineteenth century occupied twenty-five blocks of land just south of downtown San Antonio, and was characterized by picturesque gardens and grand old Victorian houses shaded by big leafy trees. The elegant charm of the community drew in busloads of tourists, who browsed in the quaint shops, ate in the restaurants, toured the historic Guenther House Museum, and cozied up in one of the local bed-and-breakfasts for a relaxing stay within easy driving distance of the famed Riverwalk.

Ten minutes after bartering the keys to one of the newer unmarked Crown Vics—this one with functioning air-conditioning—Sebastien pulled up in front of a large brick Victorian painted in a shade his grandmother would call, in her lilting accent, sèvres blue. The house came complete with a columned wraparound porch and two-story bay windows. Giant cypress trees nestled close to the house like protective older brothers, and flowers bloomed in riotous profusion from planters hung above the porch.

As Sebastien started up the walk, he ran an appreciative eye over the candy-apple-red Lexus convertible parked in the driveway. INDY JNS, the license plate read.

Indiana Jones?

Chuckling softly, he wondered just what kind of character Dr. F. Lee Purnell would turn out to be. As he climbed the wide porch steps and pressed the doorbell, he envisioned a balding, middle-aged man sporting black horn-rimmed eyeglasses and a white lab coat with an ink-stained pocket, an introvert whose daring alter ego had talked him into buying the hot ride.

While he waited for someone to answer the door, Sebastien turned once again to admire the vehicle, and to contemplate how the professor could afford both the car and the expensive home on a teacher's salary.

Clearly, Sebastien mused, *he* was in the wrong line of business.

When no one appeared after another minute, he rang the bell again, then rapped his knuckles lightly on the etched-glass window of the door. It was then that he heard the noise, the low whirr of an electric appliance coming from the backyard.

Stepping off the porch, Sebastien followed the sound to a white lattice fence at the side of the house. He unlatched the gate and stepped through, announcing his presence by calling out, "Hello? I'm looking for Dr. Purnell?"

He scanned a small yard framed by more of those ancient cypress trees, tall manicured shrubs, and garden beds teeming with a vibrant palette of roses, azaleas, impatiens, and pink hydrangeas that perfumed the air. It was over one of these flower beds that a woman knelt, pruning roses with a handheld electric trimmer. She wore a white T-shirt under denim overalls and a wide-brimmed straw hat to shade her head from the punishing heat of the sun, which was already baking Sebastien's scalp.

"Hello?" he called a second time. "Ms. Purnell?"

The woman didn't respond or even glance over her shoulder. Thinking she couldn't hear him over the noise of the trimmer, Sebastien started across the brick path toward her. As he drew closer, he couldn't help but notice—and admire—the shapely roundness of her bottom, the denim stretching snug across her butt whenever she leaned forward.

Bon Dieu.

By the time Sebastien reached the woman's side, his mouth was watering, and he was convinced that F. Lee Purnell had to be the luckiest man in all of Texas if he came home to the sight of *that* ass every night.

"Ms. Purnell?"

The woman's head snapped up, and startled dark eyes stared at him behind black horn-rimmed spectacles.

With a jolt, Sebastien recognized the woman from the Espuma Coffee and Tea Emporium.

The dowdy librarian with an ass that put Beyoncé to shame.

His throat went dry. "I'm sorry," he said thickly. "I didn't mean to startle you."

Shutting off the electric trimmer and setting it down, the woman scrambled to her bare feet, the top of her head barely reaching his shoulder. Quickly she yanked off a pair of earphones connected to the iPod tucked into the front pocket of her overalls, and Sebastien realized that the reason she hadn't heard him was that she'd been listening to music.

"What are you doing here?" she demanded, sounding more baffled than frightened at the appearance of a strange man on her property.

Her voice surprised him. Smooth, husky, with a hint of a southern drawl he hadn't anticipated. He wondered what other surprises were in store for him. It couldn't get much better than the sweet apple-bottom.

Still somewhat distracted, he reached inside his jacket pocket and withdrew his badge, which he showed the woman, who was by now frowning at him.

"Detective Sebastien Durand," he introduced himself. "I apologize for scaring you, ma'am. I rang the doorbell, but no one answered. I'm looking for Dr. Purnell. Is he home?"

Those thick-lashed eyes widened a fraction beneath the low brim of the hat. "What's this about?"

"I wanted to ask him a few questions about a case I'm working on. Are you his wife?" *Please say it isn't so*, he silently begged. *Please tell me you're his daughter, or baby sister, or gardener.*

She pushed her glasses up on her slender nose, the thick rims skimming the high, sharp slope of her cheekbones. Full, lush lips threatened to send his imagination into overdrive, and her chin bore the faintest cleft, as if God Himself had brushed a gentle thumb across her face while she slept in the womb. Tufts of chestnut-brown hair peeked from beneath her wide hat, and Sebastien wondered how long it would take for an errant curl to wiggle free.

"Dr. Purnell is my father," she answered, "and, no, he isn't home."

"Do you know when he might be back?"

"He's out of the country." She hesitated. "For a year."

"I see." Disappointment washed over Sebastien. It had been a long shot, anyway. But why hadn't the secretary at the university's entomology department told him that Dr. Purnell was out of the country? She could have saved him a trip, albeit a short one.

"Is there anything I can help you with?"

"I don't think so." At least, not anything remotely related to the purpose of his visit. "Thanks for your time, Ms. Purnell."

"I'll walk you out," she offered. No doubt to make sure that he did, in fact, vacate the premises.

As she fell in step beside him, she asked, "If you don't mind me asking, Detective, exactly what kind of questions did you want to ask my father? I mean, I know he's not in any kind of trouble—"

Sebastien shot her a look. "You sure about that?" At her stricken expression, he laughed. "Sorry, I couldn't resist. Your father's not wanted by the law, Ms. Purnell— at least not that I know of. I was hoping to tap into his expertise with spiders."

She frowned. "But my father's not—" She stopped midstride, staring at him. "Wait a minute. Did you come here looking for Gordon Purnell?"

Sebastien shook his head, turning to face her. "I was looking for F. Lee Purnell."

"Oh! Well . . ." With a shy smile, the woman thrust her hand forward. "Francesca Lee Purnell. Nice to meet you."

Well, well, well. Things are looking up after all.

Before he could shake her hand, however, she snatched it back with a throaty chuckle that made his pulse skip. "Sorry," she muttered self-consciously, wiping her hands down the front of her overalls. "Almost forgot I've been digging in dirt for the last hour. Would you like to come inside for a glass of lemonade, Detective Durand?"

He smiled. "I'd love to."

As she led him across the terrace toward a pair of French doors, he lamented the fact that the baggy overalls no longer clung to her butt. But, considering the atrocity she'd been wearing the first time he saw her, the overalls were a huge improvement. Maybe the *next* time he ran into Francesca Lee Purnell, she'd be decked out in a leather bustier and Daisy Duke shorts that barely covered the ripe swell of her ass.

Sebastien gave an inaudible sigh. A guy could dream, couldn't he?

* * *

Hands in the pockets of his trousers, the detective followed Francesca into the large kitchen, his gaze skimming over the stainless steel appliances, custom cherry cabinetry, marble countertops, and center island with an electric cooktop and space for four bar stools. Francesca waved him into one of the chairs while she washed her hands at the sink, wishing she could slip away and freshen up without seeming to do so for his benefit.

She still couldn't believe that the gorgeous stranger from the coffeehouse, the man whose bold, intense gaze had lingered in her memory for the past three days, was actually here, in her house. One minute she'd been listening to Chopin while pruning her mother's prize roses; the next minute she was drowning in a pair of piercing eyes with irises the color of storm clouds.

Detective Sebastien Durand, he'd introduced himself in that dark, smoky drawl that sent a thrill pulsing through her veins. The way he'd pronounced his name—*Doo-rond*, with the second *d* barely audible—was unmistakably Cajun.

"This is quite a house you have," he commented. Even in the spacious high-ceilinged kitchen, he struck an imposing figure with his broad shoulders and hard-muscled chest. He was wearing a tailored sport jacket, pleated charcoal trousers, and a white broadcloth shirt without a tie. He also wore a shoulder piece, though the cut of his jacket was good enough that it nearly concealed the bulge of the weapon. He didn't sit down at the center island, as she'd offered, but stood resting his hip against the counter, the very essence of masculine power and grace.

Francesca filled two tall glasses with fresh-squeezed lemonade and walked over to him, all too aware of the way he watched her with those smoky, hooded eyes of his. She wondered what he saw when he looked at her, and contented herself with a fantasy that he found her as sexy as she found him.

She handed him a glass of lemonade, their fingers brushing during the transfer. Heat rushed to her belly. Their gazes locked for several charged moments before Francesca, clearing her throat, took a step backward in cowardly retreat.

"Um, thanks," she said, belatedly remembering his compliment about her home. "It actually belongs to my parents. I'm house-sitting for them while they're out of the country."

Sebastien took a sip of lemonade. "Where are they?"

"In Cairo. Digging up human remains."

"Come again?"

Francesca laughed. "My father is an archaeologist. A few months ago, he was asked to participate in a major archaeological excavation over in Egypt. Seems a group of scientists came across skeletal remains they believe belonged to Montezuma's descendants. The story was in the news not too long ago."

Sebastien nodded. "Sounds vaguely familiar. So your father was chosen for the excavation team? That's pretty cool."

"He thought so, too. Within a week, he and my mother were packed up and on a plane to Africa."

"Your mother's an archaeologist too?"

"No, just a groupie. She retired from corporate America several years ago and now travels everywhere with my father. They're inseparable." A wry smile touched her mouth. "Makes life a whole lot easier for me."

Sebastien chuckled low in his throat. "I would imagine. Are you an only child?"

"No, I have a younger sister," she said, easing onto a stool opposite him at the center island. She began to remove her straw hat, then considered the state of her hair—matted and damp with perspiration—and thought better of it. Presenting hat hair was *not* a way to win points in the sexy department.

Sebastien raised his glass to his lips and drank, his gaze never leaving hers. As she drew in a deep breath of his clean-scented male warmth, erotic images stole through her mind, a seductive fantasy that began with her knees drifting slowly apart and Sebastien stepping between them, his large, callused hands cupping her face as he slanted that sensual mouth over hers.

"This is the best lemonade I've ever had."

It took Francesca a dazed moment to realize that his words had not been part of her fantasy, that he'd actually spoken them aloud.

"Thanks," she croaked out, her face flaming as red-hot as her fevered imagination. "I, um, made it this morning."

Humor, and a touch of something wicked, glinted in his gray eyes. "Mmm. You make fresh-squeezed lemonade, you keep one helluva garden." He shifted closer, redoubling her awareness of him as he murmured huskily, "What other talents do you possess, Francesca Lee Purnell?"

Her throat felt tight, and her insides burned hotter with his nearness. She gave him a saucy smile, surprising herself. "Doesn't take much to impress you, does it?"

He threw back his head and laughed, a deep, smoky rumble that made her toes curl against the cool tiled floor. God, he was sexy.

"Depends on who's doin' the impressing," he drawled. "Me, I've always been a sucker for a smart tongue in a beautiful face."

Francesca smiled, as entranced by his words as the lazy, liquid accent that shaped them. "Where are you from, Detective Durand?"

"New Orleans."

She nodded. "I figured as much. How long have you lived in San Antonio?"

"Two years in August." Something like pain flickered in his eyes, disappearing so swiftly she might have imagined it. But she knew she hadn't, a hunch that was confirmed when he added quietly, "My family was one of many displaced by Hurricane Katrina."

"I'm sorry," she murmured softly.

"Don't be." He held her gaze with the compelling force of his own. "San Antonio, as I'm discovering, has a lot to offer."

Francesca's heart thumped. She could feel the heat between them, a heat as scorching as the summer sun. Every nerve ending in her body tingled as if he'd reached out and touched her. He was virile, strong, and all male. Pure, unadulterated, *dangerously* male.

Drawing in a shaky breath, she reeled in her thoughts. "You said you wanted to ask me about spiders?"

"That's right." As he straightened from the counter, preparing to shift gears, his eyes communicated a veiled promise that the mating dance between them was not over. Not by a long shot.

Francesca reached for her glass of lemonade and took a long, fortifying sip, wishing she had something stronger.

"I'm investigating the homicide of a woman who was found stabbed to death in a local motel," Sebastien explained.

"I heard about that. The tourist from California, right?"

He nodded, removing a photo from his jacket pocket. "There was a tattoo of a spider on her arm, the most unusual-looking spider I've ever seen. I haven't been able to find any photos of it, and I was hoping you could help me. I understand you're an authority on arachnology?"

"I don't know about all that," Francesca demurred, pleased that he'd done his research and was familiar with the term *arachnology*. Most people she knew reacted with a glaze-eyed look whenever they heard the word. Of course, most people she knew weren't entomologists.

"There are eleven extant and five distinct orders of arachnids," she explained, "which means that the different species of spiders number in the thousands. As much as I'd like to think so, Detective, I haven't seen them all."

"I'll keep that in mind," said Sebastien, with an amused look that conveyed what he thought of her modest attempt to downplay her expertise. He slid the photograph across the counter. "This is an actual picture of the tattoo found on the victim's arm. Do you recognize this spider?"

Adjusting her eyeglasses, Francesca leaned down to examine the photo.

After a moment, she looked up at Sebastien. "I do recognize the spider. It's called a Mexican Blood Walker, named for the unusual red markings on the abdomen." She paused, pursing her lips thoughtfully. "It's supposed to be cursed."

Chapter 4

For several moments the only sound in the room was the ticking of the antique grandfather clock in the hallway. Across the counter, Sebastien studied Francesca with an expression that gave nothing away.

"What do you mean by 'cursed'?"

"I read about it in a journal article last year. The Mexican Blood Walker is—*was*—indigenous to a very small region of the Yucatan Peninsula."

"Was?"

She nodded. "About three years ago, the entire species was supposedly wiped out in a fire. None survived, according to the article."

Those piercing gray eyes narrowed on her face. "What happened?"

Francesca frowned, trying to remember the details. "It all took place in Xeltu, a tiny fishing village in the Yucatan Peninsula. That summer, there was an epidemic of deaths caused by the Blood Walker, a rare, highly poisonous spider. The villagers were terrified. According to local folklore, the spider was believed to bear the hieroglyphic symbol of an ancient Mayan curse. During prehistoric times, anyone bitten by the Blood Walker died once, only to return to life inhabited by an evil, cannibalistic spirit."

She paused, carefully watching Sebastien's face, gauging his reaction. "I know it sounds like superstitious mumbo jumbo, but those people really believed their lives were in danger."

One corner of his mouth lifted in wry humor. "You're talkin' to the great-nephew of one of the most famous voodoo priestesses in N'Awlins. Believe me, I've seen and heard just about everything."

"Really?" Intrigued, Francesca was tempted to ask him more, but he merely smiled and said, "Some other time, *chère*, when we've gotten to know each other better. I don' wanna scare you away."

Francesca's pulse drummed at the idea of becoming better acquainted with Sebastien Durand, who had to be the sexiest, most compelling man she'd ever met in her life.

"I don't think there's anything you could say or do that would scare me away." She heard the words leave her mouth before she could stop them. Heat flooded her cheeks as she watched Sebastien's smile turn wolfish.

Briskly she cleared her throat. "As I was saying, the villagers were very superstitious. When victims died from a spider bite, their bodies were immediately burned to prevent them from coming back to life. This precaution also helped to reduce the spread of disease from the corpses. This continued for several months before the villagers came up with a solution to the crisis."

"And what was that?"

"To exterminate the Blood Walkers."

Sebastien frowned. "How do you exterminate an entire species of spiders?"

"They were systematically lured to a warehouse over the course of thirty days. Once they were trapped, a chemical pesticide was released into the air, killing the spiders and their eggs. Even if a few somehow managed to escape, they would carry the poison back to their nests and be dead within hours. After the warehouse was sprayed, the building was set on fire. That was the end of the epidemic. According to eyewitnesses, there were no more sightings of the Blood Walker after that."

Sebastien glanced down at the photo on the counter. "Until now."

"Yeah," Francesca agreed, following his gaze. "Until now. What an eerie coincidence."

"Could be that, or something else."

"Like what?" Francesca stared at him. "Wait a minute. Are you saying . . . Do you think one of those *villagers* is responsible for killing this woman and tattooing her body? Or someone who was in Xeltu during the epidemic?"

"I don't know. It's too early for me to draw any conclusions."

"Yeah, because *anyone* could have learned about the spiders the same way I did, by reading the journal article."

"True," Sebastien said, tipping his head to concede the point. "And that's what I'm hoping to find out. Do you still have it, by the way? The journal article?"

"I think so. Let me check in the study." As she started from the kitchen, Sebastien hung back politely. She glanced over her shoulder at him. "This may take a while. Most of my books are still packed away in boxes."

Accepting the unspoken invitation, Sebastien followed her from the room and down the hallway. As Francesca walked, she imagined she could feel his hot gaze on her back, specifically her rear end. But she knew that was ridiculous. Good-looking men didn't ogle Francesca Purnell, least of all when she was dressed like Farmer Bill in baggy overalls and a big straw hat.

Her father's study was located at the end of the hallway, a large room that boasted a twenty-foot ceiling and cherry-paneled walls that contained rows and rows of books, the upper tiers accessible by a pair of ladders on wheels. Dust motes swirled in the pale shaft of light that slanted into the room from a tall, narrow window. Several boxes filled with more books littered the floor, waiting to be unpacked.

Francesca knelt before one of the opened boxes and began rummaging through the contents. "I've been so busy with classes that I haven't had a chance to unpack and get settled in."

Sebastien propped a shoulder against the door frame and swept an appraising look around the room. "Did you grow up in this house?"

"No. My parents bought it eleven years ago. It was a fixer-upper, needed a lot of work. They poured blood, sweat, tears, and a small fortune into renovating it, but it paid off. This place is their pride and joy."

"Oh, I don' know about that," Sebastien countered mildly. When Francesca glanced up at him, he nodded toward the framed family photographs arranged on the massive cherry desk. In one photo, a smiling, bespectacled Francesca posed with her younger sister, Tommie, who'd refused to smile in protest of the braces she'd been forced to wear.

"Seems to me you and your sister are your parents' pride and joy," Sebastien observed.

Francesca chuckled. "Maybe, but this house is definitely a close second." Not finding what she was looking for, she got up and moved to the next box.

"Where were you living before you agreed to house-sit for your parents?"

"In an apartment complex closer to the university. I'll probably move back there when my parents return from Africa."

"Ever consider staying here with them?"

"No," Francesca said unequivocally. Just because she often dressed like an old maid didn't mean she had to *live* like one. "I haven't shared the same address as my parents since I graduated from college, and our relation-ship has been the better for it."

Sebastien chuckled, and damn if it wasn't the sexiest sound she'd ever heard. "I know what you're saying. I left my folks' house when I was fifteen. I couldn't have imag-ined goin' back again."

Francesca wanted to ask him why he'd left home at such an early age, but his cell phone rang. Murmuring an apology, he stepped into the hallway to take the call. As she listened to the low vibration of his voice through the open doorway, she found herself wondering if he was single. A man like Sebastien Durand could have any woman he wanted, and probably did. Beautiful, alluring, sophisticated women.

All the things Francesca wasn't.

She located the copy of *Texas Scientific Quarterly* just as Sebastien returned to the room. "I knew it was in here somewhere." Rising to her feet, she flipped to the first page of the article detailing the Mexican Blood Walker epidemic. "The article was authored by an American sci-entist who was residing in the village at the time. He was there with a team of other entomologists as part of a fed-eral research grant."

"Thanks," Sebastien said as he accepted the book from her. "I'll make a copy of the article and return this to you as soon as possible."

"Take your time," Francesca said. Out of the corner of her eye, she saw her father's Xerox machine and real-ized she could make copies for Sebastien herself. But then she wouldn't have an excuse to see him again.

How pathetic you are, an inner voice mocked.

"I should be getting back to my roses," she blurted.

"Of course. I've taken up enough of your time." Sebastien reached inside his jacket pocket and pulled out a card. "If you think of anything else, give me a call."

Francesca nodded, accepting the card from him. She

walked him to the door and stood on the porch as he made his way to a midnight-blue Crown Victoria waiting at the curb. Before climbing into the car, he glanced over at the red convertible parked in the driveway and grinned at Francesca.

"Nice ride," he said. "Yours?"

She considered lying to him, thinking she'd win major points in the sexy department if he believed she owned such a hot little number.

But she'd never been a very good liar. "It belongs to my father. He bought it for his fifty-ninth birthday last year."

Sebastien nodded, his grin widening. "Your father, the archaeologist. Explains the license plate."

Francesca grimaced. "Yes, unfortunately." The INDY JNS license plate had become the bane of her existence, ever since she'd been forced to junk her old car and drive the Lexus while her father was out of the country. She couldn't count how many times strangers had pulled up beside her at traffic lights and called out laughingly, "Indiana Jones! That's a good one!"

Sebastien climbed into his cruiser and slid on a pair of mirrored sunglasses. With his wicked good looks and killer smile, he could have starred in a Hollywood blockbuster. "I'll be in touch," he said.

Francesca could only nod and lift her hand in a slow wave as he drove away.

Figures, she mused as she headed back inside the house. Sebastien Durand was the first man in ages who'd shown any interest in her, and all she had to offer him was her knowledge of extinct spiders.

When Sebastien returned to the police station, Rodriguez met him in the noisy corridor and followed him back to his office.

"Looks like your hunch might be right about the spider tattoo," he announced as Sebastien set down his book and claimed his chair behind the desk. "I just got off the phone with two of Christie's best friends, and they both insisted that Christie never would have gotten a tattoo. Not only did she hate them, but she was also terrified of needles."

Sebastien grinned at the detective. "Kills you to admit I was right, doesn't it?"

Rodriguez scowled. "They also said Christie had a big argument with her boyfriend, Tad Cotter, before she left town. She felt as if Tad had been neglecting her, and she threatened to break up with him. He told her she needed time to cool off and think things over. If she still felt the same way when she returned from her trip, he'd accept her decision to end the relationship."

"Sounds reasonable enough. What do the friends think of Cotter?"

"They think he's an arrogant, self-absorbed, over-achieving jerk. But they also believe he genuinely cared about Christie and would never hurt her. As for his whereabouts on the day she was murdered, he was at the hospital the entire time. His resident surgeon confirmed it. Course, that doesn't mean he couldn't have hired someone to follow his girlfriend all the way to San Antonio and kill her, but it's a long shot." Rodriguez folded his arms across his chest and propped a shoulder against the door frame. "Where'd you run off to earlier? O'Hara says you flew the coop like a bat outta hell."

Sebastien rummaged through the paperwork on his desk for the Snodgrass case file. "I went to speak to a local spider expert about the tattoo."

Rodriguez arched a brow. "A spider expert?"

"Yeah. An entomology professor who teaches spider biology at TABU. I came across an article she'd written about spiders, so I wanted to see if she could identify the tattoo on Christie's body."

"Did she?"

Sebastien nodded, locating the manila folder. "She not only recognized the spider, she had one helluva tale to go along with it." He quickly relayed Francesca Purnell's account of the Mexican Blood Walker and the havoc the venomous spiders had wreaked on the village until they were destroyed.

When he'd finished, Rodriguez gave a long, low whistle. "You're right. That's quite a story. So what're you thinking? Our perp was there during the epidemic?"

"It's possible. I'm not ruling it out."

"Okay, humor me for a moment. The perp tattoos his victims, carves them up, then what? Hangs around to see if they come back to life?" Rodriguez frowned. "Wouldn't it make more sense if they were actually *bitten* by the spider?"

"Not if he doesn't have one handy. According to the article, they were all killed in the warehouse fire."

"So maybe our guy kept one for himself. These scientist types never destroy everything. They always keep a sample for research and testing."

"I thought the same thing. So, if this theory proved correct, perhaps the next question might be, does the perp plan to use the spider on his next victim? Or is he saving it for something else—some grand finale?"

In grim silence the two men regarded each other across the room. Neither had to guess what the other was thinking. Serial killers who left calling cards did so to taunt the police, to feed their own warped egos, and to create fear that they would kill again. The fact that Christie Snodgrass's murderer had taken the time and effort to brand her body with such an elaborate, sinister tattoo revealed a level of premeditation that didn't sit well with either detective.

Still, it was too early to tell what, or who, they were dealing with.

Sebastien held up the journal Francesca had loaned him. "I'm gonna track this guy down, see what else he can tell me about the Blood Walker."

"Good idea. And maybe you can ask the professor to talk to some of her colleagues to see if anyone else recognizes the spider. Might give us some leads."

"It's worth a shot. I need to return her book, anyway." He made it sound like nothing more than an errand, but the truth was that he definitely wouldn't mind seeing Francesca Purnell again. Since leaving her house, he hadn't been able to push her image out of his mind. A beautiful woman was hiding beneath all those frumpy layers of clothing. A smart, beautiful woman who intrigued him in a way he couldn't begin to explain. He was already looking forward to paying her another visit in order to return her book. He figured the more often he saw her, the better her attire would be, until one day he'd catch her wearing those ass-clinging Daisy Duke shorts he'd been fantasizing about since discovering her in the backyard, bent over a bed of roses. Damn lucky roses.

As if he'd read his mind, Rodriguez asked, "So, what's the professor like? And what kind of chick makes a living studying bugs?"

Sebastien chuckled. "Your guess is as good as mine, but from what I understand, she's considered an authority in the field."

Rodriguez grunted, straightening from the door frame. "Sounds like we may be needing her expertise to catch this nutcase."

Sebastien nodded, and tried not to think about other, more pleasurable ways Francesca could be of service to him.

Chapter 5

Night had fallen by the time Francesca let herself into the darkened house and locked the door. She'd gone to the university to finish some paperwork and had wound up staying until her rumbling stomach reminded her it was past dinnertime.

As she reached for the table lamp in the foyer, she felt a draft—a whisper across her skin, something not quite right. She stopped short, peering through the darkness.

She wasn't alone. Someone else was inside the house.

Fear pulsed through her blood. Two summers ago, there had been a rash of burglaries in the neighborhood, the thief escaping with expensive jewelry and priceless family heirlooms. And then, just as suddenly as the break-ins had started, they stopped. The culprit was never caught, and life returned to normal in the quiet community. Except that those who'd once scoffed at the idea of equipping their million-dollar Victorians with burglar alarms had changed their tunes.

Unfortunately, Francesca's parents weren't among them.

Francesca remained perfectly still, straining to listen above the ticking of the grandfather clock, which seemed loud, deafening. Her breath was shallow, the hairs standing on the nape of her neck. Whoever was in the house would have heard her come inside. The intruder was probably hiding in the shadows, waiting for an opportunity to attack her.

Think, Francesca, think!

If she could make it to the kitchen, she could arm herself with a butcher knife. But she couldn't be sure the intruder wasn't already in the kitchen, or even closer. Her quickest route of escape was through the front door. Once she was safely outside, she'd lock herself in the car and use her cell phone to call the police.

Having formulated a plan, Francesca began easing backward, edging toward the front door.

Behind her a floorboard creaked. As she spun around, heart in throat, a dark shape emerged from the shadows.

"Boo!"

Francesca's terror quickly turned to shock, then relief, when she recognized her younger sister's voice. *"Tommie?"*

"Yeah, it's me," came the laughing response. "I got you so good!"

Francesca marched over to the console and snapped on the lamp before whirling on her sister again. "Girl, are you crazy? Are you trying to give me a heart attack?"

Tomasina Purnell was laughing so hard she had to prop herself against the wall to keep her balance. "I wish I could've seen your face, Frankie," she choked out between gasps, wrapping slender arms around her flat midsection. "I thought you were going to pee your pants!"

Francesca gave her a withering look. "Real mature, Tommie. And what would you have done if I'd gotten a knife?"

"Ducked," Tommie retorted, and burst into another fit of giggles.

Shaking her head in disgust, Francesca turned on her heel and strode down the hallway to the kitchen. After a moment her sister followed, the sharp click of her high-heeled sandals echoing through the house.

"Aw, come on, Frankie," she cajoled. "Don't be mad."

"Why shouldn't I be mad?" Francesca snapped, removing two frosted glasses from the cupboard. "You scared the crap out of me! I thought you were an intruder. Where'd you park, anyway? I didn't even see your car!"

"I parked a few doors down. I knew you wouldn't notice."

"Nice, Tommie. Real nice. Don't you remember the string of burglaries that happened in this neighborhood a couple of years ago?"

"Of course I remember," Tommie grumbled, leaning on the doorjamb with one shapely hip thrust out. A wedge of smooth brown skin peeked out from beneath a pink tube top, and low-rise denim jeans clung like a second skin to long, curvy legs. With exotically slanted dark eyes, high cheekbones, and lush, pouty lips, twenty-nine-year-old Tomasina Purnell had the looks to rival any supermodel. And if she had a nickel for every time she'd been mistaken for one, she'd be a very rich woman—instead of a struggling dancer waiting to be discovered.

"Dad never let me forget about the burglaries," Tommie said bitterly. "He practically accused Roland of being responsible."

"He did not," Francesca said, pouring lemonade over two glasses of ice for the second time that day. "Dad may not think the world of your boyfriend, but he'd never call him a thief."

"That's right, Frankie. Take Dad's side, just like you always do."

"I'm not taking anyone's side," Francesca said emphatically, walking over to the center island and setting down the drinks. "I'm just letting you know that Dad never suspected Roland of those robberies. If he had, believe me, he would've called the police. You know Dad doesn't mess around."

"Yeah, whatever," Tommie muttered under her breath.

Unperturbed, Francesca slid onto a bar stool, picked up her glass, and took a long, leisurely sip. Tommie glowered at her from the doorway for a moment, then slowly made her way over, unable to resist the lure of her sister's fresh-squeezed lemonade.

Francesca hid a knowing smile as Tommie sat down across from her and claimed her drink. Her long dark hair, streaked with golden highlights, was parted down the center and swept over one shoulder.

"Have you eaten?" Francesca asked. "I've got some leftover chicken salad in the fridge."

Tommie shrugged, sipping her lemonade. "I'm not really hungry."

Francesca's eyes widened in surprise. Since childhood, Tommie's enormous appetite had been a running joke in the family. She'd always been the first to request dessert after dinner, and if she ever skipped a meal—which was rare—she became downright cranky.

"Not hungry? Who are you, and what have you done with my sister?"

Tommie didn't laugh, idly running a manicured fingertip over the rim of her glass and gazing into the pale contents.

"Hey," Francesca said softly. "Is everything all right?"

Tommie lifted her head and ran a critical eye over Francesca's chestnut-brown hair, which she'd washed after Sebastien left. The curls had dried naturally to form a soft, thick cloud about her face and shoulders.

"When are you going to let me straighten your hair?" Tommie asked. "You'd look so much better with a relaxer."

Francesca frowned. "There's nothing wrong with my hair." True, the same couldn't be said about her taste in clothes, but her hair—at least when combed and tamed—was perfectly fine. "You're avoiding my question."

Tommie pushed out a long, deep breath. "All right, fine. I ran into an old friend from college today. Nadine Howard. She and I were both dance majors. After graduation, Nadine moved to New York and got a waitressing job while she went on auditions." Tommie paused, forcing out the next words. "She just landed a small role in *The Color Purple* on Broadway."

"That's wonderful for Nadine," Francesca said quietly. "She must be very excited."

"Of course. She was in town visiting her parents. They're throwing her a party, and the *Express-News* is doing a story on her. She'll be famous before opening night."

Francesca's heart constricted at the abject misery on her sister's face. She knew Tommie would have given anything to be in her friend's shoes. Ever since she was a little girl, twirling around the house in a pink tutu and matching tights, she'd dreamed of performing on Broadway. But after years of her taking choreography classes and earning a bachelor's degree in dance, Tommie's onstage performances were limited to amateur campus productions and a brief stint in a local dance troupe, now defunct due to mismanagement.

"I know what you're thinking," Tommie said, a bitter note of accusation in her voice. "You're thinking I should've moved to New York like Nadine did. You think I'm not ambitious enough, or talented enough, to go after what I want."

Francesca shook her head slowly. "What I think," she said, reaching across the counter to touch her sister's arm, "is that you should stop trying to be a mind reader, especially since you're so lousy at it. I've never thought you lacked the talent or ambition to become a professional dancer."

Tommie stared broodingly into her glass. "I'll be thirty next year. What do I have to show for it? Credit card debt, a dead-end job as a secretary, a loser boyfriend. You don't have to deny it," she said when Francesca opened her mouth to protest. "I know Roland is a loser. He drives a delivery truck and still lives at home with his mother. Not exactly Mr. Right material."

Roland Jackson had been a source of contention between Tommie and her father ever since she'd started dating him two years ago. Gordon Purnell thought his daughter could do better, and had even gone so far as to blame Roland for Tommie's "lack of direction." Francesca had done her best to remain neutral and to keep her opinion about Roland to herself—no matter how often her father beseeched her to "talk some sense" into her sister.

But now she couldn't help but ask, "If you think Roland is such a loser, why are you still with him?"

Tommie lifted one shoulder in a dispassionate shrug. "I care about him, and he treats me well and accepts me for who I am. Aren't those good enough reasons?"

"That's not for me to decide," Francesca murmured.

Tommie snorted rudely. "Yeah, especially since you haven't exactly found *your* Mr. Right." Seeing Francesca flinch, she was instantly contrite. "Oh God, I didn't mean that, Frankie. I'm so sorry—"

"No, you were right," Francesca said mildly. "I'm not the most qualified to be dispensing advice on anyone's love life." Not when she could scarcely remember the last time she'd been on a date. Not when she seemed destined for the life of a spinster, surrounded by books on entomology and insects housed in glass jars.

Tommie tugged her full bottom lip between her teeth. "Frankie—"

Abruptly Francesca rose and walked to the sink with her glass of lemonade, barely touched. "I think I'll go to bed early tonight. It's been a long day and I'm beat. You're welcome to stay if you like."

"Come on, Frankie, please don't be mad. I didn't mean—" The rest of Tommie's apology was cut short by the sudden blast of a popular hip-hop song. She jumped up, peeling her cell phone out of the back pocket of her jeans and hurrying from the kitchen to take the call.

Francesca busied herself with washing dishes while her sister made arrangements to meet friends at a local nightclub. Even in high school, Tommie—though three years younger than Francesca—had been the one with the active social calendar, while her sister had spent many Friday nights alone in her room with her nose buried in a book.

"I'm heading out, Frankie," Tommie announced, returning to the kitchen and crossing to where her sister stood at the sink. She paused beside her, then draped an arm around Francesca's shoulders, the familiar gesture emphasizing their differences in height. While Francesca was petite at five-three, Tommie's body was poured into a voluptuous five-eight frame that turned heads wherever she went.

She gave Francesca a rueful smile. "Just because I'm feeling like a failure doesn't mean I have to take it out on you. Forgive me?"

Francesca smiled wanly. "Nothing to forgive. Well, unless I count that little stunt you pulled earlier, scaring me half to death."

Tommie chuckled. "I'm just glad you weren't wielding a knife."

"Would've served you right. Now get out of here before I change my mind about not being mad at you."

Tommie grinned, backing out of the room. "One of these days I'm going to drag you out to the club with me. You need to learn how to let down your hair and have a good time, Frankie."

"So you've been telling me for the past sixteen years. Lock the door on your way out."

After her sister left, Francesca finished washing dishes and cleaning up the kitchen, swiping crumbs and coffee spills from the granite countertops. Remembering Tommie's half-empty glass on the center island, she walked over to retrieve it. Spying a slip of paper on the floor, she bent and picked it up, turning it over to read the front. SIRENS AND SPURS GENTLEMEN'S CLUB was printed in gold lettering across the black business card, along with an address, a phone number, and the name of the proprietor. The card must have fallen out of Tommie's back pocket when she pulled out her cell phone.

Francesca's nose wrinkled in distaste. So now her sister was hanging out at *gentlemen's* clubs? What could Tommie possibly get out of watching other women strip in public?

Don't be such a judgmental prude, she could almost hear her sister saying. And she'd be right. Just because Francesca had no desire to ever step foot in a gentlemen's club didn't mean Tommie and her friends should feel the same way. Free-spirited and adventurous, Tommie had never suffered from the inhibitions that plagued her older sister. *She* wouldn't have gotten tongue-tied around Sebastien Durand. She would have been confident, sexy, and charming. By the time the detective left the house, Tommie would've had him wrapped around her pretty little finger. And if Francesca were more like her sister, she'd be getting dressed for a hot date right now, instead of facing another solitary evening at home.

You need to learn how to let down your hair and have a good time, Frankie, Tommie's admonishment echoed in her mind.

Francesca frowned down at the card in her hand.

Tommie might be right about her nonexistent social life, but Francesca had no intention of going to a strip club.

She'd leave *that* to her free-spirited, adventurous sister.

Tears blurred Tommie Purnell's vision as she sped away from the King William District in her sporty little Mazda coupe. The latest hit single from the Pussycat Dolls blared from the CD player, but Tommie wasn't in the mood to sing along. What she needed at that moment was a pint of Blue Bell ice cream, a box of Kleenex, and a good, long cry.

Running into Nadine Howard that afternoon had really done a number on her. She knew it was petty and ungracious of her to begrudge Nadine her good news, but Tommie couldn't help feeling somehow cheated. In college it was Tommie, not Nadine, who'd always landed the lead roles in the campus dance productions. An instructor had once waxed eloquent about the way Tommie embodied each performance piece through the "grace and lyricism of her movements." She was far more talented than Nadine, yet *she'd* never been called back for a second audition in any local production, while Nadine would soon make her debut on Broadway, the most celebrated stage in the world.

It wasn't fair, Tommie silently fumed, scraping tears from her eyes with the heel of her hand, momentarily veering into the next lane before pulling back into her own. When was she going to get *her* big break? What would it take to make *her* dreams come true? Did she have to move to New York and moonlight as a waitress while she went on auditions, as Nadine had done?

Maybe what she'd suggested to Frankie was true. Maybe Tommie *did* lack the talent and ambition to pursue her dreams, to make things happen in her life instead of waiting passively on the sidelines.

Tommie frowned, suffering a sharp pang of guilt at the reminder of her sister. The way she'd lashed out at Frankie had been mean-spirited and uncalled for. After all, it wasn't Frankie's fault her younger sister was a colossal failure, although she hadn't exactly made things easier for Tommie by setting the bar so high. Frankie, a perpetual straight-A student who'd won her first national science competition at the age of nine and received a scholastic achievement award from the governor that very same year, had always been a hard act to follow. She'd sailed through college in three years and earned her doctorate degree by the time she was twenty-seven. And since becoming the youngest faculty member at her alma mater, she'd published a ton of articles in prestigious scientific journals, picked up a few more awards, and had been invited to lecture at various international conferences.

It hadn't been easy for Tommie to grow up in the shadow of such brilliance. So after a while she'd stopped trying, choosing instead to forge her own identity. But no matter how many performances she starred in or how many beauty pageants she won, she'd never seen her father's eyes glow with pride the way they did over Frankie's accomplishments. Gordon Purnell and his firstborn were as close as any father and daughter could be. From the time Frankie was old enough to understand what her father did for a living, the two had bonded over discussions about archaeology and their mutual love for all things science. It hadn't taken Tommie long to realize that Frankie was the apple of their father's eye, the one he'd taken with him on archaeological digs during the summers, the one he shared his rare artifacts with when he returned from his trips. The one he'd entrusted to look after his house *and* prized convertible during his yearlong absence.

Francesca—the smart, mature, sensible daughter.

Tommie's lips twisted in a parody of a smile. Her best friend, Shauna Sutton, often told her she had unresolved issues, the kind that needed to be worked out on a therapist's couch. She was probably right.

But how could Tommie explain to a total stranger what she could hardly admit to herself, that while she loved and adored her older sister, a part of her secretly rejoiced in Frankie's frumpiness? For years Tommie had been acutely embarrassed by her sister's abominable taste in clothes, to the extent that she'd denied being related to Frankie at school and whenever they went to the mall together. When Frankie got her driver's license at seventeen, Tommie had begged her mother not to send Frankie to pick her up from cheerleading or dance practice, afraid of what her sister would show up wearing. And then one day, after being left out of yet another intellectual discussion between her father and Frankie, Tommie had a revelation. While she might never possess her sister's genius IQ or dependability, she would always have one advantage over Frankie, an unexpected advantage where genetics had otherwise failed her.

Tommie had her looks.

While her beauty had been known to stop traffic, Frankie, upon entering a room, barely earned a second glance, blending into the background like beige wallpaper. It wasn't that she was unattractive, not with her doe eyes, high cheekbones, and a killer body she hid beneath those tacky muumuus she insisted on wearing. No, Frankie Purnell could hold her own in the looks department.

But she didn't have a clue.

And as long as she remained in the dark about her natural assets and clung to her homely appearance like a security blanket, Tommie could enjoy her status as the beautiful, popular, outgoing sister.

She'd take whatever advantage she could get.

Her cell phone rang, the music of her favorite rapper

colliding with the Pussycat Dolls. Keeping one hand on the steering wheel, Tommie dug inside her back pocket and retrieved the phone.

"Hello?"

"Hey, Tommie," came the low, muffled greeting. "It's Gloria."

"Hey, girl." Tommie frowned. "What's wrong with your voice?"

"I have the flu. I've been in bed all day, too damned weak to do anything."

"Sorry to hear that," Tommie said, easing her foot off the gas pedal as she passed a darkened police cruiser parked on the side of the highway. "Were you on the schedule tonight?"

"Yeah, that's why I'm calling. I was wondering if you could do me a huge favor and fill in for me."

Tommie groaned. "Girl, you have the worst timing in the world. I was on my way to the club with—"

"Please, Tommie? I wouldn't ask if it wasn't really important. I called Jennifer first, but she's studying for an exam and can't work tonight. Yelena says if I can't find a replacement, I'll have to drag my butt in, flu and all. You know what a bitch she can be."

"Yeah, I know," Tommie grumbled, thinking about their manager at the Sirens and Spurs Gentlemen's Club, where Tommie had been moonlighting as an exotic dancer for the last three months. In that short period of time, she'd had more run-ins with Yelena Slutskaya than all the other dancers combined, due in large part to the fact that Tommie was the only one who had the courage to stand up to the strict, domineering Russian woman. Tommie took a certain amount of satisfaction in knowing that the only reason Yelena kept her around was that the customers loved her. She was beautiful and charming, and her dancing skills surpassed those of any other girl at the club.

When Tommie stepped onstage, no one could take their eyes off her.

"She'd kill me for telling you this, but Yelena's the one who suggested that I call you," Gloria confided, then loudly blew her nose.

A triumphant smile lifted the corners of Tommie's mouth. "Don't worry. Your secret's safe with me."

"So you'll do it? You'll fill in for me?"

Tommie swerved around a motorist who was testing her patience by driving too slow. Luckily, the police cruiser staked out on the side of the road had long since receded from her rearview mirror.

"Tommie?" Gloria tentatively prodded.

Tommie heaved a resigned sigh. "All right, I'll fill in for you. But you owe me big time. I was looking forward to hanging out with my friends tonight, not working."

Gloria sniffled. "I know, and I'm really sorry, Tommie."

Tommie felt another pang of guilt. "Hey, it's not your fault you got sick. Besides, I could use the extra money. Get some rest, and I hope you feel better soon."

She hung up and tossed the phone onto the passenger seat, then drummed her fingertips on the steering wheel, pondering the evening ahead. Instead of working it out on a dance floor with her girlfriends, she'd be working a stage before a roomful of leering men, smiling gamely while they groped her body and tucked dollar bills into her G-string.

Tommie chuckled mirthlessly as she steered her Mazda into the far right lane and approached her exit. She supposed if she was going to be ogled and groped by strange men, she might as well get paid for it. Not that money was the only reason she worked as a stripper.

Last year, one of the dancers at the Sirens and Spurs had been discovered by a talent agent, who happened to be out for a night on the town with some business associates. After watching Allison's performance, he'd approached her with the offer of a lifetime, the opportunity to be represented by his agency. Before long, Allison was starring in commercials for local car dealerships and grocery chains. Then a few months ago she'd signed a lucrative contract with one of the top modeling agencies in Houston.

All that because she'd been in the right place at the right time.

After hearing that story from her friend, Jennifer Benson, who worked as a dancer at the club and waitressed at a local café to put herself through school, Tommie had needed little convincing to apply for a job at the Sirens and Spurs.

She'd been keeping it a secret from her family ever since. For one thing, she knew her parents would die of embarrassment if any of their uppity friends and neighbors found out their daughter moonlighted as a stripper. Gordon Purnell would find a way to blame Roland, citing Tommie's decision to work at a strip club as another example of her poor judgment and "lack of direction." And Frankie, with her antiquated notions about sex, wouldn't understand why her sister would willingly *choose* to bare her body to a roomful of strangers.

As far as Tommie was concerned, her family need never know about her secret gig. She was almost thirty years old, too damned old to be answering to others. What she did in her private life was nobody's business but her own. Once she became rich and famous, being the black sheep of the Purnell family wouldn't matter to her, anyway.

Or at least that's what she told herself.

Thick smoke hung over the darkened nightclub and stung the stranger's eyes as he watched a tall, voluptuous brunette sashay onto the stage in ice-pick heels. A coquettish smile curved her lips as she launched into her dance routine, which consisted of gyrating her hips and shaking her buttocks to the beat of a vulgar rap song he'd never heard in his life—and hoped never to hear again.

Every table in the place was occupied, filled with leering men and more than a handful of couples out on a date. He'd chosen a table strategically located in a shadowy corner near the stage. Close enough to accomplish his mission, but obscure enough to avoid drawing attention to himself. And although he detested the taste of alcohol, he ordered a beer and nursed it while he watched the performers onstage.

He'd already dismissed the first three prospects as unsuitable. Two of them had tattoos, and the other bore a small raised scar on her ankle.

He'd initially balked at the idea of finding perfection in a strip club. Surely the one he sought couldn't be discovered in such a seedy place, where the tables were coated with cigarette ash and the floors were sticky from spilled beer and God only knew what else. But he'd soon realized the wisdom of visiting the Sirens and Spurs Gentlemen's Club. After all, where else could he openly view women's naked bodies in order to make an informed selection? And weren't the most precious diamonds found in the coarsest bowels of the earth?

The dancer onstage had stripped down to a red G-string. Her large, firm breasts barely moved as she worked one side of the stage, shaking and shimmying in a way guaranteed to please her male customers. When one lewdly grinning man beckoned to her with a crisp bill, she sauntered over to him and lowered herself to a crouch to give him a better view of what he was paying for. He apparently liked what he saw, for he began to tuck folded bill after bill into her G-string, letting his fingers linger upon her hips as he did so.

The stranger watched for several moments with

mounting impatience. It seemed an eternity before the girl glided to her feet and spun slowly in his direction.

When her dark eyes met his, he held up a bill and inclined his head in the barest hint of a nod. He needed to get an up close and personal look at the merchandise.

Anticipation heated his blood as the brunette sashayed toward him, a sultry smile on her lips.

Time to go mining for diamonds.

Chapter 6

Friday, June 15

When Sebastien stepped through the front door of his one-story brick rambler at two A.M., he wasn't surprised to find his seventy-five-year-old grandmother fast asleep in her favorite armchair in the living room, nestled beneath one of her knitted blankets. An antique lamp glowed softly on the small table beside her. On the television, CNN was reairing an episode of *Larry King Live*. A humorless, pinch-faced Condoleezza Rice was discussing the war in Iraq and defending the U.S. military's continued occupation.

Sebastien walked over to the coffee table, picked up the remote control, and turned off the television, knowing Augustine Durand wouldn't appreciate waking up to the sight of ole Condie—her least favorite person in the world.

Grinning wryly at the thought, Sebastien crouched in front of his sleeping grandmother and reached up to remove her eyeglasses, which were slipping off her arrow-slim nose. As his hand neared her face, she said without opening her eyes, "Thank you for shutting it off. I swear dat woman's voice was startin' to give me nightmares."

"I figured as much." Sebastien chuckled, gently pushing her glasses back into place. "Even after all these years, *Mamère*, you're still a light sleeper."

Behind the thick lenses her eyelids lifted, and a pair of smoky gray eyes smiled into his. "I'm old, not comatose."

Sebastien laughed. He remembered, as a rebellious teenager, trying to sneak into his grandmother's house past curfew. After years of practice, he'd learned how to negotiate the old floorboards, knowing which ones creaked and which were safe to step on. But no matter how stealthy he was, the moment he tiptoed past her bedroom door, she'd call out sternly, "Boy, have you lost your everlastin' mind? Do you know what time it is?"

The punishment for breaking curfew included washing windows, scrubbing floors, cleaning the attic, mowing the lawn—and not just at his grandmother's house, either. Standing on the porch with her fists planted on ample hips, a medley of Cajun French tumbling from her mouth, she'd often sent him next door to offer his services to the neighbor, an elderly widow who'd welcomed the free labor. Sebastien became so accustomed to tending Mrs. Thibodaux's house and yard that it was often one of the first things he did when he came home from LSU on the weekends. *She* looked forward to his visits almost as much as his grandmother.

Augustine glanced at the clock mounted on the wall and frowned. "*Il est après duex heures.* Why you home so late?" she asked, though Sebastien rarely ever made it home before midnight, especially when he was working a big case—which the Snodgrass murder promised to be.

"Had a bunch of paperwork to catch up on," he answered, figuring his grandmother didn't need to hear the gruesome details of homicide cases that consumed his every waking thought.

Straightening from his crouching position, he leaned down to drop a kiss on top of Augustine's head, which was lumpy from rollers and covered with a teal satin bonnet. As she watched, he removed his shoulder holster and Glock, making sure the weapon was secured before laying both items on the sofa table. He tugged his shirttail from the waistband of his trousers and ran a hand around the back of his neck, trying to dislodge a cramp that had bugged the hell out of him all day.

"You look tired, *cher*," his grandmother observed, thick dark eyebrows knitted together in a worried little frown. "You don' get enough sleep."

"Look who's talkin'," Sebastien teased, making his way down the hall to the kitchen. "Who's the one staying up, watching TV at all hours of the night?"

He heard the creak of the armchair as Augustine got up and followed him. "Are you hungry? I can fix you a plate. I made some baked chicken and stuffing."

Sebastien's stomach growled in anticipation of the mouthwatering fare he'd grown up on. Every Sunday after church, his grandmother had prepared enough food to feed a small parish. Red beans and rice, steamed crawfish, gumbo, fried catfish and chicken, mustard and collard greens, sausage and corn bread, and yellow cake with chocolate icing served for dessert. Cousins, aunts, and uncles—five generations of south Louisiana relatives—had filled the tiny wood-frame house on Metairie Street, bringing anecdotes of wayward children, juicy gossip, and plenty of laughter and love.

Hurricane Katrina had scattered many of those same relatives around the country and destroyed the only home Sebastien had ever known, leaving nothing but a pile of rubble in its wake.

Shoving aside the painful memories, Sebastien mustered a smile for his grandmother, who hovered in the doorway, waiting to fix the promised plate. "I'd better not eat this late, *Mamère*. But I'll definitely take leftovers for lunch. Everyone'll be jealous."

She clucked her tongue. "Take enough to share, like I done taught you."

Chuckling, Sebastien opened the stainless steel refrigerator and snagged an ice-cold bottle of Heineken, then trailed his grandmother back to the living room. The floral silk of her housedress made a soft swishing noise as she walked, her slippered feet padding along the hardwood floors.

She reclaimed the armchair, and Sebastien settled down on the sofa. "How was your day?" he asked, opening his beer and tipping the bottle toward his mouth.

"Jus' fine. Had choir practice this evenin'. Guess what happened?"

Sebastien took a swallow of beer. "What happened?"

Her eyes shone with pride. "Minister Paige chose *me* to sing a solo next Sunday in church."

"Hey, that's wonderful, *Mamère.* The congregation's in for a special treat."

"Oh, go on with you, boy," Augustine said, blushing like a schoolgirl even as she waved off the compliment.

Which only made Sebastien shower her with more. "You know I've always enjoyed hearin' you sing, *Mamère.* Growing up, that was the best part about being dragged to church with you every Sunday. Your solos used to bring down the house."

"Pastor Brazelton's *sermons* brought down the house," his grandmother corrected, quick, as always, to share credit with others. "I jus' served as an instrument of praise and worship, dat's all. And I don' remember draggin' you nowhere, *p'tit boug.* Talk about!"

Sebastien grinned. "That's because you're gettin' old. And if memory serves me correctly, *Mamère,* the only thing Pastor Brazelton used to bring down were folks' eyelids."

Augustine laughed, a warm, welcome sound from a

woman who'd endured enough tragedy and suffering to test the faith of Job.

"What I'm gon' do with you, T'Bas?" she asked, her eyes twinkling with mirth as she shook her head at him.

Sebastien smiled at the familiar nickname. "You been askin' that question since I was seven years old. You ain't figured it out yet?"

"*Mais non*, I haven't," she agreed, rising from the armchair with a little effort. "Maybe it'll come to me in my sleep. And speakin' of sleep, don' you stay up all night goin' through that stuff," she warned, nodding toward the thick manila folder Sebastien had dropped on the table in the foyer when he got home. "It's already late, *cher*. You need to get some rest."

"I will," Sebastien promised, then winked at her. "Scout's honor."

"Humph. You ain't never been a Boy Scout. They wouldn'ta known what to do with the likes of you, T'Bas." Shaking her head, she leaned down and planted a kiss on his cheek, then patted it gently. "See you in the mornin', baby."

"Night, *Mamère*." Sipping his beer, Sebastien watched as his grandmother shuffled down the hallway toward her bedroom. Beneath the long housedress she wore, she looked small, almost fragile—two words that had never been used to describe Augustine Durand.

Affectionately known as "Mama August," she'd been the matriarch of her Lower Ninth Ward neighborhood, the woman everyone came to for recipes and advice on marriage, careers, and childrearing. Life had blessed—or cursed—her with the wisdom to dispense counsel on such matters, because by the time she was thirty years old, she had buried two husbands and three stillborn babies. Refusing to succumb to grief, she'd thrown herself into raising the two children God had spared her, working tirelessly to feed, clothe, and eventually put them through college.

And years later, when her firstborn came to her seeking help with his rebellious fifteen-year-old son, Augustine had taken the boy in, vowing to whip him into shape. She'd done just that, disciplining Sebastien with an iron fist that was tempered by the love and affection his parents had seldom shown him.

His parents' Cadillac had been swept away by violently surging floodwaters when Hurricane Katrina struck.

Sebastien lowered his beer bottle and closed his eyes, his gut clenching painfully at the memories that followed.

His grandmother had never forgiven herself for her role in the tragedy that claimed his parents' lives. On that fateful morning, Leonide and Bernice Durand were on their way to Augustine's house to pick her up, although in a previous phone conversation she'd adamantly refused to leave the city with them, not wanting to abandon her home and friends. At first they'd accepted her decision, knowing how stubborn she could be when it came to being uprooted.

As they headed out of New Orleans, planning to spend a few days with friends in Houston until the storm blew over, they'd told themselves Augustine would be all right. She'd survived the tragic loss of several family members and lived through her own share of wars and natural disasters. No hurricane named Katrina would pose a serious threat to the indomitable Mama August.

But as Leonide and Bernice sat on the freeway jammed with other motorists fleeing the Gulf Coast, as the weather forecasts grew more dire and every radio station reported news of the mayor's mandatory evacuation order, they realized they'd made a terrible mistake in leaving Augustine behind.

By the time they turned around and hurried back to the city, it was too late. Katrina had made landfall.

Unbeknownst to them, Sebastien had already arranged transportation out of the city for his grandmother and several of her neighbors. He hadn't accepted Augustine's decision not to evacuate before the hurricane. With a stubbornness to rival her own, he'd barged past her into the house, thrown some of her belongings into a suitcase, then herded her and her friends onto a bus bound for Houston.

Hours later, he'd joined his fellow police officers in search and rescue operations, never imagining that his own parents would be among the dead.

Augustine had been devastated to learn that her son and daughter-in-law had come back for her. Inconsolable with grief, she'd blamed herself for refusing to evacuate the city with them. If she hadn't insisted on staying behind, they all would have arrived safely in Houston, instead of just her. The knowledge that she'd survived while they had perished in a watery grave—on their way to rescue *her*—was too much for her to bear. While she'd accepted the deaths of two husbands and three stillborn children as part of God's divine plan, she'd placed responsibility for this latest tragedy squarely upon her own shoulders. Guilt and sorrow had ravaged her body faster than any tumor could have, leaving nothing but a shadow of the strong, vigorous woman Sebastien had always known and revered.

Opening his eyes, Sebastien looked down to find that he'd spilled some beer on his shoes. Swearing softly under his breath, he removed the leather loafers, got up, and walked to the kitchen to discard his empty bottle and grab some paper towels.

Returning to the living room, he knelt and mopped at the spill, grateful that the rug was dark. He didn't think his grandmother would be pleased to know he'd spilled beer in the living room. When he was younger, she'd banned him from eating or drinking in the parlor, an immaculate room filled with antiques, chintz furniture covered in protective plastic, and the only color television in the house. He'd defied her mandate at least once a week, mostly on Sunday afternoons when the Saints were playing and his grandmother stayed behind after church to help clean up or to go visit the sick and shut-in.

Armed with a can of soda and a bag of chee wees, he'd settled down for a lazy afternoon of watching football, careful not to leave a single trace of evidence that he'd broken the rules.

A grim smile now curved Sebastien's mouth. If only life were still as simple as keeping his grandmother's living room clean.

With a deep, heavy sigh, he finished mopping at the beer, wadded up the paper towels, and tossed them in the wastebasket located in the powder room.

Standing in the foyer, he eyed the thick case file he'd brought home to work on. Although it was three in the morning, he knew sleep would elude him if he tried to go to bed. He had too much on his mind, saw too many ghosts whenever he closed his eyes. His dreams were haunted by the bloated faces of his parents and others who'd drowned in the raging floodwaters, of homicide victims whose cases remained unsolved.

After another moment, Sebastien picked up the manila folder and walked over to the sofa.

He couldn't bring back Leonide and Bernice Durand or the countless other victims of Hurricane Katrina, nor could he return Christie Snodgrass to the living.

But with any luck, he could find her killer before he struck again.

"Is this seat taken?"

Francesca glanced up from the grilled chicken salad she'd been picking through to find her colleague, Peter Ueno, standing at her table with a tray in his hands. She smiled at him. "Hey, I didn't know you'd be on campus today."

"Had some research to do in the lab. Mind if I join you?"

"Of course not. I could use the company."

Peter slid into the chair across from her and promptly dug into his meal, a turkey burger with French fries. "I'm starving," he said around a mouthful of food. "Haven't eaten a thing since yesterday afternoon. How was class today?"

Francesca speared a chunk of chicken with her fork and nibbled on it. "Uneventful." She surveyed Peter's mussed hair, wrinkled T-shirt, and stubble-darkened jaw. "Long night?"

He grimaced. "You could say that. Sarge kept me up for hours, whining and scratching at the door to be let out every twenty minutes. I took him to the vet first thing this morning. Turns out the old man has bladder stones."

"Poor Sarge," Francesca murmured, thinking of the sweet-tempered golden retriever that had been Peter's constant companion for the past twelve years. "He must be miserable."

"Yeah. The doctor prescribed some medication to treat the infection and reduce the frequent urinary urges. It's supposed to work really fast."

"That's good. Hopefully you'll both get some sleep tonight."

"I'll drink to that," said Peter, raising his plastic bottle of Coke in a mock toast before taking a healthy swig. Reaching for his burger again, he paused to frown at Francesca, who was absently poking at a cherry tomato. "Something wrong with your salad?"

Francesca shook her head. "I'm not very hungry." Truth be told, she'd been too preoccupied with thoughts of Sebastien Durand to concentrate on much else for the past two days. Images of him had invaded her mind at the most inopportune moments, such as that afternoon in class when she'd been explaining the differences between spiders and insects and had suddenly remembered the detective calling her beautiful. She'd stammered over her words and promptly lost her train of thought. Snickering, her students had stared at her while she racked her brain trying to recall what she'd been talking about, no doubt sealing their impression of her as a scatterbrain.

Inwardly groaning at the memory, Francesca looked across the table at Peter. "Do you remember reading about the Mexican Blood Walker epidemic in *Scientific Quarterly* last year?"

Peter paused in the middle of dragging a French fry through a puddle of ketchup on his plate. A deep furrow lined his brow. "I vaguely remember that article," he said slowly. "Rare, poisonous spiders terrorized a small village, right?"

"Right."

Peter nodded, shoving the ketchup-coated fry into his mouth. "Sure, I remember. Why?"

Francesca hesitated, suddenly realizing that the information Sebastien had shared with her might not be public knowledge. None of the newspaper articles or television reports about the murdered tourist had mentioned the mysterious spider tattoo left on her body—which meant the media had not gotten hold of this particular detail.

"Why do you ask?" Peter prompted again.

Francesca shrugged. "No particular reason. I came across the article again while I was unpacking, and I couldn't remember whether we'd discussed it before."

"We did, briefly. I thought the villagers' solution to the crisis was extreme. You disagreed, which was surprising coming from you."

She shot him a sardonic look. "Because I'm the Spider Lady?"

"No, because you're always advocating the importance of conserving spider species."

"Only when it's possible. Some species of spiders are harmful to humans, as was the case with the Mexican Blood Walkers. They were preying on those people as if their habitat had been threatened. So, yes, while as a rule I *don't* support spider species extermination, I understand why the Xeltu villagers had to take such drastic measures to protect themselves." She frowned. "Don't tell me you still disagree with that?"

Laughing, Peter held up his hands in mock surrender. "Hey, I'm not going to get into a philosophical debate with you about whether humans or spiders are the dominant species. No *way* am I winning that argument, not on two hours of sleep."

Francesca stared at him in disbelief. "This isn't about who ranks highest on the evolutionary food chain, Peter. This is about venomous, predatory spiders killing innocent men, women, and children. This is about survival."

"That survival thing goes both ways, Frankie." His mouth curved cynically. "When was the last time you heard about someone receiving the death penalty for killing a spider?"

She frowned. "You're missing the—"

"Am I interrupting something?"

Francesca looked up to find her best friend, Patricia Garza, standing at her elbow, one finely sculpted eyebrow arched as she divided a speculative look between Peter and Francesca.

Peter managed a small, cryptic smile. "Frankie and I were just having a friendly debate about her favorite eight-legged creatures."

Patricia held up a manicured hand. "Say no more. Any talk about insects over lunch is just plain *wrong*."

"Spiders aren't insects," Francesca automatically

corrected. "They belong to the *Araneae* group. *Insects* belong to the *Insecta* group."

"Okay. Whatever." Plunking down her sushi and Diet Coke, Patricia claimed the last chair at the small round table.

Patricia, who served as the director of recruitment at the university, had been blessed with creamy skin, long-lashed amber eyes, and dark, glossy curls that tumbled past her shoulders. While Francesca had zero fashion sense, Patricia was always stylishly dressed, choosing clothes and accessories that flattered her full figure, such as the red blouse and straight-legged charcoal pants she now wore with a pair of low-heeled designer pumps.

Peter glanced at his watch. "Hate to eat and run, ladies," he said, scooping up his meal tray and rising from the table, "but I've got some paperwork to finish up before the end of the day. Catch you two later."

As Francesca watched him wend a path through the bustling cafeteria and head out the door, she tried to dismiss the uneasy sensation that something was wrong with her friend. Something other than a sick dog at home.

"What was *that* all about?"

"Nothing," Francesca murmured, returning her attention to her abandoned chicken salad, which now looked about as appetizing as burnt toast.

"Didn't look like 'nothing' to me. In fact, if I didn't know better, I would think you and Peter were having a lovers' quarrel."

Francesca scowled. "Well, then, I guess it's a good thing you know better."

Patricia laughed. "Why do you act like it's so impossible for you and Peter to become more than just friends?"

"Because it is! I'm no more interested in Peter than he is in me."

Patricia arched a dubious eyebrow. "Don't be so sure about that."

Francesca leveled a gaze at her friend. "What's that supposed to mean?"

"Oh, I don't know." Patricia's eyes twinkled with mischief as she dipped her sushi in soy sauce and popped it into her mouth. "Anything can happen. You and Peter have been friends for a long time."

"So have you and I."

"You share an office together—"

"With two other people."

Patricia was undeterred. "You work in the same field, share some of the same interests."

"Doesn't mean we're secretly in love with each other."

"Maybe *you're* not," Patricia conceded, chewing thoughtfully. "But it wouldn't surprise me in the least to find out Peter is interested in you."

Francesca snorted, shaking her head in exasperation. "Girl, you're delusional."

"Why?"

"Look at me," Francesca said, then wished she hadn't as Patricia ran a critical eye over her unkempt ponytail, oversize T-shirt, and baggy jeans. "Do I *look* like the kind of woman men secretly pine over?"

"Not at the moment," Patricia admitted with a disapproving frown, "but that's purely by choice. If you wanted, Frankie, you could have any man on this campus with the snap of your fingers."

Francesca laughed. "I think you've got me confused with my sister."

"Like hell. You're just as beautiful as Tommie is. The only difference between you and your sister is that she knows what to wear and takes risks, and you don't."

Francesca made a face but offered no rebuttal. What was there to refute? Patricia was absolutely right about Francesca and her sister. Tommie had always been the risk-taker, while Francesca preferred to play it safe. Safe and predictable.

She had a fleeting image of the business card her sister had left behind at the house two nights ago. SIRENS AND SPURS GENTLEMEN'S CLUB, the card had read. *Where your pleasure is our promise.*

Without thinking, she blurted, "Have you ever been to a strip club?"

Patricia paused, a piece of sushi halfway to her mouth, brows lifted in surprise. "A strip club?"

Francesca nodded, throwing a self-conscious glance over her shoulder to make sure no one had overheard her. She could only imagine what her colleagues and students would think if they knew what she was contemplating.

Good Lord. What *was* she contemplating?

"I've gone to see male strippers," Patricia answered, a wicked grin tugging at her mouth. "*That's* always an experience. But I've never been to a gentlemen's club, if that's what you're asking."

"Why not?"

Patricia shrugged. "I don't know. Breasts aren't really my thing. I've got a perfectly fine pair of my own."

Francesca laughed, her gaze inexorably drawn to the scooped neckline of her friend's blouse. Patricia made no secret of the fact that her double-D-cup breasts— proudly dubbed "The Girls"—were, in her opinion, her best attributes.

"Wait a minute." Patricia's eyes narrowed suspiciously. "Are *you* thinking about going to a strip club, Frankie?"

Heat flooded Francesca's face. "Of course not! I was just . . . um, curious, that's all. My sister . . . She and her friends . . ."

Patricia gave her a knowing grin. "Don't be embarrassed about wanting to take a walk on the wild side," she teased.

"I never said anything about wanting to walk on the wild side," Francesca grumbled. But even as the denial left her mouth, her mind was filled with vividly erotic images of Sebastien kissing and caressing her, making love to her.

"I need to get back to the office," she muttered, standing so abruptly that she nearly tipped over her chair.

Patricia gave her a quizzical look. "Is everything okay?"

Everything's just fine, other than the fact that I've suddenly turned into a horny adolescent who daydreams about sex twenty-four hours a day!

As she and Patricia left the dining hall, Patricia sent her a sidelong grin. "If you're really serious about going to a strip club, Frankie, I'd be more than happy to take you. There's a place downtown—Hardbodies—that has the hottest male strippers around. I'm talking *sizzlin'* hot. It'll be fun."

"I'll think about it," Francesca said halfheartedly.

The only man she wanted naked and gyrating in her face was Sebastien Durand.

And that's when she knew she was in deep trouble.

Chapter 7

"Thank you for agreeing to see me on such short notice, Dr. Fincher," Sebastien said as he settled into the proffered chair across from a large desk cluttered with papers, file folders, and a hodgepodge of textbooks. An oak bookcase behind the desk was crammed with editions of every scientific journal imaginable. Potted plants arranged on the windowsill baked under the bright sunlight that poured through the paned glass, keeping the room temperature several degrees too warm. Sebastien resisted the urge to tug at the silk noose around his neck, wondering what had possessed him to wear a tie in the first place when it was ninety-eight degrees outside.

"Would you care for some coffee, tea, or water, Detective Durand?"

Coffee or tea? In this damned heat? "Water would be great, thanks."

Norman Fincher made his way over to a mini refrigerator tucked into a corner of the office and removed an eight-ounce bottle of water. As he walked back over and handed it to Sebastien, he smiled ruefully. "I know it gets rather warm in here. My colleagues call this office the 'greenhouse room' for the way it traps heat."

Sebastien chuckled. "Great view, though," he said,

nodding toward the window that overlooked the beautifully landscaped campus grounds filled with students hurrying to class or loitering around in small groups, laughing and making plans for the weekend.

Sebastien twisted the cap off his water bottle and took a swig as Fincher sat behind the desk and folded his hands atop a stack of papers. As chair of the entomology department at the San Marcos university where he'd taught for twenty-six years, Dr. Norman Fincher was in his late fifties with thinning gray hair, sharp features, and a trim physique. Shrewd blue eyes flecked with silver regarded Sebastien across the length of the desk.

"On the phone you said you wanted to ask me about an article I wrote for *Texas Scientific Quarterly.* Is that correct?"

"That's right. I'd like to learn more about what happened in Xeltu. I understand you were there with a team of other researchers as part of a federal grant."

Fincher nodded. "We were there to study the vertical stratification and beta diversity of arthropods in the rain forests of the Yucatan, one of the most biologically diverse habitats in the world. The project was jointly funded by the National Science Foundation and the Smithsonian Tropical Research Institute. As described in my article, our objectives were to study elements of the beetle fauna, conduct research on *Satyrinae* butterflies, and gather specimens for the university's insect collection, which is available to other researchers through our loan program. Our field station was located in the village of Xeltu, which, as you know, is where the epidemic occurred."

Sebastien nodded. "According to your account, the first casualty was a seven-year-old boy."

"Tragically, yes. He was outside playing by himself when he was bitten by the Mexican Blood Walker." Fincher's expression turned grim. "I can still hear his mother's hysterical wails as she pleaded for her son's body not to be burned, to be given a proper burial. As I explained in the article, village custom dictated that the body be cremated at once."

"Because of the ancient curse."

"Precisely." Those silvery blue eyes narrowed thoughtfully on Sebastien's face. "Are you a superstitious man, Detective Durand?"

A lazy smile tilted one corner of Sebastien's mouth. He was always amused by that question. Damn right he was superstitious. He'd never met a Cajun who wasn't.

"If you're askin' whether or not I think those villagers were crazy for believing what they did," he replied, "the answer is no."

Fincher nodded slowly. For a moment his gaze drifted past Sebastien, to the window beyond his left shoulder. When he spoke, his voice was remote, as if he'd been transported back in time to that tiny Mexican village. "I'm a scientist, trained to believe that every phenomenon has a rational explanation rooted in hard, cold fact. I've never been superstitious, and quite frankly I'm skeptical of those who are. But after a month in Xeltu, even *I* began to wonder if there was any credence to the legend of the Blood Walker."

Sebastien said nothing, studying the man across from him, hoping the professor would reveal more in the ensuing silence. But after another moment Fincher chuckled wryly, as if embarrassed by his own admission. His gaze returned to Sebastien. "You can imagine the kind of stress we were dealing with, trying to live and work under those extreme circumstances, always wondering which one of us might be next. If not for the important project that brought us there, I have no doubt that some members of our research team would have gone home the first chance they got. They were understandably traumatized, and I wouldn't have faulted anyone for packing up and leaving."

"But you weren't going to," Sebastien surmised.

Fincher shook his head. "The thought of leaving never crossed my mind."

Frowning, Sebastien sat forward in his chair. "I'm having a hard time understanding something, Dr. Fincher. According to everything I've read, spiders don't attack in herds, and they don't lie in wait and attack people. They only bite humans when they're scared and are trying to defend themselves. But these Blood Walkers seemed to be preying on the villagers, deliberately stalking them. How do you explain that?"

"I can't," Fincher said simply. "As you stated, spiders are not predators of humans. They generally prefer to live in undisturbed areas where they can catch insects in peace. The level of aggression we witnessed in the Mexican Blood Walker was unprecedented, like nothing we'd ever seen before. Those spiders behaved as if their natural habitat was under siege, and they had to protect it at all costs.

"The most logical explanation I can provide for what happened in Xeltu is that spiders are ectotherms, which means that changes in temperature alter their activity levels. In other words, temperature can affect their ability to hunt if it varies too much from their norm. So spiders may show higher levels of activity when exposed to higher temperatures, and activity will *decrease* when they are exposed to cooler temperatures."

Sebastien nodded slowly, digesting the information. "So what you're saying is that the hotter it gets, the more predatory these spiders become."

"Theoretically."

Sebastien wondered if the same pattern would apply to Christie Snodgrass's killer. Would the predator become more bloodthirsty as the summer wore on, as the temperatures kept rising?

Dread coiled in his gut at the mere thought. Just that morning, the weatherman had declared no end in sight

to the punishing heat wave that had gripped South
Texas for over a month.

"Interestingly enough," Fincher calmly continued, "it
was warmer in the Yucatan that summer. Not drastically
warmer, but enough, perhaps, to have upset the balance
of the spiders."

"And turn them into killing machines," Sebastien muttered grimly.

Pursing his lips, the professor leaned back in the chair
and lightly tapped his fingertips together. "Contrary to
popular belief, Detective, only a small number of spiders
possess venom that is fatal to humans, which is what
made the Mexican Blood Walker so extraordinary. The
venom released by this rare, deadly species caused severe
necrosis and systemic failure in the victim, resulting in
sudden paralysis and death. Even if an antivenom had
been available, by the time the victim was discovered it
would have been too late."

Sebastien remembered that the journal article had
contained gruesome photos of the ravaged body of a vil-
lager who'd been bitten by the Blood Walker. The
spider's venom had attacked the man's tissue cells like
a swarm of piranhas, causing lesions that covered over
eighty percent of his body.

Sebastien frowned. "Something's still bothering me.
The timing of the spider attacks, the suddenness. The
species was indigenous to that region, had been for cen-
turies. Had anything like this ever happened before?"

Fincher shook his head. "Not that I'm aware of. Ancient curse notwithstanding, what happened in Xeltu
three years ago was the first time in recorded history that
the Blood Walker preyed on humans." He glanced at the
gold watch peeking from beneath the starched cuff of
his shirt. "I'm afraid we'll have to wrap this up, Detective.
I'm giving a lecture in Austin this evening, and I still

have a few things to complete before I head out to battle that god-awful traffic."

As Sebastien stood and shook the professor's hand, he said, "Can you provide me with the names of the other researchers who were part of the expedition? I'd like to speak to them as well, if possible."

Fincher hesitated, then gave a slight nod. "I'll have my secretary e-mail the list to you, although I don't know how helpful it will be. Of the twelve team members who traveled to Xeltu, only two remain at this university. The rest are scattered around the country, teaching at other schools or working in the public sector. But I suppose you could still interview them over the phone." His shrewd gaze probed Sebastien's face. "I've answered all of your questions, Detective, but you still haven't answered the one I asked you over the phone. Why is my article on the Mexican Blood Walker of such interest to a homicide detective in the San Antonio Police Department?"

Sebastien paused at the door, tucking his hands into his pockets. "That's what I intend to find out, Dr. Fincher." Knowing it was an unsatisfactory response but not inclined to offer more, he thanked the professor for his time and left the office.

It was six o'clock by the time Sebastien made it back to San Antonio, nearly an hour after leaving Norman Fincher's office. He returned to the police station to check his voice mail and drop off a plastic evidence bag containing the now-empty water bottle he'd gotten from Fincher. Though he hadn't treated the professor as a suspect, Sebastien believed in covering all his bases, which meant having Fincher's fingerprints checked out against any prints lifted from Christie Snodgrass's crime scene.

After returning a few phone calls, Sebastien left the

station and headed toward the King William District, taking a chance that Francesca Purnell would be home.

When he pulled up in front of the large house, he was relieved to see her father's red convertible parked in the driveway. He grabbed the borrowed journal from the passenger seat and climbed out of the car.

As he started up the walk, he surveyed the quiet, tree-lined street with its elegant Victorians, pretty little gardens, and manicured green lawns. It was a far cry from the Lower Ninth Ward neighborhood he'd grown up in, where old shotgun houses and tiny corner grocery stores and Laundromats had provided a bleak landscape for the city's poorest blacks.

It was safe to assume, from the expensive car in the driveway to the million-dollar home she lived in, that Francesca Purnell had never experienced poverty, had never gone to bed hungry or been forced to fend off homeless drunks on her way to school. She and Sebastien were as worlds apart as two people could ever be.

So what did he care? It's not like he had marriage on his mind.

Shaking his head at the turn of his thoughts, Sebastien pressed the doorbell and waited.

Moments later, the heavy oak door swung open. Behind the horn-rimmed glasses she wore, Francesca's dark eyes widened in surprise at the sight of him standing on her porch.

That was the first thing he noticed.

The second, and by far the most important, was that her legs were bare. And they were glorious. Firm, shapely thighs and sleekly toned calves, the kind of legs any man would kill to have wrapped around his waist during hot, mind-blowing sex.

Sebastien's body reacted in a surge of pure, unadulterated lust.

"Sebastien?" Francesca blurted out in surprise, and

the sound of his name on her lips, in that soft, husky voice of hers, made his erection throb against the zipper of his pants. *Mon Dieu.*

"Wh-what are you doing here?" she stammered.

Behind his mirrored sunglasses, Sebastien reluctantly dragged his gaze away from her magnificent legs and held up the book. "Brought it back safe and sound."

"Oh." She reached for it, and he deliberately let their fingers brush during the exchange, the satin warmth of her skin heating his blood. Their eyes held for a moment, and then she cleared her throat self-consciously. "Did you, um, find it helpful?"

"Very," Sebastien murmured, slowly removing his sunglasses and tucking them into the front pocket of his shirt. "Thanks for loaning it to me."

"You're welcome." Her naked toes curled against the gleaming hardwood floor as she stood there, hugging the book to her chest. She wore a white T-shirt that was three sizes too big and caught her at midthigh, and for the first time Sebastien glimpsed a pair of navy blue shorts underneath. While they weren't the skimpy cutoffs he'd been praying for, she was at least showing some leg. *A lot* of leg. Progress had definitely been made, although, with his body still thrumming with lust, Sebastien didn't think he could handle the sight of Francesca any less clothed than she was now.

She stepped back, opening the door wider. "Would you like to come inside, Detective?" she offered, tacking on the formal address as if belatedly realizing she'd called him by his first name a minute ago.

As he brushed past her into the house, he caught a whiff of her scent, soap mingled with a hint of night-blooming jasmine. Even *that* turned him on.

"Did I catch you at a bad time?" he asked as he stepped into the wide foyer of carved mahogany paneling and spied two empty cardboard boxes pushed against the wall in the hallway.

"Not really," she said, closing the door behind him. "I was just doing some unpacking. At the rate I'm going, by the time my parents return from Africa next year, I'll still be living out of boxes."

Sebastien chuckled. "On the bright side, at least you'll be ready to move right back out."

She laughed, a warm, husky sound that made his mouth run dry. "Good point. Can I offer you something to drink, Detective?"

"No, thank you. Actually," he drawled, turning around to face her, "I was wondering if you'd like to have dinner with me."

Her eyes flew wide in a manner that was becoming endearingly familiar. "Dinner?" she echoed, as if he'd spoken in tongues. "Tonight?"

He smiled, dipping his hands lazily into his pockets. "Yes, dinner. Tonight." He paused. "If you don't already have plans, that is."

She shook her head. "No."

He waited a beat. "No, you won't have dinner with me? Or no, you don't have plans?"

"No, I don't have any plans. But . . . well . . . I can't have dinner tonight."

He arched an amused brow. "You fasting, *chère?*"

She laughed. "No, of course not."

"Then you can have dinner with me."

She hesitated, scraping small white teeth over the lush curve of her bottom lip. "I really need to finish unpack—"

"You've put it off this long. What's a few more hours?" When she continued to hedge, he dropped his voice to a silky caress. *"Si vous plaît?"*

He watched her dark eyes soften and tasted victory even before she murmured, "All right." Self-conscious, she smoothed a hand over her messy ponytail, where wisps of chestnut-brown hair had escaped to frame her face. "I'll, uh, need to change first."

"No problem. I don't mind waiting."

"Okay. But no place fancy," she warned. "I don't have anything dressy to wear."

Sebastien reached up, unknotted his silk tie, and tugged it free from his collar, then loosened a few buttons on his shirt. "Problem solved."

With a shy smile, Francesca turned and headed up the winding staircase. Sebastien stood watching through the open cherry railing until those killer legs disappeared from view. Then, shaking his head in wonder, he wandered into the large living room that boasted an eclectic mix of African artifacts, English antiques, and hand-carved furniture made of dark, glossy woods.

He was studying an elaborate oil on canvas painting when Francesca returned to the living room ten minutes later. He turned, a question about the artist on the tip of his tongue. At the sight of Francesca, he promptly lost his train of thought.

She had changed into one of those gauzy peasant blouses with a scooped neckline and full, billowy sleeves, which made her look soft and feminine. Nice.

What *wasn't* so nice was the long brown Gypsy skirt she wore. He hated it. Not because the skirt was unattractive, but rather, because it was so damned *long*. He felt cheated, like a starving man who'd been served a lavish meal, only to have the plate snatched away as he reached for a fork. If Sebastien could have arrested Francesca and charged her with the crime of concealing those beautiful legs, he would have.

Beneath the spoiler skirt, she wore a pair of brown sandals with a short wedge heel, no open toe. She'd done away with the untidy ponytail and arranged her hair into a neat, sensible twist that accentuated the slender curve of her neck.

An improvement, yes, but he'd have given anything to see those thick, silky tresses loose and tumbling about her face and shoulders.

And he would, Sebastien decided in that moment.

After all, he made a living exploring mysteries and uncovering people's secrets. One way or another, he would uncover the mystery that was Francesca Purnell, peel away every layer, literally and figuratively, until the sexy, beautiful woman hiding beneath was revealed.

"Are you ready?" she asked, a note of apprehension in her voice.

Sebastien's mouth curved in a slow smile as he started across the room toward her. "*Allons, chère,*" he murmured softly. "Let's go."

Chapter 8

Francesca was a nervous wreck.

As she sat ramrod straight in the passenger seat of Sebastien's unmarked cruiser—knees pressed tightly together, hands folded neatly in her lap, face averted to the tinted window—she wondered how on God's green earth she was going to get through the evening without making a complete fool of herself.

It was one thing to *fantasize* about being with Sebastien; it was quite another to actually find herself on a real date with him. The last time she'd been on a date was three years ago, and it hadn't really been a date, not in the traditional sense of the term. She'd been at a science conference in Beijing, and one of the other attendees, whom she'd chatted with between sessions, had invited her to have drinks with him one evening. She and Jarvis Watkins had been the only two black entomologists present out of only a handful of Americans in attendance, so naturally they'd gravitated to each other.

Over cocktails in the hotel lounge, they'd swapped stories about their work and discussed scientific advances in the field of entomology. He'd been a perfect gentleman, making no overtures as he walked her back to her hotel room and wished her good night. Early the next morning, Francesca ran into him coming from another guest's room, a beautiful blonde he'd apparently met after parting company with Francesca the night before. They were draped all over each other in the doorway when Francesca stumbled upon them on her way to the elevator for the early-bird breakfast. She would never forget the guilty expression on Jarvis's face when he looked at her, then down at the rumpled clothes he'd been wearing just hours ago.

He'd avoided her like the plague for the rest of the week.

That painfully awkward incident had confirmed Francesca's growing belief that while some men might appreciate her intellect, very few were interested in pursuing her romantically—or even sexually. Although Jarvis had enjoyed talking shop with her, he'd sought out another woman to spend the night with, to satisfy his needs. He'd obviously determined that the only stimulation Francesca could provide was of a cerebral nature, and he'd had enough for one evening.

Which was why Sebastien Durand was such an enigma.

Where Jarvis had only been marginally attractive, Sebastien was gorgeous, breathtakingly so. He could have *any* woman he wanted, whenever he wanted, wherever he wanted. But for reasons unknown to Francesca—and probably the rest of the population—he'd set his sights on *her.* "Frumpy Frankie," as she'd once been called by a group of laughing, pointing classmates as she got dressed in the locker room after gym, donning a checkered corduroy skirt over purple stockings that bunched at her ankles. She wondered what those same girls would say if they could see her now, being driven to a restaurant by a man whose dark good looks rivaled any Hollywood heartthrob's. No doubt they would question Sebastien's sanity—as she herself was now doing.

Not only had he asked her out on a date, but then

he'd refused to take no for an answer. And he'd played dirty, too, speaking French to her in that deep, black-velvet voice of his. Just thinking about it made her shiver and cross her legs tightly.

The sudden movement drew Sebastien's inquisitive gaze. "Are you cold?" At her nonplussed look, he nodded toward the dashboard, where the frigid air pumping through the vents battled the sweltering heat outdoors. "Too cold for you?"

She shook her head. "I'm fine." Glancing out the window, she realized they were heading away from downtown. "Where are we going, by the way?"

"You'll see."

Her lips relaxed into a smile, and she felt some of the starch leave her spine. "Are you always this mysterious, Detective?"

He chuckled softly. "Only when it suits my purposes."

She laughed, then glanced around the roomy interior of the Crown Victoria, not only surprised by how clean it was, but also how "unofficial" it looked. Among discarded fast food containers and coffee-stained paper cups, she'd expected to find handcuffs dangling from the glove compartment, a police-issue shotgun at the ready, and a wire mesh or glass divider separating the front seat from the back. But other than a sticker in a corner of the windshield bearing the SAPD logo, the occasional crackle of the police band radio, and the fact that Sebastien was armed, she might have forgotten her date was a cop.

She turned her head just a little and studied him with a sidelong glance. He wore dark trousers and a gray-and-white-striped broadcloth shirt open at the collar to reveal the strong column of his throat. The sleeves were rolled up to muscled forearms dusted with smooth black hair. Her gaze followed the line of his thick wrist to settle on his hands, which rested lightly on the steering wheel.

Big, strong, capable hands, guiding the vehicle with the relaxed ease of someone who spent a great deal of time behind the wheel. As she stared at his hands, she found herself remembering the brush of his warm, slightly callused fingers when he'd returned her book to her. She'd been yearning for his touch ever since.

As if sensing her silent appraisal, Sebastien glanced at her. "What's on your mind, baby girl?"

Inside her sandals, her toes curled at the endearment. "I was just thinking that I could have driven," she lied. "I don't want you to get in trouble for taking the car on personal business."

His lips curved in a slow, lazy grin. "I won't get in trouble," he drawled. "And I wouldn't have let you drive, Francesca. Not on our first date."

Her heart tripped. "Our first? Meaning there'll be more?"

Those smoky gray eyes pinned hers. "If I have anything to do with it," he said huskily. "And believe me, *chère*, I will."

His words, and the glittering promise in his eyes, sent a tingle of pure sexual awareness dancing up her spine.

Not for the first time, she wondered what Sebastien saw when he looked at her. Though his expression had given nothing away, she'd sensed his disappointment earlier when she returned from changing her clothes.

After she'd rummaged around in her walk-in closet for ten minutes, the blouse and skirt she'd settled on had seemed like the best choice. Not that she had many options. As she'd stood in her closet surrounded by a drab collection of shirts, slacks, and skirts—with a couple of halfway decent suits worn strictly for interviews and conferences—she'd realized, perhaps for the first time, just how woefully limited her wardrobe was.

Francesca frowned, plucking a piece of lint from her skirt. Maybe she'd finally accept Patricia's offer to take her shopping. If she and Sebastien really did have a second date in their future, she wanted to be prepared.

As they headed out of the city, the sun dipped lower behind them, shooting streaks of red across the sky that stretched above miles of rolling green ranchland.

Sebastien drove to a little waterside restaurant off the beaten path, well away from the tourists and crowds that routinely flocked to the Riverwalk. They were seated outside at a cozy round table covered with linen and adorned with a single white candle in a glass globe.

After the waiter took their orders and bustled away, Francesca stared across the table at Sebastien. "How did you find this place?"

He smiled at her. "Do you like it?"

"It's beautiful," Francesca exclaimed, gazing out at the shimmering lake surrounded by lush green forest. A young couple strolled along the shoreline, holding hands and talking quietly. It was postcard-perfect.

"I'm glad you approve," Sebastien said, leaning back in his chair and watching her, pleased by her reaction.

"I've never been here before. Lived here all my life and never even knew this place existed, right outside the city."

"It's a hidden treasure. Keeps the crowds away."

Her gaze swung back to him. "How'd *you* find out about it?"

A soft, enigmatic smile touched his lips. "I can be very resourceful when I want to be."

Francesca made no comment as she picked up her glass and took a sip of water. She wondered how many other women Sebastien had brought to the cozy lakeside restaurant since moving to San Antonio. With its romantic ambiance and scenic lakefront views, this was the kind of spot that guaranteed thank-you sex afterward. Not that Sebastien needed any help getting a woman into bed, she thought gloomily.

"You're the first."

Her eyes snapped to his face. "First what?"

"The first woman I've ever brought to this restaurant." He paused. "In case you were wondering."

"Oh." Francesca feigned nonchalance, even as her insides warmed with pleasure at his words. "I wasn't. Wondering, that is."

"No?" The knowing gleam in his eyes told her he knew better.

Thankfully, the arrival of their meals spared her from answering. In silence she watched as the waiter served their entrées and poured white wine into their glasses with an elegant flourish before slipping away.

As Francesca dug into her blackened tilapia, she asked conversationally, "Were you on the police force in New Orleans, Detective?"

"Sebastien."

She blinked, fork halfway to her mouth. "Hmm?"

"Call me Sebastien, the way you did earlier. I liked it."

"All right . . . Sebastien."

"Much better," he said approvingly, gazing at her. "You have an incredible voice. Anyone ever tell you that?"

"*Me?*"

"Yeah, you. It's soft, a little throaty. Sexy as hell." His eyes darkened as he added huskily, "I've been hearing it in my dreams ever since we met."

Heat pooled between Francesca's legs. Their gazes locked across the table. She had never before been so acutely, physically aware of a man as she was in that moment, almost breathless from the impact on her senses.

"That goes both ways," she told him softly, then watched his eyes grow heavy-lidded with desire.

He lifted his glass and took a sip of wine, holding her gaze over the rim. The look in his eyes was so powerfully seductive that if he'd picked her up and carried her out of the restaurant that very moment, Francesca wouldn't have protested.

Slowly setting down his glass, he picked up his fork and knife. "Eat your food, *chère*," he murmured, "before I do something that might embarrass us both."

Oh God. Beneath the table, Francesca's knees trembled hard. Bowing her head slightly, she drew in a deep lungful of air and willed her heart rate to slow down.

After several moments, Sebastien said, "To answer your original question, yes, I was in the NOPD before I came here. For twelve years. Joined right after college."

Francesca nodded, swallowing a succulent bite of tilapia. "I've always wondered something."

"What's that?"

"Does everyone who goes into law enforcement do it because they've always felt a calling? It's certainly not the type of career you just stumble into."

He chuckled, the sound so warm her stomach began to melt again. "I can't say that I've always felt a 'calling' to be a cop," he admitted, cutting into his steak. "In fact, there was a time in my life when I was doing everything in my power to be on the wrong side of the law."

"Really?"

His mouth twitched. "Don't sound so surprised. I wasn't always the clean-cut choirboy you see before you."

"Choirboy?" Francesca laughed, making an exaggerated show of looking around the restaurant. "I don't see any choirboys."

His teeth flashed white in an irreverent grin as he forked up a bite of steak.

"Seriously, though, Sebastien. Were you really a bad boy growing up?"

He grimaced. "Bad enough to get tossed out of my parents' house when I was fifteen."

Francesca frowned. "I remember you mentioning that

you'd moved away from home at an early age. I didn't know that was the reason."

He nodded grimly. "I was on the fast track to a life of crime. Getting into fights, skipping school, experimenting with drugs. Wish I could say I was just following the crowd, but most of the time I was the ringleader."

"Why?" Francesca asked gently. "What were you rebelling against?"

"Who, you mean." His mouth twisted sardonically. "I was hardheaded, had a chip on my shoulder the size of Lake Ponchartrain. Nothing but the grace of God kept me out of prison. That, and my grandmother's iron fist. Living with her was like being in boot camp."

Francesca smiled. "But her tough love worked, didn't it?"

"Like a charm." He chuckled softly. "By the time she shipped me off to LSU, I was a changed man. Missed her so damn much I came home practically every weekend."

Francesca's heart stirred at the gruff-tender admission. "She sounds like quite an extraordinary woman. Where is she now?"

"Now?" He glanced at his watch and grinned. "Right now she's probably makin' a killing playing bingo at church. She goes every Friday night."

Francesca laughed. "Way to go, Grandma! Does she live here in San Antonio?"

He nodded. "I bought her a house to replace the one she lost back home."

"That was very sweet of you, Sebastien. And your parents? Are they here, too?"

A shadow crossed his face. "No," he said quietly. "They didn't make it out."

Francesca's heart constricted. "I'm sorry."

"Yeah," he murmured, picking up his wineglass, staring into the twinkling contents for a moment, "so am I."

Those four simple words held enough sorrow, anger, and guilt to make Francesca wonder about the demons that must haunt him every day. Had he and his parents ever reconciled? Had he made peace with them before the hurricane struck, claiming their lives and throwing his own into turmoil?

"Don't," Sebastien said softly, and for a moment Francesca didn't understand what he was telling her. Shaking his head slowly, he reached across the table and gently ran his fingertip down the curve of her cheek, then took her chin between his thumb and forefinger. "No tears for me, *chère. Si vous plaît?*"

Francesca blinked, and realized with some surprise that her eyes were moist. She sniffed, dabbing at the corner of her eye. "I'm sorry." She offered him a small, self-deprecating smile. "My father calls me an empath."

Sebastien chuckled. "Like the Betazoids on *Star Trek?*"

She laughed in surprise. "Yes, exactly. We used to watch the show together all the time. Were you a Trekkie too, Sebastien?"

"I was, though there was a time you couldn't have gotten me to admit such a thing."

She grinned. "Not cool enough for you, huh?"

"Nah. I had a rep to maintain."

"Of course," Francesca said with mock sobriety. She cut into her tilapia, then teased in a singsong voice, "*Sebastien was a Trekkie, a Trekkie, a Trekkie.*"

He pretended to scowl. "Quiet, woman, before someone cool hears you."

Francesca paused. Then, like a recalcitrant child, she repeated the little tune under her breath.

Sebastien threw back his head and laughed, drawing mildly curious smiles from some of the other diners.

As they finished their meals and lingered over coffee and dessert, they talked and laughed, sharing memories of their favorite *Star Trek* episodes, enjoying the simple pleasure of each other's company.

By the time they left the restaurant, night had fallen.

Stars glittered in the sky like diamonds sprinkled across black velvet, and the moon shone bright and full. After two glasses of wine, Francesca felt deliciously relaxed as they headed back to her house. She couldn't remember the last time, if ever, she'd had so much fun on a date. She didn't want the evening to end.

So when they arrived at her house, she invited Sebastien inside for coffee, though they'd already had two cups apiece at the restaurant. When he accepted, the heated look in his eyes told her he had more on his mind than coffee. She felt a shiver of anticipation.

Once inside the house, she paused in the foyer to step out of her sandals, then padded barefoot to the kitchen. As she switched on the coffeemaker and reached for the Folgers, she felt Sebastien approach her from behind.

Her nerve endings tingled from his sudden nearness as he stopped behind her, trapping her against the cabinet with the pressure of his warm, muscled body. She trembled as gentle, callused fingers cupped the back of her neck and began to caress her skin in lazy, tantalizing strokes. Sighing, she closed her eyes and let her head fall limply forward, the coffee all but forgotten.

"I've wanted to do this all night," Sebastien murmured as his mouth trailed down the exposed column of her neck, nibbling and raining hot, bone-melting kisses along her quivering flesh.

She moaned softly, her hips moving of their own volition as she rubbed her buttocks against his groin, feeling the rigid length of his arousal. He groaned, his hands encircling her waist to hold her closer.

Swept away on the racing tide of her pulse, she turned in his arms and gazed up at him. The eyes that met hers were smoldering, liquid pools of smoke. As she watched, breath lodged in her throat, he removed her eyeglasses and laid them on the counter.

His eyes roamed across her face, devouring her. "You're so beautiful," he said huskily. "So damn beautiful."

Heat sizzled through her brain as he leaned down and pressed a soft kiss to one closed eyelid, then the other. When his warm, sensual mouth covered hers, she nearly melted through the floor. This was what she'd been fantasizing about, and now that it was finally happening, she could hardly believe it.

His lips molded hers, a gentle, tormenting caress that drove her slowly insane with need. Suddenly she wanted his tongue, wanted it so bad that she drew her arms around his neck and pulled him closer, deepening the kiss herself. He gave a low growl deep in his throat and took the initiative from her. His tongue delved inside her mouth, hot and sweet, and the pleasure was sharp, splintering, making her moan aloud. His tongue moved deep and sure, taking, and hers danced around it, softly teasing. A delicious, painful ache filled her loins. Her breasts throbbed; her hips undulated a little, rocking against him, instinctively seeking relief from the exquisite torture.

Without breaking the kiss, he lifted her into his arms and carried her over to the center island. Wanting to feel the hardness of his chest against hers, she parted her knees and he stepped between them. She wrapped her legs around his waist and pressed her breasts to him, feeling her nipples pinch with pleasure. He groaned softly, his fingers grazing the underside of her breasts before reaching up to cradle the back of her head.

"Why do you do this?" he whispered raggedly against her mouth.

She could hardly think straight. "What?"

"Keep all this beautiful hair pinned up. It oughtta be a crime." He slipped one hand into the thick pile of her hair, working at the twist until the pins loosened and popped free, scattering across the floor. He made a rough sound of masculine approval as her hair tumbled to her shoulders. He sank his hands deep into the curly mass, working the kiss at a more erotic angle. Francesca's head spun drunkenly.

His hands moved from her hair to caress her back, roam down her spine. He grasped her skirt and hitched it all the way up to her waist, then slid his hands downward to clasp her bottom. She arched forward, gasping soundlessly. His fingers rhythmically kneaded her buttocks, half lifting her off the counter as he ground her hips into his, letting her feel the bulge of his erection straining against his pants. Francesca felt positively feverish with need, the power of which astounded her. She wanted him to rip off her clothes and make love to her, wanted it with a reckless abandon she'd never imagined was possible.

Her breath caught sharply as his finger reached beneath her cotton underwear, parted the damp, springy curls, and slipped inside. She writhed against him as pleasure swept through her body, throbbing in her womb to the beat of his skilled strokes.

His finger reached deeper inside her, pressing upward. Simultaneously his thumb stroked her slippery feminine folds, circling the engorged nub of her clitoris. Heat poured through her, drawing her upward like a bow. Her thighs shook uncontrollably, tightening around his waist as an exquisite pressure built inside her.

"*Sebastien . . .*" She clung to his shoulders with desperate hands, her hips pumping frantically against his hand, her heart pounding against her rib cage.

"Open your eyes, little one," he commanded, low and husky.

Her eyelids felt incredibly heavy as she raised them. She saw his face above hers, dark and powerfully seductive. He pushed a second finger deep inside her, sending her over the edge. Her body bucked as she climaxed, and Sebastien's mouth captured the wild, breathless cries that tore from her throat.

After several moments he broke the kiss and gazed down into her flushed face. His expression was set, his eyes narrow and piercing, his mouth fiercely sensual.

Without a word, he swept her into his arms. Really, she could think of no other way to describe how he plucked her off her feet and strode purposefully from the kitchen.

"The bedroom," he growled.

"Upstairs," she panted, suckling his bottom lip. "Second room to your right. Hurry."

He reached the second floor in a matter of a few long strides, his eyes never leaving hers, as if he thought blinking or glancing away would cause her to disappear. Inside her bedroom, he set her down gently on the floor, tugged off her shirt, then knelt to slide her skirt and panties down her legs.

"Step out," he whispered as the skirt pooled around her feet. She obeyed without question, too far gone to feel shy or self-conscious about her nudity. He picked her up and carried her over to the queen-size bed, awash in the silvery moonlight that poured into the room from a pair of French doors. He laid her gently on the cool, satin sheets before stepping back to remove his own clothes and put on a condom, holding her captive in the heat of his intoxicating gaze.

"I wanted you from the moment I saw you," he said huskily. "Don't ever forget that, *chère*."

There was nothing about this night Francesca would ever forget. Every detail, from the wild beating of her heart to the sight of Sebastien's hard, sculpted body bathed in moonlight, would be permanently etched into her memory.

The mattress dipped beneath Sebastien's weight as he joined her in the bed. She reached out and touched his stomach, feeling his hot, smooth skin and the hard pad of muscle underneath. A tremor passed through him as her hand drifted lower, finding the engorged length of his erection. He shuddered convulsively, his breath hissing out of him as her fingers closed around his penis— long, thick, and impossibly hard. As she grasped the base of his shaft and began to stroke him, she wondered when she had become so bold, so uninhibited, to do such things with a man she'd known less than a week.

"*Arrète*," Sebastien groaned in agony, snagging her hand and bringing it to his mouth. "Stop before you kill me, woman."

Dazedly Francesca watched as he kissed her fingertips, one by one, then deftly unclasped the front hook of her bra and slid the straps off her shoulders.

"Beautiful," he uttered thickly, his eyes glittering with desire as he drank in the sight of her breasts. Leaning down, he licked her right nipple, then drew it into the silken heat of his mouth, making her gasp sharply. He sucked at her, pressing the tight nipple against the roof of his mouth while his tongue worked at it. She writhed helplessly as waves of indescribable pleasure blazed through her. He buried his face in her breasts, kissing, teasing, suckling, while his big hands roamed all over her body.

She clung to him, her fingers raking down the sinewy cords of his back as he slid on top of her, muscular thighs parting her knees, his body rising above hers in the moon-silvered darkness. The first touch of his penis to her was startling, a stark reminder of just how long it had been for her. He held her gaze and entered her with one deep, steady thrust, sheathing himself to the hilt. She cried out, her body arching in feminine shock at the force of his penetration, at the feel of him buried deep inside her.

His gaze intent on her face, he withdrew a little and

thrust again. She moaned at the resulting sensation, the pleasure that was almost torment. Her legs tightened around his waist, her hips lifting to meet his next powerful stroke. He groaned as she began to move to his rhythm, and as she did, the room seemed to melt away, the universe centering on the single spot where their bodies were joined.

Her breathing was shallow, her blood hot, her skin on fire as she yielded to the fierce intimacy of Sebastien's lovemaking. As he thrust into her, he whispered endearments in that dark honey voice of his, a ballad of hot, erotic French.

Soon they were both panting, sweat pooling on their skin as they rocked against each other, faster and harder. Incredibly, for the second time that evening, Francesca felt that same delicious pressure building inside her, boiling upward like lava from a volcano.

"I'm . . . *coming!*" she cried out, throwing back her head as her body convulsed in the grip of an intense orgasm. She sobbed Sebastien's name, seized by spasms so violent she thought she would faint.

He rode her hard through the waves of sensation, pounding into her until he reached his own powerful release. His back stiffened beneath her hands, and he called her name hoarsely as he came.

Gasping for breath, he collapsed on the bed beside her, then drew her protectively into his arms. Francesca nestled against him, deliciously sated and boneless with exhaustion. *So this is what real lovemaking feels like,* she thought dreamily. It had been well worth the prolonged drought.

The night, thick and warm, wrapped around them as their breathing gradually slowed. After several moments, Sebastien levered himself on one elbow to gaze down at her, looking slightly dazed. "Are you all right?" he murmured huskily. "Was I too rough?"

"Mmmm. Not at all. Now I know what all that wining and dining were about."

He chuckled softly. "You figured it out, huh?"

"Yep. The cozy little restaurant by the lake was a dead giveaway."

"Damn. I must be losing my touch if you can figure me out so easily." He smiled down into her eyes. "You're an amazing woman, Francesca Purnell."

Her lips curved. "You're not too bad yourself, Sebastien Durand."

He bent his head, kissing her gently at first, then with increasing hunger as his hand tightened around her waist and his penis hardened against her thigh.

Oh yeah, thought Francesca, wrapping her arms around his neck and opening her mouth to the erotic invasion of his tongue, *this has definitely been worth the drought.*

"Perfection awaits me if only I seek it."

The words, soft as a whisper and laced with conviction, were uttered in the candlelit gloom of the basement where the stranger knelt at an altar. Candles burned and flickered in glass holders on a side table, their waxy scent thick in the air.

On the altar before him, meticulously arranged upon a white lace runner, were a tattoo machine, a supply of needles, a pair of latex gloves, some sterilization products, and an assortment of inks in small plastic bottles.

As he gazed upon the tools spread before him, a slow, deliberate smile curved his mouth. It wouldn't be long now. He was close, so very close. He could taste it, could smell it as surely as the hot wax pooling on a nearby table.

He felt his blood begin to heat at the thought of his mission. After five days of watching, and patiently waiting, he was a step closer to finding her. The one who would bear the ancient symbol. The one who would share his destiny. The one who embodied perfection.

The One.

A thrill swept through him at the realization that his search might soon be over. After all this time, after toiling with shameless imposters, the one he sought was within reach.

Beautiful. Untouched.

Perfect.

He lifted his gaze to a shelf hung on the wall above the altar. There, inside a glass aquarium, was a large black spider perched on a severed tree branch. On the creature's abdomen, three red lines ran horizontally over a tiny circle—the ancient Mayan code for "one who walks through blood."

As he gazed into the glass, the spider did not stir. It merely regarded him with glassy black eyes, eyes that held infinite knowledge of the creature's lethal prowess. Supremacy.

Slowly he raised his hand to the aquarium, stopping inches away from the glass. His fingers trembled as anticipation wound through his bloodstream. Soon he would make his selection.

Soon, and very soon.

Closing his eyes, he licked his lips and whispered a second time, "Perfection awaits me if only I seek it."

He had sought.

Now it was time to find.

Chapter 9

Saturday, June 16

The evidence report from Christie Snodgrass's crime scene was waiting on Sebastien's desk when he arrived at the office on Saturday morning. He slid into his chair and picked up the folder, not expecting to learn anything that would help crack the case, but hoping for a miracle, anyway. But as he sifted carefully through the pages of the report, his hope grew dimmer and dimmer, like the flame from a cigarette lighter that was low on liquid butane. Just as he'd expected, the crime scene unit had collected an inconclusive number of fibers, hair strands, and latent prints from the motel room where Christie had been murdered. Finding her killer would be like trying to find the proverbial needle in a haystack.

Assuming the killer had left any trace evidence behind.

"Shit," Sebastien muttered under his breath.

"My sentiments exactly."

He glanced up as Rodriguez, wearing faded blue jeans and a black T-shirt, sauntered into his office and sat in one of the visitors' chairs. "I read it this morning," he said, hitching his chin toward the report in Sebastien's hand. "We got nothing. *Nada.*"

"Tell me about it." With one final disgruntled glance, Sebastien closed the folder and set it aside on his cluttered desk. "How're the parents doing?"

"As well as can be expected. They're ready to fly Christie's body back to California and begin making funeral arrangements. I told them it'll be a few more days." He stretched out his long legs. "How'd things go with Fincher yesterday? Was it a wasted trip?"

"Not at all. It was very informative, as a matter of fact." Leaning back in his chair until it creaked, Sebastien recapped everything Norman Fincher had told him about the Mexican Blood Walker and the Xeltu epidemic.

When he'd finished his account, Rodriguez shook his head in amused disbelief. "Sounds too loco to be true, *mi amigo*. An ancient curse, heat-crazed killer spiders. Next you'll tell me the nutcase we're looking for was actually there, in the village, three years ago."

"Joke all you want," Sebastien grumbled, "but right now the spider connection is the only tangible lead we have."

Rodriguez tipped his head in concession. "So you think this Fincher guy could be our perp?"

"Don't know. I'm having his prints run through the system to see if we get any matches from the crime scene."

"Even if we do, he'll just claim he once stayed at the motel."

Sebastien shrugged. "Then we'll pin him down for a date, and subpoena the motel's guest reservation computer records. In the meantime," he said, tapping a hardcover book on his desk, "I'm going to learn everything I can about the Xeltu epidemic."

First thing that morning, he'd gone to the public library to check out any materials related to the Mexican Blood Walker. Well, technically, the *first* thing he'd done that morning was make love to Francesca. Sweet, beautiful, wallflower Francesca, who'd rocked his world into the wee hours of the night, then awakened before dawn wanting more.

Just thinking about it got him hard again.

"At the rate you're going," Rodriguez said, nodding toward the pile of books that had occupied a corner of Sebastien's desk all week, "you'll be able to open your own library soon."

"Very funny, George Lopez. Speaking of that, I put in a call to a friend at the bureau. I'm gonna ask him to get me some library records, see if we can find out who else has been reading about the Xeltu epidemic—starting with a list of people who've checked out this book from our friendly local libraries. I'm also asking for a list of people reading books on how to apply tattoos. Maybe our guy's still honing his craft."

Rodriguez nodded. "Good idea. And I think it's time we put out a BOLO to other law enforcement agencies to see if there have been similar killings in other jurisdictions. There's no telling when and where else our perp may have struck."

"Good point." Sebastien reached for a legal pad buried beneath a mound of paperwork. "Heard from any more of Christie's friends and colleagues?"

"Yeah, but none of them had spoken to her since she left for her trip. They just said she'd always wanted to visit San Antonio to see the Alamo and Riverwalk, which we know she did. What we *don't* know is at what point she attracted the attention of the psycho who butchered her."

Sebastien grimaced. "That's the sixty-four-thousand-dollar question."

Rodriguez stood, stretched his spine, then started for the door. "Read your books, Durand. In the meantime, I'm going to see what I can dig up on Norman Fincher and see about that BOLO."

"You do that."

After the detective left, Sebastien listened to his voice mail messages and leafed through a pile of papers that had accumulated on his desk overnight—routine notices, memos, and reports he had requested on other cases.

As he scribbled notes onto a legal pad, his thoughts strayed once again to the amazing night he'd spent with Francesca.

He hadn't meant to take things to the next level so soon. He'd been planning a slow seduction, one in which he finessed her, showed her how beautiful and desirable she was, before coaxing her into bed. But the moment she answered the door and he got an eyeful of those wondrous legs, his libido had kicked into overdrive. It had taken every ounce of self-control he possessed to keep from seducing her right then and there, and he'd had a hell of a time keeping his hands to himself during the romantic candlelight dinner. When she'd invited him inside at the end of the evening, he couldn't resist helping himself to more than just coffee.

Hours later, he was still a little dazed by what had happened. He'd expected Francesca to be reserved in bed, to control her sexuality as fiercely as she concealed her beauty from the rest of the world. How wrong he'd been. Last night, she'd shed her inhibitions and morphed into one of the hottest, sexiest women he'd ever slept with— and there had been plenty. He couldn't recall how many times they'd made love during the long, sultry night. He couldn't get enough of her, and she'd matched him stroke for stroke, demonstrating a sexual appetite that rivaled those of his most experienced lovers.

The memory of it was enough to heat his blood and make his pulse accelerate.

He scrubbed a hand over his face, chuckling mirthlessly to himself. He wondered what Francesca would think if she knew just how much she'd gotten to him. If she knew that, instead of concentrating on work right now, he was fantasizing about making love to her again.

What made it even worse was that his attraction to Francesca went beyond the physical. She had a sharp mind that challenged and fascinated him, and a witty sense of humor he found immensely appealing. He felt like he could talk to her for hours and never run out of things to say.

In the back of his mind, Sebastien knew he should leave her alone. He and Francesca were from two different worlds, and no matter how much he'd enjoyed her company, he had no burning desire to bring those worlds together—not at this point in his life. Between settling into a new police department, looking after his grandmother, and trying to pick up the shattered pieces of their lives in the aftermath of Hurricane Katrina, he didn't have the time or energy to pursue a serious relationship with Francesca, or anyone else.

But he wanted her, wanted her like no other woman he'd ever wanted before. From the moment he'd laid eyes on her in that coffeehouse less than a week ago, he'd been captivated, driven by a need to peel away the layers she used to disguise herself and get to the heart of the real woman underneath. And now that he'd had a taste of her, he only wanted more. He wouldn't be satisfied with one night of mind-blowing sex. He had to have more.

He had to have her.

"More coffee, Frankie?"

Francesca glanced up from the book she'd been trying to read to find Alfonso Garcia standing at her table with a steaming coffee pot. She looked blankly at him. "Hmm?"

"Do you want more coffee?" he asked again, indicating her empty mug.

"Oh. Sure, thanks."

Alfonso frowned at her as he refilled her mug. "Is everything okay? You've been staring at the same page for the past twenty minutes."

"I have?"

"Yeah. I know because I've been watching you."

Francesca chuckled dryly as she reached for her coffee. "Don't you have better things to do with your time, Alfonso? Especially given how busy it is in here?"

He made a face, glancing around the crowded café. Every table was occupied, the noisy din of conversations and clinking flatware drowning out the expletive he muttered under his breath. "Jennifer was supposed to be here an hour ago," he complained. "She knows how crazy it gets on Saturday afternoons. She hasn't even called to say she'll be late."

Beneath the exasperated words, Francesca detected a note of concern in his voice. She paused, coffee mug halfway to her mouth. "Have you tried calling her?"

He nodded. "She's not answering her cell or home phone." He scowled. "She's probably still in bed, trying to catch a few more hours of sleep after working at the club last night. I keep telling her burning the candle at both ends is gonna kill her someday."

"Club? Jennifer also works at a nightclub?"

"You might say that." Alfonso watched as Francesca took a sip of hot coffee and grimaced. Shaking his head, he passed her the cream and sugar before she could reach for them. "Something's definitely on your mind, Frankie. You *never* forget to sweeten your coffee. What gives?"

"Nothing," Francesca lied, pouring cream and sugar into her mug.

The dubious expression on Alfonso's face told her he

wasn't buying it. Fortunately, she was spared from further inquiry when he was called away by another customer.

She tried, once again, to bury herself in her book, but even Octavia Butler's brilliant prose and storytelling couldn't compete with the thoughts swirling around in her head.

Since Sebastien's departure from her house early that morning, she'd been unable to think of anything but him. She remembered the wet heat of his mouth on her nipples and the searing intensity of his gaze as he thrust into her. She remembered the way his big, callused hands had curved around her bottom, lifting and positioning her for his pleasure, grasping her hips as she rode him toward another earth-shattering climax. She—who'd never experimented with anything beyond the missionary position in her limited sexual encounters—had straddled Sebastien's powerful thighs, lowered herself onto his engorged penis, then ridden him until they both cried out in ecstasy. The memory of their lovemaking made her belly quiver on a swell of sexual arousal, and she could almost feel him down there, thrusting furiously into her.

Closing her eyes for a moment, Francesca blew out a deep, shaky breath and crossed her legs tightly under the table.

When she awakened that morning, she'd expected to feel shame and regret, the "morning after" regret she'd heard other women talk about after sleeping with a guy on the first date. All she'd felt, however, was a burning ache of desire for the gorgeous man asleep underneath her, his arms wrapped possessively around her waist. Surprising herself, she'd leaned up and nibbled on his earlobe, then pressed butterfly kisses to his neck and collarbone. By the time she reached his chest, he was awake and groaning softly. He had her on her back, her legs locked around his hips, before she could draw her next breath.

And that was how she'd started her day.

But now, sitting in the crowded café where she'd first encountered Sebastien, she felt the doubts beginning to creep in. *Had* she been too easy? Should she have held out a little more, made him wait longer? She'd known him less than a week, for heaven's sake. And now that they'd made love, would he move on to the next challenge—someone who might actually be more of a challenge than Francesca had proved to be?

She grimaced at the thought. A man like Sebastien Durand would want variety in his sexual partners. He wouldn't be content with just one woman. Especially an inexperienced, straitlaced woman—which, ultimately, she was, contrary to her behavior the night before. She wasn't a sex kitten, a seductress who drove men wild with her skills in bed. She couldn't explain what had come over her last night, other than to say she'd had one too many glasses of wine over dinner and had been decidedly horny after years of deprivation.

Her reverie was interrupted by Alfonso's sudden reappearance at her table. One look at his face, and she knew something was wrong.

"What is it, Alfonso?"

"I just called the Sirens and Spurs, and they told me Jennifer never made it to work last night," he said worriedly.

Francesca frowned. "Do you want to drop by her apartment to make sure she's okay?"

"Yeah, but you know I don't have a car."

"I'll drive you. It's no imposition," she assured him when he opened his mouth to protest. "I'm already familiar with where Jennifer lives, and I have some errands to run on that side of town, anyway. Come on, let's go."

* * *

Alfonso chattered nervously on the way to Jennifer Benson's apartment located in the Medical Center, a bustling area of town that comprised four major hospitals, the University of Texas Health Science Center, and a vast array of restaurants and gated apartment complexes.

"She's been moonlighting at the Sirens and Spurs club for a year now," he explained to Francesca, sitting on the edge of his seat, silently urging her to go faster in the little red convertible. "When she first told me about it, I didn't believe her. I just couldn't see sweet little Jennifer being a stripper, allowing herself to be pawed by strange men. But she told me it wasn't as bad as I thought it was, and the money was pretty good. I still thought it was a bad idea. With her being in school full-time and waitressing at the Espuma, I didn't think she needed any more on her plate. But she told me to back off, so I did." He shoved a trembling hand through his dark hair. "She's had such a rough life. Her parents died when she was seventeen, so she had to put off college and get a job in order to take care of herself. And then three years ago, her older brother died in Iraq. She's got no one left in the world but a few close friends."

"She seems like a very strong, resilient young woman," Francesca said.

"She is. I was *never* that mature at twenty-four." Alfonso turned his head to stare out the window. "I just want to make sure she's all right. Please, God, just let her be all right."

"I'm sure she is," Francesca murmured, though she couldn't shake the feeling that the young waitress was *not* all right.

The sense of foreboding intensified when they arrived at Jennifer's third-floor apartment and found the front door unlocked. Alfonso knocked, but didn't wait for an answer, opening the door and stepping quickly inside.

Francesca followed more slowly, the knot of dread tightening in her stomach.

"Jennifer?" Alfonso called out. "Are you home?"

He was greeted with silence, almost eerie in its stillness. After trading a worried glance with Francesca, he started from the small living room. "I'm going to check her bedroom."

Francesca was already pulling out her cell phone to call the police when Alfonso screamed a moment later. An earsplitting, bloodcurdling scream that sent her running down the hallway.

What she saw nearly made her lose the contents of her stomach. But before she could succumb to the violent nausea, Alfonso, his face as white as a sheet, turned and collapsed in her arms.

An hour later, the tiny apartment was crawling with crime scene technicians methodically at work, dusting surfaces for fingerprints and taking photographs of Jennifer Benson's mutilated remains. Yellow crime scene tape blocked the third-floor stairwell and the entrance to the apartment. Uniformed officers posted outside the building were keeping out the curious, and department vehicles with flashing lights clogged the parking lot, invariably drawing the attention of the media. Two news vans had already arrived, and the reporters and cameramen who'd eagerly jumped out were now interviewing residents who'd been denied access to the building.

Francesca took it all in from where she sat in the lobby facing the double-glass doors of the entrance. Nearby, huddled under a blanket bearing the SAPD emblem, Alfonso was being consoled by two detectives. His low, keening wails wrenched Francesca's heart and brought a fresh sheen of tears to her eyes, blurring Sebastien's image as he knelt in front of her.

"Drink this," he said gently, holding out a cup of Starbucks coffee that one of the uniformed officers had fetched at his request.

Francesca shook her head mutely, numb with shock and horror. For as long as she lived, she would never forget the bloody violence of the scene in Jennifer Benson's bedroom. She knew she would see the girl's ravaged corpse, and hear Alfonso's awful screams of terror, in recurring nightmares for years to come.

Sebastien wrapped her cold, stiff fingers around the paper cup of coffee. "Just one little sip. It'll warm you up, I promise."

"I'm fine," Francesca whispered faintly.

"No, you're not. You're in shock." Leaning forward, close enough for her to see the storm-cloud gray of his irises, he added coaxingly, "Do it for me, *chère. Si vous plaît?*"

Mechanically she brought the cup to her lips and took a small sip. The hot brew burned a path down the back of her throat and mingled with the meager contents of her stomach, a half-eaten vegetable pita she'd ordered at the Espuma.

"*C'est bon,*" Sebastien murmured, reaching up and gently kneading the nape of her neck. "That's a good girl."

It was the warmth of his strong fingers, not the coffee, that finally seeped into her bones, dispelling some of the chill that had gripped her for the past hour. "Thank you for getting here so quickly," she said weakly. "I—I didn't know whether it was appropriate to call you before I called nine-one-one."

"You did the right thing," Sebastien said softly.

Within twenty minutes of her desperate phone call, Sebastien had arrived with his partner, Detective Juan Rodriguez, a man bearing an uncanny resemblance to Benicio Del Toro. They'd found Francesca huddled on the floor in the narrow hallway, cradling Alfonso in her arms and whispering soothing words of comfort to him as he wept uncontrollably. When she looked up and saw Sebastien striding purposefully toward her, eyes locked on to hers, she'd nearly swooned with relief. Never before had she been happier to see another human being.

While Detective Rodriguez tended to Alfonso, Sebastien had swept Francesca into his arms and carried her out of the apartment, onto the elevator, and down to the first-floor lobby, where they'd been met by uniformed officers arriving on the scene. It was only after he'd made sure she was safe and sound that he'd returned upstairs to process the crime scene, entrusting one of the officers to take her statement.

Now, as the horrifying images rewound in her brain, she closed her eyes and shuddered. "What kind of an animal would do such an unspeakably vicious thing to another person?" she whispered, torn between anger and despair. "What kind of monster did this?"

"A very disturbed one," Sebastien answered grimly. He took the coffee cup from her trembling fingers and set it down on the floor, then wrapped his big hands around hers, infusing her with the warm, comforting strength of his touch.

"Poor Alfonso," Francesca murmured around the walnut-sized lump in her throat. "He and Jennifer had been friends for a long time."

"Did you know her?"

Opening her eyes, Francesca shook her head. "Not very well. She'd waited on me several times at the Espuma. We usually made small talk about her classes, or Alfonso's antics. She was a very sweet girl." *Oh God.* Had she just referred to Jennifer in the past tense? Was this really happening?

"From what you could tell, was she generally liked by

the customers?" Sebastien had subtly shifted from concerned lover to detective mode.

"She was a terrific waitress, so yes, I do think she was well liked."

Sebastien nodded. "Do you remember any altercations with a rude customer? Or a guy coming on to her and refusing to take no for an answer?"

She frowned. "Not that I can think of. You'll have to ask Alfonso, though, since he actually worked with her."

In silence they looked over at Alfonso, who had composed himself enough to answer questions from Detective Rodriguez. Francesca's heart constricted as she noticed, for the first time, that Alfonso still wore his green apron. In his haste to leave the Espuma and check up on his friend, he'd forgotten to remove the apron.

Francesca turned back to Sebastien. "You think Jennifer could have been killed by a disgruntled or obsessed customer?"

Steady gray eyes met hers. "I'm not ruling out anything, Francesca. According to Mr. Garcia, Jennifer Benson moonlighted as a stripper at a local gentlemen's club. It's just as likely that whoever killed her saw her at the club and became fixated on her."

A fine tremor swept through Francesca. She thought about her sister hanging out at the Sirens and Spurs with her friends. Could Tommie have come in contact with a sadistic killer and not even known it?

Her stomach clenched at the idea. But she knew that if she tried to warn Tommie to stay away from the club, her sister would call her paranoid or accuse her of being a prude and a spoilsport. Without knowing the identity of Jennifer Benson's killer, Francesca couldn't prove that Tommie was endangering herself by visiting the Sirens and Spurs Gentlemen's Club.

Struck by a new, chilling thought, Francesca stared at Sebastien. "You saw the body, didn't you?"

He nodded, a muscle bunching in his jaw.

"I know you're not at liberty to discuss the crime scene," Francesca said haltingly. "But I . . . I saw something on Jennifer's arm. It looked like a tattoo . . . a tattoo of a spider. Is that what it was?"

Before Sebastien could respond, they were joined by a tall, solidly built man with short, steel-gray hair and sharply intelligent green eyes set deep in a craggy, not-quite-handsome face.

"You must be Francesca Purnell," he said, extending a large hand to her. "I'm Sergeant Clive MacDougal."

"Nice to meet you," Francesca murmured as his smooth, warm palm swallowed hers in a firm handshake.

Sebastien straightened slowly from his kneeling position in front of Francesca, bringing himself shoulder to shoulder with the other man. "Sergeant MacDougal is my supervisor in the Homicide Unit," he explained.

MacDougal nodded, smiling gently at Francesca. "I just finished speaking to Mr. Garcia. He told me you were with him this afternoon when Miss Benson's body was discovered."

"That's correct," Francesca said quietly. "I drove him over here to check up on her. He was worried about her. With good reason, unfortunately."

MacDougal's expression softened with sympathy. "I know what a terrible shock it must have been for both of you to find your friend that way. I can assure you that we're going to do everything in our power to apprehend Miss Benson's killer. That's why I assigned Detective Durand to be the lead investigator on this case. He's one of our best."

"I can tell," Francesca said, smiling a little at Sebastien, who winked at her.

MacDougal said, "I know you've already given your statement to our officers, but I just wanted to come over and formally introduce myself." He reached inside his dark sport coat and withdrew a business card. "If you think of anything else that might help with our investigation, please don't hesitate to contact me or Detective Durand."

"All right," Francesca said, accepting the card from him. "You've been very kind. Thank you."

The sergeant's face creased into a small, brief smile. "In that case, I hope you won't mind that I have to borrow Detective Durand for a while?"

"No, of course not. I was just about to leave, actually. Poor Alfonso needs to be taken home and put to bed." She looked askance at Sebastien. "Unless we're still needed here for questioning?"

Sebastien shook his head. "I'll walk you out to the car."

When Sebastien returned to the third floor of the building fifteen minutes later, he was met by MacDougal, who'd just emerged from Jennifer Benson's apartment where the crime scene team was still hard at work. The sergeant, though he was no stranger to images of violent death, looked decidedly ashen.

"It's like a damned slaughterhouse in there," he muttered grimly, swiping a white handkerchief over his mouth. "All that blood. Damn, I was going to have a thick, juicy T-bone for dinner, too."

Sebastien gave a mirthless chuckle. "You sound like you're blaming poor Miss Benson for ruining your dinner plans, Chief."

MacDougal grimaced. "Wouldn't be the first time a woman's done that to me. Speaking of women, what was that whole scene with Francesca Purnell? I thought it was Rodriguez's job to coddle and cuddle witnesses."

"I have no idea what you're talking about, Chief," Sebastien said, straight-faced.

"Likely story," MacDougal grumbled, stuffing the

handkerchief inside his coat pocket. "Just remember what your focus should be, Durand. The brass is breathing down our necks to catch this killer before the case starts making national headlines. The mayor's worried that if CNN breaks the story, tourists will start avoiding San Antonio like the damn plague."

"Of course," Sebastien said sardonically. "Can't have tourism dollars impacted by the scandal of murder in our sleepy little town."

"Scoff all you want, Durand, but those tourism dollars help pay our salaries. And I don't know about you, but having to shell out child support for four kids gives me a whole lot of appreciation for my paycheck." MacDougal's gaze followed a passing crime lab technician carrying plastic evidence bags labeled SAPD CSU. "So, what do you make of it?"

Sebastien didn't have to ask what the sergeant meant. "It's definitely our guy," he said grimly. "Same MO as before, right down to the spider tattoo."

"Figured as much. What about the victim? Next of kin?"

Sebastien shook his head. "Parents died when she was seventeen and her only sibling—a brother—was killed in Iraq three years ago."

MacDougal groaned loudly. "Oh, great. An orphaned victim whose brother died while serving his country. This keeps getting better and better."

"If it's any consolation, we're trying to track down a distant relative in Montana to claim the body. So maybe she's not *entirely* an orphan."

MacDougal smirked. "Ever the optimist. That's what I like about you, Durand. Despite everything you've been through in the last two years, you remain an optimist." As his cell phone trilled, he dug it out of his pocket and frowned at the number displayed on the screen. "It's Lieutenant Burnside. Probably calling to chew my ass out for why the damn sky's blue."

Sebastien chuckled dryly. "Or maybe he's calling to tell you what a fine job you've been doing."

The look MacDougal shot him as he walked away to take the call conveyed just what he thought Sebastien could do with his "optimism."

Chapter 10

After Jennifer Benson's remains had been tagged, bagged, and wheeled out on the medical examiner's gurney, Sebastien returned to the bedroom to walk the scene one more time. Though the body had been removed, the stench of violent death still clung to the air—a putrid miasma of blood, bladder, and bowel content. Jennifer Benson, like Christie Snodgrass, had been found naked, gagged, and bound, her wrists and ankles tied with the same kind of cloth cord that had been used on Christie.

Entering the small bedroom, Sebastien set about the task of checking everything, opening every drawer, sifting through clothes in the walk-in closet, looking between the mattresses and underneath the twin bed, inside the bathroom medicine cabinet, searching for anything that might hint at the identity of Jennifer's killer.

But the sparsely furnished bedroom yielded few clues about the owner, let alone the lunatic who'd brutally ended her life. Jennifer Benson had been a struggling college student, and it showed. The bedroom furniture was of the basic variety bought at discount furniture outlets, consisting of a nightstand, a small matching dresser, and a narrow twin bed draped in cheap linen that was now soaked with blood. There were no photographs or paintings on the walls, as if the bedroom had not been lived in very long or else her stay was temporary. But they'd learned, from the leasing consultant Rodriguez interviewed, that Jennifer had lived in the apartment for two years.

Sebastien walked over to the nightstand and angled his head down until he was eye-level with the smooth wooden surface. A half-empty soda can resting on a coaster had been found on the table. Both items had been collected and removed by the crime scene unit. The use of the coaster told Sebastien that Jennifer had believed in taking care of her belongings, however meager they might be.

His eyes continued moving slowly across the surface, taking it one inch at a time. Black fingerprint powder revealed what appeared to be a partial handprint at the edge of the table, probably belonging to the victim. He kept looking, searching.

"What're you doing?" Rodriguez asked from the doorway.

"Checking for equipment," Sebastien murmured without glancing over his shoulder.

"Equipment?"

"The perp shows up with complete tattoo kits—ink bottles, needles, tattoo machine, the works. I want to know where he's setting up shop."

"Maybe he brings his own table. One of those foldaway types."

"Which would make him more conspicuous as he enters and exits the building," Sebastien ruminated. "Carrying a bag of supplies over one shoulder, a folding table tucked beneath his other arm. Would make him easier to identify, don't you think?"

Rodriguez shrugged. "So he doesn't provide his own table."

"Probably not." Sebastien came to his feet and peered behind the nightstand. "Damn."

"What?"

"CSU forgot to dust the outlet back here. The perp has to plug in his machine somewhere, and this one is closest to the bed, where he tattoos his victims."

Rodriguez walked over and looked behind the nightstand. "The lamp's plugged into the first socket, the alarm clock in the second."

Sebastien frowned. "Maybe he unplugged one of them before he put on his gloves. His prints could be on one of those cords."

"Or he used another outlet," Rodriguez proposed, hitching his chin toward an outlet a few feet away from the bed. "That one's close enough, and it got dusted."

Careful not to touch anything, Sebastien went through the motions of leaning over the nightstand, reaching down, and pretending to plug an imaginary cord into the socket. As he did, he visualized the killer bracing one hand on the wall, or on the edge of the nightstand—where the fingerprint tech had already uncovered a partial handprint.

Sebastien muttered another curse. Digging his cell phone out of his jeans pocket, he dialed the CSU lab and tersely requested that another technician be sent back to the crime scene. Snapping the phone shut, he resumed his inspection of the nightstand while Rodriguez made his way over to the dresser.

The detective began opening drawers, his hands shuffling through layers of neatly folded clothing. When he reached the top drawer, he gave a long, low whistle.

Sebastien glanced up from sifting through a pile of receipts and bank statements he'd found in the night-stand drawer. "What's up?"

Rodriguez held up a scrap of red lace. "Whole

drawer's full of 'em. Now we know where all her money was going. To Frederick's of Hollywood."

Sebastien shook his head at his partner. "She was a stripper. Of course she owned a lot of G-strings—that was practically her uniform." He dropped the miscellaneous receipts and bank statements inside a plastic evidence bag and closed the nightstand drawer.

"The leasing consultant I spoke to said Miss Benson was a model tenant," Rodriguez said. "Always paid her rent on time, never took anyone's parking space or threw wild parties. Other than having a couple of friends over now and then, she mostly kept to herself."

"She probably wasn't home very often. Between being in school full-time and holding down two jobs, I'll bet she used this place more as a rest stop than anything else."

"That's pretty much what Garcia told me. He said she didn't make any time for a social life, and hadn't had a steady boyfriend in years."

"What about an on-again, off-again?"

"Nope. Not even that. They used to joke that when she graduated from school, she'd celebrate by getting laid."

Sebastien followed Rodriguez from the bedroom, down the hallway, and into the equally spartan living room. A pair of uniformed cops stood guard outside the front door, which was roped off by crime scene tape.

"How did the killer gain access to the apartment?" Sebastien pondered aloud. "There was no sign of forced entry. No indication that the door lock was jimmied. So either the perp had a key, or Jennifer Benson opened the door for him."

"Which would suggest she knew him."

"Or he tricked her into *thinking* she knew him."

Frowning, Rodriguez paused by the ancient answering machine located on a glass end table. "Here's what I don't get. Jennifer was supposed to report to work at the strip club at eleven last night. When she didn't show, no one called—not until five a.m."

"Six hours later," Sebastien murmured thoughtfully. Rodriguez was right. That *didn't* make sense. "Who called?"

"The manager. Woman by the name of Yelena Slutskaya. Smoky voice, sexy as hell Russian accent. Didn't sound too pleased about Jennifer blowing off her shift. Apparently another stripper covered for her, but the manager didn't sound too happy about it. Which doesn't explain why she waited until morning to call and chew Jennifer's ass out."

Sebastien frowned. "Did you catch the name of the stripper who covered for her?"

"Tommie or something like that. We can find out when we get there." Rodriguez flashed a wicked grin as they headed for the door. "I'm dying to meet this Yelena chick. If she looks half as hot as she sounds on the phone, you're gonna have to let me do all the talking."

Sebastien chuckled grimly as he ducked under the crime scene tape. "Considering what we witnessed here today, Don Juan, 'dying' probably isn't the best word choice."

If Yelena Slutskaya was devastated to learn about the death of one of her dancers, she didn't show it.

She reacted to the news with implacable calm, taking a slow drag on the cigarette nestled between her long, elegant fingers and releasing twin curls of smoke through her nostrils. Her face was broad, her features strong, almost masculine. The heavily mascaraed blue eyes that regarded Sebastien and Rodriguez were cool and shrewdly assessing, as if she'd been fed so much bullshit in her life that she now viewed everyone with a jaundiced eye. Her dark hair was woven with silver strands and pulled back tightly from her face in a no-nonsense bun. She wore a pin-striped black business suit, and the whiteness of her sheer silk blouse provided a sharp contrast to the dusky hue of her skin.

She'd been seated behind a tidy wooden desk when they were shown into her office located in the rear of the building. The room was small and windowless, the walls decorated with framed photographs of various people—celebrities, Sebastien guessed—who had visited the club over the years.

Without rising to greet her two visitors, Yelena had motioned them into the chairs opposite her desk with an impatient wave of her hand. As she did, Sebastien saw that her fingernails were painted a deep shade of red that reminded him of the bloody violence of the crime scene they'd just left.

"How did she die?" Yelena asked in the thickly accented voice that had made Rodriguez salivate.

Sebastien traded glances with his partner, then answered evenly, "She was found murdered in her apartment this morning. Stabbed to death."

Again the woman didn't so much as flinch. "That's a shame," she said almost philosophically. "Jennifer Benson was a good dancer, one of my best. She will be missed by the customers."

"Any one in particular?" Sebastien asked.

She frowned. "I do not understand."

Rodriguez said, "We're exploring the possibility, Ms. Slutskaya, that whoever killed Jennifer Benson may have been one of your customers."

"Impossible," Yelena declared with icy hauteur. "I run a good establishment here, Detective. My patrons know better than to tamper with any of my girls."

"How can you be so sure about that?" Sebastien countered.

"Because I make it my business to be sure. Most of the

customers who walk through those doors are regulars. I know their names, who they work for, how much they earn, what their private fantasies are. I even know the names of some of their wives and girlfriends, who often accompany them to the club."

"That's all very commendable, Ms. Slutskaya," Sebastien drawled, leaning back in his chair as if he had all the time in the world, "but unless you've performed background checks on every customer you've ever had, or you assign a tail to everyone who leaves this building, you have no way of knowing what anyone does once they're off the premises."

Her lips tightened. Impatiently she crushed out her cigarette in a glass ashtray already bristling with butts. "No one here would have wanted to hurt Jennifer. She was one of the most popular dancers we had and was very friendly to everyone. I never had any attendance or tardiness problems with her—until last night, when she didn't show up for work." Something like regret flashed in the woman's eyes, but the look was so fleeting Sebastien could have imagined it.

"Why did you wait until this morning to call Jennifer?" Rodriguez asked, tapping a pen against his open notepad, which he seldom ever used, but brought out of habit. "You say she'd never been late or absent before. When you didn't see or hear from her last night, I would think that would've set off an alarm bell. Being a no-show was uncharacteristic of her, right? So why didn't you call sooner to find out where she was?"

"Because I didn't need her," Yelena said coolly. "Another dancer had agreed to fill in for her."

"But you called her this morning, after her shift would have been over, anyway."

"I wanted her to know it was unacceptable that she hadn't called to let me know she would be out." She hesitated, then added almost grudgingly, "If you must know,

Detective, the reason I didn't call her last night is that I did not want to disturb her. She had been studying hard for an exam all week and working at that coffee shop. I knew she was exhausted and could probably use a night off to rest."

Sebastien and Rodriguez exchanged speaking glances. It was the first show of compassion the woman had displayed since their arrival. Maybe she *was* human, after all.

Seeing the look that passed briefly between them, Yelena bristled. "I take good care of my girls, Detectives. Ask anyone out there. My waitresses and dancers are paid more than their peers at other clubs, which is why so many of them come to work for me. No girl is allowed to leave the building without a personal escort to her car, whether it is two o'clock in the afternoon or two o'clock in the morning. I do not tolerate drug use or prostitution—not only because it's bad for business, but because I believe my girls deserve better than that. They may not like me very much. They may call me a 'bitch in stilettos' behind my back. But they respect me. And where I come from, gentlemen, respect is something that must be earned." She glanced at a brass clock mounted on the wall. "If you have no other questions for me, I have an appointment I must keep."

"Of course," Sebastien said smoothly. "We don't want to take up too much of your time, Ms. Slutskaya. However, we'd like to talk to some of your dancers, especially those who were closest to Jennifer and the one who filled in for her last night. Is she still available, by any chance?"

Yelena frowned. "Tommie left this morning after her shift was over. But she's scheduled to return at five, if you care to wait for her." The woman stood, signaling that her visitors should follow suit.

As she rounded the desk to usher them out of the office, Sebastien was surprised to discover how short she was. Even in the black stiletto pumps she wore, Yelena

Slutskaya couldn't have been more than five-two. He'd expected a much taller woman, to match the authoritarian personality.

"If you decide to stay and watch the performances, gentlemen," she warned over her shoulder as she led them down a dimly lit corridor that reeked of assorted perfumes, sweat, and smoke, "please tip generously."

"Of course," Sebastien drawled, chuckling dryly at the lewd grin Rodriguez gave him.

A moment later, he was distracted by the sight of a tall, strikingly beautiful woman racing down the hall toward them, her long dark hair slicked back into a ponytail that swung from side to side with her hurried strides. She wore tight jeans, a low-cut red shirt that offered peeks of her midriff, and spiky-heeled sandals that did nothing to hinder her pace.

Beside him, Rodriguez whistled softly through his teeth, earning a dirty look from Yelena.

"Oh my God!" the young woman cried out as she reached them. "I just got a call from Gloria! She was crying hysterically. Is it true? Is Jennifer dead?"

"Yes, it is true, Tommie," Yelena said without inflection.

"Oh my God! No!"

As the girl burst into tears, Yelena seized her by the arms and hissed angrily, "Pull yourself together before the customers hear you out there."

"I don't care who hears me!" Tommie yelled tearfully. "I can't believe Jennifer's dead!"

The calm veneer Yelena Slutskaya had maintained throughout the interview with Sebastien and Rodriguez suddenly evaporated. "Don't you dare pretend to be sad!" she raged, her face contorted with fury. "You never liked Jennifer. You always felt threatened by her. I know very well you only *pretended* to be her friend!"

"That's not true!"

"Ladies," Sebastien smoothly intervened, stepping

between the two women before the confrontation could escalate to violence. God knows he'd seen enough bloodshed for one day.

He placed a gentle but firm hand on Tommie's shoulder, subtly drawing her attention away from her boss, who was still silently fuming.

When Tommie looked up at him, her dark eyes glistening with moisture, he felt a whisper of recognition. "My name is Sebastien Durand," he said, wondering why the woman seemed so familiar to him. "Me and my partner, Detective Rodriguez, are investigating Miss Benson's homicide. Is there somewhere we could speak to you in private? We'd like to ask you some questions about Jennifer."

"Use my office," Yelena said brusquely. "I don't want to cause a panic among the customers and the other girls. I will make an announcement when I return from my appointment."

Back inside the cramped office, Rodriguez steered Tommie over to a small red sofa pushed against the wall and sat down beside her. Sebastien, spying a box of Kleenex on a corner of the desk, picked it up and offered it to the distraught girl.

"Thank you," Tommie sniffled, plucking a handful of tissue from the box and dabbing at the corners of her eyes.

Sebastien grabbed the visitor's chair he'd vacated just a few minutes ago and nimbly straddled it.

"I know this has been a terrible shock for you," Rodriguez said in the quiet, soothing voice cultivated from years of consoling the grief-stricken.

Tommie gave a deep, shuddering sigh. "I just can't believe Jennifer's dead. Gloria called me on my way over here. At first I could barely understand what she was saying, she was crying so hard. She told me she'd just gotten a phone call from Alfonso Garcia, one of Jennifer's friends at the coffee shop where she works. He told Gloria that Jennifer was dead. Someone had broken into her apartment and killed her. Who would do that to her? *Who?*"

Sebastien said, "That's what we're hoping you can help us with, Miss—"

"Purnell. Tomasina Purnell. But everyone calls me Tommie. Spelled with an *ie.*"

Just like that, Sebastien realized why he'd recognized her. He'd seen old photographs of her at Francesca's house. Tommie Purnell was Francesca's sister.

Bon Dieu.

He wondered if Francesca knew that her younger sister was a stripper at one of the city's most popular gentlemen's clubs. Even *he* was unsettled by the idea, and he'd just met the girl.

"I'm more than happy to help any way I can, despite what Yelena said." Tommie frowned, her lush, pouty mouth turning down at the corners. "I can't believe what she said to me. Heartless bitch."

Sebastien and Rodriguez exchanged considering glances. "Why do you think Ms. Slutskaya said something like that to you, Tommie?" Rodriguez asked gently.

"Because she hates me," came Tommie's vehement response. "She's never liked me, from the day I started working here."

"Then why does she keep you around?"

"Because I'm good. Damned good. And she knows it." She paused, then added almost defensively, "Most people think there's nothing more to being a stripper than taking off your clothes and shaking your ass to music. But there's more to it than that. Dancing is a true art form, and that's what we do here—we dance." She frowned. "Some of us, anyway."

"Ms. Slutskaya says Jennifer was one of her best dancers," Sebastien said, carefully watching Tommie's face. "Do you agree with that?"

She met his gaze without blinking. "Definitely. I always

told her so. She really cared about putting on a good performance for the customers. She believed in giving them their money's worth."

"And do you?" Rodriguez drawled.

Her gaze remained locked on Sebastien. "Always," she said, the one-word promise leaving Sebastien to wonder if he'd just been propositioned.

He flicked a glance at Rodriguez, who was fighting the tug of a grin. With a mental shake of his head, Sebastien clasped his hands over the back of the chair. "Miss Purnell—"

"Tommie."

"All right. Tommie. We understand you filled in for Jennifer last night. When was the last time you spoke to her?"

"Around nine o'clock. I called to tell her about a cute guy at work who I thought would be perfect for her. All her friends were always trying to set her up with someone, because she never dated. Anyway, she'd just gotten home from the library, and she sounded completely exhausted. I knew she had to work at eleven, so I offered to fill in for her."

"That was very generous of you," Sebastien murmured.

Tommie shrugged dispassionately. "I fill in for other girls all the time. Just a few nights ago, I worked Gloria's shift when she came down with the flu. She would've done the same for me. Besides, I needed the extra cash."

"Where else do you work?" Rodriguez asked.

"A law firm. Thorne and Associates."

Sebastien raised an eyebrow at the mention of the prominent local law firm headed by Crandall Thorne, one of the most powerful criminal attorneys in the state of Texas. "I've heard that Thorne pays his employees very well. Enough to keep them from having to moonlight at other jobs."

She winked at him. "What can I say? I'm high-maintenance, Detective Durand."

And somehow, Sebastien knew the teasing remark wasn't too far from the truth. "So that was the last time you spoke to Jennifer? Around nine?"

Tommie nodded. "When we got off the phone, she said she was going to take a long, hot bubble bath before going to bed."

Sebastien wondered if that was where the killer had found her.

"Did Jennifer say she was going to call Ms. Slutskaya to let her know you'd be filling in for her?" Rodriguez asked.

"I told her not to. I promised to take care of it myself." Her lips twisted. "I didn't want Yelena giving her a hard time for calling in. I even suggested that she should ignore the phone if Yelena called her."

Rodriguez grinned. "Quite the tough girl, aren't you, Tommie?"

She shrugged. "There's a reason my father gave me and my sister names that could be shortened into male nicknames. I grew up having to be tough."

Sebastien thought about Francesca, and wondered if she felt the same way. "Wasn't Jennifer a little worried that if she didn't call Yelena herself, she'd get fired?" he asked.

Tommie gave a humorless half laugh. "Yelena wouldn't have fired Jennifer. Like she told you, Jennifer was one of her best dancers. Young, pretty, eager to please. The customers loved her. Yelena's a businesswoman. Getting rid of someone like Jennifer would've cut into her profit, and you know she wasn't having that."

"You say Jennifer was eager to please," Sebastien said, homing in on the comment. "Did anyone ever take her friendliness the wrong way? You know, see it as an invitation that she was offering more?"

Tommie shook her head emphatically. "No one ever messed with her—or any of us, for that matter. Have you *seen* our bouncers? No offense, but even you guys would think twice before looking at them the wrong way. They're huge! I think Yelena recruited them from the Russian Mafia or something."

Rodriguez snorted, hitching his chin toward Sebastien. "I bet my partner here could take 'em. He grew up on the mean streets of New Orleans and did a little boxing in college. Ain't that right, Big Easy?"

Sebastien chuckled dryly. "Whatever you say, Rodriguez."

Tommie gave him a demure smile. "I thought I recognized your accent, Detective Durand. It's nice. *Very* nice."

"Thanks. How long have you worked here, Tommie?"

"Just three months."

"Long enough to know who the regulars are?"

"Pretty much."

"Have there been any newcomers that caught your attention? Maybe someone you recognized?"

"Not really. Oh, wait," she said, snapping her manicured fingers. "One of my sister's coworkers has been here a few times in the past month. I recognized him from an award ceremony I attended with my family last year. My sister got an award for something or other, and he came over to congratulate her."

"Do you remember his name?" Rodriguez asked.

She shook her head, frowning. "I was introduced to so many people that night, I couldn't keep their names or faces straight. He probably doesn't even remember me."

"But you remembered him."

She shrugged. "He's Asian. There aren't many Asians living in San Antonio. Anyway, if you think it's a big deal, I'll ask my sister for his name." Suddenly wary, she divided a speculative look between Sebastien and Rodriguez. "Wait a minute. Do you guys think one of the customers killed Jennifer?"

"We're exploring the possibility," Sebastien said evenly, borrowing Rodriguez's choice of words. "We'll also be talking to some of her classmates and professors and coworkers at the coffee shop. You say she wasn't seeing anyone?"

Tommie shook her head. "There were no deranged ex-boyfriends lurking in the background, if that's what you're asking. She never even mentioned a cute guy in class or anything. She was totally focused on her school-work and making sure she graduated next year." Twisting the damp tissue between her fingers, Tommie drew in a deep, shaky breath. "I can't believe we're talking about her in the past tense. None of this seems real. We were just here together three nights ago, laughing and complaining about our sore feet after a long night. When Gloria called me today, I just *knew* she was lying. I told her Alfonso had to be mistaken."

"So Gloria's a dancer here as well?" Rodriguez clarified.

Tommie nodded. "She and Jennifer were pretty close, too. She's scheduled to work tomorrow, if you want to come back and talk to her."

"How well do you know Mr. Garcia?" Sebastien asked.

"Not very well. I've only met him a couple of times." Her tone turned mocking. "He didn't really approve of Jennifer working here, so he never wanted to associate with any of her 'stripper friends,' as he called us. The only reason he and Gloria were friends was that they grew up together, and Gloria would've kicked his ass if he tried to 'disown' her for being a stripper. If you ask me, Alfonso would've had no problem with Jennifer waitressing at Hardbodies—as long as she got him into the club for free."

Sebastien ignored the catty remark about Alfonso Garcia's sexual preferences. "How did Jennifer feel about his attitude toward her job? Did they argue about it?"

"A few times. But once she got mad and stopped speaking to him for a whole week. He finally got the message and backed off." Her lips twisted cynically. "His so-called disapproval of her stripping gig sure as hell didn't stop him from borrowing money from her to pay his rent or buy groceries. Struggling writer, my ass."

Rodriguez chuckled wryly. "I take it there's no love lost between you two?"

Tommie sucked her teeth. "Definitely not. I have no patience for hypocrites and liars."

Just then the door creaked open, and a tall blonde stuck her head inside. "Sorry to interrupt, Tommie, but your set's coming up soon."

"I'll be out in a minute, Ashley," Tommie said, impatience edging her words. After the door closed, she rolled her eyes and muttered, "I bet Yelena put her up to that before she left. Bitch."

As Sebastien rose to his feet, the other two followed. "We won't take up any more of your time, Miss Purnell," he said, removing a business card from his wallet and passing it to her. "If you think of anything else, please give us a call."

"I will," Tommie murmured, pocketing the card in the back pocket of her painted-on jeans. She smiled up at him, and this time there was no mistaking the bold invitation in her sultry dark eyes. "If you ever want to relax and watch a good performance, Detective, I hope you'll drop by and see me. In case you missed the slogan on the sign outside, *your* pleasure is *our* pleasure."

"You lucky bastard," Rodriguez said as he and Sebastien climbed into the Crown Vic a few minutes later. "Not one, but *two* beautiful sisters to choose from."

Sebastien, seated behind the wheel, cut his partner a lazy glance. "So you figured it out, huh? That they're sisters?"

"Yep. Didn't catch on at first, though. But once I heard the last name, I started seeing the family resemblance." He laughed, shaking his head. "What I wouldn't give to be a fly on the wall when little sister runs home bragging to big sister about the cute detective she met today. Man, I'd love to know how *that* conversation goes."

Sebastien's expression was deadpan. "What makes you think there's something between me and Francesca?"

Rodriguez shot him an incredulous look. "You're kidding, right? Let's see, could it be the way you swept her into your arms and carried her out of Jennifer Benson's apartment like her very own knight in shining armor? Or could it be the way you personally escorted her and Garcia to the car and made the professor promise to call you as soon as she gets home?"

Sebastien frowned at his watch. "Which reminds me— she hasn't called yet."

Rodriguez laughed. "I rest my case. So when did it happen, man? When did you and the spider lady hook up?"

"None of your damn business," Sebastien said mildly.

Rodriguez chuckled. "You work fast, *mi amigo*. You only met her on, what, Wednesday?" When Sebastien said nothing, he shook his head. "I gotta say I'm a little surprised. She doesn't really seem like your type, wearing those horn-rimmed glasses and that butt-ugly muumuu. Now, the sister, *she* seems more your speed. Packaging-wise anyway," he added, grinning as he sketched an hourglass with his hands.

Sebastien had no intention of telling his partner that beneath Francesca Purnell's frumpy clothing hid the body of a fallen angel. Let Rodriguez think he was slumming a little—nothing could be further from the truth.

"She already likes the way you talk," Rodriguez continued. "'I thought I recognized your accent, Detective Durand,'" he mimicked Tommie Purnell. "'It's nice. *Very* nice.' Get the hell outta here. I could hardly hear it myself."

Sebastien chuckled softly. "That's because you're used to it."

"Nah, that's not it. Whenever you put on your 'this is official police business' voice, the accent practically disappears. But whenever you're spitting mad or trying to sweet-talk your way outta something—or *into* something, if you catch my drift—the accent comes on strong. I swear, man, you use that thing like a secret weapon. I don't know how you do it."

"Took years of practice," Sebastien admitted grimly. "Believe it or not, there were certain professors at LSU who wouldn't take anyone seriously with a Cajun accent. They looked at me and saw nothing but another swamp rat on an athletic scholarship. Had to prove 'em all wrong."

"So you learned how to talk proper," Rodriguez teased.

"Let's just say I learned how to play a new game. So, what do you make of all that?" Sebastien asked, with a nod toward the one-story building they'd just left and were now staking out from the obscurity of their unmarked cruiser parked across the street. As night approached, more people began to arrive at the club, spilling from cars and trucks in large groups and pairs. Though a majority were men, there were enough females to make Sebastien wonder why any man would bring a date along to watch other women strip.

"I've never understood that," Rodriguez muttered, as if he'd read Sebastien's mind.

Sebastien shook his head. "You and me both."

Rodriguez leaned back in the seat, settling in more comfortably. "I was sixteen years old the first time I went to a strip club," he reminisced. "My uncle Raul took me for my birthday. I looked older, at least eighteen, so they didn't hassle me for any ID. I remember being excited, but scared outta my mind. And then my uncle paid one of the strippers to give me a lap dance. *Ay Dios!* I almost sprang a leak in my pants." He shook his head, a wide, lascivious grin curving his mouth. "That was one of the best nights of my life."

Sebastien laughed. "Horny bastard."

"Hell, yeah." He flicked a teasing glance at Sebastien. "What about you, Big Easy? Do you remember the first time you ever visited a strip joint?"

Sebastien grinned. "I was eighteen, went with a bunch of friends from college. It was my first year living away from home, and most of those guys I was hangin' out with were upperclassmen. They wanted to show me how fun college life could be, so they took me to this club, a hole in the wall near campus. I got drunk, shit-faced drunk. One minute I was flirting with this fine-ass waitress who'd been serving me beers all night. Next thing I knew, we were screwing each other's brains out in the bathroom. I think my friends must've put her up to it," he added with a wry grimace, "because right when I was about to come, the stall door burst open, and there they all were, laughing and taking photos of my naked ass."

Rodriguez threw back his head and roared with laughter. Sebastien chuckled a little, stroking his goatee and shaking his head at the embarrassing memory.

"What'd you do?" Rodriguez asked, wiping tears of mirth from his eyes.

"Before or after I came?" Sebastien said, which drew another round of raucous laughter from Rodriguez.

After another moment, Sebastien said, "Seriously, though. What happened after that is kind of a blur. I remember being mad as hell, and trying to take out as many of 'em as I could before I passed out drunk."

Rodriguez gave him a sidelong grin. "And what about the waitress? Did you ever see her again?"

"Nah, I was too embarrassed. But surprisingly enough, she asked the fellas for my number—which I didn't find out until months later."

Rodriguez snorted. "Some friends."

"That's what I said."

They lapsed into amused silence for a few moments, watching through the dusty windshield as more customers filed into the Sirens and Spurs. The neon sign perched above the building flickered on, a woman's bare, shapely leg in a cowboy boot with spurs outlined in electric blue.

A leggy brunette with a duffel bag slung over one shoulder was dropped off at the front entrance and greeted at the doors by a pair of tattooed, muscle-bound goons standing guard outside. She smiled at them, said something that made them laugh, then, with a playful toss of her head, she sashayed inside the building.

Rodriguez gave a low wolf whistle. "I gotta hand it to ol' Yelena," he remarked. "She's got some of the best-looking strippers I've ever seen, hands down."

Sebastien slanted him a sardonic look. "Maybe you ought to take Tommie Purnell up on her offer to watch a performance."

"I would, but the offer wasn't extended to me, remember?" Rodriguez grinned. "Who knows? If you play your cards right, Durand, maybe you'll get another shot at making it in the bathroom with another hot chick—this time a dancer, instead of a waitress."

Sebastien pointedly ignored the joke. "Speaking of Slutskaya, what did you make of her?"

Rodriguez shrugged. "She's an ice queen, the kind of woman who'd sooner put her stiletto heel up your ass than wish you good night. Tough, shrewd business-woman with more *cojones* than half the pricks working in Internal Affairs. You gotta respect that."

Sebastien nodded, agreeing with his partner's assessment of the no-nonsense club owner. But he'd also been struck by something else about Yelena Slutskaya. "She's hiding something," he said quietly.

Rodriguez looked at him. "Think so? Like what?"

"I don't know," Sebastien murmured, finally turning the key in the ignition. "But one way or another, I'm gonna find out."

By the time Yelena Slutskaya pulled her white Mercedes to a stop in front of the modest brick rambler, the back of her silk blouse was drenched, clinging to her body like a second layer of skin. But the perspiration that dampened her expensive clothing had not occurred as a result of the sweltering summer heat.

Fear, not the weather, had caused her to break out into a cold sweat.

The fear came from a place deep within her, a fear so horrifying, so unspeakable, that she'd never voiced it aloud to another living soul.

Relieved to find the driveway empty, she climbed out of the car and hurried up the walk. Her fingers trembled as she pulled out a single key from her designer purse and inserted it into the lock. She threw a quick glance over her shoulder, then stepped into the house and closed the door behind her.

The interior of the house was cast in shadows, the plantation shutters drawn closed on the waning rays of daylight. But she didn't need more light to know how immaculate the place would be, every surface polished to a shine, the pillows neatly arranged on the sofa, the current magazines fanned out perfectly upon the glass coffee table.

Meticulous. Just as she'd taught him.

If only she could be sure the other lessons she'd instilled had stuck as well.

Shoving aside the thought, Yelena made her way through the living room and past the small, utilitarian kitchen. When she reached the rear stairwell, she paused. Dread pulsed through her blood as she stared at the closed door leading downstairs to the basement.

She had to know.

Once and for all, she had to know if there was any truth to the terrible suspicions that had haunted her mind for the past twenty years.

She had to know.

Drawing a deep, quivering breath that burned in her lungs, Yelena reached for the doorknob.

Behind her, a chillingly soft voice spoke. "What are you doing here, Mother?"

Heart pumping wildly, Yelena whirled around. And screamed.

Chapter 11

Francesca eased her aching body into the old claw-foot tub in her bathroom and slowly exhaled as the hot, lavender-scented water wrapped around her limbs. The traumatic events of the day had left her tense and on edge, her muscles strained to the point of causing her pain.

She'd driven Alfonso home and stayed with him for the rest of the day, fixing herbal tea and heating a can of minestrone soup that neither of them had the appetite for. She'd remained at his apartment until eight, when the first of his friends began trickling in. Male and female, gay and straight, they'd come bearing an assortment of casseroles and desserts, flowers and sympathy cards. Mouths agape, eyes wide with morbid fascination, they'd listened as Alfonso tearfully relayed the horrifying scene he and Francesca had stumbled upon that afternoon. By the third or fourth recitation, Francesca decided she'd had enough and discreetly made her exit.

Now, as she closed her eyes, the grisly images rushed to the surface of her mind, as inevitable as the fall of night. The stench of violent death had been thick and suffocating, a rancid odor that assaulted the nostrils and clogged the throat. And the blood. Francesca had never seen so much blood in her life. She still couldn't believe that the same sweet, vibrant girl who'd waited on her less than a week ago was the mutilated corpse she'd seen that afternoon, gagged and bound to her own bed while some maniac tortured and brutally stabbed her to death.

Forcing the images from her mind, Francesca opened her eyes and stared at the window beyond the foot of the tub. A rectangle of night was visible above the half curtain, blackness beyond the steamed glass.

She was worried about her sister. She'd called Tommie twice and left messages, but so far she hadn't heard back from her.

She frowned up at the ceiling. She had been trying, for several months, to shake the uneasy feeling that she and her sister were growing apart. She could remember a time when she and Tommie had gotten together for dinner at least twice during the week. Though it was understood that her weekends were reserved for partying, Tommie had usually set aside one or two weeknights to spend time with her sister. While they cooked dinner— well, Francesca was the one who'd actually cooked, while Tommie mostly watched and snacked—they'd talked about work, their favorite television shows, and gossiped about the scandalous affairs of local politicians and community leaders, many of whom attended the same social functions as their parents.

But over the past few months, the sisters' weekly dinners had gradually tapered off, then ceased altogether. Suddenly Tommie wasn't available during the week, and whenever Francesca tried to reach her on her cell phone, there was no answer. On the few occasions that she did happen to see her sister, Tommie was a little distant, quick to criticize or lash out in anger, much as she'd done on Wednesday night.

Not for the first time, Francesca wondered if her sister was holding a grudge against her for staying in their parents' house. When they'd asked Francesca to housesit for them while they were out of the country, she'd naturally assumed the invitation extended to Tommie. But when she'd approached her sister about moving in with her, citing the benefits of not having to pay rent for an entire year, Tommie had flatly refused.

"If Mom and Dad wanted me to live in their house, they would have asked me," she'd snapped. "But they didn't ask me. They asked *you*. And you know I don't go anywhere I'm not wanted, Frankie."

Despite Francesca's repeated efforts to change her sister's mind, Tommie had stood her ground. When their parents called and pleaded with her to join Francesca at the house, she'd dug in her heels deeper. As far as she was concerned, no amount of groveling could right the wrong that had been committed against her.

Sighing heavily at the memory, Francesca rose from the water and reached for a towel.

Draining the tub, she dried off, wrapped herself in a thick terry robe, and padded down the hallway to the bedroom she was occupying during her parents' absence. The large, airy room had been decorated by her mother and was done in French provincial white with a four-poster Queen Anne bed, a Louis XVI armoire, and a small antique writing desk in the corner. A pair of French doors opened onto a private terrace that provided a view of the lush gardens below. Her mother had insisted that Francesca stay in this room, instead of the smaller bedroom-cum-sewing room she'd originally chosen for herself. Once Tommie found out where her sister would be sleeping, it had sealed her decision not to move into the house with her.

Frowning, Francesca smoothed scented lotion all over her body and put on a two-piece pajamas shorts set.

After the noisy chatter of Alfonso's friends, the silence of the big, empty house was unsettling. She turned on the television, then wished she hadn't as she saw that the lead story on the ten o'clock news was Jennifer Benson's murder. The screen was filled with a wide shot of the apartment building, the parking lot cluttered with emergency vehicles and curious spectators, one of whom was being interviewed by the reporter who'd been on the scene.

"I didn't know what to think when I got home and saw all these police cars," the woman was saying. "I thought there'd been a terrorist attack and they were quarantining the building. Now we're hearing that someone was killed in there. I'm just glad it wasn't a biological threat or something. I have two cats inside."

With a sound of disgust, Francesca shut off the television, threw on a chenille robe, and headed downstairs to the kitchen, where she poured herself a glass of wine, hoping the alcohol would take the edge off her jagged nerves and help her fall asleep. She was exhausted, mentally and physically, but she knew sleep would elude her that night. Visions of Jennifer Benson, in life and in death, would haunt her every time she closed her eyes.

Inexorably, her thoughts drifted to Sebastien. She missed him and would have given anything to have his strong, comforting arms wrapped around her, to hear his dark-honey voice whispering in her ear, telling her everything was going to be all right. Though he'd instructed her to call him, she hadn't because she knew he was busy, and making progress on Jennifer Benson's case took precedence over everything else, including Francesca's need to be held. Besides, she couldn't allow herself to become dependent on Sebastien, or to expect anything beyond what they'd shared last night. It had been a one-time thing, she told herself. One of those rare, spectacular moments when the moon is full and the planets are perfectly aligned. What had happened between them would probably never be repeated. But she would always remember, and cherish, the incredible night of passion he had given her.

Shaking her head at the maudlin turn of her thoughts, Francesca made her way down the hallway to her father's study. The room smelled of leather upholstery and the good cigars Gordon Purnell had smoked for as long as she could remember. Sipping her wine, she sat in the big leather chair behind his desk and booted up the computer to check her various e-mail accounts.

After responding to a few students' queries about next week's unit exam, Francesca switched over to her personal e-mail account. Her father had sent a message with new photographs from Cairo. She eagerly opened the attachments, her heart warmed by images of her parents, smiling and posing in front of ancient ruins and temples, perched on the backs of camels as they moved from one excavation site to another.

We're making very slow progress on the dig, her father had written in his message, *but it's nothing we didn't anticipate. I'm becoming addicted to warm karkady, a tea made from hibiscus. I think you'd like it too, so I'm going to see how much I can smuggle out of here to bring home to you. How's everything going? I hope you and your sister are taking good care of each other.*

Smiling, Francesca hit Reply and was about to compose a message to her father when she heard the front door open, followed by the smart click of heels on hardwood.

Francesca jumped up and hurried from the room just as Tommie appeared in the doorway. She was so happy to see her younger sister that she flung her arms around her neck and hugged her tightly, drawing a startled laugh from Tommie.

"Okay, sis, you really need to get out more if the highlight of your evening is me coming over," she teased.

Francesca drew back, wrinkling her nose playfully.

"And you need to start hanging out at smoke-free clubs. You smell like a smokestack."

"I love you, too," Tommie retorted, sidestepping her sister to enter the study—or "Gordon's Domain," as she liked to call it. Slipping her hands into the back pockets of her jeans, she walked toward the desk. "What're you doing?"

"Checking e-mails." Francesca hesitated. "I was about to write Dad back. Did you get the latest photos?"

"Haven't checked my messages today." Tommie lifted the glass of wine from the desk and took a long sip. Then, with only a cursory glance at the computer screen with the blinking prompt that awaited Francesca's response, she sank into the chair and bent to remove her shoes with a grateful sigh. "It's been a long day."

"Yes, it certainly has," Francesca murmured, folding her arms as she leaned in the door frame. "Did you get my messages?"

"No, I've been running around all day. What did you say?"

"Nothing important. I just wanted you to call me. I was . . . worried about you."

Tommie eyed her warily. "Worried about me? Why?"

Francesca drew a deep, fortifying breath. She dreaded having to tell her sister about Jennifer Benson, with whom Tommie was loosely acquainted through a mutual friend. But her sister deserved to hear the tragic news from her, rather than through the grapevine.

She moistened her dry lips. "It's about Jennifer, from the Espuma . . ."

To her surprise, Tommie held up a hand. "You don't have to tell me," she said quietly. "I already know what happened. My friend Gloria called me earlier, after she got off the phone with Alfonso. You must have been the next person he called."

Francesca shook her head, wishing that were true. "No, actually, I was with him . . . when he found Jennifer."

Tommie's dark eyes widened. "You mean you were there? You saw . . . Jennifer's body?"

"I'm afraid so," Francesca murmured, feeling a fresh sting of tears beneath her eyelids. "When Jennifer didn't show up for work this afternoon, Alfonso got worried and asked me to give him a ride over to her apartment. That's when . . . that's when we found her."

Tommie looked aghast. "Oh my God," she breathed. "Oh, Frankie. I'm so sorry. That must have been horrible for you. For both of you. Alfonso didn't say anything to Gloria about you being there with him."

"That's all right. I'm sure he wishes he hadn't been there himself, to see what he did." Francesca walked over to her sister and placed a gentle hand upon her shoulder. "I'm really sorry, Tommie. I know how much you liked Jennifer. Whenever I saw her at the Espuma, she always asked me how you were doing."

"She was a sweet kid," Tommie said somberly, gazing down at the Aubusson rug beneath her bare feet. "We're all going to miss her. I hope they catch the sick bastard who did this to her."

"Me too," Francesca murmured, thinking of Sebastien again. She had every confidence in his ability to find and bring Jennifer's killer to justice. She didn't stop to question where such confidence stemmed from, when she'd only known the man less than a week. It was a gut instinct she had about him, that he'd be relentless in his pursuit of the truth and would go to the ends of the earth to solve a case, especially one in which a young woman's life had been cut brutally short.

With her head still bent, Tommie plucked a piece of lint from her jeans. "So did Alfonso say anything to you . . . about me?"

Francesca pursed her lips, regarding her sister curiously.

"No, he didn't say anything about you at all. I don't even think he remembered that you and Jennifer had hung out together a few times, or he'd have called you, too."

"Oh, that's okay." Tommie blew out a slow, deep breath, and Francesca wondered if she'd only imagined the trace of relief in her sister's voice. Tommie sat back in the chair, curled one long leg beneath her, and picked up the glass of wine again.

Francesca's mouth twitched with wry humor. "Help yourself."

"Thanks." Tommie took another gulp of wine, then sat staring into the twinkling contents for a moment. "Do you believe in love at first sight, Frankie?"

Francesca chuckled, resting her hip against the corner of the desk. "Where'd that come from?"

"Do you?" Tommie persisted.

"Well, um, I'm probably not the best person to be answering this question, seeing as how I've never been in love before."

Tommie gave her a look of exaggerated patience. "Pretend you have. Pretend for a moment that you're not sensible, practical Francesca who never broke curfew to be with a guy you really liked. Pretend you were a normal teenager who hung posters of fine-ass movie stars on your bedroom walls, instead of posters of your favorite characters from *Star Trek*."

"Hey," Francesca protested, "I knew plenty of people who hung *Star Trek* posters on their walls!"

The smirk on Tommie's face conveyed just what she thought of such people. "Answer the question, Frankie."

Francesca huffed out an exasperated breath. "Fine, if you must know, I do believe in love at first sight."

"Really?"

"You don't have to sound so surprised," Francesca grumbled. "Trekkies need love, too. Anyway, why are you asking? Have you been struck by Cupid's arrow lately?"

"Maybe," Tommie said with a private little smile.

"What about Roland?"

"Roland who?"

Francesca was shocked into laughing. "Wait a minute. You mean to tell me that after two years of being with Roland and defending his honor to everyone who dared to criticize him, you're actually ready to kick him to the curb? Cupid must have done quite a number on you."

"You have no idea," Tommie purred, taking a sip of wine.

Francesca grinned, playfully slapping her sister on the knee. It was almost like old times again. "It's late. Why don't you spend the night, then tomorrow we can get up and go stuff our faces at an all-you-can-eat breakfast buffet?"

Tommie drained the rest of the wine and set the glass down. "Sounds tempting," she said, her shirt inching up over her flat stomach as she stretched her arms above her head, "but I'm really exhausted, and I'd much rather sleep in my own bed than in one of those spare guest rooms that smells like talcum powder and moth balls."

Francesca laughed. "They do not smell like that!"

"Maybe your room doesn't, but the others do. Come on, Frankie, this place is like a museum. A big, beautiful, *antiques* museum. While other people's parents downsize to condos after their children grow up and leave the nest, what do *our* parents do? They go out and buy a dilapidated old house with more bedrooms and square footage than they'll ever need or use. What kind of sense does that make?"

"I think it makes plenty of sense. They wanted a special project they could work on together after retirement, so they invested in a fixer-upper."

Tommie rolled her eyes. "That's just a pretentious way of saying they had too much time on their hands, so they went out and bought a crumbling piece of junk they could pour all their hard-earned money into making pretty again."

Francesca chuckled dryly. "You always did have a unique way with words, Tommie-girl."

"It's called honesty. You should try it sometime."

"Honesty? That's funny, because sometimes I could swear it sounds more like bitchiness."

Her sister's eyes flashed with temper. "Hey, don't get mad at me just because I don't want to sleep in this old museum. If you wanna spend the next year of your life serving as your parents' curator, be my guest. But don't expect me to hang around just because the walls are closing in on you."

Stung to the quick, Francesca raised her hands in mock surrender. "Fine. Forget I asked." She paused, then couldn't resist adding, "God, Tommie, when did it become such a crime to want my sister's company every once in a while?"

"Hey, I'm not the one who called you a bitch!" Tommie said hotly.

Francesca mentally counted to ten, then said evenly, "You're right. I'm sorry for that comment. It was uncalled for."

Tommie swiveled away from her to face the computer. "You're not sorry," she said, furiously typing in her user name and password to access her own e-mail messages. "You're just trying to be the bigger person, like you always do."

Surprisingly, Francesca felt an impudent grin tugging at her lips. "You should try it sometime," she said low under her breath.

Tommie whipped her head around. "*Excuse* me?"

Francesca snagged the empty wineglass from the desk and started for the door. "I said I'm going to pour myself some more wine. Would you care for your own glass this time?"

Tommie's eyes narrowed suspiciously. "That's not what you said, but since you're being so nice, yes, I would like a glass of wine. And don't even think about spitting in it, Frankie."

"I wouldn't dare," Francesca said with exaggerated sweetness.

Inside the kitchen, she closed her eyes for a moment and wearily pinched the bridge of her nose. She could feel the onset of a headache, brought on by stress and the near confrontation with her sister. It was probably for the best that Tommie had turned down her invitation to spend the night. After the day she'd had, Francesca wasn't in the mood to deal with her sister's little bouts of hostility, which were getting really old, really fast.

Francesca was reaching for a bottle of Pinot Grigio when the doorbell rang. Her eyes flew to the clock mounted on the wall. It was after eleven o'clock. Who could be visiting her at this late hour?

As she passed the study on her way to the front door, she could hear Tommie conversing on her cell phone in the low, silky voice she used when talking to Roland. So much for Cupid and his arrow.

But when Francesca opened the door and saw who stood there, *she* definitely felt pierced by something.

Sebastien wore the same low-slung jeans and black New Orleans Saints T-shirt she'd seen him in earlier, but now his square jaw was darkened with a five o'clock shadow that made him look ruggedly male, and more than a little dangerous. Especially with that Glock holstered to his waist.

Heavy-lidded gray eyes roamed across her face. "You didn't call," he said softly.

"I know." Her voice came out in a breathless rush. Mortified, she snatched a quick breath and tried again. "You were busy. I didn't want to disturb you. Besides, it's not your job to—"

He leaned down, cupping her chin in his hand and slanting his mouth over hers. She gasped a little as he kissed her slowly, deeply, drugging her senses. She let her lips part beneath the pressure of his, allowing him access, shivering as he took possession with hot, sensual sweeps of his tongue against hers.

When he drew away, she whimpered softly in protest and leaned into him, chasing the heat of his body. He chuckled low in his throat, brushing the pad of his thumb against her lower lip.

"Invite me inside, *chère*," he murmured. The deep, husky timbre of his voice made it clear he wasn't just talking about an invitation into her home.

Pulse racing, Francesca opened the door wider and stepped aside to let him enter. It was only when his gaze traveled past her shoulder that she remembered she wasn't alone in the house.

She turned her head to find Tommie staring at Sebastien in openmouthed shock. Shock and a touch of something else, something that slid away when she caught Francesca's gaze.

Francesca closed the door and quickly performed the introductions. "Tommie, I'd like you to meet Sebastien Durand. Sebastien, this is my sister, Tommie."

Tommie made no move to step forward and shake his hand. "Hello, Sebastien. It's nice to meet you."

He inclined his head in the barest hint of a nod. "Likewise."

Francesca didn't know how to interpret the look that passed between them, so fleeting she could have imagined it. Or had she?

Clearing her throat, she said, "Sebastien is a detective with the SAPD. He's investigating Jennifer's murder."

"Is that right?" Smiling politely, Tommie divided a curious look between Sebastien and her sister. "So the two of you met today—at the crime scene?"

"Not exactly," Francesca said, with a shy glance at Sebastien. "We met on Wednesday."

"Monday," he countered softly, gazing down at her. "Just because we didn't exchange words doesn't make it any less of an introduction."

Francesca's belly quivered. If she could have kissed him right then and there, she would have.

Out of the corner of her eye, she could see her sister giving her a deliberate once-over, taking in Francesca's makeup-free face, messy ponytail, and bulky blue robe. She knew Tommie was wondering how on earth she'd captured the attention of a man like Sebastien Durand. Francesca supposed she couldn't fault her sister for wondering. She'd been doing the same thing herself for days.

"So, Sebastien, what brings you to this neck of the woods in the middle of the night?" Tommie asked lightly. "Are you taking a break from searching for Jennifer's killer?"

"Tommie," Francesca said tersely.

"That's all right," Sebastien drawled, unfazed by the question. His expression was vaguely amused as he regarded Tommie across the living room. "I'm off duty, but I'm always on call, Miss Purnell, so put your pretty little mind at ease."

Tommie said nothing, looking slightly deflated.

Francesca turned to Sebastien. "Can I offer you something to drink? I was just pouring myself a glass of wine, if you'd like some."

"Sounds good. Lead the way."

To Francesca's utter relief, Tommie didn't follow them into the kitchen, returning to the study instead.

As Francesca refilled her own glass and poured wine into another, she wondered if Tommie would change her mind about spending the night. She felt a pang of guilt for hoping her sister would leave—and soon.

"I'm sorry about that," Francesca murmured. She walked over and passed Sebastien a wineglass, then settled onto a bar stool at the opposite end of the counter. "She didn't mean to be rude. She knew Jennifer as well. Her death came as a shock to all of us."

"You don't have to apologize for your sister," Sebastien said softly. "Believe me, it takes a whole lot more than what she said to offend me. However, I will be offended if you don't bring your beautiful self back over here so I can kiss you."

Francesca blushed with pleasure. "Shhh, not so loud," she whispered. "I don't want Tommie to hear you."

"All right, then," Sebastien said, his smoky eyes glinting wickedly. "Where can we go to get some privacy? And I suggest you think fast, *chère*, or your sister's gonna be hearin' *a lot* of things in a minute."

Choking back a laugh, Francesca jumped up from the table so quickly that she sloshed a little wine onto the counter. Ignoring the spill, she went over to Sebastien, grabbed his free hand, and led him from the room. As they crept past her father's study and climbed the winding staircase, Francesca felt like a naughty schoolgirl sneaking a boy into the house while her parents were asleep. It was a thrilling sensation.

By the time they reached the top landing and rounded the corner, her lungs were bursting with the effort to contain her airless giggles. Sebastien backed her into the bedroom, one deliberate step at a time, and kicked the door shut behind them.

With one arm, he pulled her against him and crushed his mouth to hers, swallowing the laughter that finally bubbled up from her throat. His lips were warm and sweet, tasting of wine and his own delicious male flavor. The searing intensity of his kiss sent a rush of dizzying pleasure through her.

"Let's sit out on the terrace," Francesca whispered

into his mouth. He nodded, and she turned and led him through the French doors.

The temperature had cooled a little, enough to make it bearable for them to sit outside for a while. The air was thick with the perfume of flowers from the garden below, and the moon shone brightly from where it hung in the starry night sky.

Bypassing two white wrought-iron chairs, Francesca and Sebastien walked over to the balcony and stood in companionable silence, sipping their wine and listening to the lazy drone of nocturnal insects. It was so romantic, so perfectly tranquil, that Francesca could almost forget that somewhere out there, a sadistic killer was on the loose, waiting for the next opportunity to strike.

A small shudder ran through her. Sebastien, standing so close the hair on his arms tickled her skin, gazed at her silent profile. "Don't think about him, angel," he murmured. "Don't give him any more power than he's already taken."

"I'm trying not to," Francesca said quietly. "But every time I close my eyes, all I can see is what that monster did to her. And I keep thinking, what if he goes after my sister next? She likes hanging out at the Sirens and Spurs. What if that's where the killer first saw Jennifer?"

For a prolonged moment Sebastien said nothing. Then, "How close are you and your sister?"

"What do you mean?"

He searched her face in the moonlit darkness. "How much do you share with each other? Would she tell you if she thought her life was in danger?"

"I think so." She frowned, then heaved a long, wistful sigh. "I don't know, to be perfectly honest with you. There was a time I could have answered that question with an unequivocal yes, but now . . . everything's so different. Tommie's different."

"In what way?" Sebastien asked, hearing the pain in her voice that she couldn't mask.

"She's angry. Resentful. Hostile."

"Toward you?"

Francesca nodded. "Don't get me wrong," she said ruefully, "we've never been best friends. We're nothing alike, in case you didn't notice. She's always been into clothes and boys, and because I never was, we had very little in common growing up. But as we've gotten older, we've come to respect and appreciate each other's differences. Or at least that's what I thought."

"And now you're not so sure?"

She shook her head. "These days, being around my sister is like walking through a minefield, never knowing when the next bomb will go off. I spend more time dodging verbal attacks than having an actual conversation with her." Hearing the bitterness in her own voice, Francesca grimaced. "I'm sorry. I don't mean to dump on you like this, Sebastien. God knows you've got enough things to worry about."

"And you're one of them," he said gently. "What concerns you, baby girl, concerns me."

Her heart constricted. "Sebastien . . ."

Reaching out, he took her glass from her hand and set it down beside his own on the balcony ledge. Then, gently turning her to face him, he took her chin between his thumb and forefinger. The searing intensity of his gaze stole her breath.

He said huskily, "I can't explain this . . . I feel like I've known you all my life."

Her heart soared traitorously, foolishly.

Not trusting her voice, she lifted her hand and touched his face with her fingertips, lightly tracing the strong bridge of his nose and the hard line of his cheekbones, before trailing lower to the soft, enticing curve of his lips. He held himself still, watching her from beneath those sexy, heavy-lidded eyes.

Reaching on tiptoe, she brushed her mouth against his, softly and tenderly. Feeling his breath quicken, she drew her arms around his neck and boldly flicked her tongue against the seam of his lips. He groaned, his arms banding around her waist and holding her tightly against him as he deepened the kiss. Hungrily their mouths meshed and parted, fueled by a passion that burned hotter, faster, wilder.

Breaking the kiss, Sebastien rested his forehead against hers and gazed down at her, his lower lip slick and shining, his nostrils flaring slightly. He looked uncivilized—dangerous, untamed, raw. Francesca felt a thrill of excitement, a heady rush of desire that pulsed between her legs.

Still, when he reached to remove her robe, she tensed. "Not out here," she whispered self-consciously. "Someone might see us over the fence."

His eyes glittered. "Then let's go inside."

She hesitated, biting her lip, tasting him as she did so. "Tommie's still in there. I feel weird . . . doing this with her in the house."

He made a sound that was half groan, half chuckle. "Your sister's a grown woman. I'm sure she can handle the idea of her big sister being sexually active." When she wavered, he leaned down and kissed her—a long, deep, provocative kiss that slowly melted away her resistance.

Tasting her surrender, he slipped her robe from her shoulders and let it fall to the cobblestone ground. Then, kneeling before her, he reached up and slowly inched her brief shorts down her legs. All thoughts of impropriety evaporated as he pressed a hot, open-mouthed kiss to the soft spot below her navel. The sensation was electric. She trembled hard, closing her eyes as he slid his hands around to cup her buttocks, then dragged the kiss lower to the sensitive area just above the neat triangle of springy black curls, then lower.

She gasped at the touch of his lips on her, at the bold probing of his tongue. She instinctively tried to edge away, but he held her in place, his fingers stroking, kneading, pulling her closer, tilting her hips into the shocking intimacy of his kiss. The intensity of the pleasure stunned her.

She clutched at his big shoulders, then his smooth head, pulling him tighter against her. The need for this act, for this man, burned within her, wild, hot, too intense to be contained. Before meeting Sebastien, she'd never known what it was to let go of her self-control completely, but now, once again, she felt it sliding away from her. The feeling was both terrifying and exhilarating.

He stroked his tongue over her slick feminine folds, bringing her right to the edge, then drawing back, making her whimper in protest.

When he rose to his feet to unfasten his jeans, she pushed his hands away from his belt buckle and unfastened it herself. Her fingers trembled as she eased the zipper down. She touched him through the soft cotton of his boxers, savoring the feel of his hardness straining against her hand.

Sebastien endured her delicate teasing with a clenched jaw, holding on to his control until he could take it no longer.

"Touch me, *chère*," he growled, closing her hand around his penis, guiding it slowly up and down the engorged length of him. A deep, tortured groan rumbled up from his chest. "See what you do to me? Can you feel how much I want you?"

A sense of feminine power swelling inside her, Francesca followed his lead, reveling in the feel of him in her hand. Hot, hard, thick, pulsing. She traced her fingertips over the swollen tip and found a spot that made him suck in his breath sharply. With his hand still curved over hers, she reached down and cupped him. He swore, low and guttural, a shudder rippling through his whole body.

He dug into his pocket and fished a condom out of his wallet, then sheathed himself with impatient fingers. He backed her toward the nearest chair, then turned her around and sat down in one fluid move.

Hands at her waist, he guided her astride him. She eased herself down, taking him deep, her fingernails digging into his shoulders. As he filled her, she bit her lower lip to keep from crying out at the exquisite pleasure of it. Slowly, erotically, they began moving together, without words, the warm, ethereal glow of the moonlight cascading over their bodies.

Eyes locked on to hers, Sebastien reached beneath her tank top and fondled her breasts, teasing and caressing her nipples until they puckered in response. Heat poured through her limbs, drawing her backward like a bow. With her head thrown back, she braced her palms on his muscled upper thighs and gave herself completely over to him as he thrust harder, faster, deeper with every stroke.

Though she tried to remain quiet, it was a losing battle. A moment later, her wild cry pierced the night as her climax tore through her in blinding waves of ecstasy. Tears pricked her closed eyelids. She wrapped her arms around Sebastien's neck and clung to him as he came just after her, moaning her name and gripping her bottom.

Several moments later, as the spasms ceased and the tension began to ease from Francesca's body, she tightened her hold on him, afraid of what she would feel when she let go—not *wanting* to let go.

Fortunately, Sebastien had no intention of releasing her.

"Let's find a bed and finish this," he said huskily. With their bodies still joined, and her legs still wrapped around his waist, he stood and carried her back into the bedroom.

Chapter 12

Sebastien awakened at seven the next morning—hours later than he'd planned, hours sooner than he'd wanted.

Francesca lay half atop him with her soft, curly hair spread across his chest and one silky leg burrowed between his thighs—just south of the growing erection that had roused him from a deep slumber.

Smiling a little, Sebastien reached out to stroke her hair, then stopped, realizing that once he touched her, he wouldn't be able to stop. He'd roll her gently onto her back, slide between the glorious haven of her legs, and bury himself deep inside her wet heat.

Much as he'd done throughout the night.

Francesca stirred, sighing softly in her sleep. Sebastien held his breath as she shifted on top of him, then rolled away to curl into a ball at his side, taking the covers with her.

Carefully, so as not to awaken her, Sebastien swung one leg over the side of the bed, then the other. Soundlessly he rose and gathered his clothes from the floor, then dressed quickly, grimacing as he zipped his jeans over his throbbing erection.

Bon Dieu, he thought. The first thing he'd do when he got home was take a damn cold shower.

He paused at the door, gazing down at Francesca. Bars of early morning sunlight slanted through the French doors, gilding the soft curves of her body. Every inch of her was beautiful, from her high, round breasts, gently muscled belly and shapely legs, to the sweet, curvy ass that had fulfilled the promise of his fantasies. He wanted her so bad he ached with it. But he couldn't stay any longer than he already had. He had too many pressing things to do—phone calls to make, paperwork to sort through, leads to pursue.

Tearing his gaze from the enticing vision of Francesca in the bed, Sebastien left the room quietly, closed the door, and headed down the hallway. He was halfway down the stairs when he heard the creak of a floorboard behind him, followed by the soft whisper of his name.

He glanced over his shoulder to find Tommie Purnell standing at the top of the stairs, clad in nothing more than the low-cut shirt she'd worn yesterday and a pair of black lace underwear. Her long dark hair looked as if she'd combed it, then deliberately fluffed it with her fingers to achieve a sexy, tousled look.

Sebastien would have to be dumb and blind not to notice just how beautiful she was. But she was also trouble. Trouble with a damn capital *T*.

She gazed down at him with those exotically tilted dark eyes, as at ease with her sexuality as he was with a gun. "Good morning," she murmured.

He inclined his head. "Mornin'."

"I wanted to thank you for not telling my sister about you-know-what yesterday."

"It's not my place to tell her," Sebastien said evenly.

"I know, but thanks, anyway. She wouldn't have understood."

"Maybe you're underestimating her."

"Trust me, I'm not. I know what a Goody Two-shoes my sister can be." She paused, her eyes narrowing thoughtfully on his face. "Which is what makes this situation so . . . interesting. The Frankie I know would never have a man sneaking out of her bedroom early in the morning. Or at any other time, for that matter."

The ghost of a wicked grin touched Sebastien's mouth. "Like I said, don't underestimate your sister."

"Oh, believe me," Tommie purred, her eyes raking over him in slow, deliberate appraisal, "I'll *never* underestimate her again."

"Glad I could help." Sebastien tipped his head, then turned and sauntered down the stairs and out of the house.

As he reached the Crown Vic parked at the curb, his cell phone rang. He dug it out of his pocket. "Durand."

"Detective Durand," said a deep, familiar voice. "This is Rafe."

Sebastien grinned, unlocking the car door and sliding behind the wheel. "How the hell are you, Santiago?"

"Life is good, my friend." The soft murmur of a woman's voice could be heard in the background, then Rafe added, a distinct smile in his voice, "Life is *real* good."

Sebastien chuckled. "Don't rub it in, you lucky bastard. And how is the lovely Mrs. Santiago?"

"Korrine's doing well. She sends her regards. Hey, listen, sorry I didn't return your call on Friday. I was out of town all week. We just got back late last night."

"Oh yeah, that's right. Last week was your one-year anniversary, wasn't it? Congratulations, man. Where'd you two lovebirds go?"

"Oaxaca, where it all started. We stayed at the same little bed-and-breakfast where we spent our honeymoon."

"Nice," Sebastien said approvingly.

"Very. If you're ever thinking about Oaxaca for a romantic getaway, I highly recommend that place. Ouch!" The connection was muffled, as if Rafe had covered the mouthpiece. A moment later, he came back on the line chuckling ruefully. "On second thought, *mi amigo*, find somewhere else. Korrine says that's *our* special place."

Sebastien laughed. "Tell her not to worry. The last time I took a date to Oaxaca, it was for your damn wedding. And I spent the next two months having to hear about how 'beautiful and perfect' the ceremony was, and how it was the 'most incredibly romantic' wedding she'd ever been to. It took another two months just to convince that chick I wasn't interested in marrying her. You think I plan to step foot anywhere near Oaxaca again? Hell no."

Rafe chuckled. "You sound like Paulo. The woman he took to the wedding harassed him for a long time, too."

"Yeah, I know. When I ran into him last month, we got into this long conversation about why it's never a good idea to bring dates to weddings—especially 'perfect, beautiful, incredibly romantic' weddings held in Mexico."

"I hear you, my friend. But you know what? As amazing as the ceremony was, nothing compares to the journey that starts afterward, being able to spend the rest of your life with the incredible, beautiful woman who was crazy enough to marry you in the first place." Rafe sighed, and it was a sound of pure, unadulterated satisfaction. The kind that comes from deep within a man's soul.

Something stirred in Sebastien's chest, and for a moment his eyes drifted toward the house he'd just left. He imagined Francesca sleeping soundly on a bed of satin, just as he'd left her. And then he imagined what it would be like to wake up beside her every day, and to have her in his arms, warm and trusting, every night before he went to sleep.

Shaken by the turn of his thoughts, he tore his gaze away from the house. "Hey, Santiago," he joked, "it's too early in the morning for you to be waxin' poetic about your wedded bliss. Save those sonnets for the love of your life."

"Don't be jealous, *mi amigo*," Rafe drawled. "Seriously, though, your message sounded pretty dire. *Que paso?*"

"I'm working a case, and I need access to some library records. Think you can help me out?"

There was a pause on the other end. "You know I need a search warrant to get my hands on library records," Rafe said mildly.

"How long would that take?"

"Depends on the judge. Could be days, or weeks."

"You know I don't have that kind of time."

"Yeah, we never do," Rafe said quietly. He paused for a moment, then asked, "What're we looking for?"

Sebastien gave him a quick rundown of the case and the Mexican Blood Walker. When he'd finished, Rafe blew out a long, deep breath. "Damn. Another one."

Sebastien didn't have to ask what Rafe meant by "another one." Last year, five members of a local secret society had been murdered by a ruthless serial killer bent on revenge. The case of the "Weekend Killer," which had captured national headlines, had been investigated by Rafe and his wife, Korrine, FBI agents at the San Antonio field office. Rafe and Sebastien had met while serving on a joint task force during that time. As the only two members of the team who didn't give a damn about politics and appeasing bureaucrats, they'd bonded at once, and had been friends ever since.

Sebastien knew Rafe would understand, better than anyone, his urgency to track down the sadistic predator now stalking and murdering innocent women in their city.

"Tell you what," Rafe said. "Give me a few days, and I'll see what I can do about getting those records."

"Thanks, man."

"Don't mention it—literally. Oh yeah, before I forget,

Korrine says I should invite you over to the ranch for dinner sometime."

Sebastien grinned. "She finally realize she made a mistake by marrying you instead of me?"

Rafe snorted. "In your dreams, Durand." There was the sound of muffled feminine laughter in the background, as if Korrine, lying in bed beside her husband, had overheard Sebastien's comment.

"Now if you'll excuse me," Rafe drawled, "I'm going to show my beautiful wife just why she made the right choice in marrying me."

Sebastien grinned. "Give her my best."

"Better yet," Rafe said lazily, "I'll give her mine."

Chuckling softly to himself, Sebastien snapped the phone shut and stuffed it back inside his pocket.

Contrary to his teasing remark, Sebastien had known within moments of seeing Rafe Santiago and Korrine Friday together that they were perfect for each other. Their wedding guests had known it, too. It was all they'd talked about throughout the day—that, and the bride's stunning gown, the beautiful flowers, the quaint charm of the hillside chapel where hundreds of their friends, colleagues, and family members had gathered to see the happy couple exchange their vows.

Watching Rafe and Korrine at the altar, Sebastien had realized, perhaps for the first time in his life, that it was possible for two people to be soul mates, a concept he'd once mocked. Not necessarily because he didn't believe in romance—he *was* French, after all. No, his cynicism in this regard stemmed from the simple fact that he hadn't had many examples to learn from. Since his grandfather had passed away long before he was born, Sebastien had been deprived of the opportunity to see his grandmother in the role of loving, doting wife. And his parents, though they'd been married for over thirty years before their death, had been too absorbed in their demanding careers to model the behavior of two people who were clearly destined for each other. Sebastien could count on one hand how many times he'd seen them kiss or embrace or exchange teasing, affectionate words. They'd been like polite strangers, and their cold interactions with each other had spilled over into the way they dealt with their only child.

Pulling his mind from those painful recollections, Sebastien glanced toward the house again, where Francesca was probably still asleep in bed. Francesca, who was warm, soft, giving, and seemingly without a jaded bone in her beautiful body.

Sebastien drummed his fingertips on the steering wheel. Though he was off duty that day, he had every intention of working. Now that the killer had struck again, he couldn't afford to let the trail grow cold. He needed to interview Jennifer Benson's classmates, professors, coworkers—anyone who had a connection to the victim was vital to the investigation. He also planned to compile a comprehensive list of regional retailers of tattoo supplies, to see if he could track large shipments to private residences within the past three months. He had a lot of work to do, and time was of the essence. He couldn't allow any more distractions. . . .

Before he could stop himself, Sebastien climbed out of the car and slammed the door, then strode purposefully across the lawn. The front door swung open just as he stepped onto the porch, as if Tommie Purnell had been watching him from the window.

"Did you forget something?" she asked, a little breathlessly.

Sebastien barely spared her a glance. "Yeah," he muttered, brushing past her and heading for the staircase. "Your sister."

Francesca was still sound asleep when he entered the

bedroom. He locked the door behind him, kicked off his boots, and quickly undressed.

As he crawled beneath the covers and drew her into his arms, she mumbled sleepily, "Where'd you go?"

He brushed a kiss across her temple. "Outta my mind," he murmured softly.

Yelena Slutskaya's hand trembled as she held a gold lighter to her fourth cigarette of the morning.

After tossing and turning all night, she'd risen before dawn, showered and dressed, then driven across town to the Sirens and Spurs. Although the club didn't open until two p.m. on Sundays, it had long been her practice to arrive early to finish paperwork and take care of other business before the first customers began to trickle in.

At the age of fifty, Yelena not only managed the popular gentlemen's club; she was co-owner. And if all went according to plan, she'd soon be able to buy out her partner, a real estate magnate with principal interests in several local establishments, including a hotel, a residential apartment building, and a restaurant along the Riverwalk. He'd recently set his sights on purchasing and developing an upscale retirement community in Arizona, which meant he and his wife would, in all likelihood, relocate to the area. Which meant he'd be more willing to sell his half of the club to Yelena, fulfilling a dream she'd nurtured for ten years.

When she fled from Russia twenty years ago, she'd been forced to start over. Faced with a new life in a foreign country, with little money and no family to speak of, she'd made it her priority to learn the language and customs as quickly as possible, knowing this was her only chance of survival. She'd taken menial jobs and worked tirelessly to save enough money to put her son, Yuri, through college. And because she'd been blessed with an eye for talent and a head for business, she'd had no trouble landing a full-time job as manager of a little-known strip club called Classic's. It was Yelena who'd suggested a new name for the place, coming up with Sirens and Spurs because it was catchier, more memorable, and captured the flavor of San Antonio. She'd made other drastic changes as well, replacing the current stable of strippers with younger, prettier, sexier girls who embodied *her* definition of an exotic dancer. Though she'd made enemies in the process, it had paid off. Within months, business had picked up dramatically, and it wasn't long before the Sirens and Spurs Gentlemen's Club gained the reputation of having the best dancers and waitresses in South Texas.

Two years later, she'd approached the owner about buying a share in the business. And in that defining moment, she'd determined that someday she would become the sole proprietor of the Sirens and Spurs.

Everything finally appeared to be on track in her life.

Everything . . . except for the horrible fact that her son might be a cold-blooded killer.

A shudder swept through Yelena. Her hand shook as she took a drag on her cigarette and exhaled on a long, shaky breath. Lying on the desk before her was the Sunday edition of the *San Antonio Express-News*, open to an article about the murder of Jennifer Benson.

She'd read the story twice already, and each time she finished, the sick knot of dread in her stomach tightened.

She'd been unable to sleep a wink last night, haunted by images of her son's face when he'd discovered her at his house yesterday.

"Why are you screaming?" he'd asked her in that calm, implacable manner she'd always found so unsettling.

Yelena had pointed a trembling finger at his hands, which were coated with a red substance. "What . . . what is that?"

Slowly he'd glanced down at himself, then back at her. "It's paint. I was in the backyard painting a birdhouse." Seeing the doubt in her eyes, his mouth had hardened. "What else could it be, Mother?"

She couldn't say it, couldn't bring herself to utter the word.

"It's paint," he said a second time, low and succinct. "If you don't believe me, follow me outside and I'll show you the birdhouse."

And she had. God help her, she'd followed him just to see for herself that he was telling the truth.

What kind of mother would do such a thing? What kind of mother would suspect her own flesh and blood of brutally murdering innocent women?

The very same woman who'd once endured the vicious beatings of a man who claimed to love her. A man who'd threatened to hunt her down and kill her if she ever left him. She'd stayed, paralyzed by fear not only for herself, but for her ten-year-old son.

And then one day she came home late from work and found her husband lying in a pool of blood, in the very same bed in which he'd raped and beaten her on several occasions. There had been an empty bottle of rum on the bedside table, making it clear that someone had stabbed him to death while he lay in one of his drunken stupors, too inebriated to defend himself. Although Yuri was nowhere in sight, Yelena had known, with horrifying certainty, that her emotionally traumatized son had finally decided to take matters into his own hands.

In a moment of sheer, blinding terror, she'd panicked. Instead of calling the police, she'd wrapped her husband's body in the bloody bedsheets, then dragged the corpse outside to her car and loaded it into the trunk, using the dark night as her cover. She'd driven to a remote lake fifty miles from her house and disposed of the body, then returned home and scrubbed the place clean until her knuckles were raw and swollen. Yuri had quietly materialized and stood in a corner of the room, not speaking or asking any questions, just watching his mother with an eerily vacant expression she would later identify as shock.

She'd packed up their belongings, called her family to tell them she was leaving her husband while he was away on business. And then she'd done the only thing a mother desperate to protect her child could do. She'd taken Yuri and fled the country, knowing she would never step foot on Russian soil again.

To this day, she'd never asked her son if he'd killed his father.

But the terrible secret was always there between them, a grim, silent specter that loomed over their lives.

Although Yuri went on to lead a seemingly normal childhood, making friends and excelling at school, Yelena knew, with a mother's intuition, that her son was a damaged soul, broken beyond repair. But she couldn't take him to see a psychiatrist, lest the truth of what he'd done—what *they'd* done—should be brought to light.

After all, if she'd had the courage to leave his abusive father long ago, Yuri wouldn't have been pushed over the edge, driven to commit murder in his desperation to protect his mother. The knowledge that she bore as much responsibility for her husband's death as if she'd actually wielded the knife had filled Yelena with tremendous guilt. She'd compensated by raising her son the best she could, doing everything in her power to shelter him, to make sure he never suffered again.

When he first began appearing at the club last week, she hadn't discouraged him. Even when he seemed to take an inordinate amount of interest in Jennifer Benson, she'd thought little of it. After all, she'd told herself, Jennifer was a beautiful, desirable girl who was favored by a majority of the customers. Why should her son be any different?

And then one night Yelena had spied Yuri sneaking backstage to the dressing room. She'd discreetly followed him, then watched from around the corner as he slipped a folded piece of paper inside Jennifer's storage locker. After he left, Yelena had used her master key to open the locker and retrieve the note.

What she'd read had made her blood run cold.

YOU ARE THE ONE FOR ME, her son had typed in bold, capital letters. WILL YOU BE MINE?

Yelena shivered at the memory of those words. Her hand trembled violently as she stubbed out her cigarette in the glass ashtray on her desk.

Folding up the newspaper, she looked across the small office, her gaze coming to rest on a framed photograph of herself posing with a former Dallas Cowboys player who'd frequently visited the Sirens and Spurs. Concealed behind the photo was the entry to the safe where she stored all important documents.

That was where she'd hidden the note.

She thought about the two detectives who'd shown up at the club yesterday to interview her about Jennifer. If they ever learned about her son's obsession with the dead girl, they'd take him down to the police station for questioning, and in the course of interrogating him, they'd not only find out about the note—they would uncover the truth about the past.

Yelena couldn't let that happen. She had to do whatever it took to make sure the letter never saw the light of day.

She rose and walked across the room. Removing the framed photograph from the wall, she quickly unlocked the safe and reached inside. She withdrew the note, and without reading it again, she did what she should have done in the first place—she ripped it into tiny pieces.

Chapter 13

Monday, June 18

"I thought I'd find you in here."

Francesca glanced up from making notations in a logbook to see Peter Ueno standing in the open doorway of the entomology laboratory. "Come on in," she called, smiling and waving him over.

"Am I interrupting anything?" he asked as he approached, threading his way through a maze of counters lined with sterilized tubes and beakers, microscopes, and a host of other specialized equipment used in the collection and identification of arthropods. Various species of spiders and insects were housed in glass aquariums tucked into shelves along the walls.

"I'm just recording some data," Francesca answered, perched on a stool at the counter as she scribbled furiously in her lab book. "I'm almost finished."

"How's the research experiment coming along?" Peter asked, nimbly straddling a stool beside her. "Is *Portia* as smart as you think it is?"

"Even smarter," Francesca said, unable to keep the excitement from her voice. As part of her postdoctoral studies, she'd spent the last four months conducting research into the cognitive abilities of a genus of jumping spiders from Malaysia called *Portia iabiata.*

Peter arched a brow. "Smarter? How so?"

"Well, basically, what I've found is that *Portia* is able to do an image search of its prey based on mental templates," she explained. "In other words, this spider is consciously making intelligent choices and decisions—not relying solely on instinctive behavior. And after *Portia* makes a kill, it finds it easier to spot prey of the same species and becomes less attuned to other types of prey."

"Like selective attention," Peter observed.

"Precisely. And they only need to make one encounter in order to remember the image. This is probably aided by the fact that *Portia* belongs to the jumping spider family, which has extremely good eyesight."

She'd set out to prove four hypotheses about *Portia*: that the predators had evolved an innate predisposition to form search images for prey from the preferred category; they relied on optical cues as opposed to chemical cues; they became more dangerous to the type of prey for which they had formed search images; and while they were using a search image for one prey type, *Portia's* attention to other prey types was diminished.

"That's pretty fascinating research," Peter said thoughtfully.

"I think so, too," Francesca agreed, bending over her notes again.

Once she'd completed her experiment, she would concentrate on getting the results published in a leading trade journal. Although she wouldn't be the first to demonstrate search-image use by a spider, her findings were no less significant. And in the world of academia, especially at a research-based institution such as TABU, the key to reaching the exalted ranks of tenured faculty was getting published—the more, the better.

Peter said, "The reason I came looking for you, other

than to see how things were going, is that I was wondering if you could pinch-hit for me tomorrow morning."

"You want me to teach your nine o'clock class?"

"Yeah. I have some pressing matters to take care of and won't be able to make it to campus until later in the day."

"Sure, that's no problem," Francesca said easily. "If I remember correctly, that's why we agreed to stagger our classes during the week. So we could help each other out whenever necessary." Her tone gentled. "How's Sarge doing?"

He grimaced. "Not so good. The vet thinks he might need surgery to remove the bladder stones. They aren't responding to the medication he prescribed."

"Oh no. Poor Sarge."

"I know. But he's a trooper—he'll be all right." Keen dark eyes searched her face behind rimless lenses. "How was your weekend?"

"Umm . . ." Where should she start? How could she begin to describe the rollercoaster ride of the past three days? The weekend had started off like a dream, with the romantic candlelight dinner with Sebastien, followed by the most incredible night of passion she'd ever experienced in her life. Within a matter of hours, though, the dream had turned into an unspeakable nightmare with the gruesome discovery of Jennifer Benson's body. The pall of the girl's brutal murder had tainted the rest of the weekend, though Francesca and Sebastien had certainly done their best to escape into another universe, where nothing and no one existed but the two of them.

It was a weekend she would not soon forget, for more reasons than one.

Watching the play of emotions that crossed her face, Peter laughed. "All right. Forget I asked." He glanced at his watch. "You'd better get a move on before you're late to class."

"Oh! Thanks for reminding me." As Francesca scooped up her notebook, the Sirens and Spurs business card she'd stuck between the pages earlier fell out.

Peter bent to pick it up from the floor. Before passing the card back to her, he idly scanned the front. One brow lifted in surprise. "A gentlemen's club? Why, Frankie, I didn't know that was your thing."

An embarrassed flush heated her face. "It's not," she said quickly. "The card belongs to my sister. She left it at my house last week, and I keep sticking it in odd places thinking I'll remember to give it back to her."

Peter grinned. "Your sister's card, huh? Likely story."

She laughed. "Hey, you met her yourself at the awards banquet last year. *You* tell me which one of us is more likely to be adventurous enough to visit a strip club."

He gave Francesca a once-over, taking in her bespectacled face and white lab coat, complete with an ink-stained front pocket where her pen had leaked. His grin widened. "I see your point."

Francesca chuckled. "Thank you." As they walked out of the lab together, she sent her colleague a sidelong look. "What about you, Peter? Ever visit a strip club?"

He turned his head to meet her teasing gaze. "Can't say that I have," he said softly. "It's not really my thing."

Sebastien spent the first half of Monday morning on the campus of the University of Texas at San Antonio, talking to Jennifer Benson's classmates and professors. He'd learned that Jennifer had been an exemplary student and well liked by her peers, always willing to share her class notes and take the lead on group projects. Everyone he spoke to had been genuinely devastated by the tragic news of her death. No one could imagine why anyone would want to hurt her.

Sebastien left the campus, empty-handed and frustrated,

and headed back to the police station. Upon his return, the secretary, a middle-aged Hispanic woman seated behind a large metal desk littered with files, arched a finely sculpted brow at him.

"You have a visitor," she said with barely concealed displeasure. It was the same tone she used when screening calls from pushy reporters.

In spite of his grim mood, Sebastien couldn't help but flash a crooked grin. "Uh-oh. That bad, huh, Esther?"

"Worse." Esther Rivera scowled, motioning toward his office at the end of the corridor bustling with police officers changing shifts or escorting suspects to interrogation rooms. "Wouldn't leave a message or talk to anyone else. Insisted she had to wait for *you* because she had important information pertaining to one of your cases."

Sebastien paused to swipe an evidence submission slip off her desk. "She?"

Esther nodded, sucking her teeth in disgust. "Better not keep *Miss Thang* waiting any longer."

Chuckling softly, Sebastien continued down the hall to his office. He wasn't at all surprised to find Tommie Purnell occupying one of the visitors' chairs. After yesterday, he'd known he hadn't seen the last of her.

"Miss Purnell," he drawled, strolling into the room and rounding his desk. He dropped the pilfered evidence submission slip onto a growing pile of reports, case files, and other miscellaneous forms cluttering the surface of the desk, then sat down and leveled his gaze at his visitor. "Esther tells me you have some important information for me."

"Yes," Tommie said with a coy little smile, "but I'm not going to tell you anything if you keep calling me Miss Purnell."

Sebastien propped his elbow on the desk and leaned back in his chair, regarding her through narrowed eyes. She wore a pink halter top and a denim miniskirt that showed off a good amount of thigh when she slowly, deliberately, crossed her long legs. Sebastien, who'd been the recipient of more than his fair share of propositions, found himself amused by Tommie Purnell's lack of subtlety. Amused and a little annoyed, because he had a ton of work to do and couldn't afford to have his time wasted.

"Shouldn't you be at work?" he asked.

She shook her head. "I took the day off. I knew I wouldn't be able to concentrate on anything today, not after what happened this weekend."

He nodded. "What would you like to talk about, Tommie?"

She tucked an errant strand of dark hair behind one ear. "I've been thinking about our conversation on Saturday, when you and Detective Rodriguez were asking all those questions about the customers at the club."

Sebastien said nothing, his silence prompting her to continue.

"Well, after I got home on Sunday, I remembered something that had happened last Monday night when I arrived at the club." She paused, a note of censure lacing her next words. "I would have called you yesterday, but I didn't know whether you and Frankie had gotten back from your breakfast date yet."

Sebastien remained impassive. "I can always be reached on my cell phone if you have information about the case."

Her lips curled in a parody of a smile. "Even if you're in the middle of screwing my sister's brains out?"

Sebastien lifted one shoulder in a lazy shrug, refusing to rise to the bait. "What can I say, Tommie? That's why voice mail was invented."

Her mouth tightened, and for a moment her gaze strayed to the wall behind him, where a bulletin board was strewn with Polaroids of homicide victims whose cases remained unsolved.

When she spoke again, her voice was a low murmur. "Last week at the club, when I was walking across the parking lot with a few other dancers, I had this feeling that someone was out there watching us. It was creepy."

Sebastien studied her face like a poker player, trying to gauge whether she was telling the truth or just blowing smoke up his ass to get some attention. "Around what time was this?"

"Nine o'clock. My shift had just started."

"Did you see anything unusual or notice anyone loitering around the club?"

"No. It wasn't anyone I heard or saw." She frowned. "I just had this eerie feeling we were being watched. You know, like a gut instinct."

Sebastien nodded. "Did anyone else feel the same way?"

"I don't think so. No one said anything, and neither did I. We were all running a little late, so we just hurried inside and went about our business. I had forgotten all about it until yesterday . . . after Jennifer . . ." She trailed off, unable to finish.

Sebastien nodded his understanding. "Thank you for sharing this with me, Tommie."

She bit her lip. "I know it's not much, but, well . . . maybe you're right about the killer being one of our customers."

"I said it was a possibility," Sebastien said evenly.

"Which means it's possible that my life is in danger. Am I right?" Her dark eyes searched his, demanding an honest answer.

Sebastien hesitated, then nodded grimly. "Yes, it's possible."

"What are you going to do about it? Can you arrange police protection for me and the other girls at the club?"

"I wish it were that simple, Tommie."

"It *is* simple!" Her voice climbed an octave. "One of

my coworkers just got killed by a psycho who's probably staking out the place as we speak, choosing his next victim. And you're telling me there's absolutely nothing the police department can do about it? Why? Because we're a bunch of strippers nobody gives a damn about?"

Sebastien clenched his jaw. "You need to calm down—"

"I don't *want* to calm down! This is unbelievable! How can you people—"

"Tommie!" Sebastien's voice cut across the desk like the sharp crack of a whip.

She flinched and blinked at him, promptly shutting her mouth.

Leaning forward, he said calmly and succinctly, "I'll do everything I can to see about arranging surveillance for the club, but I can't promise anything. Unfortunately, it's not as simple as requesting a squad car to monitor the Sirens and Spurs twenty-four/seven. I wish I could tell you it was, but I'd be lying."

Tommie pulled her bottom lip between her teeth. "I'm scared, Sebastien," she admitted.

"I know," he murmured gently. "Maybe you should consider crashing with your sister or a friend for a while."

She nodded, holding his concerned gaze. "Or maybe you could look after me. You know, sort of like a personal bodyguard—when you're not working, of course." She offered him a soft, tremulous smile. "I know I'd feel safe with you around, Detective Durand."

Before Sebastien could respond, Rodriguez stuck his dark head in the open doorway. "Got a sec? Oh, Miss Purnell," he said, as if belatedly noticing who was seated in the visitor's chair. "I didn't realize you were here. To what do we owe the pleasure of this visit?"

Tommie barely spared him a glance over her shoulder. "I came to speak to Detective Durand about the case."

"Oh?" Rodriguez arched a brow at Sebastien, whose

expression was inscrutable. "Well, if you ever have any problems reaching my partner, don't forget you have my card as well. Do I need to give you another one?"

"No, thanks. I still have it." Tommie rose from the chair, gave her skirt a discreet little tug, then slowly walked to the door. Rodriguez stepped aside as she paused and gazed back at Sebastien, the dark curtain of her hair falling over one side of her face. "I really hope you'll give my suggestion some thought, Detective Durand."

Sebastien inclined his head briefly. "Have a good day, Tommie."

As she walked out, more than one officer craned a neck to watch her swing by in her midriff-baring halter and tight little miniskirt. Rodriguez backed into the office, whistling softly as he stared after Tommie's departing form—specifically her ass.

"*Dios mio!*" he exclaimed under his breath. "That is one fine, sexy woman."

Shaking his head in amusement, Sebastien reached for a folder buried beneath a pile of half-finished reports.

When he made no comment, Rodriguez turned and gave him an incredulous look. "Come on, man. Tell me you don't want a little piece of that action."

Sebastien chuckled dryly. "Don't get me wrong. She's a damned beautiful woman, no doubt about it."

"But?"

"I don't know. She doesn't really do it for me." He shrugged dispassionately. "I must be gettin' old."

Rodriguez snorted. "Old, my ass. The reason you don't have the energy for Tommie Purnell is you're too busy, as she put it, screwing her sister's brains out."

Sebastien scowled. "You heard that?"

"I was standing out there waiting for a fax. What can I say? Voices carry."

"Thanks for bailing me out a lot sooner," Sebastien grumbled.

Rodriguez grinned, leaning a hip against a metal file cabinet near the door. "I was waiting to see how long she'd beat around the bush before coming out and asking you what she came here for in the first place. 'I know I'd feel safe with you around, Detective Durand,'" he mimicked in an exaggerated falsetto. His grin turned lascivious. "Beating around the bush—pun definitely intended."

Sebastien chuckled grimly. "You need to get laid, Don Juan. I think you got too much sex on the brain."

"We can't all be as lucky as you, Big Easy. If you wanted, you could be having a hot little ménage à trois this very minute. What a waste," he lamented, shaking his head in disgust. After a moment he brightened. "Hey, you think Tommie Purnell would settle for yours truly if I offered my services? I bet I'd make one helluva bodyguard."

Sebastien grinned. "Yeah, just as long as you remember you're supposed to be *guarding*, not mauling, her body. All kidding aside, though, I did believe her when she said she thought someone was watching her and her friends last week."

Rodriguez arched a brow. "You sure about that? That chick strikes me as one very talented actress who knows how to turn it on when she really wants something—you, in this instance."

"No," Sebastien murmured thoughtfully, "that was real fear I saw in her eyes. Somethin' spooked her that night."

"Something she conveniently forgot to mention until she figured out a way to use it to her advantage."

"Maybe." Sebastien scrubbed a hand over his face, then motioned toward the piece of paper his partner had been clutching in his hand. "What's that?"

"The fax I was waiting for." Rodriguez's dark eyes glittered with triumph as he held up the printout. "I did some checking around on our friend Norman Fincher, and you'll never believe the interesting tidbit of information I came across."

"Try me."

"Seems he was a keynote speaker at a higher education conference held in Berkeley this past spring. I'll give you three guesses as to who else was in attendance."

Sebastien sat forward in his chair. "Christie Snodgrass."

"*Ding, ding, ding!* Give that man a door prize." Rodriguez, obviously pleased with himself, stroked his stubble-darkened chin. "What are the odds that Fincher, who was in Xeltu and wrote the article on the Mexican Blood Walker, would be at the same conference with a woman who was murdered and marked with a tattoo of the spider? What're the odds?"

"Slim," Sebastien agreed, frowning. "But it doesn't explain how Fincher could have known that Christie was coming to town."

"What if they met at the conference and kept in touch? What if Fincher's the one who suggested San Antonio as a great place to visit? What if she called him a few days before she arrived, or even after she got here, to see if they could hook up for drinks?"

Sebastien's frown deepened. "We checked out her cell and motel phone records, remember? Other than a few calls home to her parents and a couple of friends, she didn't call anyone once she got here."

"But we're still waiting on her home phone records," Rodriguez reminded him. "And her parents promised to check her e-mail messages and report back to me when they returned to California. Christie could just as easily have e-mailed Fincher to let him know she'd be in town."

"That's true." The muscles in the back of Sebastien's neck tightened. Thinking aloud, he said, "So now we have to consider the possibility that he may have visited the Sirens and Spurs at some point, which is how Jennifer Benson came into his crosshairs."

Rodriguez straightened from the file cabinet. "I'll make another trip down to the club with Fincher's photo," he volunteered, then heaved a long, dramatic sigh. "Man, I just hate my job sometimes, being forced to hang out at places crawling with naked, beautiful women."

Sebastien chuckled wryly, already reaching for the phone to make some calls. "It's a tough job, my friend, but someone's gotta do it."

"And it might as well be me," Rodriguez added with a wink before heading out the door.

"What do you think of this one?"

Francesca lifted her head from the clothing rack she'd been sifting through to find Patricia on the other side, holding up a shirt for her inspection.

Francesca pursed her lips, eyeing the severely low cut silk silver blouse. "Very . . . interesting," she said diplomatically.

Patricia chuckled. "Which is Frankie-speak for 'I wouldn't be caught dead wearing something like that.' Which is also why you're getting it," she declared, adding the blouse to the growing pile on her arm.

Francesca sputtered. "What? I can't buy that, Patricia."

"Why not? It's on sale."

"I don't care about the price. Look at it! If I wore that shirt, my breasts would be hanging out!"

A passing Macy's employee smiled at her scandalized comment.

Flushing with embarrassment, Francesca lowered her voice to a terse murmur. "Where would I wear something like that? I mean, can you see me walking into a classroom with that shirt on?"

Patricia grinned. "You'd never have another problem keeping your male students interested, that's for damn sure." At Francesca's scowl, she laughed. "Seriously, though, Frankie, you're supposed to be thinking outside the box, remember? You already have a closet full of safe, conservative clothes. The reason we're here this evening is to get you out of that rut. This," she said, lifting the shirt from her arm and holding it up again, "is the complete opposite of anything you've ever worn before. It's fun, sexy—"

"Indecent," Francesca interjected.

"It is not. Look, if you're worried about your boobs hanging out, that can easily be remedied with some tape or—"

Francesca groaned. "Great. I'd have to strap myself in every time I wanted to wear the darned thing."

Patricia grinned. "I never said being sexy didn't come with a price. Anyway," she said, moving on to a new clothes rack, "you're getting the shirt and that's final."

"Fine," Francesca muttered under her breath, "but don't expect it to see the light of day."

"I heard that," Patricia said over her shoulder. "And I not only expect you to wear the shirt, Frankie. I expect you to wear it with *attitude*. I know you can pull it off. I have faith in you."

Which was more than Francesca had in herself. Tommie could pull off a shirt like that—she'd gotten away with wearing much less, in fact. But Francesca wasn't her sister, and never would be.

"You can wear it with one of the new pairs of jeans you bought," Patricia was saying as she sifted through a rack of brightly colored summer skirts.

Francesca frowned. "You mean those skintight jeans you forced upon me?"

"Yeah, one of those. Once again, the complete opposite of the baggy, unflattering jeans you usually wear. If I had your booty, Frankie, I'd *live* in skintight jeans. Now stop complaining. You're the one who asked me to go shopping with you, remember?"

Francesca heaved a resigned sigh. "I know, I know. And I'm sorry for being such a whining ingrate."

"It's all right," Patricia said gently, lifting her head to gaze at her. "I know you've been through a lot these past few days. When you called this afternoon and invited me to go shopping with you, I figured there was more to the story than you having a fashion emergency."

Upon leaving the campus that afternoon, the two women had driven to the Shops at La Cantera, an upscale retail village that drew affluent shoppers from across the state and from as far south as Mexico. Over dinner, Francesca told Patricia about the harrowing experience of finding Jennifer Benson's mutilated remains in her apartment on Saturday. Patricia had listened with a mixture of sympathy and horror.

"I couldn't stop thinking about it all day," Francesca murmured now, absently fingering the hem of a gauzy pink skirt. "Every time I looked at my students in class today, all I could think was, what if it had been one of them?"

Patricia frowned. "Well, based on the article I read in the paper today, it doesn't sound like this serial killer is only targeting students. The first victim was that tourist from California."

"I know," Francesca said quietly.

She wondered if any progress had been made in the investigation. She hadn't spoken to Sebastien all day, which was just as well. They'd spent several hours together on Sunday, strolling down to the Guenther House for a leisurely breakfast of the buttermilk pancakes that had made the historic restaurant so popular. Afterward they'd taken a tour of the quaint old mill house before returning home, where they'd tumbled back into bed, alternately making love and dozing until late afternoon.

Francesca's cheeks flushed at the memory of how often, and how passionately, they'd made love. Over the course of three days, she'd more than compensated for years of being sexually deprived. And though she wished she could say the past weekend had been about satisfying a long-neglected itch, she knew better.

No doubt about it, she thought, pushing out a deep breath. It was definitely for the best that Sebastien hadn't called her all day. He needed to concentrate on the murder investigation, and she needed . . . well, she needed to concentrate on anything but him. Which was why she hadn't breathed a word about him to Patricia. She figured the less she talked about Sebastien, the less she'd think about him. And the less she thought about him, the less likely she was to do something utterly foolish.

Like fall in love with him.

Patricia's voice pulled her from her reverie. "The article was saying that, other than their ages, there were few other similarities between the two women. One was a blonde, the other a brunette. One was a teacher from an upper-class family, the other an orphaned college student who moonlighted as a stripper."

"I know," Francesca murmured. "I couldn't believe it when Alfonso told me that Jennifer was a dancer at the Sirens and Spurs. Not to sound judgmental, but she just never struck me as the type to do that sort of thing. She always seemed a little shy to me."

"Well, she was doing whatever it took to make ends meet and put herself through school. You have to respect that kind of determination."

"I do," Francesca said solemnly. "I just hope it didn't cost her her life."

Patricia, sorting through the rack once again, shot her a curious glance. "Why do you say that?"

Francesca hesitated, then answered truthfully, "The police believe the killer may have encountered Jennifer at the strip club and become fixated on her."

"Really?" Patricia's hand stilled on the skirt she'd just reached for. Slowly she turned her head to look at Francesca. "If that's true, then are you going to talk to your sister?"

Francesca made a face. "About hanging out at the Sirens and Spurs with her friends? I've been seriously thinking about it. I know she's going to get mad and tell me to mind my own business, but her safety *is* my business."

Patricia was watching her with the oddest expression on her face. "You don't know, do you?"

Francesca frowned. "Know what?"

"All this time, I just assumed you knew. I heard it from a friend who saw her there a while ago, but I never mentioned it because I figured if you wanted to talk about it, you'd bring it up yourself. And then the other day, when you asked me if I'd ever been to a strip club, I thought you were asking because Tommie had talked you into going to see her."

A chill of foreboding swept through Francesca. Though she dreaded hearing the answer, she had to ask. "What are you talking about, Patricia?"

"Your sister's not just hanging out at the Sirens and Spurs." Patricia paused, her expression grim. "She works there. As a stripper."

Tommie smiled to herself after listening to the message Francesca had left on her cell phone. Her sister's voice had been noticeably strained as she asked Tommie to return her call, saying it was "important."

Tommie had a pretty good idea what her sister wanted to discuss with her, and it had everything to do with a certain e-mail Tommie had sent to their father last night, in which she dropped hints about "feeling uncomfortable" at the house while Frankie "entertained strange men."

Oh, she knew it was childish, even spiteful, of her to have ratted out her sister like that. After all, they weren't teenagers anymore, so it wasn't like Frankie would be grounded for "sneaking boys" into the house when their parents were away. But Frankie had always been a staunchly private person, and the few crushes she'd had during high school had been closely guarded secrets. The embarrassment she'd suffer when their father began grilling her about Sebastien Durand was, in Tommie's opinion, worth risking her sister's wrath. After what Frankie had put her through over the weekend, a little payback was definitely in order.

Though she'd given Frankie a hard time about spending the night at their parents' house on Saturday, once Sebastien arrived Tommie knew there was no way she was leaving. She'd been shocked and dismayed to discover that the sexy detective who'd shown up at the strip club hours earlier to question her was not only acquainted with her frumpy sister, but was actually *attracted* to her. Even a blind man couldn't have missed the sexual tension that crackled in the air between them when their eyes met. They'd wasted no time stealing upstairs to Frankie's bedroom, and after a few minutes, Tommie's curiosity had gotten the best of her and she'd followed them. When she heard no sounds through the closed door, she'd tiptoed downstairs and crept outside to the backyard. And then she'd stood in the moonlit shadows, shamelessly eavesdropping on her sister and her lover. The breathless moans and cries she'd heard had both enraged and aroused her. She'd stomped back inside the house, called her boyfriend, Roland, and picked a fight before hanging up on him. Then she'd masturbated herself to sleep, imagining Sebastien was thrusting in and out of *her*, instead of her sister.

It was downright maddening, Tommie thought darkly as she cut in front of a crawling Buick and flipped off the indignant driver who blared his horn at her.

She had never, ever been interested in the same men as Frankie, who'd rarely dated in high school or college. The few men her sister liked had been bookworm types, reasonably attractive but too shy and nerdy to warrant a second glance from Tommie.

Sebastien Durand was nothing like those duds. He was gorgeous, for starters, tall and powerfully built with those piercing bedroom eyes, sinful lips, and strong, rugged features. He was smart, confident, and sexy, oozing virility in a way that should be outlawed. And that dark, liquid drawl—Lord have mercy—made her mind rush straight to the gutter.

Sebastien wasn't Francesca's type. He was Tommie's type. And the fact that he was knocking boots with the wrong sister was a problem. A *big* problem.

One she intended to do something about.

The stranger was inconsolable.

Three days after yet another failed attempt to find The One, he still hadn't recovered from the shock and despair that had sent him into a violent rage, causing him to stab Jennifer Benson until she was nearly unrecognizable. Even now, as he knelt before the altar in his basement sanctuary, a fresh wave of fury rolled through him.

How could he have been so wrong about her? He'd been so patient this time, returning often to the club to watch her, to ensure he made the right selection. He'd studied every inch of her beautiful body as she performed for him, slithering to the floor and spreading her legs wide as he stood over her, so absorbed in his inspection of her that it didn't occur to him to become aroused. The only excitement he'd felt was the thrill of discovery, for he'd finally found what he was looking for. The girl's skin was young, supple, and smooth, without any tattoos or the kind of birthmark that had doomed the other imposter. Unblemished.

Perfect.

Or so he'd thought.

The faint scar on the sole of her right foot had told a different story. Once he discovered that, he began to see other imperfections as well.

He squeezed his eyes tightly shut in an effort to obliterate the memory. A dull headache throbbed behind his closed lids.

For the first time since he'd embarked upon his mission, an awful suspicion began to whisper at the back of his mind. What if The One he sought simply didn't exist? What if it was impossible to find a perfect specimen, one whose body didn't bear the scars of childhood scrapes and bruises, blemishes from old mosquito bites, and bouts with acne? What if he was chasing fool's gold?

The thought made him break out into an icy sweat. No, it couldn't be true, he mentally vowed, fighting the doubts knifing through his brain. He couldn't give up hope. Just because he'd been deceived by clever imposters didn't mean his mission was in vain.

Somewhere out there, The One he sought was waiting for him. Waiting for him to find her, and reveal her destiny to him.

It had been three years in the making. Three long, excruciating years of wandering aimlessly, searching . . . trying to find his soul.

He couldn't succumb to despair. Not now, not when he was so close. There was too much at stake.

Fate demanded that he find her.

And he'd never been one to test the sovereign hand of fate.

Chapter 14

"What the hell is this?"

Sebastien glanced up as Sergeant MacDougal charged into his office and slapped a newspaper down on his desk. "What the hell is this?"

After a lazy glance at the item in question, Sebastien answered calmly, "It's a newspaper. Specifically, it's a copy of today's *Express-News.*"

"Don't be a smart-ass, Durand," MacDougal growled, jabbing a thick, blunt-tipped finger at the paper. "You know damned well I'm talking about that article, front and center of the Metro section, that refers to the spider tattoo from the crime scenes. I thought we agreed to keep that detail out of the press."

"We did," Sebastien said in the same imperturbable tone, though hours before when he read the article, he'd gone ballistic himself. "Seems we have a leaky faucet, Chief. Wouldn't be the first time."

"Hell," MacDougal muttered in disgust, shoving his hand through the steel-gray cap of his hair. "Now, thanks to that damned article, we're going to have every kook in the city flooding our phone lines with calls about all the 'unique, mysterious' spider tattoos they've ever seen."

"I know," Sebastien said, with a grim nod toward the stack of phone messages Esther had handed him when he arrived at the station that morning. "They've already started."

MacDougal scowled, eyeing the pile on the corner of the desk with the withering beam of a gaze that should have incinerated everything in its path. Sebastien half expected the pile itself to go up in smoke. "Someone's head is gonna roll for this," MacDougal grumbled, though he and Sebastien both knew they had a snowball's chance in hell of finding the leak, even if it came from within their own department. Whenever a murder occurred, people got excited. Uniforms talked, EMS workers talked, evidence techs talked. Sebastien had even known of well-respected detectives who purposefully leaked details to the media in order to thwart an investigation.

Hell, when it came to homicides, the only thing the police *could* guarantee was that leaks would happen.

"Since I'm already here," said MacDougal, folding his arms across his thick barrel of a chest and leaning against the wall, "bring me up to speed on the case."

Sebastien gave his boss a quick rundown of everything, from the history of the Mexican Blood Walker to the possible connection between Norman Fincher and the two victims.

"Yesterday, Rodriguez showed Fincher's photo to some of the waitresses and dancers at the Sirens and Spurs Gentlemen's Club where Jennifer Benson worked," Sebastien explained. "Lo and behold, they all recognized him."

MacDougal lifted a hairy eyebrow. "Had he been there recently?"

Sebastien nodded. "Twice last week. They said he tipped well and mostly kept to himself."

"Did he take a special interest in Jennifer Benson?"

"Well, that's just it," Sebastien said with a grimace. "Jennifer Benson was a very beautiful girl, and well liked by all of the customers. In fact, according to the manager, Jennifer was one of the most popular dancers there."

"Strippers," MacDougal corrected dryly.

Sebastien's mouth twitched. "They prefer to be called dancers."

The sergeant rolled his eyes. "Christ, what is the world coming to when you have to be PC about women who shake their asses in tittie bars for a living?"

Sebastien arched a brow. "Careful, Chief. You're starting to sound like a misogynist."

"Yeah, that's what my first wife used to tell me. Of course, considering that she left me for a stripper half her age, her opinion doesn't really matter. And to think," he added bitterly, "she and her lesbian 'soul mate' won custody of the kids while *I* got stuck with supervised visits. Where's the justice in that?"

"Life's a bitch," Sebastien murmured.

MacDougal snorted. "And I married the leader of them all. Anyway," he said, pushing off the wall, "when you get the results of Fincher's fingerprint analysis from both crime scenes, bring him in for questioning. Let him explain how his connection to two dead women is mere coincidence. And keep me posted."

"Will do."

After the sergeant left, Sebastien returned his attention to the paperwork he'd been reviewing before the interruption. As he reached for a file across the desk, he deliberately ignored the stack of phone messages from "concerned citizens" claiming to have important information about the spider tattoo cited in the *Express-News* article. Based on the notes Esther had scrawled on each slip of paper, there was nothing any of those callers could share with him that would lead to a break in the investigation.

He had to focus on more tangible pursuits, things that might actually produce results. With Esther's help, he'd begun compiling a list of regional retailers of tattoo supplies to track large shipments to local residences within the past three months. Once Rafe came through with the public library records that showed who was reading about the Xeltu epidemic and learning how to apply tattoos, Sebastien planned to compare the three lists—the tattoo supply retailer list and the library lists—to see if he got any matches. He knew it was probably a long shot, but he figured it was worth the effort, anyway.

Opening a folder marked with Jennifer Benson's case file number, Sebastien pulled out the crime scene photos and slowly spread them across his desk. Examining Jennifer's wounds in detail, he was struck by the same realization he'd had on Saturday. Jennifer had been stabbed more times than Christie Snodgrass, evidenced by the increased number of knife wounds across her torso. The killer had been even more enraged than before, nearly carving the girl up in his fury. What had been different this time?

Sebastien frowned, his gut tightening as he studied the graphic images. What kind of monster was on the loose? He'd seen more than enough carnage in his days with the NOPD, which, at one time, had boasted the highest number of murders per capita in the U.S. He was no stranger to gruesome violence and death, and yet, these recent killings had crawled under his skin and begun to fester there. There was something about the two crime scenes that niggled at the back of his mind. Something important about the two women he couldn't quite put a finger on. Why did the killer take the time to brand his victims with such elaborate artwork? The amount of painstaking detail he'd poured into each tattoo design suggested a very personal connection to the spider he was immortalizing. What *was* that connection? And was it mere coincidence that both of his victims had been twenty-four years old, though, as the newspaper article had rightly pointed out, there'd been few other similarities between the two women?

Sebastien blinked, scrubbing a hand over his face. Maybe he'd get a clearer picture of things once he attended Jennifer Benson's autopsy, which was scheduled for later that afternoon.

Sebastien glanced at his watch and saw that it was already ten thirty. For the first time that morning, he allowed his thoughts to stray to Francesca. He hadn't spoken to her since he left her house on Sunday—two days ago. He'd been tempted to call her several times, but had talked himself out of it. He had a lot of work to do, he'd reasoned. He couldn't afford to be distracted by thoughts of a woman who wreaked such havoc on his concentration.

He eyeballed the phone for a moment, then reached for it before he could change his mind.

When Francesca answered on the second ring, he couldn't help but smile. "Hey, girl," he murmured.

"Sebastien." She sounded surprised.

He chuckled softly. "Forgot me already?" he teased, though the answer meant more to him than he cared to admit.

"Of course not. I just didn't expect to hear from you for a while. I know you're really busy with the case."

"Doesn't mean I can't call to check up on you, see how you're doing."

"I'm fine," she said, but there was a subdued note in her voice.

Sebastien frowned. "Francesca?"

"I'm here. Sorry. I'm a little distracted. I just got out of class."

"I thought you only teach on Mondays, Wednesdays, and Fridays."

"I do. I was filling in for a friend." Her voice gentled. "Hey, listen, I saw the article in today's paper. I want you to know that I didn't tell anyone about the Mexican Blood Walker tattoo."

"I know you didn't," Sebastien said softly. "The thought never crossed my mind."

And it hadn't. Not once. What did that mean?

"Thank you," Francesca murmured, the hint of surprise back in her voice. As if she, too, understood the importance of having earned his complete trust after knowing him less than two weeks.

He cleared his throat. "Listen, I'd better go. I just wanted to make sure you were all right. Call me if you need anything, okay?"

"Okay. Thanks for calling, Sebastien."

"No problem."

Sebastien stared at the receiver for several moments after he'd disconnected. *No problem?* After the incredible weekend he and Francesca had spent together, was that the best he could come up with? *No problem?*

Frowning, he shook his head at himself. This was why he didn't need the distraction of a relationship. He'd spend way too much time second-guessing himself and worrying about that other little pesky matter of not falling in love.

He needed that like he needed a hole between the eyes.

As he began stuffing the crime scene photos back into the folder, Esther appeared in his doorway. "You've got a call on line three."

Sebastien cocked an amused brow at her. "Another one?"

"Yeah, but I think you should take this one. What she says about the tattoo sounds legit."

Sebastien reached quickly for the phone, relieved to have an excuse to shove aside unsettling thoughts of Francesca.

The thirty-something woman who greeted Sebastien at the door of Ink-Antations Tattoo Studio was short and thin with a narrow, bony face and wide blue eyes that were heavily lined with black, the lashes stubby and crusty with mascara. Her short hair had been dyed a shocking shade of purple and stood in spiky, mousse-sculpted layers on her head, and at least ten pairs of tiny silver hoop earrings marched along each ear.

When she opened her mouth to speak, Sebastien expected to hear a chain smoker's rusty rasp. He was un-prepared for the smooth, cultured voice that flowed from the woman's mouth. "Detective Durand? Hi, I'm Tara Weston. Thanks for coming."

"Thanks for calling," Sebastien said, flashing his badge before stepping inside the tiny shop. It was a hole in the wall nestled between a liquor store and an adult megaplex on the south side of town, one of many tattoo shops he and Rodriguez hadn't gotten around to visiting when they were making their rounds.

"When I saw the article in the paper today," Tara said, "I knew I had to call you guys. Would you care for some water or anything? I know it's blazing out there."

"No, thanks. I'm good." Dipping his hands into his pockets, Sebastien swept an idle glance around. Stock illustrations of tattoos were stapled to the walls, leaning toward the more traditional variety—skulls and bones, roses, hissing snakes, Chinese dragons. Signs declaring NO MINORS—WE ID and TATTOOED PEOPLE COME IN ALL COLORS were posted throughout the shop. The small interior could only accommodate three tattooing stations, all of which were currently vacant and unmanned.

"Everyone's out to lunch," Tara explained. "It's been a slow day."

"How many tattoo artists are employed here?" Sebastien asked.

"There're six of us. I'm the manager, but I still take clients. Here, let me show you what I was talking about on the phone." She walked over to the last tattooing station and disappeared behind the shoulder-high divider that offered customers semi-privacy while they were getting tattooed. She emerged a moment later carrying a thick binder.

"This is a portfolio of everyone's work," she said, flipping through the laminated pages as she made her way over to the small reception counter where Sebastien stood. When she neared the end of the binder, she plunked it down on the countertop and pointed at the open page, her long fingernail painted the same shade of purple as her hair. "This is one of Jeremy Dillon's designs. Does this look anything like the tattoo that was described in the article?"

Sebastien leaned down to inspect the illustration, which was an intricately drawn rendition of a black widow spider. Though the creature depicted in this design was not the Mexican Blood Walker, there were distinct similarities between the two tattoo drawings—enough to make Sebastien's pulse accelerate.

"Anyone can stencil an outline of an illustration onto your skin," Tara explained, carefully watching his reaction. "The skill in the artistry comes in the shading, use of colors, and other subtle things that set an artist apart from a simple tattooist."

Sebastien agreed. He'd practically grown up as an apprentice in his uncle's tattoo shop. After the many lectures he'd endured, he ought to know the difference between an artist and a tattooist.

He lifted his head to pin Tara Weston with a look. "Which one was Jeremy?" he asked, though he already knew the answer.

"Jeremy was an artist. He was probably one of the most talented tattoo artists I'd ever met, and he had the moody temperament to go along with his talent."

"Give me an example."

"Of his moodiness?" At Sebastien's nod, she frowned. "Well, for starters, he had a hard time understanding the concept of giving the customers what they wanted. If someone walked in and asked for a heart inscribed with his girl-friend's name, Jeremy would always try to talk the customer into something different, something he felt was more 'worthy' of his skills. That was a major problem, and one of the main reasons I fired him a month ago."

"How did he take being fired?"

"Surprisingly well. He was very gracious about it, said it was for the best because he'd never really fit in with the other tattooists, anyway." Her mouth twisted sardonically as she added, "Hard to do when you think you're better than everyone."

Sebastien turned to the next page, finding another elaborate illustration of a spider. "Is this his design as well?"

Tara nodded. "The rest of them are. He was really into spiders, almost to the point of being obsessed. That was one of the first things he always tried to talk people into getting—a spider tat."

"Did he have any tattoos himself?"

"Ironically, no. It was really weird. He had this thing about not messing with his skin, yet he made a living 'mess-ing' with other people's. Just bizarre. We all thought so."

"Did any of you ever feel uncomfortable around Jeremy?"

Tara pursed her lips for a moment. "If you're asking whether we felt physically threatened by him, the answer is no. There's only one other female who works here, and the rest of the tattooists are guys. If Jeremy had ever tried anything, they would've kicked his ass. A couple of them were looking for an excuse to do that anyway," she added with a wry chuckle. "But getting back to your question, Detective, Jeremy never came across as threatening. In fact, other than his inflated ego and weird quirks, he could be pretty friendly when he wanted to be. Quite honestly, I'm not even sure he's capable of the kind of violence described in that article. Those women were tied up and butchered like animals."

"Yes, they were," Sebastien murmured as he continued flipping through the binder, examining one intricate spider illustration after another. None, however, were of the Mexican Blood Walker.

Closing the book, he returned his attention to Tara Weston. "So tell me this. If you don't believe Jeremy is capable of murder, why did you feel the urgent need to call the police? Was it just the spider tattoo connection?"

She shook her head, her expression grim. "If it'd been just that, I probably wouldn't have called. Most tattoo artists have one or two favorite subjects, things they like to specialize in. And plenty of people like spiders. But there was something else I just couldn't dismiss after reading the article."

"What's that?"

"The photo of one of the victims, the college student, looked familiar to me. And then I remembered why. She was here a little over a month ago."

"Jennifer Benson came here to get a tattoo?"

"No, she was with a friend, and her friend was thinking about getting a tattoo. Anyway, they went to Jeremy because everyone else already had a customer. Basically, the girl wanted a tiny red ballet slipper on her ankle, which I thought was kinda cool because she said she was a dancer. But Jeremy, in his usual aggressive way, tried to steer her in a different direction. I'll give you three guesses as to what he wanted her to have."

Sebastien didn't need three guesses. "A spider," he murmured.

"Right. He told her a toe shoe was 'too tame for someone as exotically beautiful' as she was. He said he could give her a tattoo of an exotic African spider, something no one else would have."

Sebastien grew very still. "Jennifer Benson's friend was African-American?"

Tara nodded. "Tall, beautiful. Looked like a supermodel. I could tell she was a little intrigued by the idea of getting a tattoo no one else would have, but Jennifer was offended by Jeremy's suggestion that her friend should get an African spider tattoo simply because she was black. She talked her out of it, and when they left, Jeremy was furious. I'd never seen him that mad. He cursed up a storm and knocked some of his supplies around. But I was pissed off, too. I told him his pushiness with customers was costing us valuable business, and he'd better stop or I'd fire him." She shrugged. "He didn't stop, so a few days later I made good on my threat."

An awful kernel of suspicion had taken root in Sebastien's mind, stretching his nerves taut. "Did you happen to catch the name of Jennifer Benson's friend?"

Tara shook her head apologetically. "But I'd definitely remember her if I saw her again. Like I said, Jeremy was livid when they walked out of the shop. It was almost as if he took it personally—even more so than he usually did when customers turned down his suggestions." She frowned, biting her lower lip. "When I read about those recent murders and recognized Jennifer Benson's photo, I couldn't help but wonder if . . ." She trailed off, guilt filling her wide blue eyes as she stared at Sebastien. "Do you think Jennifer's friend is in danger?"

Sebastien remembered the haunted expression on Tommie Purnell's face when she'd told him, *I'm scared, Sebastien.*

His mouth tightened grimly as he looked at Tara Weston. "I need a home address for Jeremy, as well as anything else you can tell me about where I might find him."

Chapter 15

When Francesca stepped through the doors of the Sirens and Spurs Gentlemen's Club that evening, it was as a last resort.

Since yesterday, she'd been trying to reach her sister, but Tommie had not returned any of her phone calls. When Francesca stopped by the downtown law office where her sister worked, she was informed by the receptionist that Tommie had called in sick for the past two days.

"Tell her we miss her and hope she feels better soon," the woman chirped with a smile that didn't quite reach her eyes.

Francesca left the building feeling more worried than ever. When she arrived home, she'd pulled out the business card she'd been meaning to return to her sister for over a week. The person who answered the phone at the Sirens and Spurs Gentlemen's Club told her Tommie wasn't on the schedule until six o'clock. And that's when Francesca knew what she had to do.

"I'm here to see Tommie Purnell," she said to the freckled, gum-popping cashier manning the counter in the front entrance of the club.

"Who isn't here to see Tommie?" the young redhead retorted. She held out a hand. "That'll be ten dollars."

Francesca laughed. "No, you don't understand. I'm not here to watch her, uh, perform. I'm her sister."

The girl eyed her dubiously. "You're Tommie's sister?"

"Yes," Francesca said through gritted teeth, "hard as it is to believe. Anyway, it's important that I speak to her. Is there any way you can get her for me?"

"Sorry. I'm not supposed to leave the cash register." The gum crackled and popped. "But you're more than welcome to go inside and get her."

"Oh, thank you. I—"

"Ten dollars, please."

Francesca gaped at the girl. "You mean I still have to pay?"

"Sorry. House rules."

Scowling, Francesca fumbled out the money from her purse and passed it across the counter. "Is there someone—"

"Ask for Yelena."

Summarily dismissed, Francesca turned and made her way toward a pair of large wooden doors that looked like something out of a cantina, behind which loud, throbbing music could be heard.

Taking a deep, nervous breath, Francesca nudged the door open and stepped inside. The darkened interior was obscured by a fog bank of cigarette smoke that stung her eyes and made her blink rapidly, stumbling into a passing waitress balancing a tray of drinks. "Hey, watch it!" the blonde snapped at her.

"Sorry," Francesca mumbled sheepishly. Pushing her glasses up on her nose, she forced herself to continue walking, painfully aware of the curious stares of customers seated at small round tables around the dark, smoky cave. She knew she looked as out of place as a nun in the modest white blouse, pleated gray skirt, and flat, sensible shoes she'd worn that day to meet with a group of visiting scientific scholars from Japan. It occurred to her, belatedly, that she probably should have changed her clothes before leaving the house, but she'd been in such a hurry to talk to Tommie before her shift began that she hadn't given her attire a second thought. Which was nothing new.

But as out of place as Francesca looked at the club, nothing could compare to how out of place she *felt*. On the small stage, a topless dancer was sliding up and down a long silver pole to the sultry, pounding rhythm of Sheena Easton's "Sugar Walls." Blushing furiously, Francesca averted her gaze and kept walking, scanning the room for someone, anyone, who could help her locate her sister.

"May I help you?"

Francesca whirled around to find a petite, dark-haired woman in a killer red pantsuit watching her expectantly. "Yes, I'm here to see Tommie Purnell."

Cool, shrewdly assessing blue eyes met hers. "What do you want with Tommie?" the woman demanded in a smoky, thickly accented voice.

"She's my sister. I need to talk to her. Please, it's very important."

Those icy blue eyes narrowed on her face. "You are her sister?"

Here we go again. "Yes. And, yes, I do realize we look nothing alike—"

"No," the woman calmly agreed, "you are prettier."

Francesca stared at her in dumbfounded silence. A slight, cryptic smile flitted around the woman's mouth, painted a deep scarlet. "You do not hear this very often, I can see."

"No, I—" *Often?* She'd never heard it at all. Recovering her composure, Francesca cleared her throat and said, "I was told by the cashier out front to ask for Yelena."

"I am Yelena Slutskaya, the manager here. Tommie goes onstage in twenty minutes." Again that enigmatic smile briefly appeared. "And that is why you are here to talk to her, is it not? To tell her not to work here anymore?"

Caught off guard a second time, Francesca could only stare at the floor.

"Come," Yelena said mildly. "I'll take you to your sister."

Francesca followed the woman backstage, through the smell of assorted perfumes mingled with sweat. The dancers shared one dressing room lined on both sides with long mirrors and communal counters, which were covered in a messy sea of cosmetics, candy, feminine hygiene products, and other items that looked suspiciously like sex toys.

If Francesca had expected to find a somber tableau in the aftermath of Jennifer Benson's murder, she was mistaken. The room was abuzz with laughter and simultaneous conversations about cheating boyfriends, hard-to-find G-spots, stubborn toddlers, and customers who gave cheap tips.

When Yelena appeared in the doorway with Francesca, some of the voices grew hushed, several girls throwing curious glances at the newcomer before dismissing her as insignificant. For one sickening moment, Francesca was transported back in time to the girls' locker room in high school, where she'd never fit in with her classmates as they discussed cute boys and compared bra sizes.

"Frankie?" Tommie's shocked voice pulled her out of the painful reverie.

As Francesca watched, her sister emerged from behind a rack of brightly colored costumes. Looking like a *Playboy* centerfold in skimpy black lingerie and a pair of six-inch stilettos with a clear wedge heel, she stalked across the room toward Francesca, appearing none too pleased to see her. "*What* the hell are you doing here?"

Francesca actually retreated a step. "I have to talk to you."

"Can't it wait?" Tommie snapped, gesturing expansively around the room. "As you can see, I'm kinda busy right now."

"You wouldn't return any of my phone calls," Francesca accused. When several pairs of eyes swung in their direction, she realized the other dancers had probably misinterpreted her words as the complaint of a scorned lover.

The same thought must have occurred to Tommie. "Chill out," she tossed over her shoulder to the other girls. "She's my sister, all right?"

Heat flooded Francesca's cheeks as the speculative whispers turned into snickers.

Tommie glared furiously at her. "I am *so* gonna kill you for this, Frankie."

Standing just behind Francesca, Yelena looked vaguely amused. "Tommie, take your sister to my office," she said serenely. "It sounds like you two need some privacy."

Tommie grabbed Francesca's arm and yanked her down the hallway and into a small office, kicking the door shut behind them. "How dare you show up here and embarrass me!" she lit into Francesca.

"I wasn't trying to embarrass you," Francesca grumbled, rubbing her sore arm where her sister's angry fingers had bit into the flesh.

"Like hell you weren't! You're *always* trying to embarrass me!"

"How have I embarrassed you?" Francesca asked, striving for a calm she didn't feel. "Are you telling me no one else who works here has ever been visited by a friend or family member?"

"Not looking like Glenda the Good Witch," Tommie said scornfully, raking her sister with a look of scathing contempt. "Just once, Frankie, could you at least *try* to make yourself presentable before showing up at the same places where I'll be?"

Stung to the quick, Francesca snapped, "I'm not here to impress your stripper friends, Tommie. I came to see *you.*"

The moment the caustic words left her mouth, she knew she'd said the wrong thing.

Tommie's face contorted with fury. "That's exactly why I didn't tell you I was working here! I knew you'd get all judgmental and preachy."

"I'm sorry," Francesca said wearily. "That came out wrong—"

"No, it didn't. It came out *exactly* the way you meant it. My 'stripper friends.' That's what you think of them!"

"Tommie—"

"Poor Francesca," Tommie sneered. "How does it feel to know your own sister is nothing more than a stripper at a tittie bar?"

"Damn it, Tommie. This isn't about that. I came here because I'm worried about you."

"Of course you are," her sister mocked. "You're worried that I've lost every last ounce of decency and morality our parents worked so hard to instill in us. You think I'm going to hell for taking my clothes off in front of strange men—and actually enjoying it."

Francesca frowned. "There you go putting words in my mouth again. If you honestly believe the reason I've been trying to reach you for two days is to give you a lecture about your 'disintegrating morals,' then you obviously don't know me very well. Wake up, Tommie. There's a killer on the loose, someone who may be sitting out there this very minute waiting to choose his next victim. And that could be you!"

Tommie scowled. "You think I don't know that?"

"Then act like it, damn it! Use your head. Your friend Jennifer is dead, possibly by someone who visits this club on a regular basis."

"We don't know that. We don't know who the guy is."

"And you don't know who he isn't! Why put yourself in unnecessary danger, Tommie? Why? It's not like you need the money."

"You don't know what I need!" Tommie raged, nostrils flaring. She took a menacing step toward her sister, towering over her in the six-inch heels she wore. "You don't know the first thing about me *or* my needs, Frankie. So stop pretending like you do!"

Francesca stared up at her as if she were seeing a complete stranger. "Where is all this coming from, Tommie?" she whispered.

"Don't give me that wounded doe-eye look, Frankie. You started this, remember?"

"All I came here to say—"

"Fine, you've said it. I get it. You don't want your baby sister dancing in a strip club because some psycho might take an interest in me and decide to follow me home and butcher me in my sleep."

Francesca frowned. "Why are you making light of that?"

Tommie's lips twisted cynically. "I'm not. I'm making light of *you* and your so-called concern for me. We both know the real reason you're here is Sebastien."

Francesca's frown deepened. "Sebastien? What does he have to do with this?"

Tommie's expression turned smug. "Did he tell you he called me this afternoon to check up on me? And did he also tell you that he's coming by this evening just to make sure I'm all right? Ohhh, I can tell by the look on your face that you didn't know. I figured as much." In a voice dripping with malicious satisfaction, Tommie leaned close to confide, "Just between you and me, Frankie, I think your boyfriend's using the murder investigation as an excuse to see me again. But don't take my word for it. Stick around for a while, watch what happens when he gets here."

Francesca felt tears burning at the base of her throat. She backed toward the door. "I—I have to go."

"Of course," Tommie purred. "And it's almost time for my set, anyway. Who knows? Maybe Sebastien will 'conveniently' arrive just in time to catch my performance." With a provocative smile, Tommie traced a finger down the strap of her black lace bra. "Lucky man. He'll get to see not one, but *two* sisters naked in the same week."

Francesca's stomach roiled. "I'm sure you'll enjoy entertaining him," she managed coolly.

Tommie lifted one bare shoulder in a lazy shrug. "That's what they pay me for. You know," she added thoughtfully as Francesca turned and reached for the doorknob, "maybe if you had a little more courage to experiment with *your* sexuality, Frankie, you'd have less trouble keeping a man interested."

Without another word, Francesca yanked the door open and plowed right into Sebastien, who had just reached the office with Yelena Slutskaya. His arms came up to steady her as she stumbled backward and nearly lost her balance.

"Hey there," he drawled softly, gazing down at her in surprise. "I didn't know you were here."

Francesca's hands stilled against his wide chest, where she'd braced them during the collision. The warmth and solidity of muscled male flesh beneath her splayed fingers sent heat coursing through her body, and for one insane moment she was tempted to lean into him, close her eyes, and pretend they were somewhere alone, far, far away from this place.

She pushed aside the thought, as well as Sebastien's arms. "I was just leaving," she said stiffly. Out of the corner of her eye, she could see her sister lounging in the open doorway in her sexy black lingerie, a beautiful seductress waiting for her lover to arrive.

Sebastien glanced over at Tommie, then back at Francesca. "What—"

"I have to go." With a polite nod toward Yelena, who'd watched the entire three-way exchange with eyes that saw too much, Francesca hurried down the corridor without a backward glance.

He watched from the shadows. Saw her shoot out of the glass doors of the building and rush across the crowded parking lot. As she reached inside a large leather purse and pulled out her car keys, he saw that she was visibly shaken, her hands fumbling in her haste to unlock the door of a little red convertible.

He frowned. The car was ill-suited to her, much like her presence at the strip club. For even without the dowdy clothing she wore, he knew she didn't belong there. She was out of place.

Like him.

His muscles tensed at the realization, the blood heating in his veins. He sat up straighter in the driver's seat, his gaze fastened alertly on the woman.

What was she hiding beneath that long skirt? Would her skin be smooth and unblemished? Would it be . . . perfect?

Did he dare speculate?

He watched as she climbed beneath the wheel and slammed the door shut, then reopened it a moment later to release the edge of her snagged skirt. What, or who, had upset her? he wondered with mounting curiosity. What had brought her there, to this particular club, on a night when he'd almost let disillusionment keep him away?

He swallowed, trying to lubricate his suddenly parched throat.

Had he been looking for the wrong signs all along?

Should he have relied more on his instincts, that intangible stir of recognition that came from deep within the soul, and not necessarily from sight?

The little red convertible had come to a stop at the exit of the parking lot. As the woman waited for a break in oncoming traffic, he started his car.

When she pulled out onto the street, he slowly followed.

Francesca made it all the way home without crying.

She made it out of her clothes and into a pair of pajamas without shedding a single tear. But when she clicked on the television to an episode of *Star Trek*, the dam finally broke.

She crumpled in a heap on her bed and wept like her heart was breaking. And maybe it was. She couldn't imagine it remaining intact with so much pain knifing through it.

She'd known, after her brief phone conversation with Sebastien that morning, that he'd already lost interest in her. When he didn't call on Monday, she'd told herself he was busy with the case. But when he called that morning, and couldn't get off the phone fast enough, her worst fears had been confirmed. Now that they'd made love and he'd satisfied his fleeting curiosity about her, he'd moved on to the next conquest.

She honestly didn't know what hurt her more. The idea of Sebastien with another woman, or the idea of Sebastien with her very own sister.

Looking back, she realized she had no reason to be surprised. Hadn't she sensed something between Tommie and Sebastien on Saturday night when he showed up at the house? Hadn't there been a look that passed briefly between them, a look she'd wondered about? And now that she thought about it, where had he disappeared to on Sunday morning? Though she'd been half asleep, she was vaguely aware that he'd been gone at least half an hour before he returned to her bed. Had he snuck off to be with Tommie?

Francesca's body curled tighter into a fetal ball. She'd never had to compete with her sister, because they'd never had the same taste in men. Tommie liked them smooth, tough, and irreverent, while Francesca preferred the quiet intellectual types. But she'd always known, on some unconscious level, that if she and her sister ever found themselves interested in the same guy, there'd be no competition—Tommie would come out on top every time.

Oh God, Francesca groaned miserably. She didn't want to think about Tommie *on top* of anything, least of all Sebastien. But could she really blame him for being attracted to her sister? Few men could resist Tommie Purnell, especially while she was looking like a voluptuous, scantily clad Victoria's Secret angel. Of course Sebastien would find her irresistible. And being the Alpha male he was, he'd naturally want to protect her from any and all danger.

Francesca knew it shouldn't bother her that he'd called her sister to check up on her—just as he'd called Francesca—then driven all the way over to the Sirens and Spurs to personally make sure she was safe. She hated the fact that she resented Sebastien's concern for Tommie, when she herself had been worried out of her mind for the past two days.

Because she knew his concern would soon evolve into something more—if it hadn't already.

Tommie's cruel taunt whispered across Francesca's mind. *Maybe if you had a little more courage to experiment with your sexuality, you'd have less trouble keeping a man interested.*

Although she'd spoken out of pure malice, Francesca knew her sister was right. She could no more hold the interest of a man like Sebastien Durand than she'd been able to hold the interest of Jarvis Watkins during the conference in Beijing.

The only difference was that Sebastien had actually hung around long enough to get her into bed.

On that final depressing thought, Francesca drifted off to sleep and awakened some time later to the chime of the doorbell. Pushing herself into a sitting position, she squinted at the alarm clock on her nightstand and saw that it was after eleven. Her eyes felt swollen and her mouth tasted like cotton.

She stumbled groggily from bed and crept halfway down the stairs. Through the etched-glass window of the front door, she could see the tall outline of a man. But not just any man.

Sebastien.

What was he doing there? she wondered. And, more to the point, what had he been doing for the past four hours?

Watching Tommie, of course. In all her glorious, naked splendor.

The thought brought a fresh sting of tears to Francesca's eyes. As she stood there debating what to do, Sebastien pressed the doorbell again, more insistently this time.

Francesca didn't move. She remained frozen on the staircase, her heart pounding painfully against her rib cage, choking the air from her lungs.

Go away, she mentally chanted. *Go away, go away, go away.*

When he finally did, she turned and made her way back to her bedroom, where she calmly and deliberately set about the task of changing the linens.

The first step to getting Sebastien Durand out of her head, she decided, was to get his scent out of her bed.

Chapter 16

"She must've really done a number on you."

Slowly lowering the binoculars he'd been peering through, Sebastien turned to glance at Rodriguez, who was reclining in the passenger seat of the Crown Vic with his arms folded behind his head as if he were lying on a beach in Cancún. Two half-empty coffees sat cooling in the cup holders between them.

"Who did a number on me?" Sebastien asked.

Rodriguez grinned. "Play dumb all you want, but I know better. I know a whipped man when I see one, and you, my friend, are definitely whipped."

Sebastien scowled. "You don't know what the hell you're talkin' about."

Rodriguez chuckled, shaking his head sympathetically. "Denial. That's one of the first stages of whip-dom."

Sebastien lifted the binoculars and retrained them on the three-story stucco house they'd been staking out for the last hour. "It's too damn early in the morning for riddles, Don Juan. If you got somethin' to say to me, just say it."

"All right. I'll say it. You've been sulking for the past

two days. Esther told me, and I've seen it with my own two eyes."

"If I've been 'sulking,'" Sebastien muttered without lowering the binoculars, "it's because I'm champin' at the bit to interrogate Norman Fincher, but MacDougal won't cut us loose until the latent print results are back from the lab, even though we both know if Fincher's the perp, he was smart enough not to leave behind any fingerprints. And if I'm 'sulking,' it's because this kid, this tattoo artist, has been givin' me the slip since Tuesday, and it's driving me crazy."

Rodriguez considered his stony profile for a moment, then shook his head. "Nah," he said lazily, "that's not what's driving you crazy, Durand. Things have gotten sticky between you and the spider lady, and *that's* what's getting to you."

A muscle clenched in Sebastien's jaw. He said nothing. What *could* he say? Rodriguez was right. He hadn't seen or spoken to Francesca in almost two days, ever since she'd collided with him at the Sirens and Spurs, then fled from the place as if the devil incarnate were on her heels. He'd taken one look at Tommie Purnell's face, seen the triumphant gleam in her eyes, and realized she was up to no good. But when he asked her what was wrong with her sister, she'd batted her long eyelashes at him and claimed ignorance. He'd left the club twenty minutes later, intent on getting the truth from Francesca. But halfway to her house, he'd gotten a call about a murder-suicide on the east side, and that was where he'd spent the next few hours. By the time he finally made it over to Francesca's place, she'd already gone to bed.

Or so he'd told himself at first.

But after nearly two days of trying unsuccessfully to reach her on the phone, he finally realized she'd ignored the doorbell on purpose.

She was punishing him for a crime he couldn't remember committing.

And, yes, damn it, it was driving him crazy.

"So what happened?" Rodriguez asked.

"Hell if I know," Sebastien growled. "My guess is that she and her sister argued, and Tommie somehow gave Francesca the wrong impression about us."

Rodriguez lifted a brow. "What kind of impression?"

Sebastien shot him a look. "What do you think?"

Rodriguez grinned. "Yeah, I can see why that would be a problem, your girlfriend thinking you're nailing her sister." He paused. "You're not, are you?" When Sebastien glowered at him, he laughed. "Hey, I had to ask! You just never know. That's how love triangles get started, man."

"There's no love triangle here," Sebastien grumbled, then lowered the binoculars to pinch the bridge of his nose wearily. Barely seven a.m. and he already had a migraine. "*Merde*," he swore under his breath.

Rodriguez chuckled. "Why don't you just tell Tommie to set the record straight with her sister?" he suggested, as if the matter were as simple as adjusting the air conditioner.

"For starters," Sebastien said, "she's denying that they argued at all. Besides that, I shouldn't have to tell Tommie to say anything. Francesca should know better."

"Of course," Rodriguez said wryly. "Because she's known you for so long, she should just automatically assume you're not going to nail her beautiful sister behind her back."

Sebastien scowled. "Damn it, Rodriguez. This has nothing to do with how long we have—or haven't—known each other. This is about *trust*, about being innocent until proven guilty."

"You don't really believe that load of crap, do you?" Rodriguez wagged his head at him. "You're a cop. You should know better than that."

Sebastien rolled his eyes. "Why do I even bother trying to have serious conversations with you?" he muttered in disgust.

Rodriguez laughed. "Beats me. Especially this early in the morning." Sobering after a moment, he gave Sebastien a sidelong look. "You should cut the professor some slack. So maybe she's a little insecure. Can you really blame her, having to grow up in the shadow of a sister who throws her sex appeal around like it's going out of style?"

"Francesca's got more sex appeal in her pinky finger than most of the women I know," Sebastien grumbled.

Rodriguez looked thoughtful. "I believe that. There's something hot about a beautiful woman who leaves a lot to the imagination. Makes a man wanna go on a treasure hunt, if you know what I mean."

"I do, unfortunately." Peering through the binoculars, Sebastien straightened suddenly in the seat, his muscles tightening with alertness. "Well, well, well," he intoned softly. "The eagle has finally landed."

"No kidding?" Rodriguez quickly pulled his seat into an upright position and scrubbed a hand over his stubble-roughened face. He slanted a look at Sebastien. "You ready for good cop, bad cop?"

A slow, predatory grin curved Sebastien's mouth. "Aren't I always?"

They climbed out of the Crown Vic and made their way up the quiet residential street marked by large stone and stucco houses surrounded by impeccably manicured lawns that remained lush and green, although SAWS had imposed a mandatory water restriction that had pretty much killed most lawns around the city.

"How does an unemployed tattoo artist afford a place like this?" Rodriguez demanded somewhat peevishly as they stepped onto the wide porch of the three-story house they'd been staking out for the last hour.

"He doesn't," Sebastien said, pressing the doorbell. "I told you earlier. The house belongs to his parents. According to the friendly neighbor I spoke to on Tuesday, the Dillons are on vacation until the end of the month."

Suddenly the front door cracked open, and a pair of dark brown eyes in a pale, angular face peered out at them. "Yes?"

"Jeremy Dillon?" Sebastien asked.

"Who wants to know?" came the belligerent response.

Sebastien and Rodriguez flashed their badges with practiced flicks of the wrist. "We'd like to ask you some questions about a case we're investigating," Rodriguez explained.

"What kind of case?"

"Why don't you invite us inside, Mr. Dillon?" Sebastien suggested in a mild tone. When the door didn't budge, he added, "Unless you want the neighbors to tell your parents you were visited by the police during their absence."

The threat worked like a charm. The door swung open to reveal a frowning dark-haired man in his late twenties. He was medium height with a wiry build—thin enough to appear nonthreatening to the casual observer, but strong enough to subdue and violently attack an unsuspecting woman. He wore gray jogging sweats, the shirt collar rimmed with perspiration from the run he'd just returned from.

"What kind of case are you investigating?" Jeremy Dillon asked as Sebastien and Rodriguez moved past him into a cavernous entry hall awash with early morning sunshine and light from a massive wrought-iron chandelier that hung from the second-story ceiling. Augustine Durand would cluck her tongue at the waste of electricity and automatically reach for a light switch, Sebastien thought with a wry inner smile.

"Nice place," Rodriguez casually remarked, browsing the artwork on display in the hall.

"Thanks," Dillon said shortly. "It's not mine."

"But you live here," Rodriguez countered, "so, in a way, it's kinda yours, too."

Dillon shrugged, eyeing Sebastien as he awaited an answer to his question. He clearly had no intention of inviting them to sit in the living room—so Sebastien took the liberty of inviting himself, wandering into the large, expensively furnished room and taking a seat on the chintz-covered sofa. Rodriguez, the "good cop," waited a polite beat before following his lead, trailed by their frowning host.

"I hope this won't take long," Dillon said coldly. "I have an appointment at nine and I can't be late."

"What kind of appointment, Jeremy?" Sebastien asked casually. "A job interview?"

Dillon's mouth tightened. "I really don't see how that's any of your business, Detective . . . ?"

"Durand. And this is Detective Rodriguez. Sorry, we should have gotten those preliminaries out of the way up front," he said, flashing a sheepish smile that was about as genuine as a nine-dollar bill. "The reason I asked about your appointment is that you seem to be a very busy man. I've been trying to catch up with you since Tuesday, but every time I rang the doorbell, no one answered. Is that your Lincoln Continental parked in the driveway?" he asked, though he already knew the answer.

Dillon shook his head, claiming an armchair opposite them. "It belongs to my parents. I've been using it while they're on vacation."

"So you don't own a vehicle?"

"Not at the moment. I'm between jobs right now." He frowned. "What's this about, Detective?"

"We understand you used to work at a tattoo shop called Ink-Antations," Rodriguez said, producing a pen and his trusty notepad.

Dillon hesitated, then gave a slow, cautious nod. "That's right. I worked there for over a year."

"Until you were terminated about a month ago. Is that correct?"

There was a flash of anger in Dillon's eyes, disappearing as swiftly as an extinguished flame. "That's correct," he said evenly. "The manager and I had different philosophies about the art of tattooing."

"She said you were pushy with customers," Sebastien said bluntly. "You tried to impose your design choices on them, then became irate if they didn't comply."

He lifted one shoulder in an unaffected shrug. "If that's how she chooses to interpret things."

"How would *you* interpret things, Jeremy?"

He calmly studied his clean, short fingernails. "Getting a tattoo is a lifetime commitment, a permanent decision. I felt it was my duty to steer my clients in the right direction by presenting them with design options they'd be happy with, even if that meant something other than what they already had in mind."

"You really had a thing for spiders," Sebastien said.

Those dark brown eyes met his unflinchingly. "Maybe I was a spider in a past life."

Sebastien held his gaze. "You believe in past lives, Jeremy?"

"Maybe." He paused. "Who's to say we weren't here in another time, in another incarnation?"

"Who indeed?" Sebastien murmured.

"So is that why you wanted to tattoo all of your customers with a spider?" Rodriguez asked, pen poised above his notepad. "Was that your way of paying homage to your, uh, former incarnation?"

Dillon frowned. "I did more than spiders. And what does any of this have to do with the case you're investigating—which, by the way, you still haven't told me about?"

Sebastien and Rodriguez exchanged glances. "We're

investigating the recent murders of two women," Rodriguez said. "The killer left a calling card on their bodies."

"Elaborate, intricately designed tattoos," Sebastien elaborated. "Looked a lot like yours, as a matter of fact."

Dillon divided a wary look between them. "What are you implying? Are you suggesting *I* killed those women?"

"We're not suggesting anything," Rodriguez answered mildly. "We're covering our bases by talking to anyone who may have a connection to this case."

"Do you know how many tattoo artists there are in this city? Anyone could have tattooed those women!"

"True," Sebastien agreed, "but how many came in contact with one of our victims a few weeks before she was killed?"

A single bead of sweat skimmed down the side of Dillon's face. "I didn't kill anyone," he said tersely.

"Do you remember Jennifer Benson coming into Ink-Antations?" Rodriguez asked. "She was with a friend who wanted to get a tattoo. You tried to talk her into an African spider."

"That was over a month ago."

"But you do remember," Sebastien prodded.

"So what if I do? They were beautiful girls. Of course I remember them."

"And do you remember being royally pissed when they left after Jennifer talked her friend out of getting the tattoo?"

A muscle ticked in Dillon's tightly clenched jaw. "I got over it."

"Did you?" Sebastien asked.

"Of course. Why wouldn't I?"

"I don't know. Maybe you've got a short fuse, and that encounter just pushed you over the edge. I mean, you *did* lose your job over it."

"I lost my job," Dillon said through gritted teeth, "because that bitch Tara felt threatened by me. She and the rest of those losers were jealous of me."

"Because you were so talented," Sebastien said, dead-pan. "Because your designs were so distinct, so unique, that few others could imitate them."

"Exactly. I—" Dillon broke off abruptly, his pale face flushing as he realized, too late, that he'd walked right into Sebastien's trap.

The corners of Sebastien's mouth lifted in the feral smile of a hunter closing in on its prey. "Where were you on the night of Sunday, June tenth, and Friday, June fifteenth, between the hours of ten and three a.m.?"

Dillon lurched to his feet. "I don't have to answer that! You can't just barge in here and interrogate me in my own home. I want you both to leave."

"Not until we're finished," Sebastien said in a voice edged in steel. "Sit down, Mr. Dillon."

His nostrils flared. "I'm calling my lawyer."

"Why would you need a lawyer?" Rodriguez inquired, all innocence. "You're not under arrest. We're just asking a few simple questions, trying to get to the bottom of this mystery. If anything ever happened to you, your parents would expect the same thoroughness from any detective assigned to the case."

Dillon wavered, glaring balefully at Sebastien. "I'm not a murderer."

Sebastien's eyes narrowed shrewdly on his face. "That remains to be seen," he said softly.

Dillon marched to the door and yanked it open. "You've overstayed your welcome, Detectives."

As Sebastien and Rodriguez got slowly to their feet, Rodriguez gave his partner a look meant to convey his disgust with Sebastien's lack of diplomacy.

"By the way," Sebastien said casually as he walked toward the door, where Dillon stood fuming. "Have you ever been to the Sirens and Spurs Gentlemen's Club?"

Dillon looked him straight in the eye. "No, I haven't," he said coolly.

"Are you sure?"

"I'm positive."

"That's odd," Sebastien said, exchanging perplexed glances with Rodriguez.

"What's odd?" Dillon asked warily.

"Jennifer Benson's friend swears she saw you one night at the club last week."

Something flickered in Dillon's eyes. "It wasn't me."

"Yeah," Sebastien murmured thoughtfully. "Must've been someone else. Another tattoo artist who tried to talk her into getting an African spider on her ankle."

Dillon's expression hardened. "Unless you come back here with an arrest warrant, Detective, I have nothing more to say to you."

Sebastien inclined his head, a hint of menace in the smile that curved his mouth. "We'll be in touch."

Peter fell in step beside Francesca and Patricia as they walked across campus toward the dining hall that afternoon. "Mind if I join you ladies for lunch?"

"Hey, Peter," the two women chorused in unison.

"Haven't seen you all week, stranger," Francesca said, bumping him playfully on the shoulder. "How's Sarge doing? Still recovering okay from surgery?"

Peter nodded. "No complaints. He's been sleeping like a baby. Thanks again for pinch-hitting for me on Tuesday. My class really enjoyed having you. I got several e-mails from students raving about your lecture on invertebrate pathology."

"Really?" Francesca said, brightening for the first time in days. She bit her lip guiltily. "I know I strayed a little from your syllabus—"

"Don't worry about it. You were great." Peter smiled

easily at her. "You really should be teaching upper-level courses."

She issued a long, plaintive sigh. "Maybe in a few years."

"Or maybe sooner. I was thinking about approaching the dean about the possibility of us team-teaching a course in the fall."

"Really? You'd talk to Dr. Liebherr for me?"

"Not just for you," Peter said with a laugh. "I'd get something out of the deal, too. A co-instructor who's as knowledgeable and passionate about the field of entomology as I am."

Francesca beamed a smile at him. "Thanks, Peter. I really appreciate that."

On the other side of her, Patricia made a loud gagging noise. "I hate to interrupt this mutual admiration society, but, Frankie, I'd be derelict in my duties as a friend if I didn't draw your attention to the positively scrumptious specimen walking straight in our direction."

Francesca turned her head to find Sebastien striding purposefully toward them, his steely, intoxicating gaze locked on hers. Her heart leaped to her throat, and for one moment she was tempted to turn tail and run. But she couldn't move, could only stand there and drink in the sight of him. He wore loose khaki trousers and a black T-shirt that stretched across his broad shoulders and sinewy biceps. She remembered kissing those biceps, watching the sensual glide and flex of muscle beneath her exploring hands and mouth.

Beside her, Patricia made a low feline sound in her throat. "*Yum-my.*"

Francesca swallowed and willed her heart rate to slow down as Sebastien approached, stopping directly in front of her.

She stared up at him. "Wh-what're you doing here, Sebastien?"

"You've been avoiding me," he said, a husky reprimand.

Heat stung her cheeks. Belatedly she remembered her companions and performed the introductions.

Peter exchanged coolly polite greetings with Sebastien. "A detective, huh?" he said. "Where did you and Frankie meet?"

"Detective Durand is investigating Jennifer Benson's murder," Francesca answered.

Peter nodded slowly. "Tough case."

"Yeah," Sebastien murmured.

"What happened to Jennifer and that woman from California was absolutely horrifying," Patricia chimed in. "I hope you'll catch the monster responsible for their deaths."

"Believe me, Ms. Garza, I'd like nothing better," Sebastien said quietly.

"Call me Patricia," she said with a warm smile. "Any friend of Frankie's is a friend of mine."

He inclined his head. "Thank you, Patricia."

"Peter, why don't we go grab a table in the cafeteria before it gets too crowded?" Without waiting for his consent, Patricia snagged his arm and led him away, tossing over her shoulder, "It was nice meeting you, Detective Durand!"

Sebastien chuckled. "Likewise."

"I'll catch up with you guys in a minute," Francesca called after them.

"Actually," Sebastien said softly, stepping into her line of vision, "I was hoping you'd have lunch with me. Can you get away for a while?"

"No," she blurted out. Then, in a softer, less panicked tone, "I mean, I can't leave campus. I have a meeting at two."

"It's barely noon," he said with a lazy glance at his watch. "I'll have you back in time."

She shook her head emphatically. "I can't, Sebastien."

His eyes narrowed, his gaze a silvery laser beam locking on to hers. "Can't," he challenged, "or won't?" When she said nothing, he smiled with a sardonic twist to his lips. "Don't mind me. I have this annoying little habit of wanting to know why a person suddenly hates my guts."

Her throat constricted. "I don't hate your guts, Sebastien."

"No? You don't return any of my phone calls, you don't answer the door when I show up at your house, you refuse to give me an hour of your time. What's a guy to think, Francesca?"

She drew a breath that burned in her lungs. "Sebastien—"

"If this is about your sister—"

"It's not. No, really, it's not," she said when he arched a dubious brow. "I mean, it was about her at first. When I saw you at the club the other night, I *did* believe you were there to see Tommie for purely personal reasons, and it bothered me, I'll admit that. It bothered me a lot. But then it made me realize something about myself." She drew a deep, shaky breath, then forged bravely ahead. "I'm too insecure for a man like you, Sebastien. If it wasn't my sister, it would have been another woman. I'm not the jealous type, but being with you would turn me into that. Because no matter what you tell me, I'd always be wondering, deep down inside, what you're doing with me, when you could have any other woman you want. See, that's the level of insecurity we're dealing with here. I don't want to put you through that. Heck, I don't want to put *myself* through that. So, while I *have* enjoyed spending time with you, Sebastien, I think it would be best if we were just friends."

Throughout her monologue, Sebastien had remained silent, watching her with an unreadable expression that offered no insight into his thoughts or emotions. When she'd finished speaking, she unconsciously held her breath, bracing herself for his reaction—whatever it might be.

"Just friends?" he murmured in a voice without inflection.

She hesitated, then nodded jerkily. "Just friends."

"That's too bad, *chère*," he said quietly. "For a minute there, I thought we could've had something special."

And then, without another word, he turned and sauntered away, leaving Francesca with a hollow ache of regret in her heart.

Chapter 17

For the rest of the afternoon and into the evening, she immersed herself in research. The laboratory was where she belonged, surrounded by the exotic creatures that were so familiar and fascinating to her. The spiders she studied and nurtured would never hurt or betray her, or scare her senseless with the depth of her feelings for them. The laboratory was her sanctuary, and within its sterile walls she felt safe, secure, confident. Totally in her element.

When she returned home that night, the last thing she wanted, or expected, was to find her sister camped out in their father's study using the computer, her designer snakeskin pumps kicked off and peeking from beneath the desk.

Tommie glanced over her shoulder as Francesca stuck her head inside the room, and for a moment their eyes met and held.

Without a word, Francesca continued down the hallway to the kitchen, her heart thudding as she heard her sister rise from the chair and pad after her in her bare feet.

"I was checking my e-mail messages," Tommie explained, appearing in the doorway. "My Internet's down at the apartment. I didn't think you'd mind."

"It's not my computer," Francesca said tonelessly, reaching into the cabinet for a wineglass. She crossed to the refrigerator, pulled out a chilled bottle of Bordeaux, and filled her glass.

Tommie leaned on the door frame and watched her for a moment. She was effortlessly chic in the sleeveless leopard-print silk blouse and pencil-slim skirt she'd worn to the office that day. Her long black hair was swept off her neck into an elaborate twist that managed to be hip and sophisticated at once.

"Dad sent some more pictures from Cairo," she cheerfully announced. "He and Mom really look like they're having fun."

Francesca said nothing, sipping her red wine as she sorted through a stack of mail on the center island.

Tommie frowned. "You're still mad at me, aren't you?"

Francesca walked over to the trash bin and began dumping the junk mail.

"Look, Frankie, I'm sorry about—"

Francesca whirled around, her eyes flashing with controlled fury. "You don't get to be sorry, Tommie. Not this time."

Tommie recoiled as if she'd been struck. "What's that supposed to mean?"

"It means that for once in my life," Francesca snapped, "I'm not accepting your half-assed apology."

Tommie sputtered in disbelief. *"Half-assed—"*

"You heard me." Francesca stalked over to the center island, plucked up her glass of wine, and started purposefully from the kitchen. "Lock the door when you leave."

"Wait a minute!" Tommie cried, reaching out to grab Francesca's arm on her way out.

As Francesca jerked away to evade her sister's grasp, she jostled her glass, sloshing red wine all over the front of Tommie's silk blouse.

Her sister sucked in a sharp, horrified breath. "Look what you did! Do you know how much this shirt cost me?"

Francesca was seized by a nasty urge to throw the remainder of the wine in her sister's face. Instead she said coolly, "Next time, think twice before you grab someone holding a glass of *red* wine."

As Tommie gaped at her, she lifted the half-empty glass to her lips, took a long sip, then turned and started down the hallway.

"I can't believe you're acting like this!" Tommie hurled after her departing back. "I never thought you'd let a man come between us, Frankie!"

Francesca spun around so fast she nearly spilled wine on herself this time. "He wasn't just *any* man, Tommie. And what 'came between us' happened long before Sebastien entered the picture. What came between us is the fact that you're jealous of me!"

"Jealous of *you?*" Tommie gave a harsh, mirthless laugh. "I hate to break it to you, Francesca, but I'm not jealous of you."

"Oh yes, you are, *Tomasina.* Your attitude's been bugging the hell out of me for months, but I finally figured it out. You're jealous of my relationship with Dad, you're jealous that he and Mom asked me to house-sit for them, you're jealous that I have a career I actually love, and you're positively jealous that a man like Sebastien Durand might actually be interested in me instead of you!"

Tears welled in Tommie's eyes. At another time, that would have stopped Francesca cold in her tracks. She'd never been able to handle the sight of her younger sister's tears. Even when they were children fighting over a favorite Barbie doll, at the first wobble of Tommie's chin Francesca had always capitulated, not wanting to make her sister cry.

But the Francesca who now stood before Tommie had

made one too many concessions in her life and had
been pushed too far. At that moment, she was beyond
caring whether or not she hurt her sister's feelings and
caused her tears. What about *her* feelings? What about all
the tears she'd shed on Tuesday night, and would probably shed in the days and weeks to come?

"If you really believe Sebastien's so interested in you,"
Tommie challenged, her lips twisting in a sneer, "then
why didn't you stay and fight for him? Why'd you run
away like a coward?"

Francesca fell silent for a prolonged moment. "That's a
very good question, Tommie," she murmured. "In fact, it's
probably the smartest thing you've said to me in years."

As Tommie frowned at her, she turned and went quietly upstairs.

Later that afternoon, Sebastien stood in the brightly
lit coffee room of the police station with Rodriguez and
two other detectives working the four-to-midnight shift.

Running the length of one wall hung a large rectangle of white paper that was divided into three sections to
represent the different shifts that fell under the
Murder/Attempted Murder detail of the Homicide
Unit. To the untrained eye, the homicide board—also
known as the HOMBO—appeared to be a complex
matrix of names, case numbers, and initials scrawled in
black and red felt marker. But to the four sergeants and
thirty-nine detectives that composed the entire unit, the
purpose of the board was clear enough—to tally homicides and their clearance rates, and provide fodder for
competition between the detectives assigned to the different shifts.

After returning from the campus of TABU, where he'd
had his heart ripped out by Francesca, Sebastien had
holed himself up in his office to pore through autopsy

reports and finish paperwork from the murder-suicide case he'd caught on Tuesday night. Determined to obliterate thoughts of Francesca from his mind, he'd worked relentlessly for hours, surrounded by brown paper evidence bags containing the miscellany from the autopsy he'd attended yesterday morning: shoes, bloodied clothes, scrapings from the victim's fingernails for conclusive DNA or blood typing—though the rambling note left by the husband made it abundantly clear he'd killed his estranged wife before turning the .38 on himself.

Around six o'clock, two hours after his shift should have ended, Sebastien had emerged from his office and gone in search of coffee, craving a change of scenery more so than the shot of caffeine. He'd found Rodriguez and two other detectives huddled around the HOMBO, cradling cups of black sludge scraped from the dregs of the office coffeepot. They were discussing the most high-profile case on the board. That, of course, being the "Spider Tattoo" case, as the media had eagerly dubbed it.

Rodriguez was recounting the details of their early-morning interrogation of Jeremy Dillon, while Sebastien set about the task of brewing a fresh batch of coffee.

In the time it took the coffeepot to fill, Rodriguez had engaged Detectives Shane Merriman and Burt Jackson in a lively debate about reincarnation.

"This kid really thought he was a spider in a past life," Rodriguez drawled in unconcealed amusement. "I could see it in his eyes. He really believed that crap."

"Why does it have to be crap?" asked Merriman, a thin blond man in his early thirties. "Millions of people believe in reincarnation. Doesn't make 'em serial killers."

"Uh-oh," Rodriguez intoned. "Something you wanna tell us, Merriman? Were you, uh, an iguana in a past life?"

This drew a snicker from Burt Jackson, a short, dark-skinned African-American man with the stocky build of a former college running back.

Merriman scowled. "Seriously, though. Those shrinks—what're they called? Parapsychologists. They've been studying the phenomenon of reincarnation for decades. What they do is put subjects under hypnosis and regress them to early childhood, infancy, and past lives. In many cases, these patients dredge up some crazy shit, stuff they couldn't possibly have known unless they'd actually lived through it. Like that woman in Ohio who remembered being a fighter pilot and flying a Boeing B-29 during World War Two. Under hypnosis, her voice changed to the pitch of a man's, and the details she provided about the events leading up to the aircraft being blown up were so dead-on accurate they couldn't be disputed. Don't believe me? Medical journals have documented hundreds of incredible cases of people regressed to former lives." At Rodriguez's skeptical expression, Merriman looked to Jackson. "Help me out here, man."

"Hey, don't look at me," Jackson said, holding up his hands. "I was born and raised Baptist, remember? Reincarnation goes against every biblical scripture I've ever been taught."

"So does fornication," Merriman pointed out dryly, "but that's never stopped you from plugging your johnson into every willing socket you can find."

Rodriguez roared with laughter while Jackson could only grin and shake his head, unable to refute his reputation as a skirt-chasing letch.

"What about you, Big Easy?" Merriman said, hitching his chin toward Sebastien, who'd been heretofore silent throughout the discussion. "Do you believe in reincarnation?"

"Don't ask *him*," Rodriguez interjected. "Didn't you know Durand's great-aunt was a big-time voodoo priestess back in the day? He probably believes in reincarnation and a whole bunch of other weird shit."

Sebastien chuckled. "No weirder than your grandma

cracking an egg into a bowl and performing cleansing rituals over you after you've had a string of bad luck."

This time it was Rodriguez's turn to scowl as Merriman and Jackson howled with laughter. "Hey, man, *ojo* is real!" Rodriguez protested. "If someone gives you an evil eye, you're done for, my friend."

Merriman clapped a hand to his shoulder. "That's the point I was trying to make about reincarnation, man. You can't thumb your nose at people who believe in it when so many in the Hispanic culture hold to beliefs and superstitions the rest of us might find—"

"Featherbrained?" Jackson supplied, and the two men chortled again at the reference to the cracked egg.

"Tolerance, gentlemen," Sebastien said in the nasal, patronizing monotone of the department's diversity training consultant. "'Let's all endeavor to understand and respect one another's differences. After all, these differences are what make each of us unique.'"

This drew another round of raucous male laughter.

It was at that moment Sergeant MacDougal chose to enter the room. He took one look at his four detectives, three of whom were bent over in stitches, and shook his head grimly. "Good to know the ugly business of homicide hasn't tarnished your collective sense of humor," he muttered.

"We do whatever we can to cope, sir," Rodriguez said, straight-faced.

MacDougal snorted, shaking his head again as Merriman and Jackson dispersed, followed shortly by Rodriguez.

Drawn to the scent of freshly brewed coffee, the sergeant made his way over to the coffeepot, where Sebastien filled a paper cup and passed it to him.

"Thanks," MacDougal said, taking a grateful sip. Propping a hip against the counter, he looked across the room at the homicide board, his sharp green eyes narrowing on the names of Christie Snodgrass and Jennifer Benson scrawled in black Magic Marker.

"This Dillon kid," he said with a sideways glance at Sebastien. "Rodriguez told me about the interview this morning. What did you make of him? Think he could be the perp?"

"Don't know," Sebastien answered honestly. Jeremy Dillon was definitely hiding something, and if Tommie Purnell was to be believed, Dillon had lied about his recent visits to the Sirens and Spurs. But lying about being at a strip club didn't necessarily make him a psychopath, or the same would apply to every husband who'd ever blown wads of cash on lap dances, then gone home to the wife and lied about his whereabouts.

"We're running out of time," MacDougal said grimly. "You heard what the FBI profiler said this morning. He not only predicted there would be more pronounced signs of violence with subsequent killings, but he said that the intervals between each murder would get shorter, as the perp becomes increasingly desensitized and needs more to satiate him. We've gotta find this son of a bitch before it's too late, before he escalates into a spree murderer like Ted Bundy."

"I know," Sebastien said quietly. He felt the urgency of it, the race against the clock. Every detective in the Homicide Unit had been there before, working 130-hour weeks as the primary investigator on a case that simply didn't add up, a set of facts that wouldn't solidify into a suspect no matter how hard the detective tried to make the pieces fit. The "Spider Tattoo" case was a prime example. It had been nearly two weeks since Christie Snodgrass's body had been found in that motel room, and they were no closer to finding her killer than they'd been then.

"The latent print results came back negative on Fincher," Sebastien said aloud.

MacDougal nodded. "No surprise there. It was a long shot, anyway." He sipped his coffee. "I spoke to the lieutenant yesterday, and he wants us to steer clear of Norman Fincher unless we've caught him red-handed with the smoking gun, or, in this case, the bloody knife. We're just lucky Fincher hasn't complained to the brass about the visit you paid to his office last Friday. If you'd gone there kicking down doors and questioning him like a suspect, we'd both be cooling our heels in the unemployment line right now. You get what I'm saying?"

Sebastien nodded tersely. Norman Fincher, as he and MacDougal had discovered that morning, was a major donor to the San Antonio Police Department and a personal friend of the mayor's, which meant one thing: He was virtually untouchable. MacDougal's boss, Lieutenant Rick Burnside, whose long-term aspirations had him assuming the position of police commissioner, had proven time and again that he was perfectly willing to hinder investigations in the name of securing his own political future.

Sebastien had learned early in his career that knowing how to play the game of politics was as integral to surviving in law enforcement as being a smart cop. It had been that way in New Orleans, and it was no different now.

MacDougal wandered over to the HOMBO, one hand thrust in his pocket, the other cradling his cup of coffee. "Talk to me, Durand. What else have you got?"

"I'm checking out the manager at the Sirens and Spurs. She has a thirty-year-old son named Yuri. He's in a doctorate of history program at UTSA—"

"The same university Jennifer Benson attended?"

"Yep. But that's not all. According to what Tommie Purnell told me, Yuri showed up at the club for the very first time last week."

"Last week?"

Sebastien nodded. "His mother's been the manager

there for ten years. Why'd it take him ten years to check out where she works?"

MacDougal frowned. "Good question. What'd Tommie Purnell tell you about him?"

"She said he's an introvert, keeps to himself and doesn't seem to have many friends. Even when he comes to the club, he sits alone at a table and doesn't interact with any of the dancers or waitresses, even though his mother is their boss. Course," Sebastien added dryly, "that could also be the reason he *doesn't* talk to them. Maybe his mother warned him beforehand to look but don't touch. She's a real ballbuster."

MacDougal grimaced. "Poor kid. Having been married to two ballbusters, I can definitely sympathize. So, when was the last time you spoke to Tommie Purnell?"

"Tuesday night, when I went there to question her about Jeremy Dillon and get a positive ID."

"I heard she wanted a bodyguard—specifically you."

Sebastien frowned. "Tommie Purnell wants a lot of things she can't have," he muttered darkly.

"I've arranged for a squad car to periodically cruise by the club, but that's the best I can do at this point with the limited resources we have."

Sebastien nodded. "I told her to crash at her boyfriend's place. Hopefully she heeded my advice."

MacDougal chuckled wryly. "Women seldom do what we want them to."

"Ain't that the truth?" Sebastien grumbled, thinking about Francesca. And then, because thinking about her only raised his blood pressure, he left the coffee room—minus the cup of coffee he'd gone in search of in the first place—and returned to his office to bury himself in more autopsy reports.

Chapter 18

Two hours later, Rodriguez appeared in his doorway, pulling on his jacket over his holstered shoulder piece. "Remember that BOLO I put out on Saturday?" At Sebastien's nod, he said, "I just got a call from San Marcos PD. They've got a body in a house located near the university where our very own Norman Fincher works."

The words were barely out of Rodriguez's mouth before Sebastien grabbed his Glock and followed him quickly out of the room.

They made it to San Marcos in record time and soon turned down a tree-lined residential street already clogged with police and emergency vehicles, their flashing red and blue lights illuminating the night sky like an early display of fireworks. Neighbors hovered in doorways and gathered on sidewalks to watch the unfolding drama with mingled expressions of curiosity and dread.

Sebastien and Rodriguez parked half a block away and walked up the street. As they approached the address, Sebastien knew that the quaint charm of the small clapboard cottage, with its window boxes filled with bright flowers and an American flag fluttering over the entrance, would be forever tainted by the scene of gruesome violence that awaited them on the inside.

They flashed their badges at the young uniformed officer guarding the entrance. "SAPD," Rodriguez explained. "Detective Kemper called us."

The uniform hesitated another moment before lifting the yellow police tape barring the front doorway.

Sebastien and Rodriguez stepped into the house, which was crawling with uniformed officers and plainclothes detectives who eyed them curiously until one detached himself from the group and came forward.

"Detectives Durand and Rodriguez?" he inquired, quickly shaking their hands in turn. "Wes Kemper. Glad you could make it."

"Thanks for calling, Detective," Rodriguez said.

Wes Kemper was medium height and trim, with a thatch of sandy brown hair and slumberous dark eyes. "The crime scene techs are in there now, and the ME's on his way," he said, leading them down a narrow hallway ripe with the stench of blood. "I'll ask them to step out for a few minutes so you can have a look at the body."

At first glance, the scene was jarringly familiar. The victim, a blond-haired white woman in her mid-twenties, was nude, gagged, and bound, her arms stretched taut above her head and fastened to the center bedpost, her wrists and ankles tied with the same kind of cloth that had been used on Christie Snodgrass and Jennifer Benson. She'd been repeatedly stabbed across her neck and torso, the satin bedspread beneath her body stained crimson with blood. Tossed upon the wrought-iron bench at the foot of the bed were a white lab coat and a pair of white drawstring pants—a nurse's uniform.

Everything about the scene appeared to bear the signature of the same killer.

Except, as Sebastien stepped farther into the small room, he realized what was missing.

A tattoo.

He and Rodriguez noticed at the same time, their eyes meeting in silent speculation.

"Victim's name is Mary Ott," Detective Kemper said. "She worked as a nurse at McKenna Memorial Hospital. A friend she worked with had been trying to reach her all day to share the results of a board exam she, not Mary, had recently taken. When Ott never answered the phone, the friend got worried and called the police around seven o'clock p.m. An officer arrived at the scene and found the front door unlocked."

"No sign of forced entry?" Sebastien asked, making his way carefully to the bed.

Kemper shook his head. "None whatsoever. The back door and every other window in the house were securely locked."

"Did she live here alone?" Rodriguez asked.

"Yes. According to the neighbors we questioned, she arrived home from her night shift around eight this morning, which was her usual time. No one saw any unfamiliar vehicles or individuals around the property, not even so much as a UPS deliveryman."

Rodriguez asked, "What about a boyfriend? Ex-lover? Anyone who might've had a motive for hurting her?"

"We're looking into it. The friend thinks she may have been seeing someone at the hospital, an X-ray technician. Of course, we'll be questioning everyone she worked with."

Sebastien knelt at the bedside and examined the body. The woman had been dead for some time, rigor mortis having come and gone. He studied the pale, smooth skin of her right arm. Not even a hint of the beginnings of a tattoo.

He glanced over his shoulder. "Next of kin?"

"Her parents and an older sister are driving up from El Paso as we speak." Kemper divided a speculative look between Sebastien and Rodriguez. "Think this could be your guy?"

Before either could respond, one of the crime scene techs appeared in the doorway. "We need to finish up in here before the ME arrives."

Kemper nodded, then said to Sebastien and Rodriguez, "Let's step out into the living room. I want to compare notes."

"So, what do you think?" Rodriguez said to Sebastien an hour later as they left the house and returned to the car. "Think this is the work of the same perp?"

"I don't know," Sebastien answered honestly. "If it weren't for the absence of a tattoo, I'd definitely say yes. But that missing piece of evidence is bugging the hell out of me."

"Maybe that's what he intended," Rodriguez suggested. "To throw us off the scent of his trail."

"It's possible." Sebastien frowned as they sat in the shadowy darkness of the car. "It just doesn't make sense. If you ask me, our guy is making a statement with the spider tattoo, building toward some sort of grand finale. Why change direction midstream? I'm sure he's been following the news. He has to know we're nowhere close to making an arrest."

"So maybe it wasn't intentional. Maybe something interrupted him before he could apply the tattoo."

"Maybe," Sebastien murmured, unconvinced. The predator they were dealing with was too calculating, too methodical, to allow any unforeseen developments to interfere with his mission. If he'd decided not to tattoo one of his victims, there was a reason.

"If this is our guy," Rodriguez said, "he's a long way from home."

"Or maybe not. Norman Fincher lives and works around the corner from here."

"I was getting to that. What if he parks his car down

the street, walks the rest of the way to Mary Ott's house, then when he's finished, he drives back home, showers and changes his clothes, and returns to campus before anyone even misses him?"

"It's entirely plausible," Sebastien said, adding sardonically, "We may never know, of course, since he's virtually untouchable. MacDougal told me I'd be looking for another line of work if I even *thought* about approaching Fincher again."

Rodriguez scowled. "So we've got a dead body practically in the man's backyard—not to mention proof of his connection to two other victims—and there's not a damn thing we can do about it?"

"Pretty much."

"Son of a bitch," Rodriguez growled.

"My sentiments exactly."

In the brooding silence that lapsed between them, Sebastien contemplated the timeline of the murders. Christie Snodgrass had been killed June 11, Jennifer Benson less than a week later on June 16. Today was the twenty-first. If this latest killing was the handiwork of the same perpetrator, then he was right on schedule.

Sebastien wondered if, as the FBI profiler had predicted, it was only a matter of time before the killer escalated his crimes.

If that happened, God help them all.

Chapter 19

Friday, June 22

Francesca slid a tube of deep red lipstick over her mouth and finger-combed her hair before stepping back from the full-length mirror to examine her reflection. The beautiful, sexy woman staring back at her through smoky eyes was someone she didn't recognize, a stranger in an indecently low cut silver blouse and a denim miniskirt with a rhinestone belt draped loosely around her waist. Her horn-rimmed eyeglasses had been replaced with contact lenses, and her thick, unruly hair had been straightened to fall in long, heavy layers that skimmed her shoulders. The ankle-strap wedge sandals she wore added at least three inches to her height and accentuated her legs, making them appear longer and curvier.

Definitely someone she didn't recognize.

And that was fine. For what she was about to do tonight, she needed to become someone other than conservative, straitlaced, painfully self-conscious Francesca.

Grabbing her car keys, she left the house before she lost her nerve.

Even at seven-thirty p.m., the parking lot of the downtown police station was still a beehive of activity. Francesca swept through the double glass doors of the building and encountered a uniformed desk sergeant behind a raised desk. He took one look at her and broke into a wide, toothy grin.

"Who're you here to see, sweetheart?"

"Detective Durand," Francesca answered, fully expecting to be waved into a chair in the waiting area.

He pointed over his shoulder. "Homicide offices are straight back and to your right. Big Easy's at the end of the hall."

Francesca flashed a demure smile at the desk sergeant. *Maybe there's something to this sex-symbol business after all*, she thought.

She had never been inside a police station before, her impressions shaped by what she saw on television cop dramas and movies. She expected something approaching chaos; what she encountered were ringing phones, people sprawled in chairs, clouds of cigarette smoke, and the bitter odor of strong coffee.

As she wound past a maze of cubicles, desks, and cramped offices, curious heads swung in her direction, cops and suspects alike. Someone gave a low whistle of appreciation, making Francesca blush. If she could've kissed the culprit, she would have.

At the end of the bustling corridor, she found Sebastien's office. He was seated behind a large metal desk cluttered with books, papers, and file folders. He was in shirtsleeves with his silk tie tugged loose around his collar, as if he'd been meaning to remove it but hadn't gotten around to it yet. He looked tough and more than a little tired, frowning as he read the contents of a report.

As he was about to bite into an Italian sub, he caught a glimpse of her in the doorway. He did a double take, his eyes widening as they roamed down her scantily clad body, then back up to her face. The look on his face sent a thrill of pure feminine satisfaction through her. It was priceless.

"*Mon Dieu,*" he breathed, his sandwich forgotten. "Francesca?"

She leaned in the doorway and struck what she hoped was a casually sexy pose, with one foot lifted slightly behind the other. "I was in the neighborhood and thought you might like to go for a ride with me," she recited the line she'd rehearsed all the way over there, complete with the smoky voice. "If you're game, meet me out at the car in five minutes."

Without awaiting his response, she turned and walked away. *Please let him come,* she mentally prayed. *Please let him come. Please, please . . .*

He came.

As he caught up to her with those long, ground-eating strides, she slid him a sultry smile. "Atta boy," she purred.

His response was a low, husky chuckle.

As Francesca pulled away from the police station, she could feel Sebastien's eyes on her. The heat of his gaze made her belly quiver with anticipation.

"Where're we going, *chère?*" he murmured.

"You'll see," she said, echoing the words he'd spoken to her on their first date. When he smiled, she realized he remembered as well. Her heart soared.

With the convertible top down and the wind tossing up her hair, she felt beautiful, seductive, powerful. As something edgy and pulsing poured from the stereo, Sebastien seemed content to just sit back and watch her, and she could tell he liked what he saw. It was utterly exhilarating.

Twenty minutes after leaving the police station, they arrived at a secluded spot surrounded by lush, rolling hills and majestic trees. Perched high on a bluff that overlooked the San Antonio River, where moonlight shimmered on the surface like strands of pearls, Canyon Cove had once lured young lovers who wanted to make out far away from the prying eyes of adults. In high school, Francesca had overheard her classmates whisper and giggle about clandestine forays to the cove with their boyfriends and cute guys they were trying to win over.

Though it was a warm summer night, perfect for stargazing and cuddling, there were no other cars parked at the cliff when she pulled up. She couldn't have planned it better herself. And she wasn't wasting any time.

Sebastien had barely unfastened his seat belt before she was out of her seat and straddling his powerful thighs. He made a sound deep in his throat, surprise mingled with pleasure as his hands lifted to her waist. "Francesca—"

"Shhh. Let me look at you for a moment." She cradled his face between her hands, her gaze tracing the rugged, masculine features cast in silvery moonlight. "I love your face," she whispered softly. "So strong and beautiful. I love everything about it." She brushed her lips across his forehead, then kissed his closed eyelids, the strong bridge of his nose, the hard line of his cheekbones. His breath quickened as she skated her open mouth along his jaw, then kissed her way back to the seductive curve of his lips.

Sebastien groaned as she covered his mouth hungrily with hers. He thrust his hot, sweet tongue into her mouth and she suckled it like candy, greedy for the taste of him. The bulge of his erection pressed against the crotch of her thong underwear. She gyrated her hips and he moaned again, reaching down to slide his hands beneath her miniskirt. She gasped as he palmed her bare buttocks and gently squeezed. The heat of his touch seared her, sweeping through her body like an out-of-control brush fire. She wanted him inside her, hard and deep.

Without breaking the kiss, she reached down and caressed his muscular thigh, sliding her hand to the inside, then upward. A faint shudder ran through him. The bulge in his pants grew, and as it did, so did the pressure between her legs.

Through the fabric of his trousers, she closed her hand around him. He sucked in a sharp breath, tightening his hold on her bottom as he pressed her closer. She eased his zipper down and slipped her hand inside his pants, then his boxers, until she found his smooth, rigid erection and curled her fingers around him.

He swore under his breath, low and guttural. His pelvis tilted and he thrust upward, into her palm. As she slid her hand up and down his hardened length, she flicked her tongue in and out of his mouth with light, sensual strokes that matched her movements.

He groaned, cupping her buttocks so hard she was sure he'd leave permanent handprints. *"Francesca . . . Mon Dieu . . ."*

"You like that?" she murmured, her voice naturally throaty with desire.

"Mmmm . . . Damn, woman. You're gonna get us arrested."

She gave a husky little laugh. "Is that even possible? You're one of them."

"Oh . . . yeah."

Moisture beaded the tip of his shaft, and she used her index finger to swirl it around his throbbing hardness. He moaned loudly.

She scooted off his lap and knelt between his legs. Because he was so tall, the seat was already pushed back as far as it could go, giving her a little wiggle room in the tight space.

Holding his gaze, she took him inside her mouth. He threw his head back against the seat with a savage oath that made her feel immensely powerful. *"Francesca . . ."*

She explored every delicious inch of him, sucking and flicking and swirling her tongue as if she'd been doing this for years, instead of for the first time. She grasped the thick base of his penis with her hand and kneaded his testicles at the same time, unbearably stimulated by the ragged sounds of pleasure that tore from his throat. She'd never imagined in a million years that she, "Frumpy Frankie," could have this effect on any man, let alone a virile, sexy man like Sebastien Durand.

He rocked his hips, thrust deeper into her mouth, then gripped the back of her head and pulled her away. His eyes glittered in the moonlight, fierce with arousal. "Enough," he ground out, the word so low and husky it was almost a growl. "If you don' stop, woman, I'm gonna come."

A wanton smile curved her lips. "But I want you to come." To prove it, she leaned down and locked her lips around him once again.

"*Merde*," he groaned hoarsely, enduring another minute of torture before grasping her arms and lifting her quickly onto his lap to straddle him.

He dug into his pocket and withdrew a condom from his wallet, then sheathed himself with hands that trembled slightly with anticipation. Francesca knew the feeling. She was so turned on she was already on the brink of an orgasm.

Sebastien lifted her skirt over the swell of her bottom and nudged aside the wet strip of silk between her legs. She gasped, arching upward as his fingers stroked the slick, pulsing folds of her sex. Her hips writhed, grinding rhythmically against him.

Their gazes locked as he thrust high and deep inside her. She cried out his name and threw back her head, riding the waves of erotic sensation, riding him. They were both already so aroused that a few hard, desperate thrusts later, they exploded. Their loud moans rang out together, bouncing off the surrounding hills as they clung tightly to each other.

Moments later, panting and trembling, Francesca dropped her head onto Sebastien's shoulder and burrowed her face in the crook of his neck. She could feel the galloping race of his heart, as rapid as her own. He held her in his arms, running his hands up and down her back as their bodies remained joined.

After a while he drew back slightly and angled his head to gaze down into her face. His heavy-lidded eyes glinted with mirth. "If this is your idea of friendship . . ."

She laughed sheepishly. "Oh yeah, about that. Forget what I said. Blame it on temporary insanity." She lifted her head to search his face. "You're not mad, are you?"

He chuckled, a low, sexy rumble. "Do I look mad?"

She smiled. "No, I guess not. Although, for a minute back there, I was worried you wouldn't follow me."

He shook his head. "Sweetheart, nothin' could've kept me from following you," he drawled huskily. His fingers flirted with the hem of her miniskirt, which remained rucked up over her thighs. "In case I didn't mention it before, I like the skirt."

"I figured you might," she said demurely.

"I like the shirt, too." He ran a fingertip up and down the plunging neckline of the blouse, trailing a path of fire along her nerve endings and making her breasts tingle.

"What about the shoes?" she asked, leaning a little to the right so he could see them. As she moved, his breath caught sharply. "You like them, too?"

"Oh, most definitely." His voice was tight as he lifted his hands and cupped her naked bottom. "I think you're tryin' to drive me outta my mind, *chère.*"

She bit her lip naughtily. "Is it working?"

"Like a charm. Can't you tell?"

She could. His penis had grown thick inside her once again, hard and throbbing. Her body tightened around him.

As they gazed at each other, his fingers slipped beneath her buttocks and slid toward her wet heat. She shivered and moaned softly as he began to stroke her clitoris and the slippery feminine lips that were stretched wide to accommodate his hardened length. The sensation was so sublimely erotic, she felt an orgasm building inside her.

"Sebastien," she breathed, closing her eyes. *"Sebastien."*

"You make me so damn hot," he said huskily. "I can't get enough of you."

Her head fell back as he reached inside her blouse with his other hand and covered the swell of one breast, while his mouth latched on to a throbbing pulse on her neck. "When I was in high school," Francesca said breathlessly, "this used to be the favorite make-out spot."

"Yeah?"

She nodded jerkily. "Tonight was the first time I've ever been here."

"Well then," Sebastien murmured, thrusting deep inside her, "I guess we've got a lot of catching up to do."

After "catching up" a second and third time at Canyon Cove, blanketed by the stars and pale moonlight, they somehow made it back to her house and tumbled into her bed for another round of hot, frenzied lovemaking.

When Francesca awakened hours later, naked and sprawled upon Sebastien's back, she couldn't remember how she'd wound up in that position. For several moments she reveled in the smooth, muscled hardness of the male body beneath her, marveling at how perfectly they fit together. Lying on top of him like this, she realized just how much he dwarfed her in size. She felt warm from the inside out, warm and deliciously exhausted. If she could have lain there forever, she would have.

Sebastien stirred just then, lifting his head slightly to glance over his shoulder at her through heavy-lidded eyes.

"How did we get like this?" Francesca leaned up to whisper in his ear.

He chuckled low and deep in his throat, the vibration of it making her belly quiver. "I think you were giving me a massage."

"I must be a lousy masseuse," she teased. "Falling asleep on my clients."

"You were perfect," he murmured. "It was the best massage I've ever had in my life."

She smiled, nibbling his earlobe. "And you, sir, were the best client I've ever had."

"Even though I had my way with you?"

"Even more so."

"Mmmm. You're a very naughty girl, Francesca Purnell."

"You bring out the naughty in me," she purred, dipping her tongue inside the soft shell of his ear as he put his head back down on his arms. "Before I met you, I never would have done something like what I did tonight. Strolling half naked into a police station and whisking you away to make out in the middle of nowhere."

The low, husky rumble of his laughter reverberated through her body again. "We did a little more than make out, *chère*. And I'm glad you showed up the way you did tonight—although I'm probably gonna have to beat up some of the fellas who couldn't keep their tongues in their mouths when they saw you. They're gonna have wet dreams about you for a damn long time."

Francesca chuckled softly. "I'm not used to being sex-symbol material." She gave a thoughtful pause. "I think I like it."

"Don' like it too much," Sebastien growled half seriously, "unless you *want* to see me gettin' into fights all the time."

"Of course not. Besides," she said with a sigh, "being sexy all the time would probably get pretty old really fast."

"Sweetheart, you *are* sexy all the time. You just don't know it."

Francesca warmed with pleasure at his words, however untrue they might be. "You're very kind, but—"

"I thought you were sexy the first moment I saw you," Sebastien said in dark, velvety tones that made her pulse accelerate. "I wanted to know why you were hiding beneath that god-awful muumuu, because I knew your body would be like heaven. I wanted to free your hair from that ponytail and watch it tumble across your face and bare shoulders. I wanted to wrap a fistful of it around my hand, hold your head back, and watch your face as I entered you slowly." He paused with a husky little laugh. "Should I tell you what else I wanted, beautiful one?"

His provocative words had robbed her of speech, turning her insides to molten lava. Her nipples pinched painfully against his back, and she was acutely aware of her pelvis pressed against the muscled sleekness of his butt, a butt you could bounce quarters off of. She burned everywhere their bodies touched, which meant she burned all over.

"Francesca?"

She squeezed her eyes shut. "Give me a sec. And don't move a muscle."

He did, of course, turning around to pull the front of her body flush against his. If she hadn't already been so aroused, that alone would have done her in. But by the time his wicked fingers reached between her thighs, she was already coming.

The orgasm shook her entire body. She could only hang on to him as it overtook her, could only suck her bottom lip into her mouth to hold back the scream that rose in her throat as Sebastien laughed softly.

As the spasms gradually tapered off, he gathered her into his arms. Weak and satiated, she snuggled against him, fitting her head beneath his chin and draping her arm across his wide chest.

"I can't believe I almost gave this up," she murmured dreamily.

"Nah, I wouldn't have let you go."

That pleased her. Pleased her so much she felt tears sting her eyes. "I was jealous of my sister," she admitted shyly. "Jealous of you liking her better than me."

Sebastien kissed the top of her head. "I don't even think that's possible."

"Anything's possible."

"Not that, *chère*. Your sister's a beautiful woman, but I'm not interested in her. I'll never be interested in her. *Comprenez vous?*"

"*Oui, je comprends.*" She smiled. "I love it when you speak French, Sebastien." She paused. "You know, a lot of people believe Cajuns can only be white."

"It's a common misperception, since, yes, the majority of Cajuns *are* white. You ready for a quick history lesson?" At her nod, he explained, "All Cajuns are descendants of French immigrants from what was known as Acadie in Canada back in the early 1600s and 1700s, which is now Nova Scotia. Pierre Thibodaux was the first person from France to settle in Acadie. My maternal great-grandfather was one of his descendants—Baptiste Thibodaux from Opelousas, Louisiana. So, yes, there are definitely black Cajuns."

She nodded, intrigued by the account. He was the

most compelling man she'd ever met. She wanted to know everything about him. "And what about your father's side of the family?"

"A complicated mix of Cajun and Creole. Someday I'll break down the family tree for you."

"I'd like that." Francesca hesitated, then said softly, "You must miss your parents."

She felt him tense beneath her arm, and for a moment she feared she'd said the wrong thing. They were supposed to be enjoying pillow talk, not rehashing his painful past.

But then Sebastien said quietly, "I do miss them. More than I ever thought I would."

Francesca was silent, waiting for him to continue.

"There was a time I wanted nothing more than to have my parents out of my life. When they sent me to live with my grandmother, all I could think was, good riddance."

"Why?"

"My parents and I didn't have the best of relationships," he said grimly. "They were both into their careers, and I was, well, I was an afterthought. Now, that doesn't justify my rebellious behavior as a teenager. It just provides some context."

Francesca nodded slowly. "You were starved for affection," she said gently. "At the risk of my sounding like a therapist, you probably acted out because you were seeking attention from them."

"There's probably some truth to that," he murmured, absently running his finger back and forth across her arm. "Anyway, it didn't work. They had little patience for my antics, so when I was fifteen they threw me out of the house. We didn't speak for a very long time after that."

Francesca angled her head to study his stony profile in the soft lamplight. "How long?"

"Put it like this. When they attended my college graduation, my mother was surprised by how tall I'd grown."

Francesca's heart constricted. "Oh, Sebastien . . ."

"Don' go getting all teary-eyed on me, *chère*," he said gruffly. "I'm not telling you any of this to gain your sympathy."

"You lived in the same state and didn't see your own parents for at least seven years. I think you deserve a little sympathy."

"It's not that I didn't see them during those years. I did. Just not very often, and not for long periods of time. At first my grandmother went out of her way to arrange 'accidental' meetings between us, but after a while, when she saw how miserable those little visits made all of us, she stopped. When I asked her about it one night, she told me that in God's perfect time, my parents and I would reconcile on our own."

"And did you?" She held her breath as she gazed at him.

After a prolonged moment of silence, he shook his head. "No. We didn't reconcile. Not for lack of trying, though. When I came home from LSU, my father tried to get me interested in the insurance business. But I already knew what I wanted to do. When I joined the New Orleans Police Department, my folks didn't approve. They thought I could do better for myself. When I graduated from the academy, the only one who attended the ceremony was my grandmother. That pretty much did it for me. I decided if my parents couldn't accept the career I'd chosen, they'd never accept me. After that, we became little more than polite strangers. We kept abreast of one another's lives through my grandmother."

"I'm so sorry, Sebastien," Francesca murmured, her throat tight.

"Don't be. It was probably for the best that we stayed out of each other's way. Being polite strangers was better than being enemies, or at least that's what I always told myself."

"But you wanted more. Deep down inside, you wanted a relationship with them."

"Maybe. Maybe not." He slanted her a knowing look. "It's hard for you to fathom otherwise, because you *do* have that close relationship with your parents." He paused, then added a touch sadly, "Don't ever take it for granted, *chère*."

"I won't," she promised, more to herself than him.

Silence lapsed between them for several moments; then Francesca ventured almost timidly, "Sebastien?"

"Hmm?"

She swallowed. "Why didn't your parents make it out of New Orleans?"

His chest lifted beneath her cheek as he drew in a breath and slowly expelled it. "It's a long story."

"I'd like to hear it," she said softly. "That is, if you don't mind sharing it."

He hesitated another moment, but she didn't look at him, just waited for him to begin speaking. When he did, his voice was low and remote, laced with the pain of his memories. "They were on their way to Houston to stay with some friends while they waited out the storm."

"The storm hit while they were on the road?"

"No. If they'd continued to Houston, they would have made it. But they turned around and headed back home."

"Why?"

"To get my grandmother. She wasn't with them."

"They left town without your grandmother?" Francesca kept her voice carefully neutral, without judgment.

"You have to understand something about what happened during that time. When Hurricane Katrina was first announced, there were a lot of people who thought nothing of it. My grandmother was one of those people. She refused to leave her home, and her friends, for a storm that was going to blow over in a matter of hours." A sardonic smile tugged at his lips. "If you ever meet my grandmother—which you will—you'll see how stubborn she can be. Growing up, I used to think Mama August could've talked God out of the Ten Commandments if she'd been around."

Francesca smiled, too distracted by the story to register his promise to introduce her to his grandmother.

"Anyway," Sebastien continued, "after trying to convince her to go to Houston with them, they finally gave up and left without her. She told me that when they hugged and kissed her good-bye, their last words to her were 'We'll see you in a few days. Try not to give Katrina too much of a hard time.' They, like many others, expected the storm to just blow over."

Francesca looked up at him. "What about you?"

His expression was grim. "In my line of work, I've learned to expect the worst, and pray for something a little better. I wasn't taking any chances on Katrina, so I packed up my grandmother and some of her friends and put them on a bus headed for Houston. We both tried repeatedly to reach my parents on their cell phones to let them know not to worry about Mama August, but the lines were down, or the circuits were overloaded. Either way, they never got the message. By the time they made it back to New Orleans, it was too late. Katrina had arrived in full force. They drowned when their car was swept away by the floodwaters."

"Oh, Sebastien," Francesca whispered mournfully. "I'm so sorry. You must have been devastated. And your poor grandmother. Oh God. She must have blamed herself."

"She still does," Sebastien said quietly. "And nothing I can say or do will ever change that."

Francesca's heart swelled with sorrow for Augustine Durand, who would probably carry that burden of guilt for the rest of her life. And Sebastien, though he might never admit it to anyone, would always regret that he and his parents had never truly reconciled before their deaths.

"I'm sorry," she whispered again, tightening her arm around his chest and drawing him closer. He curved his arms around her waist and brushed a kiss across her temple that was so achingly tender, one would think *he* was comforting her.

"*Je t'aime*," he murmured softly.

For one heart-stopping moment, Francesca wasn't sure she'd heard right. She froze in his arms, her eyes searching his face. "Wh-what did you say?"

Sebastien gazed down at her with a look of such adoration that tears filled her eyes even before he said, "*Je t'aime beaucoup*. Or, if you prefer it in the language of my people, *Mi aime jou*. Either way, what I'm saying is, I love you, Francesca."

A surge of joy welled up inside her. Curving her arms around his neck, she drew his head down to hers and kissed his mouth, pouring all her feelings into the kiss, making him groan softly with pleasure.

Drawing back a little, she gazed into his smoky, heavy-lidded eyes. "I love you, too," she whispered fiercely. And, God help her, she did love him. With an intensity that at once frightened and liberated her.

He whispered her name, softly and reverently, as he slid between her legs. His mouth came back to hers, and she opened. Opened everything, so that when he thrust inside her, he entered not only her body, but her heart as well.

Chapter 20

At seven o'clock the next morning, Sebastien climbed from Francesca's little red convertible, skirted the fender, and leaned over the driver's seat to kiss her, though he'd already kissed her before stepping out of the car. He couldn't stop kissing her, touching her, holding her. And somehow he knew it would always be that way.

"You sure you don't wanna come inside and meet Mama August?" he murmured against the exquisitely soft pad of her lips.

Her dark eyes danced with mirth. "Not dressed like this," she said, indicating the sexy, low-cut blouse and miniskirt he'd coaxed her into putting on that morning for the fifteen-minute drive over to his house. If he'd thought she looked like a goddess last night, she was even sexier with her hair tousled and her face glowing from hours of good lovemaking. No, not just good. Mind-blowing.

"Unless you want your grandmother's first impression of me to be that I'm a cheap hussy," Francesca teased, "I'd better take myself on home."

He chuckled. "She'd never think that about the woman I love."

Francesca stilled, her gaze softening on his face. "Say it again," she whispered.

"I love you," he said huskily. He covered her lips again, not really kissing her this time, just letting their breaths mingle sensually. He reached between her legs where the short skirt ended, and she clamped her warm thighs together, trapping his hand there. His body stirred, his erection straining against the fly of his pants.

"*Mon Dieu*," he groaned hoarsely. "Will I ever get enough of you, woman?"

She laughed softly. "I hope not."

With a supreme effort, he pulled away and straightened from the car. "I'll pick you up at six."

"I'll be ready. Are you sure we shouldn't bring anything?"

He winked at her. "Just your beautiful self. Rafe and Korrine will take care of the rest."

"All right." She hesitated, then added with a shy smile that warmed his heart, "I'm looking forward to meeting your friends, Sebastien."

"And they're looking forward to meeting you, *chère*. Now go, before I give in to temptation and ravish you right here in the driveway."

She giggled, throwing the car into reverse and backing out onto the street. He lifted his hand in a brief wave, then stood watching until she'd disappeared around the corner before he made his way into the house.

As he stood in the foyer sifting absently through a stack of mail, he heard the approaching shuffle of his grandmother's footsteps. "Dat you, T'Bas?"

He glanced up to smile at her. "G'mornin'. What're you doin' up so early?"

"Shoot. When have you ever known me to be a late riser?" Wearing a housecoat, slippers, and her satin bonnet, she shuffled over to him, and he dropped a kiss on her smooth forehead.

"You been workin' so many hours," Augustine complained, rubbing his back, "I hardly ever see you anymore."

"I know," he murmured. "This case I'm investigatin', it's been consuming all my time."

"The one that's been all over the news? Even your uncle Henri heard mention of it on CNN. He called today. Said you ought to know how to solve the case on account of all dat trainin' you got in his tattoo shop years ago."

Sebastien chuckled dryly. "If only it were that simple, *Mamère*."

"Life never is," she agreed, with a quiet little smile. "Want some breakfast before you head back to the station?"

"That sounds good," Sebastien said, setting the mail down on the console. "But don' go to the trouble of fixin' anything. I'm gonna take you out for breakfast this mornin'. Anywhere you wanna go."

She smiled. "I'd like that very much."

"Good. Let me grab a shower and we can go." As he started down the hall, his grandmother called his name. He turned back to look at her.

Augustine's gray eyes were twinkling. "She's very pretty, T'Bas. When am I gon' get to meet her?"

Startled, Sebastien could only grin sheepishly. "You looked out the window."

"Uh-huh. And now it all makes sense, the way you been mopin' around here like a lovesick fool for the past few days."

"You've hardly seen me," Sebastien protested.

"I've seen enough, *cher*." His grandmother's eyes were filled with the keen wisdom and intuition that people had sought out for years. "I'm thinkin' she must be very special to make my handsome, devil-may-care grandson pine after her."

"She is," Sebastien said softly.

Augustine smiled serenely. "I'm also thinkin' maybe it's time you moved into your own place. Not that I haven't enjoyed sharin' the same roof with you these past two years, but you must admit it's been a big adjustment for you, to go from havin' your own nice apartment in the French Quarter, to livin' in a house with your ol' maw-maw again."

Sebastien scowled, feigning affront. "I don' believe this. You kickin' me out, Mama August?"

She chuckled. "Well, I can't really do that, seein' as to how *you* bought this place. But I know you don' have the heart to put me out of a house I've grown to love, so since one of us has to go, I'm thinkin' it should be you, *cher*." She paused, her tone gentling as she gazed at him. "That money your parents left you ain't goin' nowhere, T'Bas, no matter how hard you wish it away."

"That money," he said darkly, "should have been left to you."

"Nonsense," she clucked, waving a dismissive hand. "I'm an old woman. What I'm gon' do with eight hundred thousand dollars?"

"More than I've done with it," he grumbled.

"You haven't done anythin' with it."

"Exactly."

Augustine frowned, shaking her head slowly at him. "Your parents wanted you to have that money, *cher*. For you to reject it is jus' plain foolish." When his expression remained mutinous, she softened her voice. "I know how upset you were when you found out how much they'd left you. I know you felt like this was their way of tryin' to make up for not showin' you all the love and affection you wanted so desperately as a child. And I know, darling Sebastien, that deep down inside, you feel like you don' even deserve the money. But Leonide and Bernice loved you dearly, though it didn't always seem that way. They worked hard hopin' to give you a better life than they'd ever had. They wanted something better for you than the Lower Ninth Ward." She shook her head sadly. "They didn't realize, until it was too late, that what a child needs from his parents can't be bought with all the money in the world."

Sebastien's chest felt tight. He pushed out a deep breath, leaned his head back, and closed his eyes for a moment. "I don't know what I want to do with the money, *Mamère*. Maybe I'll give it away to charity, or help you rebuild your house if you ever decide to go back home."

"I'm not goin' back home," Augustine said with a note of finality that made him open his eyes and look at her. Her jaw was set, her lips pressed firmly together.

Sebastien frowned in confusion. "We've always discussed the possibility of returning—"

"Not anymore. San Antonio is my home now, T'Bas. I've made new friends, found a lovin' church family." Her voice hitched, and for a moment tears glistened in her eyes. "Don' misunderstand me, baby. I'll never forget the life we had in New Orleans, but I can't keep lookin' back, or the memories—the bad ones—will suck me right under. I'm an old woman. I have to make the most of the time I've got left on this earth, whether that's a few months or a few years." Her gaze turned imploring. "I hope you can understand my need to move on, Sebastien."

He could. He understood it better than he'd ever imagined was possible. Meeting and falling in love with Francesca had already changed him in ways he couldn't begin to measure.

A soft smile touched his mouth. "I think," he said reflectively, "that San Antonio is very lucky to have you, Mama August."

She smiled, walking over to him. Tenderly she reached

up and curved a hand against his cheek. "And I think," she murmured, "you're about to make a certain young lady the happiest woman in the world."

Rafe and Korrine Santiago lived on a sprawling estate nestled deep in Texas Hill Country. The two-story stucco ranch house with a red-tiled Spanish roof was perched on a hillside overlooking the valley, lush and green like a rumpled velvet blanket against the backdrop of rugged mountains.

Sebastien and Francesca arrived as the sun was setting, spreading vibrant flames across the sky.

"Oh my God," Francesca breathed in awe. "That is the most beautiful thing I've ever seen."

"I agree," Sebastien murmured huskily, but when Francesca glanced over at him, he was gazing at her, not the stunning sunset. She blushed with pleasure at the frank male admiration reflected in his eyes, which he'd scarcely been able to take off her since arriving at her house to pick her up an hour ago.

For dinner with the Santiagos that evening, she'd donned a slim-fitting linen skirt with a modest slit up the front and a turquoise tube top with braided straps that tied around the back of her neck. A beaded turquoise bracelet from New Mexico, courtesy of Patricia, encircled her wrist, and she wore a pair of wood-heeled wedge sandals and had painted her toenails a bold, sassy shade of red. She felt beautiful, chic—and still sexy.

And if Sebastien didn't stop devouring her with those bedroom eyes of his, she'd have to drag him into the nearest bathroom and have her way with him. Not exactly the kind of first impression she wanted to make with his friends.

The woman who answered the door smoothing down her black shoulder-length hair was tall and exotically beautiful, with dark, almond-shaped eyes and skin the color of cinnamon blended with chocolate. She wore cream slacks that accentuated her curvy figure and a salmon-colored summer top that Francesca noted, upon closer inspection, was buttoned crookedly, as if she'd dressed in haste.

She beamed a welcoming smile at them. "You made it! We were worried you'd gotten lost or something."

Sebastien chuckled. "Now, how could I get lost, as many times as I've been here?"

"Smart-ass." Grinning, the woman gave Sebastien a quick bear hug, then reached for Francesca's hand. "You must be Francesca. It's so nice to meet you. I'm Korrine Santiago."

"Hello, Korrine," Francesca said warmly. "Thank you for inviting me for dinner this evening."

"Thank *you* for accepting. Come in, come in," Korrine urged, opening the door wider. As they stepped past her into the cool interior of the house, she called out over her shoulder, "Rafe! Our guests have arrived."

A moment later, a tall, broad-shouldered man appeared from the back. With close-cropped dark hair, skin like burnished copper, and piercing eyes that turned to the color of whiskey when the light hit them, he was as devilishly handsome as his wife was beautiful.

He sauntered across the room with fluid, relaxed strides and gently grasped Francesca's hand. "Rafe Santiago," he introduced himself in a deep, warm drawl. "A pleasure to meet you, Francesca."

She smiled, and couldn't help feeling a little dazzled. "Nice to meet you, Rafe. You have a beautiful home."

"Why, thank you, Francesca." He reached out, clapping Sebastien on the shoulder with a broad grin. "Durand, my friend. How the hell are you?"

"I'm good, Santiago," Sebastien said with an easy smile.

"Real good. Sorry we're running a little behind. I left the station later than I'd planned."

"No problem," Rafe said, curving an arm around his wife's waist and drawing her gently against his side. "Korrine and I made good use of the extra time, isn't that right, sweetheart?"

Korrine's dark eyes twinkled with mischief as she gazed up at her husband. "We sure did. We put the finishing touches on dinner . . ."

"And got started on dessert," Rafe murmured.

Sebastien chuckled wryly. "I'll bet you did. Come, let me show you this amazing view," he said to Francesca, taking her hand and leading her farther down the hall. The entrance spilled into a large, high-ceilinged living room punctuated by wide glass windows that provided a panoramic view of the surrounding valley.

As Francesca glanced over her shoulder, she saw Rafe bend his head low to nuzzle his wife's ear, then murmur something that made her glance down at herself. Eyes widening, she clapped a hand to her mouth to smother an embarrassed giggle.

Francesca and Sebastien exchanged knowing grins as Korrine hurried from the room to fix her shirt, tossing over her shoulder, "I'll be right back. You guys make yourselves at home."

Rafe turned to his guests with an innocent smile. "Wine, anyone?"

An hour later, the foursome was cozily ensconced in the dining room, laughing and talking as if they'd known one another for years. The conversation, like the vintage cabernet sauvignon Rafe topped off their glasses with, flowed freely from politics and speculation about a controversial documentary being filmed in San Antonio, to talk of families and careers.

"So, Francesca," Korrine said, smiling easily at her. "As the only person at this table who doesn't carry a gun and hunt bad guys for a living, how did you get into the field of entomology, of all things?"

Francesca laughed, setting down her wineglass. "Call me strange, but I've always been interested in the study of insects. Before you even ask, yes, as a kid I *did* collect bugs in jars and conduct 'experiments' on them—nothing as sadistic as plucking off their legs to see which insects could crawl on their bellies, I assure you."

As everyone chuckled, she continued, "My 'experiments' were humane, like trying to find out which insects were sensitive to light, or how food supply affects the growth rate of grasshoppers." She shrugged, looking sheepish. "When I grew up and found out there was an actual profession for people like me, it was like discovering the Holy Grail."

Korrine nodded. "I think that's pretty cool," she said, and Francesca could tell she was sincere, which only made her like Korrine Santiago more.

Rafe slanted an amused look at Sebastien, who'd been gazing across the table at Francesca while she spoke, her eyes undoubtedly glowing as they did whenever she discussed her love for entomology.

"You're not afraid of bugs, are you, Durand?" Rafe drawled.

Sebastien pulled his gaze from Francesca's face to look at his friend. "No. Why?"

"Because if you ever make her mad, she could get back at you real good by dropping a few spiders in strategic places around the house—your shoes, your underwear drawer. The bed."

Sebastien chuckled. "Don't give her any ideas, man."

"Too late," Francesca said evilly, drawing another round of laughter around the table.

Settling back in her chair, Korrine divided a curious

ook between Sebastien and Francesca. "So, when and
here did you two meet?"

"Almost two weeks ago this Monday," Sebastien
nswered.

Francesca smiled playfully. "He invaded my favorite
aunt—a café that's located five minutes away from my
ouse. One morning I was just minding my own busi-
ess, enjoying a cup of coffee, and then I looked up and
e was there, staring right in my face."

"I couldn't take my eyes off her," Sebastien admitted.

"He made me choke on my coffee," Francesca said ac-
usingly.

Sebastien grinned. "At least I got her attention. She
ad her nose buried in this whopper of a textbook. It
ad to be this thick—no kidding," he said, gesturing to
ncompass the width of his chest.

Francesca laughed. "What an exaggeration!"

Rafe and Korrine grinned, enjoying the back-and-
orth exchange. "So what happened?" they asked in
nison, then glanced at each other and smiled.

Sebastien said, "Well, I finally got up to go talk to
er—"

"And I was so terrified I didn't know whether to bolt
r stay put."

Sebastien smiled lazily at her. "I could see that in your
yes. It made me all the more determined to find out
our name."

"But you didn't get the chance."

"That's right. Just as I reached you, my cell phone
ang and I got called away."

"But somehow I knew I'd see you again," Francesca
murmured.

"It was meant to be," he said huskily, gazing at her, and
or a moment they forgot the other two occupants of the
oom, until Korrine, hiding a smile, discreetly cleared
er throat.

With sheepish grins, Sebastien and Francesca dragged their gazes apart and reached for their wineglasses at the same time.

"Eyes meeting across a crowded room," Rafe said, with a soft, intimate look at his wife. "Sounds familiar."

Korrine smiled warmly. "Yeah, only ours was a crowded *street*. We met during the Battle of Flowers parade last year," she explained to Francesca. "I had just been transferred to the San Antonio FBI field office. Rafe and I met over a dead body."

"Not exactly the most romantic of beginnings," Rafe said grimly.

Korrine reached over and laced her fingers through his. "But we more than compensated for that in the weeks and months to come."

"Yes," he agreed, holding her gaze as he lifted her fingers to his lips and kissed them one at a time, "we certainly did."

This time it was they who became so absorbed in each other that they forgot they weren't alone in the room. It was only when the phone rang that they remembered their company.

"That's probably my sister Daniela," Rafe said ruefully to Sebastien and Francesca. "She's going through another relationship crisis and has been calling us all day for advice."

Korrine laughed. "Or it could be my niece Julia. She became a big sister last year, and although she positively adores her baby brother, every now and then she needs a break. We'll let voice mail pick it up." She glanced around the table, pleased to see empty plates. "Did y'all enjoy the bourbon chicken?"

Everyone nodded and responded enthusiastically. "I was going to ask you for the recipe," Francesca said.

Korrine beamed with pleasure. "Absolutely! Between Rafe's godmother, Lupita, and my sister, Katherine, I honestly don't know who to thank more for my newfound culinary skills. Rafe's too kind to say it, but when we first got married, my claim to fame was that I could make the best grilled cheese sandwiches—and that's about it."

"I didn't marry you to slave over a hot stove for me, *querida*," Rafe said with a tenderly admonishing smile. "We both work hard. Cooking is a duty we'll always share."

"I know, baby. But I really enjoy it." Korrine grinned at Francesca. "My sister and I have a pact, of sorts. She's helping me become less of a tomboy, and I'm helping her become less of a pampered socialite. In exchange for cooking lessons, I'm teaching her karate." Her dark eyes danced with mirth. "If you ever meet my sister, Katherine, you'll understand why that's such an amazing sight."

Francesca laughed, feeling a pang of envy for the close relationship Korrine and her sister obviously shared. Would she and Tommie ever return to some semblance of the friendship they'd once had? she wondered sadly.

"Who's ready for dessert?" Korrine asked, and in response to the eager chorus of yeses, she grinned broadly and rose from the table. "Wait until you taste my tiramisu. Lip-smacking good."

"You're in love with her."

Those were the first words out of Rafe's mouth the moment he and Sebastien were alone on the porch after finishing dessert, which had been, as Korrine promised, lip-smacking good. The two men had stepped outside for some fresh air while Korrine and Francesca retired to the living room to pore through the couple's wedding album.

Sebastien, standing at the wood balustrade that wound around the wide porch, chuckled wryly at Rafe's pronouncement. "Is it that obvious?"

Humor tugged at the corners of Rafe's mouth as he

walked over to join him at the railing. "Only to someone who knows what that look means."

"What look?"

"The look on your face every time she walks into a room, or says something sweet or clever or unconsciously sexy. Or every time she just glances at you. You have *that* look."

Sebastien smiled a little. "Spoken with the voice of experience."

"You know it." Rafe slanted him a crooked grin. "Less than two weeks, huh?"

"Hell yeah." Sebastien shook his head. "Hit me like a ton of bricks, too. One minute all I was thinking about was getting her into bed. The next thing I knew, I was daydreaming about what it'd be like to wake up beside her every day for the rest of my life."

Rafe chuckled. "Scary, isn't it?"

"Most definitely." Arms folded across his chest, legs braced slightly apart, Sebastien gazed out into the distance. Night had fallen, casting moonlit shadows over the ranch yard and surrounding valley.

"She's the most amazing woman I've ever met," he said quietly. "So pure, open, trusting. A heart of gold. I don't think she has a malicious bone in her beautiful body. And she's one of the smartest people I've ever known. Her *brain* turns me on, let alone what the rest of her does to me. *Mon Dieu,*" he muttered, shuddering at the memory of a scantily clad Francesca sashaying through the doors of the police station yesterday, then taking him on the ride of his life—literally and figuratively. It had been like something out of an erotic fantasy, except the reality had surpassed anything his imagination could have conjured. And he'd conjured up plenty.

Grinning, Rafe clapped him on the shoulder. "You've definitely got it bad, my friend."

"*C'est vrai,*" Sebastien murmured. "That's true."

"But at least it's not one-sided. She's crazy about you, too. She couldn't keep her eyes off you all during dinner. Korrine and I both noticed."

Sebastien grinned. "How did you guys notice anything? You could hardly keep your eyes off each other. By the way, that's some powerful stuff between you two."

"It is," Rafe agreed with a tranquil smile. He was silent a moment, basking in thoughts of his wife. "We're planning to start on our family next year."

"Yeah? That's great. Congratulations, *mon ami*. I know your families must be excited."

"We haven't told them yet." Rafe made a face. "Between my mother, sisters, and godmother, not to mention Korrine's mother and sister, we'd never get any breathing room if they knew we were trying to have a child."

Sebastien laughed. "You would think they'd realize that the sooner they leave you to it, the sooner you can produce results."

Rafe chuckled dryly. "You would think."

"You still planning to have six rug rats, like you always joked about?"

Rafe grinned, stroking his chin. "We'll see. I'm still working on Korrine."

"Well, you definitely have the room for a big family," Sebastien said, gesturing to encompass the large ranch house and surrounding landscape. "You've got a slice of heaven out here, Santiago. You're a very lucky man."

"I know." Rafe sighed, surveying the land before him with the deep pride and satisfaction of one who owns the soil he walks on. And in that moment, Sebastien realized he wanted the same thing. He wanted to put down roots somewhere, claim ownership of something for the first time in his life. He wanted permanence.

He wanted a wife.

And no one but Francesca would do.

Chapter 21

Monday, June 25

"Hey, look who's here! It's my favorite customer in the whole wide world!"

Alfonso Garcia's boisterous greeting drew curious stares from the diners crowded into the Espuma on Monday afternoon.

Francesca chuckled as she slid into a chair at a table in the middle of the café. It wasn't her usual corner table, but that was okay. She'd already broken the mold in other areas of her life. Why should this be any different?

"Not that I don't appreciate being your favorite customer," she said wryly to Alfonso, "but I wouldn't say that too loudly if I were you. Unless you *want* to get stiffed on tips tonight."

"Ah, who cares?" Alfonso said with a dismissive wave of his hand. "If all goes well, pretty soon I won't be needing these people's stingy tips, anyway."

Francesca arched a brow. "Oh? Why's that?"

Alfonso's dark brown eyes glittered with excitement. "A New York editor asked to read my full manuscript!"

"Congratulations, Alfonso!" Francesca said warmly. "That's wonderful news."

"I know, I know! Ever since I received the e-mail three days ago, I've been on cloud nine. You can't even begin to *imagine*, Frankie."

Actually she could. She'd been floating up there in the clouds herself since Friday night.

Still brimming with excitement, Alfonso slid into the chair across the table from Francesca, in defiance of house rules. "Now, of course, there's no guarantee that the editor will like the story enough to offer a contract, but based on what she said in her e-mail—which I have memorized and can recite verbatim—if she loves my writing as much as she loves the premise of the story, the book is as good as published!"

"That's really great, Alfonso. How exciting for you. Now refresh my memory. What's this story about?"

"It's about the son of a migrant farm worker from Mexico who struggles to find his sexual identity and cope with his impoverished upbringing. It's full of angst, betrayal, and drama—perfect ingredients for a best seller."

"Sounds like it." Francesca grinned. "Just don't forget about us little people when you're going on international book tours and appearing on *Oprah*."

He laughed. "As if I could ever forget about you, Frankie. And speaking of superstars, look at you! You look amazing in your skintight jeans with your hair all loose and flowing. And where are your glasses? I hardly recognized you when you stepped through the door tonight. What's with the dramatic makeover? Have *you* been on *Oprah*?"

She smiled. "Not quite. I just wanted to experiment a little."

"Looks like you experimented *a lot*. Don't get me wrong, Frankie. I've always thought you were a doll, but now you're, like, a total babe." Grinning, he reached across the table and touched her arm, then snatched back his finger as if he'd been burned. "Sizzlin' hot!"

Francesca chuckled, embarrassed by all the attention. "It's really not that big of a deal. Underneath it all, I'm still the same Frankie you've always known and loved."

"That's good. Friends like you are hard to come by." His expression clouded for a moment, and Francesca knew he was remembering Jennifer.

She reached across the table and gently squeezed his hand. "She would have been very happy for you, having an editor request your full manuscript."

"I know," Alfonso said quietly. "She's the first person I thought of. I feel so torn. On one hand, I'm ecstatic about the possibility of finally landing a book contract, which has been a dream of mine for years. But on the other hand, I feel guilty for celebrating anything when Jennifer's gone."

"That's completely understandable," Francesca said sympathetically. "But you know that Jennifer would want you to be happy. Just as it was important to her to graduate from college, it's important for you to follow your dreams."

Alfonso nodded, blinking moisture from his eyes as he stared down at the table. "I've already decided that if the book ever gets published," he said, his voice thick with suppressed emotion, "I'm dedicating it to her."

Francesca smiled softly. "I know she'd like that very much."

Alfonso nodded again, then lifted his gaze to hers. "Have you been in touch with that detective who came to Jennifer's apartment that day? Detective Durand?"

"Yes, I have. And I can assure you that he and his partner are doing everything they can to find Jennifer's killer." Sebastien had called her that afternoon, in fact, to let her know he'd be late for their date that evening because he needed to follow up on a few leads. When she told him they could reschedule if necessary, he'd refused, saying he had something important to share with her that couldn't wait. She'd been unable to concentrate on anything else after that, her mind racing with speculation.

"What can I get for you this evening, Frankie?" Alfonso had jumped up from the table and was making a show of taking her order with a pencil poised above his notepad, though in all the months Francesca had been frequenting the Espuma, he'd never needed to write down what she wanted. She'd always ordered the same thing: coffee. And if she was feeling adventurous, a ham and Swiss wrap.

Puzzled by Alfonso's odd behavior, she glanced around, then grinned when she saw that his manager had emerged from the kitchen and caught Alfonso sitting at a table with a customer. Judging by the frown on the man's face, Francesca guessed Alfonso was in for a *long* afternoon.

"Frankie?" Alfonso prompted.

She hesitated another moment, then said decisively, "Let me have one of those iced Vietnamese coffees."

Alfonso stared at her. *"Really?"*

She nodded. "And a grilled pesto sandwich."

A broad grin stretched across Alfonso's face. "Comin' right up."

As he walked away humming Patti Labelle's "New Attitude," Francesca chuckled softly to herself. Alfonso was right. She *did* have a new attitude, and not just because she was wearing designer jeans that had cost her a small fortune.

For the first time in years, she felt good about herself from the inside out. By letting go of her inhibitions with Sebastien, she'd discovered a part of herself she'd never known existed, and it had liberated her from the torment of believing she could never be desirable to a man.

Such a simple thing, yet the revelation had rocked her to the core of her being and turned her world on its axis.

And she had Sebastien to thank for it. Sebastien, who she'd first encountered in this café exactly two weeks ago. Sebastien, who'd looked beyond the "Frumpy Frankie" exterior to see what others hadn't. Sebastien, who'd proven to be worth risking it all for.

With a quiet smile, Francesca reached into her satchel and hefted out the textbook he'd teased her about on Saturday night. Halfway down the first page, she found her mind wandering, turning to thoughts of the evening ahead. For the first time ever, she let herself daydream, content to believe, at least for the time being, that nothing or no one could interfere with her happiness.

As Sebastien pulled into the parking lot of the Sirens and Spurs Gentlemen's Club that afternoon, his cell phone rang. He leaned over and grabbed it from the passenger seat, where he'd tossed it after calling Rodriguez at the office.

"Durand," he clipped.

"Hi, Sebastien," purred a coy, familiar voice. "This is Tommie."

Sebastien frowned as he glanced out the window to see Yelena Slutskaya emerge from the building. "What can I do for you, Tommie?" he said distractedly, keeping his eyes trained on the Russian woman, who'd paused to speak to one of the muscle-bound goons guarding the doors.

Tommie hesitated, hearing the thread of impatience in his voice. "Did I catch you at a bad time?"

"Yeah, actually, you did. I'm out on the road. What do you need?"

A low, sultry chuckle filled the phone line. "Depends on what you're offering. I can think of several—"

Sebastien's frown deepened. "Let me stop you right here, Tommie. You and me? Never gonna happen. And do you know why?"

There was a heavy silence on the other end. "Why?" Tommie asked, her voice tight with displeasure.

"Because I'm in love with your sister. In fact, I'm going to ask her to marry me, and if I'm real lucky, she'll say yes." He paused, then asked in deceptively soft tones, "Are you going to have a problem with me as your brother-in-law, Tommie?"

She hesitated for so long he wondered if she'd hung up the phone. Finally she mumbled, "No, I guess not."

"Good girl," he murmured. "Now, then, was there anything else?"

"Yes." She sounded petulant. *Too damned bad.* "The reason I was calling is that I remembered the name of my sister's coworker who came to the club a few times."

"What's his name?"

"Peter. Peter Ueno. He works in the entomology department with Frankie."

Sebastien stilled for a moment, remembering the forty-something Asian man he'd been introduced to on Thursday afternoon when he showed up at TABU to speak to Francesca. Sebastien had thought nothing of the guy—other than the fact that he'd stood a little too closely to Francesca.

"I just thought you'd like to know," Tommie said.

"Thanks." Sebastien was distracted by the sight of Yelena Slutskaya ending her conversation with the bouncer and starting toward the parking lot. "Listen, I gotta run, Tommie. Thanks again for calling."

"Sure," she muttered sullenly.

Sebastien disconnected, tossed the phone aside, and stepped from the Crown Vic just as Yelena neared him. "Ms. Slutskaya?"

She looked up in startled surprise. The surprise

quickly gave way to suspicion when she recognized him
those imperious blue eyes narrowing on his face. "Dete
tive Durand."

He closed his car door and walked toward her. "I nee
to ask you some questions about your son, Yuri."

A shadow passed over the woman's face, disappearin
so swiftly he might have imagined it. Except he knew h
hadn't. "I don't have time to talk right now," Yelena sai
coolly. "I'm late for an appointment."

Convenient excuse, Sebastien mused. *The same one sl
used before.*

"All right, then," he said levelly. "If you're unavailabl
perhaps you can tell me where I might locate Yuri. He
not at home or at the university."

Yelena pressed her lips into a thin line. "My son is a
adult, Detective. I do not keep track of his movements.

Sebastien arched a brow. "No?"

"No." Her lips tightened, as did the manicured finger
clutching her black leather purse. "What do you wan
with him?"

"I'd like to ask him a few questions pertaining to
case I'm investigating."

"Is this about Jennifer Benson's murder?"

"Yes, as a matter of fact." He watched the woman's fac
like a poker player. "Where can I find your son, Ms. Slut
kaya?"

"I don't know," she snapped. The hand she lifted t
smooth back her silvered dark hair was trembling. "
cannot imagine what Yuri can tell you about Jennifer'
murder. He didn't even know her."

"Not according to one of Jennifer's classmates a
UTSA." Sebastien paused. "You *did* know that Jennife
and Yuri attended the same university, didn't you?"

"She may have mentioned it to me before," Yelen
said tightly.

"Well, the student I spoke to this morning told m

that one time last semester, Yuri filled in for their history professor. After class, Yuri made a point of detaining Jennifer to commend her for knowing the answer to a question he'd asked. So, actually, Ms. Slutskaya, it would appear that your son and Jennifer *were* acquainted."

"That doesn't mean he killed her!" Yelena cried.

Sebastien waited a heartbeat, his gaze narrowed on her face. "No one said anything about Yuri killing Jennifer," he said softly. "Why did you automatically draw that conclusion?"

"Because you were implying it," Yelena said angrily. But the fight was draining out of her, like a balloon with a slow leak. As Sebastien watched, tears glazed across her blue eyes, turning them into iridescent pools of sorrow.

He held himself perfectly still, though every muscle in his body was stretched taut. "Ms. Slutskaya?" he gently prompted.

Closing her eyes, she whispered, "It wasn't his fault. I should have left his father a long time ago. But I was too scared, and Yuri paid the price for my lack of courage. I will never forgive myself for that."

"Ms. Slutskaya," Sebastien murmured, "has something happened to make you suspect your son hurt Jennifer Benson?"

She hesitated, her eyes opening to settle on his face. After another prolonged moment, she nodded slowly, looking as if she'd reached an important, but difficult, decision. "Come inside with me. I have some things to share with you."

Night had fallen by the time Francesca arrived home from campus. After her office hours were over, she'd gone to the lab to finish up some paperwork. She was nearing completion of her *Portia* experiment, and couldn't wait to submit the results for publication.

Letting herself into the house, she toed off her sandals, then went about the routine task of drawing curtains and blinds closed.

It was seven fifteen. Sebastien had said he'd pick her up at eight, which gave her less than an hour to take a hot bath and get ready for their date. Anticipation quickened her footsteps as she climbed the stairs and headed into her bedroom. While she ran the tub, she got undressed and selected an outfit for the evening, a figure-hugging red sheath with a scooped neckline. She couldn't wait to see Sebastien's face when he got an eyeful of her in the dress. Hopefully they'd make it out the door in time to keep their dinner reservations.

Grinning at the thought, she padded to the bathroom and lowered herself into the claw-foot tub. Lulled by the steamy water and lavender-scented bath crystals, she soon drifted off to sleep.

It was the faint creak of a floorboard that awakened her.

By the time she lifted her drowsy eyelids and saw the intruder, it was too late. She registered a dark blur of motion; then he was at her side, a large, heavy hand clamped over her mouth as a scream rushed up her throat.

"Shhh," he whispered softly against her temple, a long knife pressed to her jugular vein. "Don't make a sound, and I won't hurt you. Do you understand?"

Francesca could hardly breathe or move, but somehow she managed to nod her head, the razor-thin blade of the knife biting coldly into her skin. As she stared at her assailant in wild-eyed terror, she felt a stir of recognition. And then she realized why. He'd been at Jennifer Benson's crime scene, speaking briefly to her and Alfonso before they left. And then she'd caught another glimpse of him at the police station on Friday night, as she passed the open door of his office.

But it can't be! her mind railed. He was sworn to serve and protect. He wouldn't do this. He *couldn't*!

The green eyes that met her panicked gaze were cold, piercing. A small, knowing smile lifted the corners of his mouth as he gazed at her. "Ah, you recognize me," he murmured. "I was hoping you would."

She shuddered as he leaned close again, brushing his lips across her hairline in a lover's caress. "I've waited so long to find you. And I almost didn't, because I was searching for all the wrong qualities."

Blood was roaring in Francesca's ears, nearly drowning out the nonsensical words he spoke. All the while, the lethal edge of the blade dug into her flesh.

Drawing back, he searched her face. "All these years . . . I want to hear you say my name, Francesca. When I remove my hand, don't scream. *Whisper* my name."

Francesca nodded jerkily. He eased the grip of his hand over her mouth, and she swallowed slowly.

Thoughts raced through her mind. How long had it been since she'd climbed into the tub and fallen asleep? Was Sebastien on his way over there, or was he striding up to the front door that very moment? If she screamed, would he hear her? Would anyone?

Sergeant Clive MacDougal was gazing at her, a feral gleam in his eyes. "Whisper my name," he said. Softly at first, and then with increasing urgency. "Whisper my name."

Francesca opened her mouth—and screamed at the top of her lungs.

Swift fury hardened MacDougal's expression. The knife clattered to the tiled floor. In a flash of movement, he reached inside his jacket pocket and whipped out a white cloth, then clamped it savagely over her face.

Francesca thrashed against him, water splashing from the tub as her arms and legs flailed in desperation. But there was no use fighting him. He was a big, strong man, holding her down as effortlessly as if she were no more than a newborn kitten.

The sweet, cloying odor of chloroform invaded her nostrils and gradually seeped into her brain. Her weak, impotent thrashing slowed, then stopped completely.

Blackness pulled at the edges of her vision, dragging her under.

Chapter 22

"How'd you get Slutskaya to talk?"

Sebastien cradled the cell phone to his ear as he quickly switched lanes. "I lied," he answered. "I told her one of Jennifer's classmates remembered Yuri subbing for their history class last semester."

"And *that* broke her?" Rodriguez asked incredulously. "A woman like Yelena Slutskaya wouldn't have cracked under interrogation by the KGB. Yet all you had to do was tell a little white lie to get her to sell out her own kid?"

Sebastien's smile was humorless. "I think she was ready to unburden herself. Twenty years is a damned long time to carry around the secret that your ten-year-old son may have brutally murdered his own father."

"No kidding," Rodriguez agreed. "Guess your hunch was right about her hiding something."

Sebastien frowned. "Guess so." But this was one time it didn't feel good to be right. The tale Yelena Slutskaya had shared with him was like something out of a Greek tragedy. As she spoke, he realized he'd never seen a more tortured, conflicted woman. She was torn between a fierce maternal instinct to protect her son, and an obligation to protect *others* from the monster he may have become. In the end, her sense of humanity had prevailed, and she'd agreed to call Yuri to ask him to meet her at his house—where Sebastien and Rodriguez would be waiting for him.

"So you really believe this could be our guy?" Rodriguez asked.

Sebastien said carefully, "I think it's a strong possibility." Thanks to the library records Rafe had given him on Saturday night, Sebastien was able to ascertain that Yuri Slutskaya's name did appear on the short list of people who'd checked out books about the Mexican Blood Walker within the last six months. That connection, combined with the fact that he'd visited the Sirens and Spurs Gentlemen's Club days before Jennifer Benson's murder, had pushed him to the top of their suspect list.

They were still awaiting more information from the San Marcos PD about the murder of Mary Ott.

"How far out are you from Slutskaya's house?" Sebastien asked.

"About five miles," Rodriguez said. "You sure it was a good idea to leave Yelena behind at the club?"

"She didn't wanna come to the house. She was too traumatized."

"What if she changes her mind about cooperating and calls her son to tip him off?"

"She wouldn't," Sebastien said, his voice edged with grim certainty. "But just to make sure, I've got a uniform babysitting her."

"Good thinking."

"I try occasionally. Anyway, you'll reach the house before me, so just lie low until I get there."

"Gotcha."

As Sebastien disconnected, his thoughts racing a mile a minute, the police radio crackled to life. As he reached over to lower the volume, the dispatcher's announcement stopped him cold. "All units in the vicinity: Possible 10-62 in progress in the King William District. I repeat, possible 10-62 in progress. Over."

King William District . . . Possible B and E in progress . . .

Sebastien grabbed the mike free of its holder, identified himself, and barked out, "What is the location of that 10-62?"

It seemed an eternity before the dispatcher's response crackled over the line. "Detective? That's 9018 East Guenther Street. Disturbance reported by a neighbor."

Sebastien's heart slammed against his rib cage. *Francesca!*

He hung up the mike and floored the accelerator, hoping there was another explanation for what the neighbor had seen or heard.

Don't let Francesca be in danger, he silently prayed, punching out her number on his phone with trembling fingers. *Let her be at home, getting dressed for our date. Please, God.*

The cell phone went unanswered, as did the house line.

Raw fear gripped Sebastien by the throat. He hurtled through a busy intersection, weaving madly between cars, praying he wasn't too late.

God help him if he was too late.

Francesca's eyes opened groggily. Her head throbbed, and her tongue felt bloated around a coarse wad of cloth stuffed into her mouth.

As she came fully awake, she realized she'd not only been gagged, but was also strapped, naked, to her own bed. Her arms were stretched taut above her head, her wrists tied to the center bedpost with the same kind of cord that had been used to bind her ankles.

And she realized, with bone-chilling clarity, that this was what it had been like for Jennifer Benson and Christie Snodgrass. The unspeakable terror she now felt was what they'd experienced before he killed them.

Just as he would soon kill her.

God, no! she pleaded, the thought filling her with a dread so deep, she thought she might pass out again. But she couldn't afford to lose consciousness. Somehow she had to find a way to escape this nightmare, before it was too late.

"Ah, good. You're awake."

Her head swung toward the chillingly soft voice. Dressed in dark clothing, her captor stood beside the bed, carefully and methodically arranging items on the nightstand—some needles, a pair of latex gloves, an assortment of inks in small plastic bottles.

As Francesca mentally catalogued each item, icy foreboding settled over her heart. She knew what was coming next. The Mexican Blood Walker tattoo.

She must have whimpered softly in her throat, for he looked at her then, his face calm and implacable. "I trusted you not to scream, Francesca, but you betrayed that trust. So you'll have to stay gagged until I decide otherwise."

At her panicked look, he chuckled softly. "Yes, I can see the questions in your beautiful eyes." Pausing in his task, he turned and sat down on the edge of the bed as if he had every right to be there. Her skin crawled as he reached out and gently stroked a hand up and down her bare thigh.

"You're not perfect," he murmured, fingering a dark mole halfway to her knee. "At least not in the sense I'd been looking for. But you're perfect in every other way that truly matters. That night when I saw you again, as you were leaving the club, I realized you were the one. Yes, Francesca, the one I'd been searching for since that day in Xeltu three years ago."

She stared at him uncomprehendingly.

"You see," he said, "I was in Xeltu three years ago during the epidemic. I know you're familiar with what happened. You're the one who told Detective Durand about the Mexican Blood Walker. That's when I should have known you were the one. You understood, better than anyone else, the power of the creature who'd given me this rare, extraordinary gift. The gift of eternal life."

Eternal life? What is he talking about?

But Clive MacDougal was no longer looking at her. Instead he was staring *through* her, his eyes glazed over. When he spoke again, his voice seemed to come from a great distance. "I was vacationing in the Yucatan near the village of Xeltu when I heard about the epidemic, people dying left and right from venomous spider bites. Being an officer of the law, naturally I felt compelled to investigate. Little did I know what awaited me."

Francesca's body was rigid, every muscle and tendon strained, stiff and quivering with fear. She tried to work the dry cloth forward in her mouth, pushing it around with her tongue without him noticing. If she screamed, would anyone hear her this time? Was it worth risking the wrath of her sadistic captor?

She froze as his eyes suddenly cleared, focusing on her face with unerring intensity. "The spider bit me," he said in a soft, reverent whisper. "The Blood Walker bit me, and I lived to tell about it. And soon, Francesca, so will you."

Icy fear slithered down Francesca's spine as his words registered. She shook her head vehemently as he rose from the bed and walked across the room, bending to reach inside a black bag he'd left by the door. As she watched, he lifted out a covered glass jar and held it up to the light.

Panic ripped through her when she saw what was inside. A large black spider striped with red.

The Mexican Blood Walker.

Terror clogged her throat. She yanked hard on her restraints, struggling frantically to escape as he came toward her, slow and predatory, his trophy raised high in the air.

"I have to make sure you're the one," he told her, a fanatical gleam in his eyes as he began unscrewing the lid on the jar. "I've been fooled by so many imposters. Just a few days ago, in fact, I put one of the imposters to the test by merely showing her the spider. She wasn't at all pleased. So I had to kill her. I don't think I can handle another disappointment, Francesca. If you live after being bitten by the spider, then I'll know you're my equal. My soul mate."

No! Francesca sobbed against the suffocating rag stuffed into her mouth. She thrashed on the bed, the cords that bound her wrists and ankles cutting into her flesh.

Just as MacDougal reached the bed, a low, deadly voice commanded from across the room, "Freeze!"

Tears of relief sprang to Francesca's eyes when she saw Sebastien framed in the doorway, his weapon drawn and aimed at MacDougal with lethal precision.

MacDougal stopped, but didn't turn around. His mouth twisted in a cold smirk. "What're you going to do, Durand? Shoot your own boss?"

"If I have to," Sebastien bit off.

"I'm unarmed. How would you explain shooting an unarmed man?"

Sebastien took a step into the room. "Put down the jar, Chief."

MacDougal laughed, a soft, chilling sound. "You can't kill me, Durand. I'm immortal."

Without warning, he dropped the jar, reached inside his jacket for a weapon, and spun around to fire at Sebastien. Francesca screamed as a shot blasted through the room, reverberating against the walls.

MacDougal's body crumpled to the floor with a dull thud.

Stepping quickly over him, Sebastien hurried to the

bed and untied Francesca's wrists and ankles, then gathered her into his arms with such force she thought her ribs would crack.

"*Mon Dieu*," he uttered raggedly. "You gave me the scare of my life, *chère*. Are you okay?"

Francesca nodded and clung to him for several moments before she remembered something else. She drew back, her eyes wide with alarm. "The Blood Walker!"

Sebastien whirled around, and their frantic gazes swept the floor for the glass jar containing the poisonous spider. Francesca sagged against him in relief when she spied the jar lying near the dresser where it had rolled when MacDougal dropped it. The lid and the spider were safely intact.

Sprawled a few feet away, Clive MacDougal stared sightlessly at the ceiling, blood oozing from a deep wound in his chest and spreading in a pool beneath his back.

As the clamor of booted feet pounding up the stairs signaled the arrival of police officers, Sebastien drew the covers around Francesca's naked body, pulled her onto his lap, and held her tightly like he never wanted to let go.

She hoped he never did.

Chapter 23

Sunday, July 22
Four weeks later

Francesca gazed out the window of Sebastien's blac
truck as they made their way down a two-lane highwa
flanked by ruggedly majestic mountains. Cattle and el
grazed in pastures so lush and green they seemed artif
cial, and in the distance, lakes shimmered in the after
noon sun like mirages.

Turning her head from the picturesque scenery
Francesca smiled at Sebastien. "You're still not telling m
where we're going?"

"Nope." He slanted a lopsided grin at her. "It's a surprise.

"That's so unfair!" Francesca protested. "You've bee
keeping me in suspense all day. Even Mama August is i
on it. She couldn't stop smiling at me in church."

"She was smiling at you because she likes you," Se
bastien corrected. "As she told me this morning, askin
you to marry me was one of the smartest things I've eve
done in my life. And I happen to agree."

"Oh, Sebastien." Francesca reached across the sea
and took his hand in hers, lacing their fingers togethe.
The pear-shaped diamond on her left hand glinted i

the sunlight slanting through the windshield. "Saying yes to you was by far the smartest thing *I've* ever done."

He smiled softly, bringing her hand to his warm lips. "Thank you for agreeing to such a short engagement. I know big, fancy weddings take time to plan, but I can't wait much longer to have you as my wife, Francesca."

Pleasure swept through her at his husky words. "Just one more week, darling, and then I'm all yours forever."

"Good." His expression darkened after a moment. "To think that I almost lost you."

"Don't think about it," Francesca murmured. "It's over now. You made sure of that."

Anger hardened Sebastien's jaw. "All that time. I never knew what that sick bastard was capable of. He fooled everyone."

It had been nearly a month since the harrowing night in which Francesca had found herself at the mercy of a madman. A search of Clive MacDougal's house afterward had revealed a basement sanctuary filled with enough tattoo supplies to last him a lifetime. There he'd erected a crude shrine to the Mexican Blood Walker—specifically to the spider that had given him the "gift of immortality." His maniacal pursuit of the perfect soul mate had been documented in a journal he'd started while in Xeltu, in which he'd rambled on and on about his desire to share his new-found destiny with a "worthy partner." He'd killed two women in Xeltu before returning to San Antonio, where his quest for the elusive soul mate had resulted in the violent murders of five more women, including Christie Snodgrass, Jennifer Benson, and Mary Ott. According to the journal, Christie was the first victim he'd tattooed, after three years of perfecting the art and, more importantly, perfecting the design of the Mexican Blood Walker. To reach his desired skill level, he'd purchased books on tattooing and experimented on homeless people, paying them not only for the use of their flesh, but to keep his identity a secret.

MacDougal's chillingly detailed journal remained in police custody, while the object of his devotion—the lone spider—had been shipped off to a government research and testing facility in Washington, D.C.

In the aftermath of MacDougal's death, the police department had been rocked by the scandal of having a deranged serial killer in its midst. The case had made national headlines and drawn more than a few morbidly curious people who'd camped out at the cemetery where MacDougal was buried to make sure he was indeed dead. His first wife was currently in negotiations with a major publisher to write a tell-all about her life with the now infamous "Spider Tattoo Killer."

Sebastien frowned darkly. "I'm not gonna be able to let you out of my sight for the next sixty years," he grumbled.

Francesca smiled, squeezing his hand. "You don't hear me complaining." Glancing out the window again, she soon contradicted herself by whining, "Come on, Sebastien. Can't you just give me one little hint about where we're going?"

"You'll see in a few minutes. We're almost there."

He slowed the truck as the road climbed in elevation, and after a few more minutes a one-story hacienda-style ranch house with a red-tiled Spanish roof rolled into view. The house was surrounded by at least two acres of lush green land shaded by large, leafy trees.

Francesca's mouth went dry as Sebastien pulled into the circular driveway. "Sebastien?" she whispered.

"Hmm?"

"Who lives here?"

"No one. At the moment." He was watching her face carefully. "Would you like to go inside and take a look around?"

Francesca nodded wordlessly, already reaching for the door handle.

The moment she crossed the threshold of the house she fell in love. Sebastien followed slowly with a quiet smile on his face as she went from room to room, oohing over this, aahing over that. She loved everything about the place—the way the large, airy rooms flowed from one to the next, the inviting warmth of the gleaming pine floors, the rustic charm of the limestone fireplaces.

"It's beautiful!" she exclaimed when they'd finished the tour.

"I'm glad you like it," Sebastien said. "I wanted to make sure before I put down a contract on it."

Francesca's eyes widened. "Oh my God. Are you telling me . . . ?"

Grinning, he spread his arms wide to encompass the living room in which they stood. "You're looking at our new home, *chère*. Just say the word and I'll make the call."

With a squeal of delight, Francesca rushed into his arms. Laughing, he lifted her off the floor and swung her around. She wrapped her arms around his neck and locked her legs around his waist as he drew her close for a long, soul-stirring kiss.

When they came up for air, she asked, "How did you find this hidden treasure?"

"Actually, Rafe told me about it. I don't know if you noticed, but the entrance to their property is up the road from here."

"Really? So Rafe and Korrine will be our neighbors?"

"Yeah. Do you mind that?"

"Not at all. They're wonderful people. I've enjoyed getting to know them better." So much, in fact, that she'd asked Korrine Santiago to be her matron-of-honor, with Tommie and Patricia as her bridesmaids.

At the reminder of her sister, Francesca smiled a little. "Before I forget, Tommie says hello."

Sebastien nodded. "How's she enjoying life in New York?"

"She says waitressing is a yucky, thankless job. Her tiny studio apartment is infested with roaches, and she hasn't been called back on any auditions yet." Francesca chuckled. "Despite all that, she said she's never been happier in her life."

Sebastien grinned wryly. "Sounds like it was a good move for her, then."

"I think so," Francesca agreed.

Tommie had been devastated to learn about Francesca's terrifying ordeal with Clive MacDougal. Whether out of pity or guilt, she'd doted on her sister for the next several days. Although she'd stopped just short of apologizing for her malicious behavior, Francesca could see the remorse in her eyes, especially whenever Sebastien was around—which had been often, as he'd hardly let Francesca out of his sight.

Although she knew she and her sister still had a long way to go in mending their fractured relationship, Francesca was optimistic that they were, at least, on the right track. If nothing else, Tommie's decision to move to New York would keep the two sisters out of each other's hair.

And speaking of hair, Sebastien had wound a fistful of Francesca's in his hand and pulled her head back so he could nuzzle her throat. Her nerve endings tingled.

She licked her lips. "So you'll call the realtor and tell him or her we want the house?"

"Uh-huh," Sebastien murmured, backing her slowly against the nearest wall. "Just as soon as we finish our tour."

"But we already did."

He shook his head slowly. "I had a different kind of tour in mind. The one I'm talking about involves tongues . . ." She shivered as he licked the seam of her lips before slipping his tongue inside, where he proceeded to go on a hot, wet exploration of her mouth. "Mmm," he whispered. "I like what I'm finding already."

Francesca made a low, strangled sound as he slid down the straps of her summer dress. "We can't do this here—"

"Why not? We're buying the house. Can you think of a better way to christen our new home?"

She couldn't. But then again, with his strong, warm hands caressing her breasts, she couldn't really think of *anything* at the moment.

She moaned as he bent, taking one taut nipple into the silken heat of his mouth. As he suckled and fondled her with one hand, he reached down with the other to unzip his pants.

"There's no furniture here," Francesca pointed out weakly.

His laugh was a low, sexy rumble that settled between her thighs. "That's what walls are for."

She closed her eyes, arching upward on a soundless cry as he impaled her with one long, powerful stroke. "I love you, Sebastien," she whispered.

"*Je t'aime*, Francesca," he groaned huskily as he began to move inside her. "*Je t'aime beaucoup.*"

Glossary of Cajun French

allons—let's go

arrête—stop

bon Dieu—good God

c'est bon—that's good

c'est vrai—that's true

chee wees—a Cheetos™ type snack made by the Elmers company in New Orleans and enjoyed by Louisianans long before there were Cheetos™

cher, chère—beloved, cherished (a term of endearment)

il est après duex heures—it's after two o'clock

je t'aime—I love you

mais—but (often used for emphasis with yes or no)

mais non—but no

mais oui—but yes

mamère—Grandmother

mi aime jou—I love you (strictly Cajun translation)

mon Dieu—my God

p'tit boug—little boy

si vous plaît—please

Grab These Other
Thought Provoking Books

Check Out These Other
Dafina Novels

507

Look For These Other
Dafina Novels